DRAGON ROAD

"One of those remarkable books that consists entirely of 'the good parts.' Non-stop fun with unexpected moments of real pathos."

Neal Stephenson, New York Times bestselling author of Seveneves

"A richly imagined story full of soaring adventure, dark intrigue, and characters you'll fall in love with."

Megan E O'Keefe, author of Inherit the Flame

"A captivating book from the first page. The world building is flawless. *Skyfarer* is non-stop action from start to finish."

The British Fantasy Society

"To say that *Skyfarer* was *Firefly* meets the Battle at Helm's Deep would be to dismiss the amazing world-building that Brassey wraps us up in, or to gloss over the intricate and intense battles we are thrust into, both on high and up close. Brassey raises the bar for everyone else."

Mark Teppo, author of Earth Thirst *and* Silence of Angels

"Brassey has created an action-packed roller coaster ride with rich characters, incredible combat scenes, and a fresh heroine audiences will love."

John G Hartness, author of the Black Knight Chronicles

"Brassey's writing is an adrenaline dump in page form."

Stant Litore, author of the Zombie Bible series

JOSEPH BRASSEY

DRAGON ROAD

A NOVEL OF THE DRIFTING LANDS

ANGRY
ROBOT

ANGRY ROBOT
An imprint of Watkins Media Ltd

20 Fletcher Gate,
Nottingham,
NG1 2FZ
UK

angryrobotbooks.com
twitter.com/angryrobotbooks
In the sky with diamonds

An Angry Robot paperback original 2018

Cover by Ignacio Lazcano
Set in Meridien by Argh! Nottingham

Distributed in the United States by Penguin Random House, Inc., New York.

ISBN 978 0 85766 679 6
Ebook ISBN 978 0 85766 680 2

Printed in the United States of America

9 8 7 6 5 4 3 2 1

To my father and mother
who first taught me
to hear the music.

CHAPTER ONE
THE PALE APOSTATE

Ishtier was beautiful. The purple rays of a setting sun vaulted off the crystalline structures of the port far below the skydock, and the countless people basking in the sunlight of a free port were a riot of colored specks. The drunken splotches of a painter throwing his brush at a blank canvas. Chaotic. Jarring.

For all this, Elias Leblanc could only process the beauty. He was very drunk. He hadn't meant to be. But a swarm of overwhelming recollections reaching up from the black void of his memory had made the bottle he'd acquired since *Elysium* docked too easy a solution to ignore. Now he stood at the railing of the skydock, white-knuckled, and gripping a metal bar that was the only thing between him and the numbness of an empty, endless sky.

Elias hadn't expected to survive. That he was alive at all was a quandary beyond his grasp, and not understanding was even worse than living.

His breath came in a slow drag as the viscous fire of the cheap brandy burned its way through his system. His eyes were red, his posture slack. He had never been one to indulge in drunkenness before, so it hadn't taken much of the poison to put him in his current state. When he'd been Azrael, when he had served the Eternal Order as its willing, brainwashed killer, he had treated his body as a temple. Now freed, the abuse he heaped upon it had intensified. Ironic. He should be taking better care of himself.

But when every waking moment walked the razor's edge of avoiding his crewmates' implacable stares, it took most of his mental energy to keep his own temper in line. When he lay awake for hours in his new cabin praying for sleep to take him, the smaller sins seemed absurd to reject. When he closed his eyes the nightmares rose again, a different color of horror every night, and the cold sweats left him parched and aching come the dawn. He would rise exhausted, head pounding, limbs burning, and begin the whole affair again.

There was nothing but vice to keep the demons away.

The bottle rested on the planks next to him. The winds whistled mournfully over its open lip. Elias's trembling left hand gripped the rail. His right held a long knife. The sunlight danced off it in a hundred dirty shades of gold that darkened as he watched to a familiar, dull red.

He hadn't come here to contemplate. The truth was he hadn't come here with any specific purpose at all, other than to escape *Elysium*. The ship, floating suspended in the heavens, was several hundred feet away. Longer by the winding catwalks of the skydocks he'd followed to get where he was.

But now he considered it. Beyond the rail there was only open sky, and a long, long fall to the lands far below. Or simply to the abyss, if the stone and dirt was missed. He thought about what it would be like to fall forever into the darkness beneath the sky. There were only ghost stories to answer that. Ghost stories, old myths, and the fearful mumblings of madmen.

The only thing Elias couldn't quite figure out was whether he was a madman, or a ghost.

The long knife gleamed in his hand. This wasn't the first time he'd thought about doing it. But every time before, it had just been conjecture. An idle thought that happened to have the weight of inevitability. *I'll get to it later,* he'd tell himself. *If I have to.*

Now he was alone, drunk, with only his knife for company. He held it before his face, stared at it with a dull gaze. It was the thinking about it that pulled him up short. That was the problem. He needed to get on with it.

Everyone would be better off.

"What're you doing, boy?"

The words cut across his thoughts, and the young man turned to see the big, burly figure of Bjorn standing a short distance from him. He was dressed in a thick coat of sheepskins and wore a pair of big clomping black boots that made Elias wonder how he'd been able to approach unheard. The alcohol, he told himself. That was why his senses weren't what they should be.

"Isnnit obvious?" Elias slurred. "mmm *voting.*"

The big man's eyes sized him up and down, something halfway between disgust and worry in their depths. Then he stepped closer and held out his hand. Elias looked at it, then at his knife with its infinite shades of gold and red.

"Give me the knife, boy," Bjorn insisted. Quiet.

"You're not letting me walk away with it, are you?" Elias asked. His fingers caressed the hilt.

Bjorn's level gaze remained on him. "I'm not."

Vision blurry, Elias turned to meet the older, more experienced stare. His head pounded and he swayed, unsteady. "I could just put it in your throat, then finish myself, you know," he said. "I'm fast enough."

"I know," Bjorn whispered. "But you won't. Because you're not Azrael. Spite isn't what drives you."

"You don't know me," Elias answered. "You don't even *like* me."

"I don't *trust* you, boy," Bjorn snorted. "That's the difference. I don't trust you because you're a half-cocked walking mess. I don't trust you because you don't trust yourself. But give me time – give them all time – and that'll come. Now give me the knife."

The last time Elias stood opposite the big man, they'd both held swords in their hands and faced one another across a rocky, blood-splattered valley floor. Bjorn still bore the bandage from the wound Elias had given him when he'd gone by the name of Azrael. He'd left that life, and that name, behind. The recollections burned in his mind, an aching, raw scar on his thoughts and emotions, but he still had the ability to say of himself that it was *the past*, and not the present. The blade longed to cut something. His hands shook.

Then he flipped it, and presented the handle to the bigger man. When Bjorn clasped the grip, however, Elias didn't let go. He met the big man's gaze and said, "There's something I need you to help me with."

Elias staggered up the gangway and into *Elysium*. His head pounded, and he leaned on the bigger man's arm so as not to topple off and into the heavens. The moment they stepped into the bay, Elias staggered away from Bjorn and caught himself on a recently loaded crate. He pushed himself up, getting his bearings. The interior of the ship was nicer, by far, than any other he'd traveled in. Warm hardwood, exposed steel beams and burnished brass were everywhere, with viewports positioned to take the greatest advantage of natural light.

In the month since Elias had joined *Elysium*'s crew – since he had turned against his former masters and abandoned the name of Azrael – Bjorn had hardly spoken to him. Even on their last mutual days spent in the infirmary, they'd avoided acknowledging one another's presence, as if even a spare glance might summon their unfinished duel from the valley floor in Port Providence. A duel that Elias had won, albeit when he was still calling himself Azrael.

"Get your clippers," Elias said. "We're going to the viewing deck after I hit my cabin."

"If you try to jump," Bjorn warned, "I swear to the gods of my ancestors I'll drag you back up by the collar of your shirt and beat you senseless."

"Too drunk to jump," Elias muttered, heading for his own room. "I'd just fall."

The primary cabins of *Elysium* had already been occupied when Elias became a permanent member of its crew, so one of the passenger cabins in the belly of the vessel had become his. Whereas the others opened their doors onto the central corridor of the upper deck, the simple, metal door to Elias's room opened directly into the cargo hold. When he stepped through, he stood for a few silent moments as a viewport-shaped slice of sunlight spilled across his living space. As far as places to lay your head went, it wasn't bad. The floor was polished hardwood, the double bed pushed against the wall. A bookcase sat opposite the viewport, bare, and a washing station and latrine were retracted into the wall. The sound of his breath and heartbeat filled the silence. Opposite him, in the room's farthest, darkest corner, a hastily made rack held the polished black steel of Azrael's armor, minus the helmet lost back in Port Providence.

He hadn't worn it since he came onboard. His reflection stared back at him from the burnished black and gold, perfectly maintained out of compulsive habit. Elias stared. The armor stayed where it was.

Someday, he thought, I will have to put it on again.

And on that day, he would be recognized. They would find him. All of them.

The thought sent a shudder through him, and he reached for the longsword that hung in its scabbard from the headboard. Its straight crosspiece was gold-chased, the lower half of its two-handed grip wrapped in wire. The broad fishtail pommel glinted in the sunlight as Elias gingerly lifted the sword called Oath of Aurum from where it hung and buckled the blade about his waist. He pulled the first few inches of hollow-ground, diamond-spined silver blade from the sheath. The steel gleamed as if lit from within, and he felt the familiar warmth of its enchantment respond to his touch. It fortified him. This, at least, he could still carry. Though it was legend in some circles, few people knew what Oath of Aurum looked like.

That Elias had taken it from the dead hands of a virtuous man he'd killed would haunt him for the rest of his life.

No, not Elias. Azrael.

He shook his head and released a fearful, measured breath into the air. Was there a difference?

There had to be, he reminded himself. And now,

with Bjorn's help, he would make that difference more pronounced.

He headed back up towards the viewing deck, still unsteady on his feet, but helped along the way by a simple conviction to get where he was going without painful embarrassment. When he got there, he found Bjorn waiting. The winds of Ishtier's vast port-bay blew the big man's coat all about him in a chaotic swirl. A sea of smaller craft hung suspended in the sky from the thousand branches of the vast, wooden dock apparatus. From this far away, the immense structure looked like a thorn-bristled beehive. It would be dark soon. The evening sky had faded from golds and reds to the deep purples and blues of twilight, and amidst the darkness of the port, the running lamps of countless ships twinkled.

Bjorn had caught the gist of what Elias intended, and the big man watched him now, his tools stuffed into his long coat pockets. The expression on his face was somber. "You sure about this, boy?"

Elias swayed, gripped the railing with his left hand to steady himself. After everything he'd been through, it was inappropriate to be disconcerted by what he was about to do. "I have to do the first part myself," he said. It was important. Symbolic.

He let go the rail, reached behind his head, and gathered his long, thick dark hair up in his hands. He pulled it into a tail at the back of his head. Then, clutching that in his left fist, he drew Oath of Aurum with his right. The blade glowed defiant in the growing darkness. A brief vision of Lord Roland swam before his eyes. His teacher. Former master. Implacable and relentless.

"I renounce you," Elias whispered. "And everything you represent."

He sliced upward with the sword's enchanted blade. Felt his hair pull at his scalp, then come loose about his face. He looked at the length of hair in his fist, then flung it into the abyss.

Then he sat back on a stool that Bjorn had fetched and, submitting himself to the trust of the man that had been his enemy only a month past, closed his eyes. Bjorn drew his clippers, grunting, "Yeah, can't have you looking like that, boy."

The snipping of shears and scissors filled Elias's ears, as bits of hair fell like rain to the deck.

CHAPTER TWO
REVELS ENDED

Walking around with nobody trying to kill her was still a luxury so far as Aimee was concerned. So as the sun dipped out of sight and the night fell over Ishtier's port, she walked beneath the soft glow of innumerable crystals suspended in the air high overhead. As if in a dream, her booted feet carried her over the long dirt road past a bazaar of shopfronts, fruit-vendors, and buildings half formed of earth sculpted by the indigenous sorcerers the local language called the Stone-Singers.

When Aimee asked Harkon why such a useful discipline had never been exported, the older mage had shrugged. "It doesn't seem to work on other lands. Only people born on Ishtier can do it, and only on Ishtier. The best minds in magic have never sussed out why."

The Third Prime of magic: things did not always happen as men understood they should.

She wore her long blue coat, and her knee-high boots had mud from the previous day's expedition with her teacher to the crystal cliffs, there to measure the growth of emerald obelisks that pushed further from the earth every year. Ishtier was less a whole landmass, and more a collection of hundreds of close-floating islands, each with its own unique biome. The name Ishtier itself referred to the main isle with its Crystal Port on which Aimee now stood. The locals had their own names for the hundreds of other, smaller islands, but she'd never learned them.

"Hey Aimee," Clutch said behind her. "Hold up. Vlana's gonna hurl again."

The pilot's dark face wore an amused expression as she brushed back blue hair from in front of her eyes and adjusted her leather jacket. A short distance away, Vlana leaned over the edge of a fountain, her thin eyes shooting glares at the pilot. The tanned face of the natural-born skyfarer had turned green. "Shut up, halfer," she muttered. "You know being on the ground makes me nauseous."

"You spent most of a day on the ground when we crashed in Port Providence," Clutch fired back. "Also, watch your mouth, ship rat."

Ship rat – Aimee had learned – was skyfarer slang for natural-born skyfarers, such as Vlana and her twin brother Vant, who had spent their whole lives on skycraft. Halfer referred to people like Clutch: skyfarers that lived and worked on ships, but came from land. Normally both terms were considered deeply offensive, but Clutch and Vlana tossed them back and forth with affection.

Vlana stuck out her tongue. "I never actually left the ship."

"Details," Clutch grinned.

"Do I want to know what someone like me is called?" Aimee asked.

"No," both answered.

They walked on, laughing. The trip portside hadn't

been intended as a girls' night for the three women, but Harkon and Vant were currently busy and Elias and Bjorn had stayed shipside. They'd already dined at a restaurant uptown that served a sort of shelled crustacean the locals called crystal-crab in a spicy sauce. Now they perused the shopfronts as the last light in the vast east faded behind the banks of immense clouds. They wandered further inland, past the immigration offices with their universal symbols of doors and hands, past the various guild Chapterhouses and the long, opal-tiled walkway that led to the governor's manor. Then they stopped at a repair shop where Vlana and the owner haggled for close to ten minutes over a rare tool that Aimee didn't recognize: a steel rod inlaid with gold filigree and capped with a multifaceted emerald that faintly glimmered in the shop's light.

It cost enough money that when Vlana handed over the slats, Clutch raised her eyebrows. "Where'd you get that kinda money?" the pilot asked as the three of them strode once more out onto the street. "A Storm-Kraken's stomach?"

"Unlike some people," Vlana said, "I save my earnings, rather than blowing months' worth on two days with an expensive prostitute."

"It's 'courtesan,'" Clutch corrected her with a grin. "And for your information, his name is Juno, and I'm very fond of him."

"Hey, I'm not judging how you spend your time or your payment," Vlana said, holding her hands up, the bag of her new acquisition dangling from one thumb. "I'm just saying – we each have our priorities. And this is going to make cleaning out the nav-panels *so* much easier.

The head of this thing is pure Ishtier Organic Emerald. I checked. Anywhere but here, an ounce of that stuff is a year's takings of a pay-grade much higher than mine. Here, though? They just grow more."

"Why haven't the guilds monopolized the production?" Clutch asked, a curious eyebrow arched. "That's usually their thing."

"That," Aimee interjected, "would be because of the Barrakha Accords. The locals get to control how much of their resources they sell, and how much they keep in free circulation here. Guilds ignore that constantly in other places, but it helps that Ishtier has all sorts of weird magic protecting the place."

Fuck the guilds, Aimee remembered her uncle saying when she was a little girl. *Evil bastards, all of them.*

Aimee followed up her words by looking up into the sky. The stars were coming out in the heavens, despite the crystal glow of the city and its port.

"Still wishing you'd seen a dragon?" Vlana asked.

"Honestly?" Aimee answered. "After everything that happened in Port Providence, I'm glad things are low-key for a change." She paused, let out a relieved breath. "The dragons will keep."

They'd walked a few feet further down the street when Aimee realized Clutch wasn't with them. Both women turned. Their pilot stood amidst several other people, staring up at the sky, her eyes wide. As Aimee watched, Clutch's mouth fell open. The young sorceress turned herself, and immediately beheld the reason. Against the darkness of the night sky, a deeper shadow – impossibly vast – blotted out the stars.

• • •

Aimee rarely lacked for words. Her upbringing was steeped in literature, in the fine speaking forms of charm-school, in the halls of the Academy of Mystic Sciences. The thing that now approached Crystal Port brought her up short. Only in Port Providence, months ago, faced with the immensity of a flying mountain known as the *Iron Hulk*, had she seen something more impressive... but the hulk – for all its terror – had been a mountain. A flying fortress built into the interior of an immense chunk of rock moving like another island through the sky.

This wasn't a mountain, it was a *ship*. A ship that – while still smaller than the *Iron Hulk* – was nonetheless bigger than the entire port it now approached. Her mind reeled, grasped about for the term she'd memorized in her hours upon hours spent studying ship types back in the academy days. She still came up short. Only Vlana's laughter shook her free of it.

"What?" the shorter quartermaster said. "Never seen a behemoth before?"

"Sure," Clutch said before Aimee could get words out. "But isn't it a bit early in the year for a proper flotilla to be showing up around here?"

Behemoth. Flotilla. Right. Aimee shook her head to rid it of the fog summoned by the vision of something so vast. Behemoths were the huge trade ships that plied the skylanes of the Dragon Road, cities unto themselves, filled with crews who were born, lived, and died upon them. They carried everything from bulk foodstuffs to the rare and exotic all across the Drifting Lands. But they never came this close. They – and the flotillas of other such ships they traveled with – would station themselves well away from the edges of the smaller ports like Ishtier and send smaller skycraft with their goods to hock. Even in Havensreach, she'd only glimpsed vessels like this at a distance. Only at the vast, mythical ports of the great powers could a behemoth hope to dock directly with the earth.

"It–" Aimee's words briefly failed her as she took several steps forward, then recovered, "–it's *beautiful*."

Abruptly, she took off jogging towards the docks, away from the shopfronts and the vendors and the restaurants and the roadside stands. Away from crystal lamps and familiarity towards – as she always did – the unknown. The pilot and the quartermaster ran behind, chasing her until she reached an unused skyjack, all battered wood and rusted metal, thrusting out into the empty heavens, a would-be bridge to the clouds.

From here the view was much clearer. Standing at the rail, Aimee could see the behemoth's colossal frame illuminated by piecemeal splashes of light amidships, and from beneath by the soft glow of Ishtier. High up above, the top of its hull vanished into the night, identifiable only by the way its outline cut off the stars, and the running lights and windows intermittently viewable as specks along the length. It was brick-shaped: long, rectangular, the bow a flat face of huge bay doors at the bottom and multistoried, cathedralesque viewports towards the top. A city's length away, her tail end could be noted by the muted glow of multiple exhaust ports, each larger than the biggest buildings in Havensreach's inner ring.

From where she stood, Aimee saw only a few windows with any clarity, but behind those, she caught glimpses of movement, and along awning-covered outer walkways and tiered, external decks, she saw the shadows of countless swarming crew-members.

Just above the bow, running lamps illuminated a name painted onto a pitted, scarred hull. Each letter was as tall as *Elysium*.

ISEULT

Aimee let out a breath she'd held unnoticed. Turning, she flashed her crewmates a grin. "It's named after one of the mythical lovers," she said. "From the pre-scriptures!"

"And she's *damn* close," Clutch said as she eyed the slowing, enormous vessel.

"Battle damage?" Vlana asked the pilot. "Here out of emergency?"

"If so," the pilot mused, frowning, "she's in the wrong damn place. There's not a drydock in all of Ishtier that could take a behemoth."

A sudden rushing noise assaulted their ears, the now-familiar blast of forward engines firing to bring the immense vessel to a halt. "Well," Clutch muttered dryly. "At least they're not planning to crush the whole port. That's good of them."

"I don't see any damage," Vlana added as her eyes traced the length of the ship. "Nothing more than the usual wear and tear of long-term service. She's been patched a lot, but most of these things get completely rebuilt over the course of their lives."

Despite the wonder of the colossal skyship blotting the night out before her, Aimee stepped back from the rail. She stretched her memory to recall what she'd learned about ships like this: their crews and passenger populations numbered in the tens, sometimes hundreds of thousands. Maybe millions. Among them could be any number of ears, informants, or – conversely – sources of information. And before they did anything else, she wagered, they should get back to *Elysium*.

"Yeah," Clutch was saying slowly as she squinted at *Iseult*. "She definitely shouldn't be here right now. Not this time of year, and not this close."

"We need to get back to the ship," Aimee said. "I need my books, and there'll be no view like the one from the common area."

Her hands itched to get the texts in hand, to review her lists of ship types, to see if one of *Elysium*'s vast ledgers had the known behemoths written down by name and history. If it didn't, she could always ask her teacher.

And if he didn't know, she thought abruptly... she could always ask Elias. The image of green eyes and a handsome face, at once the crux of a host of contentious emotions, floated momentarily through her mind before Aimee dismissed it. Not right now.

And that was when it happened: a discharge of arcane energy from the prow of the ship erupted into the air hundreds of feet above and before it. Lines of magic shot from several different tiered decks, and Aimee thought she glimpsed the silhouettes of sorcerers at the base of each flash. Twelve of them, she counted, mingling their power to create a visible display high above the tallest buildings of Ishtier's port. First came a rapid series of glyphs burning in the night sky – guild symbols, identifying the ship, her affiliations with the flotilla, the shipping guilds, the Skyspeakers' Guild, the Pilots' Guild. All the necessary credentials.

Then a face – robed, tired, immense, chalk-pale,

strong-browed, and marked with a single black bar across
the left eye – appeared in the heavens. It spoke, every
phrase repeated in the common, and local tongues.
Words flashed beneath the moving mouth to ensure the
deaf could understand, and heed what was being said.

"Ishtier, who is bountiful and beautiful," the voice
rippled, grief-thick and formal, across the port. "We are
Iseult of Flotilla Visramin. We come to you in grief for the
death of your son, Amut, who was our captain. Amut of
the kind hand. Amut, the Lion of Heaven. Amut of the
strong arm. Amut of the wise eyes. He has passed from
this world, and we have come as the wind, to lay him in
his native soil."

The message began to repeat itself. Aimee stepped
back. "Yeah," she murmured, "back to the ship."

"I agree," Clutch muttered. "Don't like being far from
my own helm and sitting in the shadow of something that
imposing."

"There is *all* sorts of subtext in that statement, Clutch,"
Vlana said with a wry laugh.

"Shut up, ship rat," Clutch said.

The three women jogged up the ramp and into the cargo
hold. Aimee didn't stop to take stock of things, she hoofed
it up the ladder and into the central corridor that spanned
the spine of the prototype warship-turned-exploratory
vessel that was her home.

"Alright!" she yelled. "Who's onboard?"

Clutch ran past her when she reached the common
area, headed for the bridge. "Vant!" the pilot called. "Did
you fall asleep on your bridge hammock again?"

"Calm your damn boots," a muffled answer came from

the exterior viewing deck. Aimee squinted, recognizing Bjorn's voice. "We're just finishing up."

Against the dim light of the port, two silhouettes could be seen on the viewing deck. Aimee did a double-take. Bjorn – discernible by his size – was standing over the angular frame of another man, seated, his back to the common area. Bjorn was holding scissors. The other silhouette – Elias, his voice confirmed – touched the side of his head. "That was *really loud*."

"Hold still, you big baby." Bjorn forced the other man to straighten before going back to grooming his hair, apparently. "Just give us a moment, Miss Laurent."

"You know what, never mind," Aimee answered, continuing up to the bridge, washing her hands of that... weirdness. "I don't want to know."

The bridge flickered to life as she stepped onto it, just in time to watch as Clutch jerked the cord at one end of a hammock hung between bulkheads, and sent a squawking Vant tumbling to the floor. "Are you shitting me?" the pilot barked. "You have a cabin!"

The engineer vaulted upwards and unleashed a cloud of curse words, half of which Aimee didn't yet know. She caught a few, though. *Sky jockey* was in there, also *Cloud-Fucker*.

Aimee had been on *Elysium* for some months and she still wasn't sure if the engineer and pilot were mortal enemies or the best of friends. Maybe they didn't know either.

"You're on night shift!" Clutch snapped back. "Sleeping is the opposite of what you do on night shift!"

"I was resting my eyes, crazy halfer!"

"In a hammock, Vant," Vlana chided her twin, crossing

the room to her navigation station.

"Look, just because I know how to optimize," the engineer grunted.

"Where's Harkon?" Aimee cut in. As funny as this was, she couldn't justify what she wanted to do without his permission.

"He's either portside giving one of those lectures he gives any school that will take him for money," Vant said, "or he's sleeping. So go find him or risk waking him up."

"The latter, if you must know," the sleep-heavy, deep voice of Harkon Bright said from behind them all, a look on his face halfway between irritated and amused. "But thank you for your discretion. It's comforting to know that my crew still can't do anything quietly."

"This one is Aimee's fault," Vlana said from her console. "A behemoth showed up and she insisted we come back. Shouting."

"Traitor," Aimee muttered.

"I keep telling people you can't trust my sister," Vant beseeched the ceiling. "Nobody *ever* believes me."

"To be fair," Clutch said, "it's close enough to port that I'm surprised there isn't panic in the streets."

"It's right up against the docks," Aimee affirmed.

"Practically fucking them," Clutch added. "The catwalks look all sorts of uncomfortable."

Harkon's brows drew together. He looked at Vant expectantly.

"What?" the engineer asked. "It's a ship coming into port. They do that."

The master portalmage turned his gaze to Aimee next, with an expression that said "please justify waking me up. Now."

Aimee drew herself up to her full height, flashed that same smile that had owned the valediction at graduation, and said, "I want to do a flyby."

Harkon frowned, considering. "Reasons?"

"One," Aimee said, "she's away from her flotilla. That's highly unusual. Two – as Clutch mentioned – she's clogging up the whole port, which has got to be making people angry. Three, according to the magical projection they just sent into the sky, their captain died and they're looking to bring him home. I think it merits a closer look."

Harkon weighed that. He arched a single eyebrow. "And it doesn't hurt, I imagine, that you've never seen a behemoth this closely before?"

"Oh, not at all," Aimee said with a grin. "But since we've got reason anyway…"

Silence. The crew looked on. Then Harkon straightened the collar of his evening robe and said, "Do it."

Vant unhooked his hammock from the bulkheads and threw it over his shoulder in the most indignant way possible. "Someone better tell the hair stylist and his client that it's about to get windy out there," he said before he vanished down the hall.

The metadrive thrummed to life moments later. There was a brief, clamorous exchange between Clutch and the dockmasters before the mooring clamps released, then the ship swept free, turning in a soft arc through the starlit sky. *Elysium* had been docked quite a distance from the central port, so they now approached *Iseult* from the rear, and well above. Vast exhaust vents glowed blue in the darkness, their dull roar audible even at range. Clutch angled the wheel forward, then aimed the ship starboard. *Elysium* dropped, turned, then began to move along the side of the city-sized skycraft. Aimee saw a vast upper deck carved deep with verandas, rich balconies, and the swells of domed structures that could be anything from houses of worship to stargazing labs to internal gardens.

"Typical behemoth," Clutch muttered. "Huge. Lower level covered in scaffolding and ad-hoc ramshackle crazy. Upper levels looking like a bunch of pretentious architects vomited all over a flying brick."

The sounds of heavy footfalls announced the arrival of Bjorn and Elias on the bridge. The former wore a long leather apron that he used for cooking and barber work. Aimee did a brief double-take. Elias's hair, previously long, thick, and falling to his shoulders, was now cut short, highlighting the angular lines of his long, thin face. There were dark circles beneath his green eyes, and the hand that gripped one of the bridge rails was white-knuckled. He caught her glance, gave her a small nod. Her small smile in response was reflexive.

"Now that thing's a sight," Bjorn muttered from the back. "Less hodgepodge than typical."

"*Iseult* is co-flagship of Flotilla Visramin," Harkon explained from just behind Aimee. "Her sister ship is *Tristan*, but it seems she came here alone."

"Not worth diverting an entire flotilla for one man's funeral?" Vlana posited.

"I imagine not," Harkon considered. "But it's still a big detour. The Dragon Road demands strict schedules."

"There are no lights running on the upper deck," Elias murmured. "Odd."

"Why?" Aimee asked over her shoulder.

"The lamps of a behemoth's upper deck are a signal to smaller craft," Elias explained quietly. "They alert other ships in the flotilla, or port, that there's something immense and covered with dwellings out there." He frowned, peering across the darkened expanse before them. "They only kill the lamps if their grid is down, or if they're paranoid about raiders."

"Raided behemoths often, did you?" Vlana muttered bitterly.

Elias fell immediately silent. A quick glance at his face showed Aimee a rapid spasm of regret and pain, before the iron curtains of discipline and control dropped, and his face was a mask again.

The panel to Clutch's right abruptly flashed, and the auto-quills started furiously scribbling across their parchment. Aimee crossed the bridge as the pilot focused on keeping them straight, checked the reading, then looked back at her teacher in surprise.

"Uh, teacher? We've got a communication incoming. Addressed to you by name."

Harkon frowned. "Let it through."

A half second later, the spell-projected image of a copper-skinned man with a wispy, pale beard hovered in the center of the bridge. A ragged scar traced from forehead to cheek on the left side of his face, the eye a jarring milk-white. When he saw Harkon, his smile – if Aimee could call it that – looked genuine. "I'll be damned. Hark, what in the name of the thousand gods are you doing here?"

"What I always do, Rachim: explore, fly, get into trouble. What are you doing on a behemoth?"

The man named Rachim seemed to shift, glanced behind him, and lowered the tone of his voice. "Long story, but suffice to say, I'm in charge of a few things on *Iseult* these days. Inter-ship relations falls under the purview. We should talk."

Harkon seemed to catch something in the tone. As Aimee watched, her teacher's frown deepened, and he said, "Name the place."

"Here," Rachim answered. "I'm issuing you and your crew a formal invitation to the funeral of Captain Amut. I'll be in touch with more details soon, but for the moment, you might want to veer off. My superiors are twitchy tonight."

"We'll be there," Harkon said, and without a further nod or comment, the projected image vanished.

"Well, *that's* not nothing," Aimee said thoughtfully in the silence that followed.

"Clutch," Harkon said. "Take us back to berth. We've got some errands to run."

His eyes swept *Elysium*'s assembled crew. "...And you all need to find something suitable to wear."

CHAPTER THREE
THE GRIEF OF ISEULT

There had to be a phrase, Elias reflected, in at least *one* of the languages he knew, for the supreme, self-conscious awkwardness of being a mass murderer attending the funeral of a good man. More likely, he acknowledged, it didn't yet exist because it hadn't yet been invented. His situation was unique.

Two days since the flyby of the behemoth called *Iseult*, and now he stood with *Elysium*'s crew upon a vast marble-tiled platform that floated between the port docks and the behemoth behind them. They stood in a line, along the edge of an open column between two clusters of mourners, waiting beneath the sun-shading vastness of *Iseult*'s immense, cathedral-like bow. All to his left, Elias's new crewmates waited in somber silence, whilst around and in front of them were spread a panoply of figures draped in importance both genuine and presumed. Many displayed the oddly-shaved heads, the elaborate jewels and spell-fashioned hodgepodge of fine, expensive clothes worn by shipboard courtiers, standing in the company of stoic, uniformed officer aristocrats. The black knight saw lips painted gold, guild brands outlined in body gems, silver and platinum adorning the delicate fingertips of men and women alike. Upon their city-ship, these people were wealthier than some land-born kings.

And Elias Leblanc couldn't stop noticing how murderously on edge every damned one of them was. Oh, none of them desperately clutched at the – largely ceremonial, occasionally real – blades hanging at their hips, nor did they finger the elaborately designed custom firearms upon their belts with the familiar terror of people about to start shooting. But to the senses of a trained killer, there were cues in abundance, when a group of people thrummed with the energy of unease and paranoia. *The smell of fear,* Lord Roland had called it.

Elias's jaw tightened at the recognition, and the dark, sardonic acknowledgment of where the skill to sense it came from. He was surrounded by a riot of mournful color, and couldn't shake the sense that it was ready to erupt into a whirlwind of red.

Then a horn sounded, and the focus changed. Elias turned and watched as two lines of crimson-robed, armored figures approached, the billowing cloth of their vestments stirring in the unique way garments did when heavy armor was worn beneath. These, then, were the Captain's Guard: the highly trained, elite warriors responsible for the defense of the behemoth's late commander. Their gauntleted hands carried tall banners, the first of which bore only the simple black glyphs of the guilds known as the Twelve. After them came a riot of heraldry as the principal households of *Iseult*'s officer class were carried forward.

Next, six figures walked with a bier on which rested the silk-draped form of Captain Amut's corpse. The petals of aurora orchids surrounded the dead man, and little objects – the keepsakes of crew and family, Elias supposed – lay on either side of him in reverence. A glass apple. A simple long knife. A crudely carved wooden comb.

Elias shifted from foot to foot, put his hands in the pockets of the black and green long coat he'd acquired for the occasion. Oath of Aurum's pommel brushed against his arm from where the sword hung on his hip. The steel was warm today, though Elias didn't feel particularly virtuous. In the face of vast ceremonial grief, his own emotions were muted by exhaustion and over-exposure. For all that it seemed wrong to feel that way, sometimes a body was just a body. He'd seen plenty.

They carried it past him. The first two pallbearers were men in black robes, silver-lipped, heavy-eyed, bearing short boarding swords. Behind them, a pair of officers in pale blue uniforms walked stoically, and last came what seemed to be a priest, and the man that had addressed Harkon on the bridge of *Elysium*. Rachim, Elias seemed to recall. He was shorter in person, with rounded shoulders, and a limp that slowed his fellow pallbearers. He must have been dear to the late captain, to be afforded such an honor at the attendant expense of the aesthetic these people clearly prized.

Elias wondered how the man had lost his left eye. He didn't seem accident-prone, nor did he look like the sort of man who went hunting. But the stance, the way his face surveyed his surroundings, the lilt of his hard-edged stoicism, those told a story. Elias felt a wan smile tug at the corner of his mouth. So, Rachim was prone to getting into fights, and often enough to pay a price for it.

No wonder he and Harkon were friends.

Elias turned and watched as they passed him, headed for the place where the delegation from Ishtier would receive the body. Glancing down the line, he had a perfect sequential view of his crewmates: the twins, Vant and Vlana, wore simple black fatigues, their boots freshly shined, brooches he'd never seen them wear before on their chests.

Clutch stood immediately to their left. The brown-skinned pilot was a study in practiced aloofness. Her blue hair was elaborately braided down the center of her head, and her leather flight jacket had been freshly patched and cleaned. Her arms were folded. Her gray eyes watched the proceedings with a lazy sort of interest.

Next was Bjorn. Him Elias understood, mostly. The old white-haired mercenary was of even height with Elias, with a barrel chest and immense hands. His beard was thick and – at least today – set with rings, and his big coat was furs and leathers sewn together. They'd hardly spoken since he'd cut Elias's hair.

Beside Bjorn, Harkon Bright cut an understated, imposing figure. Perhaps it was the legends that clung to him, or the mixture of gravitas and mischief inherent in the mage's dark eyes. Perhaps it was that Elias owed him an unpayable debt. Either way, the young man couldn't look at him for long, so instead he shifted his gaze to Harkon's apprentice.

Aimee de Laurent had laid aside her long blue coat for dark apprentice's robes that draped flatteringly over a slender, athletic figure that somehow managed to stand relaxed, poised, and yet brimming with a fierce curiosity all at once. Her gold hair was bound up in an intricate knot at the back of her head, and her silver apprentice's chain was clasped behind her pale neck. She was looking away from him, just then, her bright blue eyes fixed on the procession currently passing her with a somberness that didn't quite hide her academic fascination. Alone among the crew, she knew the full extent of the crimes he had committed, the things he had endured, and the nebulous, still foggy time before the Eternal Order had taken him.

He tried not to dwell overmuch on what that fact meant. The emotions it evoked were tempestuous at best, sharp in their pain at worst. After a handful of seconds, Elias looked elsewhere. It was no more complex than it was with her teacher: a debt was owed. He could never repay it.

Perhaps that was a lie, but lies had their uses.

A voice sounded from the priest as the coffin was laid down, and Elias turned to watch. The ceremony was beginning.

An hour later, and the young man in green and black was doing his best not to get lost in an ocean of painted faces. The ceremony had been brief. The ruling class of *Iseult* cleaved to a strain of the thousand-god faith that held the soul of the departed as a righteous burden that had to be carried to where it would rest. Having given Amut to his own people in Ishtier, they now celebrated his life with the candid relief of those who were no longer burdened.

Or, at least, that was what he'd managed to suss out from the handful of conversations he'd had. Elias stood now on the black marble steps at the far end of a vast ballroom with a ceiling enchanted to display the open sky. All around him, the officer and courtier classes rubbed elbows and spoke with the unique affectations of an upper class that fancied themselves meritocratic, but guarded the gates to their status with invisible vipers.

Elias was on edge. During his time as Azrael he had watched places like this burn to cinders in the heavens. There was no accounting for that, and deeper down, a part of him acknowledged that every second he lived was stolen time. Nonetheless, the fear pulled at him, making him tense. If any of these people should recognize his face…

It didn't do to obsess. Instead, he did his best to pick out who the power players in the room were. He watched courtiers move, their gestures and their posture. The secret language of head-lilts, eye-twitches and gesticulating fingers that all people spoke with their bodies. *Learn*, Roland's recalled voice repeated in his head, *to find the most powerful people in the room. Learn what they want.*

Elias grimaced. *I'll never be rid of you, my Lord, will I?*

He made a careful circuit of the room, affecting the stance of a simple courtier. Men and women stared at him as he passed. Eyes raked him from boots to face. That wasn't unusual. Birth had given him physical beauty. A lifetime of hard training had honed it into an effortless grace and charm. But these traits came with as many problems as benefits. It wasn't that it made going unnoticed impossible – the world was full of empty heads with pretty faces – but that managing that attention required nuance. One form of carriage could make him the focal point of everyone in the room. A small adjustment, and only *certain* people would pay any mind to the handsome man in black and green. The key was being aware of what was needed, and when.

He adjusted his posture: slack, relaxed – Gods, that wasn't easy right now – and molded his smile into something casual, self-absorbed, and not as smart as it presumed. The looks he received changed almost immediately. Only certain sorts of people eyed him now, and none of them in a dangerous way. Now he could move.

It took him the better part of twenty minutes to discern who in this room had real power, but once he'd memorized a few faces, he stopped short, briefly wrong-footed standing beside a refreshment table. He was still falling into the old patterns: learn who the powerful people were, assess them, examine them, and then what?

His own words as Azrael echoed in his ears, as if they still rang in the throne room of Port Providence. *"Absolute oblivion, majesty."*

His veneer nearly cracked. He wrested it back into place. Azrael had been trained to assess everyone in the room, find the powerful, discern what they wanted, and use it to destroy them. Elias still had the skill, but he didn't know what to *do* with it. He scanned the crowd again. Vlana and Vant were talking to a man with the brooch of the engineers' guild on his shoulder. No good. One of them was ambivalent to him, the other wished him death. Clutch he barely knew, and she was being happily chatted up by a high-collared helmsman. Bjorn was by the window getting solidly drunk.

Harkon. Harkon could make use of this. He spotted the old mage standing on the opposite side of the hall, sipping a glass of some dark, amber alcohol. Elias started towards him, only to stop halfway across the elaborately tiled floor when Rachim and two other men stepped between them, and the three began a quiet, urgent conversation that was quickly carried out onto a balcony. It was well that Elias was trying to seem a bit like a foolish courtier. Standing stumped in the center of a funerary soiree – empty-headed was how he felt.

Damn.

Move, fool, his mind reminded him. Standing here in the open like this was conspicuous. He turned and cast his eyes about for the only other person to whom he could give this information, when suddenly there she was, right in front of him. Aimee arched an eyebrow at the look on his face. "You look lost."

Elias stumbled for a moment. Her eyebrow climbed higher. He offered her his arm. "Just go with it," he muttered. She took it.

Once they'd walked to the side of the room previously occupied by Harkon, Aimee looked up at him, fixing him with the curious stare of her blue eyes. "Alright," she said. "I don't know if it's just because I know you–" they both looked briefly askance at that, it was an awkward subject "–or if you're just *that* high strung, but you look like you're ready to jump through the nearest window. Explain, please. It's making me nervous."

Elias looked away, scanning the room again. "Well," he answered, measuredly, "not the window."

"Oh for the gods' sake," Aimee placed a slender hand on her forehead. "That wasn't an invitation."

"Wasn't an offer, either," Elias replied. Before they could digress again, he launched into as clean an explanation as could be mustered. "I was trained in the arts of the court," he said, "rigorously, from just as early as… everything else. I have a trained reflex to size up the room, figure out who the resident power players are, and what they might want."

Aimee nodded, following his gaze, as if by so doing she could suck that information out of the air with her eyes. Information was a siren call to the young sorceress. "Alright," she said, folding her arms under her chest and leaning against a black pillar, "I'm not understanding the problem, though. That sounds useful."

"I learned how to do it so I would know who in the room I needed to manipulate or kill."

Understanding registered in her gaze. "Ah."

"You see my problem."

She eyed him mildly. "Assuming you're not going to–"

He frowned. "Of course not." Then he sagged back against the pillar opposite her, resting the back of his head against the cool stone. "But that's part of the problem. Absent that mission I don't know what to do with the information."

She processed that. Aimee de Laurent had a way of looking unnervingly calm when she was assessing a thing. "Well, that's obvious, then. Tell me."

"That was plan B," he admitted.

"I'm assuming plan A wasn't 'kill everyone in the room,'" she said.

"Hilarious," he deadpanned. "No. Plan A was telling Harkon."

Aimee's smile was catlike; both curious and irritated. "And now he's not here. So spill."

Elias nodded. "Fine." He shifted to face the crowd and gestured across the room. "Do you see the white-haired man covered in medals?"

Aimee shifted closer, the better to follow his finger.

She was wearing some sort of perfume. It was distracting. "Yes," she said, nodding.

"Notice the way he's responding to everyone?" Elias said. "Reserved–"

"–but cold. There's no warmth behind the smile," Aimee finished. "I track. But the way those people are surrounding him–"

"–he's someone who matters," Elias confirmed. "Someone who holds position, but elicits conflict."

Her smile was cunning. "So," she said, giving him a sideways look. "Who's he fighting?"

"When you see a grudge," Elias said, "check the shadow first."

She didn't need him to point. Her eyes flicked to the second figure. "So he's got an issue with that pale-haired Violet-Imperium fellow in the red uniform," she murmured. "And… the woman in the ochre dress, with lapis lazuli hairpins. The former of those two is more ambitious than the latter, but pretends he isn't."

Elias smiled. "That's a step further than I'd taken it."

"I'm astute."

"Perhaps," Elias suggested, "you don't actually need me to point out the others."

She frowned sideways at him. Her blue eyes narrowed. "Not fair."

"You're already taking my observations several steps forward," he said. He leaned against the pillar and leveled his gaze on her. "You're smart enough."

"That's the fun of it," she sighed in mock exasperation. "How am I supposed to enjoy myself if I'm not one-upping your assessments?"

Elias shrugged. "Birdwatching?"

She swatted his arm. The first real laugh he'd had in weeks rumbled up from his chest in retort. "The others," he relented, "are a group of identically robed individuals being sought out by half the important people in this room. They're all wearing black samite and rings with opals in them."

"A soldier," Aimee said, "a nobleman, a wisewoman, and a council of some sort." The sorceress brought a hand to her chin and pursed her lips in thought. "With the captain dead," she said, "everything in the webs of power will be bending towards who influences the choice of the new one." She held up a hand to forestall his objection. "You said the next step was figuring out what they wanted, and that's the obvious lead-in."

"Please don't follow my process to its logical conclusion," Elias said. "I don't do that anymore."

She waved away the remark, focused on her thoughts. "Everything I've heard today is that Amut's death was sudden and unexpected."

"And then there was Rachim's tone in his communique with Harkon," Elias added. "There are wheels turning here. Immense ones. The trick is seeing them."

"Why ask us here," she continued, "if not because of that?"

They suddenly looked at each other, and Elias realized in the snap of the moment that they'd both come to the same conclusion.

Then Harkon Bright reemerged from the balcony and, sighting them, made a direct line to the pair. "Get everyone together," he said in low tones. "I've just accepted a request to mediate the ruling council's deliberations to appoint *Iseult*'s new captain. When this behemoth leaves port tomorrow morning, we're going with them."

Elias's eyes flashed to Aimee's. And at the same time, they both muttered, "Shit."

CHAPTER FOUR
BEHIND THE GILDED CURTAIN

It would have been easier for Aimee to focus on the chart in front of her if Vant wasn't screaming in the middle of *Elysium's* galley. The mug of coffee steamed furiously beside her – not hot enough, it was *never* hot enough for two in the morning – and the sky outside was star-dappled blackness broken only by the glow of thousands of running lights.

"Always," Vant shouted on his third circuit around the table. "He always does this."

"Can we calm down for a second?" Vlana asked. "It's too early for yelling."

Vant slammed his gloved hands down on the table. "Could I get more than twenty-four hours' warning before I'm having to do a rush job flushing the chaos dampers? I was up all night doing that. You don't want to know the stuff that came out."

"To be fair," Vlana said, holding up a finger, "this is what you get for waiting a week to get to it."

The engineer's mouth hung open. Then it closed, and he stared at his sister through slitted eyes. "I had to wait."

Vlana sighed. "You were reading trashy Kiscadian

romances in the metadrive room."

"Oh *gods*," Aimee interjected. Her hands pressed to the sides of her head, trying to banish the mental image. "I do not want that knowledge in my head."

Vant glared, then he pointed a finger at his sister and hissed, "It is a very sensitive piece of machinery."

"*Not. Better*," Aimee said.

The engineer stalked back down the corridor, passing Bjorn on his way back up. The gunner paused in the main area and simply asked, "Do I want to know?"

"No," the two women said together.

Bjorn blinked, then shrugged. "Last bit with the portmasters has been cleared. Clutch'll be casting off in a few minutes. Best you all get to your stations."

Aimee straightened, feeling the as-yet-unbanished ache of interrupted sleep complaining in her muscles. She stretched and yawned and picked up her papers. "Where's Harkon? I've been at calculations since I got up and my brain is about ready to melt."

"Talking to Rachim," Bjorn grunted. "What are those calculations for, anyway?"

Aimee blinked twice, then held up her papers. "I decided to plot the number of jumps necessary to get us back to Flotilla Visramin based on the coordinates Harkon passed on. Not my responsibility, I know, but my brain started noodling on it last night, and I realized that the portalmages on *Iseult* aren't being efficient."

Bjorn nodded slowly. "...Aren't being efficient," he repeated.

Aimee rolled her eyes. "Oh please, don't give me that look," she rebuked the mercenary. "Their work is just sloppy in the way that bored professionals get when everything is rote repetition. I'm not about to pick a fight with *Iseult*'s portalmages, I just want to do a better job."

"You do know," the big man said, "that those are fighting words in most professions, right?"

A call came through the tubes, Clutch's voice echoing around the vessel. "Alright, kids, Hark's back aboard, so it's time to cast off. *Iseult* is departing."

"Yes, well," Aimee finished with a dismissive wave of her hand, grinning at the big man as they headed to the bridge. "If they pick it, it's hardly my fault."

Leaving port never got old. Aimee stood on the bridge as the docking clamps disengaged, and watched as the whirling sky filled the whole of the forward viewport. The metadrive growled, and *Elysium* swept into the heavens. The world tilted, and the dark, pre-dawn skies spread out before them. There, in the midst of the vast pincer-sweep of Ishtier's port, was the light-speckled vastness of the behemoth called *Iseult*. Aimee rested her hand upon the rail, taking in its sheer scale with another breath of awe.

The crew was gathered about her, sans Vant, who would be down in the engine room tending his beloved metadrive with the obsessive care of a mother hen. Mugs of coffee or tea steamed in the dim running lights of consoles and sensors.

"We've been instructed to land on pad twelve," Harkon said, standing just behind Aimee. "It's adjacent to Rachim's villa. I want us well battened down by the time they're ready to make the jump."

And then, Aimee reflected, they would be in the immensity of the deep sky. Upon the true vastness of the Dragon Road, where Flotilla Visramin was but one of many trade caravans plying the multi-year routes between the known lands.

Since childhood, the deep sky had held a grim fascination for Aimee; a place truly away from the eyes, the control, of most nations. The place from whence came monster stories, legends, and ghost tales like those her uncle had told beside the de Laurent hearth.

"She looks less paranoid this morning," Elias remarked behind her. Turning, Aimee glimpsed the angular, hungry silhouette of the black knight keeping to the back of the bridge. Hesitating to join the rest of them. He stared past her through the viewport, eyes intent. One hand gripped the ancient sword at his hip like a lifeline. He caught her gaze, and must have taken her staring as a mute request for clarification. "Her lamps are all lit," he said awkwardly.

They came in over the top of the hull. *Iseult* spread out beneath them. Topaz lights shimmered in the dark, danced about the silhouettes of columns and elaborate, beautiful villas, more city than ship. As Aimee watched, they slowed. Clutch turned the wheel, and *Elysium* arced gracefully towards a modest, dome-shaped complex that was hard to see against the pre-dawn sky. A quick series of communiques were exchanged by spell, then *Elysium* paused in mid-air and slowly lowered in front of their destination. Walls of black stone and intermittent white pillars rose about them. Then came the gentle thump of landing gear, and the winding down of the metadrive to a minimal hum.

Clutch sagged back from the wheel, then looked over her shoulder at Harkon. "What now, chief?"

"Get properly dressed," the mage replied. "We'll be meeting our host soon."

Aimee stretched, uncoiling from where she'd placed herself, and draining the last of her mug before she shot Harkon a questioning look. "What degree of formal are we talking?"

The old man gave a shrug of his shoulders as he turned and exited the bridge. "Comfortable. Functional. Cognizant."

Aimee rolled her eyes. "So helpful."

The first thing that struck Aimee about the villa was its elegant and effective use of space. Despite the domes and occasional towers that sprouted from *Iseult*'s top level, Rachim's home was recessed into the surface of the ship. The stairs from the landing pad led down and inward into spacious, art-decorated rooms lit by glow-globes that still flickered in the dim pre-dawn. A cursory glance around, however, told Aimee that during the day, the entire complex would be well lit by sunlight streaming through numerous skylights.

Their host met them in a large sitting room that seamlessly integrated the sensibilities of about nine different cultures and architectural periods. Somehow, it all blended together well, though Aimee could still hear her mother's voice inside her head, balking at the mixture of late period Imperial molding with pre-Imperial detailing. Rachim walked over the moment Harkon stepped through the door. He looked like a man that hadn't slept for days.

"You look like hell," Harkon said.

"I feel like it," Rachim growled. His eyes swept the crew of *Elysium* as they entered. Aimee met the assessing gaze, unflinching. She tried not to yawn. "I just got word that the Officers' Council has scheduled a first debate in less than an hour. I suspect to keep both myself and Lord Viltas from being awake for it. Thank the Great Currents for well-bribed political aides. You can bring two of your people with you. The rest can see about getting themselves settled in here."

Aimee felt her stomach turn, and her face twisted into a disgusted frown. "Back home the senate at least waits a few days before trying to hijack the political process," she deadpanned.

"Underhanded as it is," Rachim answered her, "I can't exactly blame them either. We're headed for the Dragon Road and the deep sky, Miss Laurent. Without a captain, *Iseult*'s choices fall to the Officers' Council. Pity the fate of a ship whose every important decision must be settled by committee."

"Still," Aimee protested.

"Still," Rachim agreed. "She's perceptive, Hark."

Aimee detected just enough sarcasm in the man's tone that she wasn't sure whether she should take it as a compliment.

"Quite," Harkon responded, amused. Then he asked, "How long do we have?"

"Little and less," Rachim replied. "Like I said, pick the two you'll be bringing with you, then we can... Young man, don't touch that."

Aimee spun on her heel. Rachim's words and gaze were directed to the rear of the group and, following them, she found herself staring at a surprised Elias. He was frozen, mid-motion, right next to an old bronze statue of a rearing manticore, and his right index finger was poised just short of its nose. Silence. Elias looked like a child caught with his hand inside a jar of cookies. After a moment, he cleared his throat and awkwardly straightened. "Sorry," he said. "I just... I don't really have an excuse."

Aimee felt a compulsive laugh rise. He looked absurd. Her teacher glanced in her direction, and she swallowed it instead, red-faced. Gods. What was *that* all about?

"My apprentice Aimee will accompany me," Harkon said. Aimee nodded.

"And my bodyguard," the mage continued. "Elias."

The entire crew stopped and stared, Aimee included. Elias looked as surprised as anyone else. "Sir?" he asked.

At Rachim's questioning glance, Harkon continued, "He is an exceptionally gifted swordsman who misses little, and he has a face made for court. That my apprentice is brilliant and capable hardly needs explaining."

Aimee looked from left to right. Clutch seemed ambivalent. Vlana's face wore a look of cold disapproval. Vant gave a slow, thoughtful nod... But it was Bjorn whose face she couldn't decipher. It was simultaneously accepting and cool. His mouth was a thin line, his eyes unreadable. He gave a slow nod.

Rachim interrupted further consideration with his own answer. "Good," he said. "It's time that you met our allies."

What opulence Aimee was accustomed to was usually understated. In her family's estate back in Havensreach, both her parents favored the reserved aesthetic ideal of the city's patrician class: white molding and broad windows to light their expansive home with natural light.

The Officers' Council of *Iseult* met in a tall, pillared room decorated with works of fine art from a thousand isles, some of which Aimee had never heard of before. As they strode beneath the high vaulted ceiling with its arched supports, the audible click of Aimee's boot-heel upon the stonework floors made her feel as if every whisper might carry from one end of the room to the other. The center of the large chamber was dominated by a circular table of pale blue stone, surrounded by a number of fine wood chairs set with teak and orichalcum. Here and there, those opal-ringed, samite-robed figures moved to and fro, back and forth between the small clusters of *Iseult*'s well-dressed officer class.

Harkon took the room in his stride, as he did so many things, and Rachim was all but immune to its charms. But a quick glance to her left, and Aimee realized that Elias was staring in quiet admiration at the paintings. "Beyond priceless," she heard him murmur.

"Your bodyguard is astute," said a voice from before them, and Aimee turned to find that Rachim had brought them face to face with a pair of men dressed in similar officers livery. The speaker was the elder of the two, a homely man with graying hair and a thick neck, bronze skin, and thoughtful brown eyes. The man beside him was young enough to be his son, and they had a similar look.

"Harkon Bright," Rachim said, "this is Lord Shipman Viltas, whose responsibilities include – among other things – relations between enlisted crew and the ruling class. Beside him is his son Vallus. Viltas was a close confidante of Lord Captain Amut before his death. We will need him."

Harkon inclined his head. "Lord Shipman, allow

me to introduce my apprentice – Aimee de Laurent of Havensreach, and my bodyguard, Elias Leblanc."

Viltas offered his hand to each of the three in turn. "As brilliant as she is lovely," he said to Aimee. She shook his hand harder than he'd expected, by the surprised look on his face. It wasn't the first time she'd heard it. It wouldn't be the last. She still didn't care for it. "Please," she said, her sweetest charm-school smile upon her face. "I'm at least twice that smart."

Viltas paused only a second, then laughed appreciatively. "Fair enough, Miss Laurent." He gave less attention to Elias. "Strapping," he said. "But young. New to the work?"

"Learned early," Elias deadpanned.

"Have they been updated on the players?" Vallus asked.

Rachim shook his head. "Do it, and do it quickly."

"There are three candidates for the throne," Vallus said. Despite having his father's look, there was something different about him, a softer mien his father lacked. An earnestness, as well. "First – and with greatest seniority – is Yaresh, Lord of the Muster. A war hero. He commands many peacekeepers and oversees the organization of countless enlisted."

"A kind term for 'disenfranchises,'" Viltas affirmed. "And 'enslaves.'"

"A captain who sees the most needy as the greatest threat is unworthy of his chair," Rachim said.

"Agreed," Aimee added, remembering certain political movements back in her home of Havensreach.

"Second," Vallus continued, "is Pentus of Aranoch. A foreigner, but well-moneyed. He was a noble in the Violet Imperium before intrigues drove him out. He purchased a title in *Iseult*'s midlevels, and rules them fairly, but often by fiat. Now he seeks the captain's throne."

"A politician," Harkon mused.

"Aye," Rachim agreed. "But a captain must be more."

"That he must," Harkon said. "And the third?"

"Diara," Vallus said. "Countess of Astronomers. She is wise, and her heart is good, but she lacks popular support, and her inscrutable card-player's face makes her seem cold. *Iseult* is hurting, and wounded people want a mother, not a frigid theorist."

Aimee frowned. "So she must be all things to them," she said, "or they will have her be none at all?"

The men of *Iseult* looked uncomfortable. Harkon smiled. "Perceptive as always."

One of the samite-robed figures with the opal ring abruptly stepped up to the table a short distance away, addressing the room. "Council, attend. Officers, to your places."

"Damn," Rachim muttered. "Quicker than I thought."

"Those–" Viltas murmured beside Aimee "–are the functionaries, bureaucrat-priests devoted to serving the Officers' Council. He will announce each of the candidates in turn."

A large number of officers had gathered about the table, each standing behind their chair. Turning, Aimee saw a gilded, empty seat at the far end.

The bureaucrat-priest's raw, tired voice announced each in turn – and within a handful of seconds, Aimee was looking sideways at Elias in time to find him glancing back her way. The candidates were precisely the three individuals the two of them had conversed about on the day of Amut's funeral.

Yaresh was the older man with a bronzed face latticed in scars. This time, however, the lord of the muster had laid aside some of his medals and exchanged the white uniform he'd previously worn for an understated one of black and red. His expression was stern, now, his dark eyes suspicious. The applause for him was nonetheless loud. He was a war hero, then, even if his wars had ended long ago. Aimee kept her face carefully neutral.

Pentus came second. The pale-haired duke had a glad-handing, theatrical look about him, and wore his well-tailored doublet and breeches with the same ease as the attention of his audience. He stood next to Yaresh, taller by a head, doing his best to seem self-effacing and humble. The lord of the muster frowned with plain dislike.

"Two for two," Aimee murmured.

Diara came next. Aimee hadn't stared too long at the Countess of Astronomers before, but she took her measure fully now: her skin was jewel-toned, like Vant and Vlana's. Her dark hair had a few streaks of white running through it, and the ochre dress of before had been replaced with a gown the color of the star-speckled night sky. Her eyes were distant and marbled brown. Her stare was opaque, and her posture conveyed a commanding indifference.

"Three for three," Elias confirmed. The look in his green eyes was uneasy.

"This council is now in session," the bureaucrat-priest said. "We yet grieve for Amut, Lord Captain, Lion of Heaven, but the work continues. Though his bridge crew yet flies us forward, *Iseult*'s throne sits empty. Three candidates for captaincy stand before you." He then gestured directly across the space to Harkon Bright.

"And the storied Magister Harkon Bright has agreed to moderate the process, that each man here feel free to speak his mind and advocate with clear conscience."

Harkon straightened. His speech was short, and Aimee spent it observing the reactions of the other officers, measuring how they responded to an outsider given such status. Her gaze swept across a riotous blend of multicolored faces wearing equally diverse expressions. Some regarded her teacher with fear as he spoke, others with admiration. None ignored him.

When he was done, all three candidates applauded with varying degrees of enthusiasm. Aimee's gaze swept the room again, and found it halted on a tall figure dressed in the red armor of the Captain's Guard she'd seen at Amut's funeral, standing at attention behind the candidates and priest. A red helm with a crest of feathers obscured both their face and gender, and the cloak draped about the armored shoulders was a rich, dark blue edged in gold. The other officers occasionally glanced at the warrior. Always with respect and a curiosity that never seemed quite satisfied.

"The person with the red armor," Aimee murmured. "Their cloak is different from the rest of the guard that I saw at the funeral. Someone important?"

"That would be the commander of the Captain's Red Guard," Vallus murmured from Aimee's left.

"Neutral, is he?" Aimee asked.

"She," Vallus corrected, "and... I don't know." The young noble's face acquired a look at once tired and exasperated. "Her name is Belit. She has held her post for three years, and the council respects her." His mouth tightened into a troubled line. "But I don't know what she thinks. We haven't spoken since before the captain passed."

"Pity, too," Rachim whispered behind Aimee. "She was deep in Amut's counsel, knew him damn well. She'd be a good ally to have right now, but she's withdrawn from politics, not that she was much of a player before."

"Not just from politics," Vallus muttered.

Aimee made note of that, and tucked it away in the back of her mind. All three candidates were to make the case for their worth. They were to proceed in order of seniority, putting Yaresh first. Aimee braced herself for long speeches.

She wasn't wrong. By the time the meeting was adjourned, she was exhausted.

It didn't make much sense to her that a council meeting should be more tiring than flying through a warzone, but Aimee dropped her coat on one of Rachim's couches with the lead weight of an old schoolbag nonetheless. She hadn't felt like this since the exhaustive theory lectures of her senior year at the Academy of Mystic Sciences. She let out a small yawn, laced her fingers together, and stretched back muscles tightened from spending so much time standing still and observant.

"So you see the situation that we're in," Rachim said to Harkon as Aimee's teacher slid into a chair near a balcony window. It was well into morning now. The sunlight cut across the vast clouds, and a flock of featherless birds native to Ishtier wheeled about beyond Rachim's villa. They weren't far from the port yet, then.

"You're faced with the task of replacing a popular ruler," Harkon mused, "and no extant choice measures up. It's not enviable."

"A soldier, a politician, and a wise woman," Aimee reflected out loud.

"That sounds like the start of a bad joke," Bjorn said, entering the room. Clutch followed behind. She had the big man's flask in her hand and looked more relaxed than usual.

"Vant and Vlana are doing a bit of exploring," the pilot explained. "They took a glimpse at the villas on the upper levels and declared in unison that there was nothing interesting up here."

Harkon let out a sharp, barking laugh. "True skyfarers to the core."

"Watch that sort of talk," Rachim added. "Most everyone on this ship considers themselves true-born to the infinite sky. The officer aristocracy doesn't take kindly to having it implied that they're not."

"Even the ones who purchased that status?" Aimee asked, quirking an eyebrow.

"Especially them," Rachim answered with a snort.

"What did you think of the speeches?" Harkon asked her next. The look on his face was contemplative, seeking another perspective.

"Yaresh is a nativist," Aimee murmured after a few moments' consideration. "Ironic for a cosmopolitan trade ship. He wants a greater share of the benefits of *Iseult*'s great trade-workings to go to her people first, rather than the collective whole of Flotilla Visramin and the guilds." She paused to chew on her lower lip for a moment. "I've heard speeches like that before. I didn't like his tone. And for one speaking for the people, he sure doesn't seem to think much of the ones who live below the top levels."

"Simplistic," Harkon agreed, "but not inaccurate. And the others?"

Aimee sighed and sank into a chair. "Pentus is good at talking a lot and saying nothing at all. If I had to guess purely on that speech, I'd say he knows how to play politics, but not how to give his politics substance. Diara has good ideas, but she's not used to having to deal with people as equals. She looked irritated that she had to make a speech at all."

"Solid analysis," Rachim sighed. "So you see the problem, Miss Laurent. And the maneuvering for votes hasn't even started yet."

"There's something I'm actually not very clear on," Aimee said then, resting her hands on the expensive hardwood table and regarding their host calmly. "What exactly are our goals here? You've said a lot about allies, factions, people who are 'with us' or 'against us,' but it's not clear to me yet what 'us' is supposed to be standing for." She laced her fingers together and met his eyes. "If we're going to be helping you, I'd like to know what we're helping you *do*."

Rachim exchanged a look with Harkon. Aimee's teacher nodded. Their host fixed her with his one-eyed gaze and said, "Keep this ship from being torn apart by sectarian violence."

The bluntness of it caught her off guard. Out of the corner of her eye, she saw Elias stir from where he was leaning with folded arms against the wall. His green eyes flashed as he looked up.

"It didn't seem *that* bad in the council, this morning," she said. "There was tension, sure, but I never felt like those people were ready to kill one another."

"You've only just arrived," Rachim sighed. "Try to understand... *Iseult* is a heavily divided society. Ninety percent of her population lives below the upper levels: the enlisted, the tenant merchant class, their families, all the transients and undocumented stowaways... Life in the lower levels is not easy, and this generation of the officer aristocracy is not as understanding as their predecessors. Amut was a uniter, an outsider who enacted reforms for the betterment of the ordinary man whilst managing to balance the ambitions and sensitivities of his officers. A balance had been established... When he died there were riots on the lower levels. We had peace, before. Now we have a lull before a storm."

"How did Amut die?" Elias asked. The question intruded on the momentary silence, cutting to the unspoken heart of the issue. When Aimee looked at him, his angular face was tired and worn, but intent.

"Painfully," Rachim said heavily. "His health had been declining for some months – he was always overworking. Against the advice of some of his councilors, he went ashore in the port of Albatross, came back with a cough that became a wasting sickness. It devoured him from the inside in under a week. Neither healing magic nor the physicians could slow its progress. The end was... messy. It's not common for our dead to be wrapped in shrouds, Miss Laurent. Amut was."

Elias nodded, silent again.

"So our allies in keeping this peace," Harkon spoke up, "are Viltas and his son Vallus. Amut's former allies. Did he have any others? In the absence of a uniter, perhaps those he most trusted can fill the void."

Rachim laughed. "What you have – myself, Viltas and

his son, and those few supporters we ourselves possess, are it."

Harkon frowned.

"And Belit," Aimee said. "Though from what you say, she's determined to remain apolitical."

"I will talk to her," Elias said softly.

"Lad," Rachim started, fixing the green-eyed young man with his single eye, "I told you, she's not a politician."

"No," Elias said. "She's a warrior. So am I. Tell me where she trains, and I will go there."

Bjorn looked at the former black knight with a carefully neutral expression. Harkon seemed to consider it.

There was a hard look on the knight's face... Then, after a moment, it relented. "Please," he said. "Let me do this."

Aimee paused. *They still don't fully trust him,* she realized. *They still see the conqueror named Azrael, the murderer, the knight of the Eternal Order.*

And what did she see? Aimee asked herself. It wasn't the first time the confusing question had been posited. More than anyone here, she knew him. In Port Providence, the Axiom Diamond – still sealed in a trunk in her cabin – had shown her the entirety of his life, how the order had taken him against his will.

"Elias is right," she said. "He's the best one to approach Belit. It would be foolish for him not to."

Her words broke the uneasy silence. Clutch took an audible swig of the flask. Bjorn looked back and forth between Elias and Aimee, then gave a small nod. Harkon gave Aimee a considering look, then said, "I agree. Do it."

Elias briefly glanced her way, inclined his head in thanks.

"She trains in the Rose Hall," Rachim said, accepting the decision. "You'll find her there many hours of the day. I hope you're good though, boy. They don't take kindly to anything less than the best in their space."

Aimee thought she saw the ghost of a smile on Elias's face before he said, "I'll manage."

"As for us," Harkon said, gesturing to Aimee and himself, "I would like to speak to the healers responsible for Amut's care, if you don't mind."

"That can be arranged," Rachim said. "But before all that, I'd like to offer you the chance to see something more relevant to your interests: Hark, Miss Laurent, I believe *Iseult* will be making its first portal jump in an hour, and I know the best place from which to view it. Will you accompany me?"

Aimee surged to her feet with renewed energy that startled even her teacher. "Born ready."

CHAPTER FIVE
THE DEEP SKY

Elias stood before a pair of elaborately carved hardwood doors set with pale marble, gold, and jewels. He had dressed in simple training attire, and carried his few weapons in a long, hardwood box loaned to him from *Elysium*'s cargo hold. To his left was a whitewashed wall of pale stone, to his right, high arched windows displayed the infinite expanse of an impossibly vast sky.

It was two days since their first jump had carried them out of Ishtier's domain, and now *Iseult* was truly upon the trackless vastness of the trade route through the deep sky men called the Dragon Road. According to their host, Rachim, one more jump would return the immense behemoth to her home flotilla.

The two days had passed much like the preceding month on *Elysium*: awkward silences, discomforted stares when he entered a room. A simple, painful uncertainty infected even the more congenial moments amongst his crewmates with stilted unease. Harkon and Aimee were in the middle of a lesson – or else meeting with Amut's former physicians – and Bjorn accompanied them. He was free to do what he had said he would do: find the red-armored, reclusive Belit, and convince her that the crew of *Elysium* wished to be her allies.

That he was at once the necessary advocate for Harkon Bright and his crew was an irony so rich that Elias wondered why he didn't choke on it. Likewise, as he stood before the door, he wondered why he was hesitating so long before pushing it open. *Fear is weakness, weakness is death,* his old master's words echoed in his mind. It made his teeth grind. "Go away," he growled to Lord Roland's echo. "Nobody asked you."

"Having trouble with the door?" The voice that intruded on Elias's thoughts was female, rich, and lower in register. Turning, he found himself facing its owner: a broad-shouldered woman with ebon skin and perceptive gold eyes. She wore no ornamentation, nor mark of status. Her thick hair was cut short, and she wore a simple canvas wrestling jacket and breeches. She was of even height with Elias, an unusual thing in itself, and her posture was relaxed.

"I'm here to train," he answered, after a moment spent in awkward silence.

"You're at the right place, then," she said. A pause. "But you'll need to open the door still. So I ask again: are you having trouble?"

Elias considered. A hundred awkward lies came to mind – veils behind which he might hide shame and pain, but then another, small echo of advice echoed through his mind in a woman's voice.

Noble and brave. Gentle and kind.

Honesty was best. He had precious little sense as to who Elias Leblanc was – who *he* was – but he at least knew what he didn't want to be. Azrael had lied. Azrael had murdered. Elias would start by being what Azrael was not.

"It has been a long time," he admitted, tired, "since I was in a proper training hall, and each has its own etiquette. I don't want to shame my hosts," he finished. *Or myself.*

"You're one of the newcomers staying in Rachim's villa," she said. It wasn't a question.

"I am."

"Rumors travel quickly on the upper levels," she said, and favored him with a thoughtful nod. "Come, I will be your guide."

She pressed her hand to the wood and pushed. A seam of light split the carvings, and the doors to the training hall rumbled inward. Elias blinked in the bright light. An arched dome rose high overhead, painted with extravagant, mythical depictions of warriors from myriad stories. At its apex, a single circular skylight flooded the chamber with sunlight that danced off the pale stone floor.

All around the far walls, practice weapons hung from pegs or rested against racks. Straight, two-handed longswords and single-edged messers such as those favored by the order, broad-bladed boarding axes, maces, spears, halberds and long rondel daggers. All of it was familiar to a student of the ancient Varengard style in which Elias was trained. *And orphaned,* a part of him reflected. When he'd turned against his masters, he'd lost the benefit of their teachings, and no one else was learned in the war-arts of the ancient masters. The order had long ago made certain of it. There were weapons in hundreds of other varieties as well: curved blades of varieties without number. He spotted steel-bladed whip swords, punch daggers and gracefully curved polearms and thick staves.

The next things his senses noted was the quality of the fighters making use of the space. Natural-born skyfarers tended on average to be shorter than those born on land, more limber, quick and dexterous. Yet here, the spread of individuals at work was startlingly diverse. Tall, short, broad and powerful, lean and swift. Elias counted more than a few with thick middles and trunk-like legs. What unified them was the unerring skill with which every one of them moved. This training hall was not for amateurs. Since coming to *Iseult*, Elias had vowed to keep his magical gifts hidden, in case some keen-eyed savant should recognize them for what they were, and identify him as the monster he'd once been. Without use of those gifts, any one of these people would be at least a middling challenge to his talents.

"You're pensive, outsider," his guide said with a small smirk. "But I know that confident look. Well trained, are you?"

"Extremely," Elias answered. It wasn't a lie.

The fighters were taking note of the pair of them now. Their eyes followed Elias, sizing him up. Some nodded in greeting, a few smiled. Most simply watched and assessed. None wore red armor. There was no sign of Belit. Yet before he could even start to properly look, one of the fighters – a tanned, bald man of middling height and copious scars – walked towards him. He pulled a long stave from one of the racks and threw it across the space between them. Elias reflexively caught it. The others, watching solemnly, nodded with approval.

"That one is Hakat, a senior member of the royal guard. I would stretch," his guide said, an amused smile on her dark face. "New blood that can walk proudly among this crowd is rare. You're going to have more than a few challengers."

Elias breathed hard. Three bouts with a stave lay behind him, followed by two with the long rondel, then two more of wrestling. This was his fourth round against a fresh fighter using a blunted steel longsword. He had been fighting continuously for what seemed near to half an hour, without calling upon his magic once. There was a familiar ache in his limbs, and his breath came even and slow.

With the stave he had sustained a handful of welts, yet won every match. With rondel and in wrestling, he had taken a bruise or two, yet come out each time in control. With the longsword in his hands, none could touch him. A wry, rueful pride filled him as he waited for his next challenger. Orphaned he might be, adrift and uncertain in the world, but one fact remained inviolate: he was still the best he had yet come across.

Taking a moment at the edge of the training ring, he took a proffered drink of water from his guide. The amused expression had never once left her face. Across the ring, another fighter was taking up a blunt steel sword – this one curved. Elias turned, letting his face sweep the assembled faces of so many different colors and shapes. Not once had he been shamed, savaged, or treated as less than an equal. The others were laughing, trading casual jokes. Hakat was grinning as the newcomer – his student by the look of it – experimentally twirled his weapon. The fight was an easy thing in which to get lost: a place of escape where he need not remember anything but the move before him, the breath, the moment. He could escape no longer. Elias put the point of his training blade in the floor and breathed out, remembering why he was here.

"Where is Belit?" he asked the crowd. "You honor me with your efforts and your courage," the words felt so awkward coming from his mouth, so foolish, "but I came seeking her. Where is the legendary commander of the Red Guard? I would see what she is made of."

Silence fell. Looks were exchanged. A small laugh came from Hakat. "You still don't know, boy?"

Elias frowned. He had seen no one receiving constant deference from the others, no warrior with a special crest, or high seat. There was nobody in this room of whom everyone was afraid. "I see no one to whom you all defer," he answered. "I see no red armor, nor marks of status."

"Then you don't look close enough," Hakat answered. "Or your experience with leaders is paltry. You want to know Belit? Find she who serves first. Who uplifts and shows by her example who is accepted."

"Hakat, enough," the voice of the dark-skinned guide said behind him, and Elias was immediately still. *Gods*, he thought. *I am such a fool.*

He turned, and the gold eyes in the dark face greeted him. Her strong arms were still folded, her expression still amused.

"You," Elias said.

"Me," Belit nodded. "Forgive my deception, stranger," she said, expression unchanging. "But my mother always taught me that if you want to know a person's character, see how they treat a person with no visible status."

"Commander," Elias began. "I have come on behalf of–"

"No," Belit said. Already she was walking away from him – but not to remove herself from conversation. The warrior stopped by a worn weapons rack, and selected from it a blunt, straight longsword, the twin of Elias's own. "You said that you wished to see what I was made of, and after witnessing your performance against my own trained fighters, I find myself curious of the same. What is your name?"

It took a moment for Elias to remember which one was right. The shade of his former self still lingered, toxic and mocking, on the tip of his tongue. "Elias," he affirmed, as much to himself as to her. "Elias Leblanc."

Belit favored him with a smile, and assumed a guard that mirrored his own, smooth and perfect. A sudden shock went through him. That was a Varengard stance. Sudden fear gripped him. Where had she been trained? Who had taught her? What was he about to walk into?

Does the order have an agent upon Iseult?

Belit's smile was panther-like. The eyes of all the room were upon them now. "Come, Elias Leblanc," she said. "You came all this way. Don't keep me waiting."

There was time neither for fear, nor hesitation. Elias banished thought, and burst forward, closing distance with a dropping cut aimed at her opposite shoulder. At the last second, his thumb – pressed to the flat of his blade – pushed, rotating from a long-edge to a short-edge strike, closing off the line. Belit moved gracefully, powerfully. Their blades met, bound. Belit pivoted back, forcing Elias's cut short. *Fast.* He wound the strike into a thrust.

Deft as a water-reed, Belit lifted her hilt high, slipped beneath his thrust, and drove her point home. Elias had the skill to see it coming, but not to stop it. His body was moving, adrenalized, his momentum forward weighted. He ran onto the blunt tip of her sword, and the blade flexed to near ninety degrees. The pain of a hard, bruising hit exploded through his chest, and Elias Leblanc slammed into the training hall floor.

He lay there for a moment, fighting to regain his breath. Habit didn't let him release his sword, and a pair of slow, deep breaths told him that nothing was broken.

Belit appeared standing over him. She regarded him for a moment, then offered her hand. "Too eager," she said.

Groaning, Elias clasped her palm and hauled himself to his feet. "The masters teach their students to always take the initiative," he said, meeting her eyes. She knew. Somehow. Yet she wasn't of the order, that much else was obvious.

She gave him an odd look. "They also teach that a sword that comes in too wrathful is easily displaced. A blade too eager for blood binds too hard, is easily offset, pushed away, or overcome."

The other fighters were still cheering for their commander, but Belit's gaze was on Elias. Still gripping his palm, she said – quiet enough to keep it between the two of them – "You fight like a demon, Elias; with fury and passion and verve, but against the calm mind, your skill unravels. Who taught you to hate so much?"

Disarmed, beaten, Elias's mouth opened and closed several times before he could form a response. "Someone utterly unlike you," he said at last. "Someone who no longer teaches me."

Orphaned. Alone. It was one of the smaller prices paid, if he was honest, and nothing against all the crimes upon his soul.

Belit gave a slow nod, then released his hand, and looked at the others. "Alright, enough watching. The ship has yet to pick her new captain, which means our duty until they do is to hone our skills. Back to work, the lot of you. First paired drills, then formation, then defensive perimeters. By day's end, you will execute all of these *flawlessly. Move.*"

The men and women jumped to obey, and the room filled swiftly with the crash of repeated training weapons and the shouts of assigned group leaders correcting their juniors on form. Elias looked around, feeling both at home and utterly alien in this place.

"I didn't say we were done," Belit said, and when he turned towards her she tossed him a messer, single-handed and single-edged. He caught it easily, then cleared his throat. "Commander," he began, "I come on behalf of Harkon Bright."

"Perhaps that is what sent you here," Belit corrected him, "but not the why. You owe me several more rounds first, so I can know the broken state of your skills in full."

Dumbfounded, Elias simply stared at the woman across from him, analytical in her gaze, fierce in her strength, but calm as well. And determined in whatever it was she'd set her mind upon.

"Why?" he asked at last. "What are they to you?"

"You're a broken orphan, Elias Leblanc," Belit answered, as if it were the most obvious thing in the world. "It's obvious in everything about you, from how you fight, to the grieving reticence with which you entered my hall. I swore a vow to the one who first put a sword in my hand and taught me its secrets, that I would always look out for the orphans, for the lost, the broken, and the forgotten. Now put up your blade, Elias. We can speak after. First I must put to mending the mess of a warrior in front of me."

The messer sang through the air. Elias stepped back, parried Belit's rapid upward cut and pushed the blade out and away from his center. He rammed the point in, aiming for her throat. She snapped her arm high and across, drew her steel back and dropped the point. A parried sword was now a wall of steel, and Elias's thrust veered away from its target. With his pressure as leverage, her blade rotated in a lightning-swift circle that brought it snapping down at his shoulder. Instead of dashing back and trying to block, Elias moved inside the range of her cut and thrust his off-hand beneath the wrist of her sword-arm, stopping the cut in its tracks. Then he went for the grab. Throw her. If he could just get close enough to *throw her*–

A brown, scar-coated set of knuckles filled his vision. The punch caught him in the side of the face, scrambled him enough to set her up for the same throw. She'd signaled her move enough that he registered what she was about to do, and instead of being slammed onto his back, Elias rolled when the world spun. He came up in a crouch as she barreled in on him, sword still in hand. She stopped short without effort, smiled, and gave a nod of approval. "Better," she said.

It was their sixth bout. Elias's arms burned and his breath came hard. He was in exceptional shape, but dueling with blunts for hits that didn't end the fight immediately took a toll... and he ruefully acknowledged that he wasn't fully recovered from his fight with Malfenshir. It had been a month since he slew his former second-in-command in the bowels of the *Iron Hulk*. A month since he'd taken a wound that should've killed him.

Perhaps he shouldn't have expected to be at the top of his game.

"Had your fill?" he asked, straightening. "I didn't actually come here to fight, you know."

"Ah," Belit answered with a correcting, raised finger. "But I did. That is the purpose of a training hall. Talking is for *after* practice. If you wish to speak," she said, "you first have to train."

A small smile perked at the corner of Elias's mouth. Whatever else might have been said of the commander of the Red Guard, he liked the way she thought.

"Go on," she said, facing him fully now. "Speak." Her gold eyes were direct, their gaze hard to meet. Elias did so anyway.

"Harkon Bright and Rachim want your help," he said. As he spoke, he watched the look on her face turn stony, reserved. A sense of sudden helplessness assailed him: he was not a diplomat. Roland had trained him in the arts of the worlds' courts, but his every skill in that sphere was intimately tied with manipulation, with deceit and with murder. Abruptly, he remembered standing in the sun-tinted splendor of Port Providence's royal palace, pointing an armored finger at a king and a prince he would soon kill, and promising them absolute oblivion.

He felt sick. So he met her gaze and said, simply, "I don't know which candidate will win your captain's chair, but I have seen what happens when a people come apart, commander." There was a lump somewhere in his throat. He swallowed it. "If you can do something to prevent it, you should. I can't say if it will work," he said, "but your conscience will be lighter."

The stone cracked slightly, but her expression was still reserved as she watched him. Somewhere a door opened as someone else entered the training hall, but Elias didn't turn to look.

"It's not appropriate," she said after a moment of painful silence, "for the commander of the Captain's Guard to involve herself in the politics of succession. Your master is the moderator of that process. I cannot be seen helping him."

Elias slowly nodded, the weight of her choice settling on him. He closed his eyes for a moment. "I will not ask you to compromise your position."

She considered that for a moment, but the sound of footsteps made her turn. Elias followed her gaze. Resplendent in his medals and uniform, Yaresh, lord of the muster, strode towards them, lightly clapping his hands.

"That," he said, "was a *magnificent* display of swordplay. I did not think to see another student of the Varengard style other than our own exceptional Belit in my lifetime." Up close, Yaresh's face was pitted and scarred. He had that combination of strong jaw and intent gaze that had likely made him very handsome in his youth, but the weight of age made skin sag off at odd angles. His nose had been broken twice, and there were scars that even the finest magical healing hadn't removed. It was his gaze, however, that set Elias's teeth on edge. He looked at the warriors in this room like well-bred birds, or adornments to his coat.

It was familiar. Yaresh fixed his stare on Elias. He was a few inches shorter than the black knight and Belit, but his presence had a weight that made up for it: this was a man accustomed to obedience.

"You are not supposed to be here," Belit said. Her tone – warm before – was frosty. "This is my hall. The Red Guard takes no part in the selection. We should not even be speaking."

"I'm not talking to you," Yaresh said with an amused smile. "Mind you, I have no particular fondness for that bit of archaic formality – as outdated as veneration for white knights and archaic trials – but I'll play along, *Commander.* Suit yourself. I am speaking to your guest.

"Now then," he turned to look fully at Elias. "You must tell me where you received your training. It *fascinates* me to find that Harkon Bright has a bodyguard of such rare martial learning. Belit is the only other student of the Varengard school I have ever met, and she was trained by the previous master of the Red Guard. There is only one other group that practices it, and they guard their secrets jealously."

He smiled. Broad. Hungry. "What other *talents* do you possess?"

The threat landed hard. Elias felt his pulse quicken. His fingers itched for the sharp blade hidden in the wooden box a few feet away. *He knows,* a panicked voice inside him started. His fist clenched beside him. Lethal spells pulled at his mind. His foot took an involuntary step forward. "My talents are sufficient."

Yaresh's eyes widened in surprise that switched to

satisfaction. "Goodness," he said quietly. "And a temper, as well. Have a care, boy. Your master's position is precarious, and my healers are exceptional."

"Yaresh." Belit interposed herself between the two of them. "This is my hall, and this man as such is my guest, not your conversation partner or your whipping boy. State your business, or get out."

Yaresh's expression darkened. He clasped his hands behind his back, as if to keep them contained. *He hates her*, Elias realized. *This had nothing to do with me*.

"I have a right to look in on my future bodyguards," he said simply. "Especially ones that *failed* my predecessor so spectacularly."

That had stung. Belit's voice abruptly raised. What had been calm and cold before was suddenly a lightning bolt that pulled every fighter in the room to attention. "Yaresh of the muster," Belit snapped, "you are *not* captain yet, and my guardsmen take no part in the selection process. Our hall is *private*, and while I don't know who invited you in, you have overstayed your welcome. Get out. Hakat, escort the Lord of the Muster to the door."

Yaresh's expression was cold contempt, but he didn't fight the bald warrior that took him by the arm, saying, "This way, my lord."

"No position is untouchable, Belit," the older man said over his shoulder. "I will be captain. There is no other fit to the challenges ahead. Do not oppose me, or it will fall upon you when I succeed."

The door closed with an audible thud. Belit turned and regarded her subordinates. "What are you all gawking at?" she asked. "Staring is not training. Back to work."

Not wishing to linger in the awkward silence, still

flushed with shame and fear, Elias walked towards his box, and removed Oath of Aurum, buckling it about his waist. His hand brushed the hilt. Warmth answered his touch, though it did little to reassure him.

"I'm sorry about that," Belit said behind him. Slowly, Elias straightened and turned. "He is forbidden to come here, but he grows bolder by the day–" Abruptly, her eyes fell upon the longsword hanging now at Elias's hip "Wait," she said. "That sword." Now she grabbed him by the arm, hauled him off to the edge of the hall, away from earshot of all the others. "How did it come into your possession?"

Elias's throat dried up. The memory of a flashing duel across the gundeck of the *Iron Hulk* played through his thoughts, and the gut-churning recollection of a noble prince's corpse falling into the inferno of his dying city. How was he to answer that question? He grasped about for an answer in his mind, before the most honest came.

"At great cost," he said, before asking a burning question of his own. "How is it that the commander of the Red Guard of *Iseult* possesses the secrets of the Varengard style? I think we both know that its only other masters aren't generous with their knowledge."

"That," Belit said after a careful pause, "is a long, complicated story. The sort that people like Yaresh think nothing more than a myth."

Elias thought about how improbable the last few weeks of his own life had been. "Try me," he deadpanned.

She examined him again. Then, apparently seeing no deception behind his sarcasm, nodded. "Very well. We will meet again, and soon. You will tell me how you came by that blade, and I will tell you the story behind my own martial lineage." She looked again, checking for listeners, and finding none, looked at him. "And, while I am still not permitted to involve myself in the selection process of the new captain, well, my second duty is to *Iseult* herself. Should Harkon Bright be acting in her interest in other ways, tell him that he may rely upon me."

She extended a hand between them. Elias hesitated for only a second before gripping it in return. "Deal struck," he said.

"Good," Belit said, firmly. "And practice, while you are away. Knowing what you know, fighting as you do, I expect everything to be thrice again as clean, when next we meet, *junk ritter*."

That phrase. He'd read it before. In the manuscripts Lord Roland kept prized in a vault in his own keep.

"As you say," Elias answered. He tried to keep his voice steady.

As he made his way back through the halls of *Iseult*'s upper levels, back towards the relative safety of Rachim's villa, the black knight felt a strange sense of hope in a place previously drowned out by despair and alcohol: he had failed, but then he had succeeded. He was bringing confirmation of a much-needed ally back to *Elysium* – and more, something else that he had never again thought to find upon fleeing the order.

He had found a teacher.

CHAPTER SIX
THE SUPPOSITIONS OF HARKON BRIGHT

Aimee stood in the expanse of Amut's royal villa and took in the curious sights. Over the past two days she'd had the chance to see several other estates of the officer aristocracy up close. As it turned out, a large number of faction partisans within the council had a vested interest in wining and dining Harkon Bright and his apprentice.

It was as if they wanted to influence the process.

Most of these palaces were opulent beyond the blushing dreams of her former Academy classmates, resplendent with the trappings of trade from across the known sky – and, some whispered, parts of the unknown. Even aboard a ship such as *Iseult*, a city unto itself, space was at a premium, so wealth tended to be concentrated in displays of expensive construction materials, art, and decorations, with treasures representing only what the highest quantities of gold could purchase. Aimee had never seen so much gilding in one place.

And that was where Amut's former residence was different. The Captain's Manse was a simple square-shaped building of black stone that stood out by its place in the center of the forward segment of the upper levels of *Iseult*. In a sea of domes, balconies, and the occasional stepped tower, it was a sparse structure that nonetheless commanded tremendous authority and presence.

And inside, it was *beautiful*. In this place of gilded finery and adorned wealth, the interior of Amut's manse was one spectacularly lovely garden. Her breath left her in a solid gasp as the doors closed behind them. Everywhere, built into the very framework of the main entryway and hall, were stunning plants, blooming flowers, and pools of fresh, clear water. For the house of a dead man, Aimee had never seen more life.

"He was not a man who took pleasure in precious stones or heaps of gold," Viltas said, with fondness in his voice. The lord shipman had accompanied them, this time. As a close friend of the late captain, he knew his home well. "But his youth in Ishtier instilled in him a great love of things that grow. The crystals of his homeland don't thrive away from their native isle, so he turned instead to botany as a hobby. Wherever we went, Amut would seek to acquire some local flora to add to his grand gardens. He planned their layout meticulously, and where plants fruited or grew food, he was always generous in donating it to the needy below."

"A noble pastime," Harkon said thoughtfully, taking in the sights. "And the whole of the manse is like this?"

"As much as could be managed," Viltas nodded sadly. "Now it is in decline. Only Amut and his master gardener knew its secrets ... and the old man passed shortly before he did."

"Two deaths in the same house, so close together," Harkon murmured, considering an osiria rose jutting from a mass of thorny branches. "Odd."

"Convenient," Aimee murmured.

"You think so?" Viltas answered, a wan smile on his face. "Good, then at least we're on the same page. Come, I will take you to his quarters. Perhaps there is something in his journals you can make sense of, or in his papers."

They passed through two more garden-halls, and a room in which the captain's portrait was displayed over a hearth, the likeness shrouded by a hanging, translucent veil that obscured the finer details. Aimee took note of sharp, intent eyes, however, and an expression with an inscrutable sort of knowing in the mark of the line.

"The painter did him well," Aimee said as they passed it.

"You never met him," Viltas pointed out. "How can you tell?"

"In my home," she said, "fine portraits are a sign of status as well. Many are beautiful, but bland. A good artist can capture a likeness, but it takes a *great* one to instill it with personality."

"Painting the soul," Viltas affirmed. The older man smiled as he walked beside her. "You know your art."

"My mother was insistent," Aimee said with a small smile.

Viltas chuckled. "Good mothers often are. My own Vallus takes more after my late wife than I, I think. Oh, he looks like me, but his essence is hers. Gentle. A peacemaker."

"You don't strike me as the contentious sort, Lord Viltas, if you'll forgive me," Harkon added as they began to climb a set of black stone stairs.

The lord shipman laughed. "Perhaps I don't, but I've had years to mellow out. Still, peaceful men don't spend their lives getting into contentious fights with their fellow officers. Before Amut came to us, I was a contender for his seat," he admitted, his voice sad – not for himself, Aimee sensed, but for a youth that had been spent making mistakes. "I wasn't born to the upper levels, you know. I married well. I wanted to make life better for those who toil beneath. Then I met Amut, and everything changed. He was a uniter. An outsider who could see how to reach both noble and common man, speak to both, represent both. Once I met him... I no longer wanted power myself. He made many reforms after he became captain, and had many more planned, but I doubt they will come to fruition now."

They crested the top of the stairs, finding themselves in a room with high arched windows facing the bow of *Iseult*. Positioned thus, the viewer had a line of sight straight down the spine of the vessel. A desk of expensive hardwood rested off to the side. Viltas produced a key from inside his vest, and knelt beside it, turning it in an archaic lock until the sound of tumblers shifting echoed through the small room. "I believe he put them in here," Viltas said. "Ah yes, there they are."

He removed a set of leather-bound, hardback journals chased with gold leaf. "He kept immaculate records," the lord shipman said. "Rachim turned the key over to me shortly after Amut passed... I think he feared being killed for it himself."

"Have you read them?" Harkon asked.

"No," Viltas shook his head and held up a refusing hand. "He was my friend, but it is not my place." His voice sounded pained. "A man deserves his secrets. Even after death. If there are things he did not tell me, I am certain he had his reasons."

"All men should be so fortunate in their friends," Harkon murmured, looking over the texts. "Hmm, that's odd. The last two pages of his final journal are blank."

"He was too ill to write," Viltas said, shaking his head, expression pained. "It burned through him quickly, whatever it was. He couldn't even speak, at the end."

Aimee turned, examining the rest of the room. Something nagged at the back of her mind. A tease pulled at the corner of her attuned magic senses. Since boarding *Iseult*, she'd grown accustomed to the ambient mystic sense of the upper levels, and the powerful – if distant – presence of its much more powerful metadrive, but this was different. The feel of magic, to Aimee, had always been warm. This, faint though it was, was *cold*. A breath of frigid winter air slipping through unseen cracks in the wall of a well-insulated house. Her eyes cast about for things that couldn't be properly seen.

"Can I walk around a little?" she asked, distractedly. The sensation, now noticed, was impossible to ignore. "I'd like to get a better sense for how he lived."

"Absolutely," Viltas answered. "You have the run of the place. Let us know if you find anything."

Aimee let the door to the beautiful room close behind her, and breathed out in her first moment of real solitude in several days of unending interpersonal work. Amut's healers had been tired sorts, each as stumped by the speed at which their captain had been taken as the one before. Harkon clearly suspected something, but he hadn't shared whatever it was yet – not that there had been time. When they were not with Rachim, they were with Viltas or his son. She'd barely seen the rest of the crew since their first day aboard. She understood Elias had made contact with Belit, but hadn't been able to talk to him about what he'd learned.

Now alone, she closed her eyes for a long span and let her hands flow through the air, summoning a simple spell to hone her senses. "Alright, little breeze," she addressed the chill she'd felt, "show me the holes in the wall."

It pulled her along. The first prime of magic dictated that magic wanted to be used. It tugged at the senses of the sorcerer, longing to be given form through spells. The same could be true of lingering spell effects. She backtracked through rooms of beautiful flora. *Iseult* flew above a thick bank of clouds today, one day from her next jump to return to the flotilla. Sunlight flowing in through the estate's windows lashed over the reaching, broad leaves of rare trees stretching towards the day. She passed the portrait again and paused, taking closer stock of it.

Something about the veiled posture of the dead captain stood out to her: he had been ebon-skinned, she saw, darker than most of the officer aristocracy by a shade. His head had been shaven, and there was something in the eyes, though she couldn't see their color through the fabric. She filed it away in her mind, made note not to forget.

Eventually she came to a door of rich dark wood set with bronze handles. The cold was stronger here, and her senses nearly dragged her forward. *Careful,* she thought, remembering the past several months, everything she had been through, the dangers of unknown magic. Harkon had taught her to refine her shielding spells since Port Providence, so she cast one: tighter, invisible to the untrained eye. The subtlety of it meant that it was weaker.

If a trap lay on the other side of the door, it would protect her from only one powerful effect, but that itself would buy her extra time. Aimee was fast when there was need. She took a deep breath, settling her nerves, and stared at the door which suddenly looked vaguely menacing. It was absurd to be afraid. She'd faced down knights of the Eternal Order and that *thing* that had called itself Esric. She let her breath out, but the fear didn't quite go with it.

Perhaps remembering the black-eyed, monstrous healer wasn't the best idea, even if she had killed him.

The handle turned in her hand, and the door creaked audibly inward. Aimee stood in the entryway to what looked like a large bedchamber. Plants lined the opposite walls, and a handful of Ishtierian crystal sculptures glimmered green near the single window with its view of the portside of the eternal sky. Nothing seemed amiss at first glance. The bed was immaculately made, the floor dusted and swept. The curtains were open, pinned, and the gentle sound of water running down the faces of carefully arranged rock sculptures cut through the silence of the dead man's bedroom.

And yet all Aimee felt was *cold*. A nameless dread hung on the air, so thick that stepping into the room was like walking into a fog that didn't let you see your own outstretched hands.

Aimee forced her nerves to settle and tried to parse the different mystic stimuli she felt. *Walk away*, her senses screamed at her when she made to step through the door. *You don't want whatever lies hidden here.*

And *that* was an even bigger red flag. Harkon's lessons on illusions sprang fresh to Aimee's mind: the most powerful deceptions were those that dovetailed perfectly with what the viewer wanted to see. A wan smile crossed her face despite her fear. "Nice try," she whispered to the empty room. "But I got over that mental hang up a while ago."

She stepped through the door, trying to sense how the framework of the illusion fit together. It took her a few moments, but she felt it, tied to whatever cold-causing magic lay beneath it. It really was a work of marvel, she reflected: so simple. Most people who had reason to be here would simply feel the innate reticence attendant to stepping into a dead man's bedroom, and walk away, thinking no more of it. It took knowing what you were looking at to even sense that something was off to begin with.

Aimee wove her hands through the complex forms of a spell of sight, and held forth her hand. "Reveal yourself to me," she commanded.

She wasn't prepared for what followed.

Every plant in the room was dead. The illusion of soft greenery surrounding a placid space fell away. In its place, black leaves, bleached-white stems and bark. Everything was gray. Subdued. Leeched of color. A terrible, bone-chilling dread filled the space. Aimee gasped. She couldn't hear the water or the wind. A quiet settled over her, so intense that the sound of her own heartbeat hammered in her ears and her breathing was a roar in the void.

At the far end of the room, just above the head of the bed, a single black mark stained the wall. A glyph that Aimee didn't recognize. It wasn't just dark; even the night sky had a color, was filled with stars or clouds. This *thing* drank the light.

She didn't remember taking the first step back, or the

second. But suddenly her heart hammered faster, her hands shook by her sides, and the ragged gasps sped up, until for the first time since she was a little girl, Aimee screamed.

Harkon was suddenly at her side. His hands grasped her shoulder, turned her to face him. Her teacher's eyes filled her vision, as one hand reached out to cup her face. "Aimee," he said. "Aimee. Look at me. *Look at me.*"

She fixed her eyes on his. Her mouth worked to form words for what seemed like eternity. Nothing came but stutters at first. Finally she managed a handful of words. "Cold," she said. "Illusion. On the room. Something–" her voice cracked, whimpering "–*quiet.* Mark on the wall."

"Stay with her," Harkon said, and Aimee heard something in his voice. A steel that made Viltas stay exactly where he stood. She sank to her knees. One hand grasped at her apprentice's badge on its chain, the other pressed to the floor. She blinked furiously, and tried to calm her racing pulse.

"What did you *see* in there?" Viltas said beside her, looking past her. "I see only the room as it was."

"Illusion," Aimee managed. Her voice was coming easier, now. The panic was receding and her mind was already racing through her repertoire of magical learning. She needed to know what that *was*. She needed to give it a name. A name put definition to nameless terrors, cut off the fear of uncertain parameters with understanding.

"The whole room is under a potent illusion spell," she finally said. "Hiding something else. All the plants are dead. The colors leeched out. There's a horrible mark above his bed. I don't recognize it."

Harkon was back with them again, kneeling on the

floor beside them. There was a look of deep worry on his face. After a moment, he said, "Yes, you do. Remember, Aimee: forbidden arts, special class, defensive segment. I insisted you take it."

She squeezed her eyes shut, not wanting to recall, but nodding at the last. She *did* remember. He was right. "I don't know the spell," she finally said, shuddering, "but I recognize the art. I just... haven't heard of it ever being *used* in the modern era."

"A little education for the non-sorcerer?" Viltas asked, straightening now.

"How many mages have examined this room?" Harkon asked. "How powerful were they?"

"Two," Viltas said, sounding concerned. "Affiliated with the functionaries. I would not call them *mighty*, but they are competent, certainly. They found nothing wrong."

"They erred," Harkon said. "Grievously. Perhaps it isn't their fault entirely. Whoever did this is... strong. Give me Amut's last journal, there is one final thing I need to check."

Viltas handed Harkon the leatherbound hardback. Harkon flipped to the last several pages, the ones that had dates but no writing. Aimee could see it, clear as day, but now she also sensed the same mystic distortion of perception. Harkon wove his hands through the motions of the same revealing spell, and inked words in the late captain's handwriting appeared, growing ever more slurred as they reached the final lines.

"I'm so cold. I can't get warm. I am cold. So cold."

A fist of ice clenched in Aimee's chest, and she felt violently ill. They had called Amut the Lion of Heaven... and he had spent his last days wasting away as a spell sucked the life from him, writing the same words over and over and over.

"We must speak with Rachim immediately," Harkon said, closing the book. "Amut was murdered."

It was hours before Aimee believed she'd feel warm again. The villa had not sufficed, and now she sat upon one of the couches in *Elysium*'s common area, a mug of hot coffee in her hands and a blanket draped over her shoulders. Harkon stood before the window, while Bjorn paced irritably back and forth. Clutch stared straight ahead, Vlana and Vant behind her. Slightly apart from the group was Elias, sitting in a chair, his long legs crossed at the ankles and his green eyes lost in thought.

Viltas, Vallus, and Rachim stood by, their faces stony and tired.

"The art died out," Bjorn growled. "With the last of its practitioners – three *hundred years ago*."

"Practices are hard to kill," Elias said quietly, "especially ones that can simply be passed from teacher to student."

"Damn, damn, *damn*," Bjorn swore, still pacing. "Fuck."

"How could you not know?" he abruptly exploded at their three guests. The old warrior's face was red with fury. "How could you have no inkling that there was a fucking *necromancer* lurking on your ship?"

"Do any of us look like sorcerers?" Rachim abruptly snapped back. "Have a care, warrior, even the greatest mages on *Iseult* are not all-seeing, and as you may have noticed: this ship is *large*, and folk aren't currently inclined to share information."

"Will you still be making those excuses when everyone on this ship is a walking *husk*?" Bjorn snarled. "Don't speak to me as if this is a simple inconvenience. I'm from *Skellig*. It's been centuries since the last of them was destroyed, and the dead still don't lie quiet in their barrows."

"Bjorn," Harkon said. "That's enough."

"Hark–" Bjorn started.

"Take a walk," Harkon said. "You need to clear your head."

The warrior stared at their leader for a moment, then grunted and stalked out of the room. Aimee released a breath she hadn't been aware of holding. "He's not entirely wrong," she said, once the warrior had gone. "If the council's division allowed this to happen, and stay hidden… everyone on this vessel is in dire peril."

"No doubt. I know only myths," Rachim said. "Now tell me what we're up against. Some sort of dead-raising psychopath?"

"Raising the dead is a *part* of necromancy," Harkon began, "but only its meanest, basest function; an expression of its greater functions, which is the control and manipulation of life-force."

"That sounds almost like the healing disciplines," Viltas mused. "And it's… familiar."

"Similar," Aimee said. Her classes on the subject were coming back to her now, and working over the problem was helping drive away the dread. "But a healer restores. Necromancy is… parasitic. It requires the sorcerer to *take* from others to fuel its magic. With such potent fuel, it can produce disproportionately powerful – and horrible – effects, but the drawbacks… the first prime affects them far more dramatically. Necromancy is deeply, maddeningly addictive. It turns even the most reserved researchers into compulsive serial killers."

Viltas sat down hard. "Do you know the story of how Amut became captain?" he asked.

"Only the bare bones," Harkon answered. "There have been limits to my time."

"They tell stories in the lower levels," Vlana spoke up. "They say a powerful sorcerer menaced this ship a generation ago, with the power to enslave the dead, and that Amut and his companions came from Ishtier and killed them. They sing songs about it," she added, a weight to her words. "He was their hero."

"Aye," Rachim nodded. "The stories are true. The officer aristocracy elected him captain afterwards, for they felt there was none more worthy."

"They tell it differently below," Vant said. "They say the officers knew that if they didn't give him the chair, they'd have a revolt on their hands. They think you lot killed him."

Rachim and Viltas both looked weary. Then, at last, the lord shipman spoke again, an exhausted look on his face. "I was one of Amut's companions, a latecomer when I saw what he might do for us," Viltas said. "He killed a sorcerer, yes. Though I never marked what kind he was. A would-be dread-lord named the Faceless that ruled some cult that faded away when Amut killed him. I do remember that he used corpses as his thralls, but one type of terrible magic looks much like another to the uneducated, and there were few magi on *Iseult* in those days beyond the portalmages. It's also true that many of the ship's rulers weren't happy to see an outsider ascend to the captain's chair, but his popularity... It was what a hero's always is."

"You're sure this *Faceless* is truly dead?" Harkon asked quietly.

Rachim shot Viltas a look. The lord shipman stared at Harkon for a long time with a very tired expression on his face. For the first time since she'd met him, Aimee reflected, he looked old. His face paled a little, and he nodded. "Amut cut him in half with an enchanted sword that rusted away to nothing after striking him down. We burned his corpse, and I scattered the ashes to the winds myself. He's gone."

Harkon seemed to accept that. "An apprentice then. Or perhaps an imitator."

Viltas looked down. "I suppose we need to start investigating, then."

"Yes," Rachim murmured, "but *quietly.*"

"Agreed," Harkon mused. "No need to tip off the aristocracy that we know there might be a necromancer in their ranks. We still don't know *why* Amut was murdered. A captain is a high-profile target, the risks are beyond reasoning. Starting tomorrow, the three of us will start going through the entire rolls of the ship's ruling class, searching for irregularities."

"That's going to take a damn long time," Rachim sighed, nodding his head. "And on top of everything *else*..."

"But it has to be done," Viltas affirmed. "As lord shipman I have access to a great number of records of names, households, heirs, bloodlines. I'll hit my books and bring you what I can in the morning."

Aimee noted that she'd been left conspicuously out of all this. Starting to stand, she said, "I'll help too."

"No," Harkon said, and with one hand, urged her back into her seat.

"Teacher–" she began to protest, feeling a rising mingling of shame and anger.

"You need to revisit your studies," Harkon said. He was looking at her sideways now, in an odd sort of way that she'd learned implied double meaning. "Talk to Vlana and Elias. There are many other things that we still have to set in order for our stay," and what he said next carried a weight of subtle emphasis. "An apprentice has her duties."

Then, rising, he started towards the door, beckoning for Rachim and Viltas to follow. "Gentlemen, I think a nightcap is in order. Will one of you be so kind as to provide me with a guide to the finer selections? It's been too long since I had something aboard a proper behemoth."

When they heard the sounds of the three men leaving the ship, Aimee stood. Clutch looked up. "Well," the pilot said. "That was blunt of him."

"Yeah, well, investigations up here in stuffy noblesville aren't exactly what the lot of us are fit for," Vant replied. A half smirk crossed his face. "Well, alright, maybe *some* of us." He flashed Clutch a wink.

"Can it, hull rat," the pilot shot back. Then she turned to Aimee. "Well, his little aside was clearly directed at *you*, so what's cooking in your head, blondie?"

Aimee chewed on her lower lip, letting the blanket fall away and putting down her mug. Harkon hadn't left her to pore over her texts, though knowing him he fully expected her regular practice to continue. She knew his methods well enough to recognize when she was being told to go off on her own.

She threw Vlana a look. "I'm going to need to know everything you saw down there, because I'm going myself. Clearly there's one half of an equation we're not going to be exposed to if we don't take the initiative. As much as Rachim and Viltas talk about advocating for the lower levels, they sure don't have any desire to go there."

"Royals so seldom do," Vlana said, with a grin forming. "Yeah, we can tell you what we saw. You want us to guide you?"

"No," Aimee shook her head. That surprised them. Her hands were moving as she explained. "I need the two of you to keep doing what you've *been* doing. Making social connections, being seen as if nothing is out of the ordinary. You too, Clutch. While Harkon is working with the known faces and names, we need to seem like we're not doing anything out of the ordinary."

"Fair," Vlana said.

"Plenty of holes to dive down," Vant echoed.

"You shouldn't go alone," Elias suddenly said. Still in his chair, Oath of Aurum resting across his lap, the tall man assessed the room after he spoke. Aimee could see the unease in his green eyes, a wall waiting to raise depending on how the others reacted.

Vlana's eyes narrowed. Vant averted his gaze. Aimee felt a small surge of irritation on their newest crewmember's behalf. Before the tension could escalate, she turned to face him, and flashed a winning smile. "I won't," she said. "You're going with me."

CHAPTER SEVEN
THE LIGHT IN THE DEPTHS

"This is a bad idea," Elias said in the dim light.

"And by bad, you mean *brilliant*," Aimee replied.

"I'm stating it for the record," Elias answered, "we're going in half-cocked and under-prepared."

Aimee turned to look at him. The lamps across the access tunnel in which they stood gave her face a soft glow, and played off the edges of her blue eyes. One of her eyebrows arched and a corner of her mouth quirked into a smile. "Like you never did things off the cuff?"

It said a lot about how much he valued the person in front of him, Elias reflected, that the small jibe about his former life made him smile, rather than flinch. "If *I'm* your legitimizing example, you have problems."

Aimee laughed, finished knotting her blonde hair into a braid, and pulled up the hood of her blue coat. "I expected you to be more eager for adventure," she said, with mock offense. Then she started walking.

"Your adventure," he said. "My exercise in keeping you alive."

"Don't worry," she replied confidently. "I believe in you."

The access tunnel was long and wide, tiled to refract the light from the dim mystic lamps across the interior. Near the entryway it had worked well, but the deeper they went, the less it seemed cleaning the walls had mattered, and the filth and soot and dirt that coated the interior dampened the illumination still further.

A few moments down the path, a tall, familiar figure stepped out of the shadows to bar their way. "What's this?" came a female voice. "A pair of up-levelers looking for a thrill?"

Elias smiled as Belit stepped fully into the light. "Her idea," he said, indicating Aimee with a cock of his head. "I'm the security."

Aimee took a step forward, extending a gloved hand with one of her brilliant smiles. "It's wonderful to meet you, Lady Belit," she said. "Thank you for coming."

Belit had left aside her armor, dressed now in a dusty longcoat with a red scarf gathered at her neck. Her longsword hung at her waist, and a dark hand wearing a fingerless glove rested casually on the hilt as the other hand clasped Aimee's. "It's just *Belit*," she said to Aimee. "No title." Turning, she laughed. "Besides, my name in my mother's language means *the Lady*. When you say that in the common tongue, you're calling me *Lady Lady*."

Aimee laughed. "Fair point. Belit it is."

They walked deeper into the tunnel. "The officer aristocracy doesn't seem to care much about the upkeep of the ship outside their sight," Aimee mused aloud as they proceeded. Elias followed her gaze. The grime was so thick where they were that graffiti was better accomplished by simply scraping away the filth to form messages.

"Their care is selective," Belit answered. "How many of our laws have you had a chance to acquaint yourselves with?" She flashed an inquisitive look.

"They have a very thick etiquette book," Aimee said. "Rachim said that being outsiders, Harkon and I aren't expected to follow most of the minutiae, but that we should know the big ones. I'm–" Elias caught a hint of schoolgirl embarrassment in her tone "–I'm still reading. They seem oddly egalitarian."

Belit gave a slow nod. "Rachim is right," she said. "Neither of you will be expected to hold to the social laws of the officer aristocracy, but you should know them. Or at least become familiar… but that's not what I'm talking about. The laws for high society and low are different, and even more so the ones for how they interact across those lines."

She paused before continuing. "There are seven basic dictates to which all enlisted are held. Excessive violence is forbidden, as is the forming of private militaries. No religion may interfere in the performance of a crewman's duties. No crewman may falsely claim the backing of his lawful superiors when he lacks it. Illness must be reported. Insurrection must be reported." Here she paused. "But first, and most important, is *do not obstruct trade*. That law derives not from us, but from the Twelve."

Elias tightened his jaw as they walked. He had ample experience with the Twelve: the twelve primary trade-guilds that lorded over all commerce in the known Drifting Lands. From kingdom to city-state, to empire, to republic, all who did business passed through their spheres of influence. The order did business with them frequently, and more than once, when he still wore the name of Azrael, Elias had stood at the side of Lord Roland as he dictated what policies the order considered unacceptable to the great lords of industry.

Despite all of the darkness of the Eternal Order in his personal experience, Elias found himself unsure which left the greater revulsion in his gut: the militaristic killers that had made him, or the apathetic lords of trade that let them have their way.

"That doesn't surprise me," he said. "The Twelve care only for their profits."

Belit gave him a curious look. Aimee stirred beside him. "My uncle used to say the same thing, but with more cursing," she said after a moment. Elias caught a quiet bitterness in her tone. "They never forgot it."

There was a story there, but it also didn't seem right to push. People's secrets were their secrets. *She has all of yours,* some part of his mind snapped back. *True,* he thought. *But that wasn't her choice.*

"I see you've both run afoul of their way of doing things," Belit said thoughtfully. "You might do better down below than you expect."

"How much experience do you have here?" Aimee asked, before qualifying the statement. "I'm sorry – I just meant, you have no noble title, but your position is... high."

"And what would one of the highest placed warriors in *Iseult* know of the lives of the people below?" Belit asked with a casual smile. "It's alright, Miss Laurent. You gave no offense." Her next words carried the slightest hint of wistfulness. "As to the answer, it's simple: I was born down there, deep as well. Near the metadrive chamber, as my mother used to tell it, before she died. I grew up running between the legs of engineers, merchants, thieves and other enlisted. After my mother passed away, my master caught me trying to pick his pocket. I didn't know it then–" she smiled fondly "–but he was the man I would go on to succeed, traveling exasperated and incognito in the company of Captain Amut. It was very common, especially in those days, for him to go about in disguise among the lower levels. *To better know the people.*"

Realization hit Elias. It seemed so obvious, in retrospect, was almost embarrassing not to have seen it earlier, but he was so accustomed to the opposite: Belit, above all else, *loved Iseult*, and its people.

"When my master passed away, Amut elevated me from the rank and file of the Red Guard himself," Belit finished, fondly.

"It sounds like he chose wisely," Aimee said. By the warmth in her voice, she'd come to the same conclusion that Elias had. The difference, of course, was that she likewise had a home to love with such unabashed affection. It made the sensation familiar to her, Elias imagined. *What was that like?* he wondered.

"That is kind of you," Belit said, her tone now tinged with a hint of deeper grief, "but that doesn't change the fact that I failed him when it mattered most. Your own investigation has shown the truth of it."

Before the uncomfortable silence could settle over Elias and Aimee, the warrior leading them gestured with a dark hand towards a greater light glimmering up ahead.

"Come, this is where we turn."

As Azrael, Elias had commanded the vastness of one of the Eternal Order's singular super-weapons. The *Iron*

Hulk he had used to break Port Providence had been a flying mountain fortress bristling with enough ether-cannons to challenge battle fleets, and containing within it an ancient, specialized weapon with sufficient power to shatter continents. He had known every part of this fortress intimately, every piece of its most minute details had been burned into his memory by months spent overseeing its operation.

It was that experience, and that alone, which gave him the context to appreciate just how vast *Iseult* truly was. They slipped through a side door in the tunnel that led to a steel-runged ladder, which dropped them down on a walkway the size of a narrow street. To their left, an immense array of doorways, ramshackle merchant stalls, and branching alleys spread out ahead and behind them as far as the eye could see. To their right was a vast span of open space from which they could see the layers of numerous levels from two above them to a vanishing distance far below. A thin fog hovered in the air between where they stood and the other side.

"That," Belit said, as both Elias and Aimee gawked, "is the foremost loading chasm. It has its own weather, when the upper and lower bay doors are closed."

"You could walk these streets and catwalks for years," Aimee said with wonder in her voice, "and never get bored or run out of things to see."

Belit laughed. "I don't know, Miss Laurent. There are some places where one brown door looks much like another." She put her hands on the rails, staring out into the fog-draped, cavernous space before them. "But we're here, so the question now is where do you want to start?"

"Vant and Vlana were down here for several days,"

Aimee said thoughtfully, staring out over the expanse. An updraft from below rustled her hair as Elias watched. "When we talked, they kept coming back to an odd rumor that reached them after digging around. A storyteller of sorts, someone who everyone seemed to know about, but always referred to in a sideways kind of way."

A memory – deep and painful – flashed through Elias's head. A rose-dappled cottage, the sound of his mother humming in the kitchen. He remembered the plucking of guitar strings, and a very simple lullaby being hummed. He'd heard the song before, he realized... many, many times, even back when he wore the name Azrael.

But this was the first time he'd heard it while he was awake. Or was it? His left hand reached up to touch the side of his head, wincing as small recollections flooded back. Yes. He'd heard it waking, as Azrael, many, many times. The memory of the icy touch of a monster masking itself as a healer made him flinch reflexively. Each time, it had been taken from him.

"Elias..." The voice was Aimee's, pulling him back. He turned, and her blue eyes filled his vision, concerned. "What's wrong?"

"Nothing," he shook his head. Both women looked dubious. There wasn't time to explain to Belit, but he didn't want to lie. "My memories of the past sixteen years are... complicated, and fuzzy before that," he said. "Every so often a new one comes back. Something about the word *storyteller* did it this time. It's not important right now."

"Maybe not," Belit answered. Her gold eyes were thoughtful, her tone quiet. "That *storyteller* your friends heard of – that's a common term for the ship's Oracle.

She's old, controversial, and the officer aristocracy denies her existence. The functionaries," she paused, "consider speaking of her tantamount to heresy."

"But you know she's *real*," Elias said, meeting the warrior's eyes.

Belit looked back and forth between him and Aimee. "...I do," she said.

"How?" Aimee asked.

Belit paused. Elias watched her posture shift in hesitation. She was about to speak of something that had – until now – been a secret. He was about to apologize on behalf of them both, when she answered. "I've seen her," Belit said. "Twice. Once as a little girl... And once in the captain's company."

"So Amut knew," Aimee said. "When the rest of his peers doubted."

"He was an open-minded man," Belit said, her voice slightly pained. Pushing herself away from the rail, she started walking. "More so than most."

"So where do you *find* this person?" Aimee asked, having to take extra steps to keep up with Belit and Elias's longer-legged strides.

"You don't, exactly," Belit explained as they walked. "You start searching, and if she wants, she finds *you*."

Laborers hurried past them, ordinary enlisted, some of them not wearing any uniform at all. At odd intervals, Elias caught a glimpse of what looked like some sort of law enforcement on patrol. Their boiled leathers were filthy, marked with insignias that it took seeing two or three of for him to mark as sorts of heraldry. They all wore the same mass-produced half-helms, though, and carried heavy cudgels.

"Who are the dome-caps?" he asked in low tones as they walked. One of them gave Elias a sour frown that deepened when he marked Oath of Aurum hanging at the young man's hip.

"Enforcers," Belit said. "To the extent that the lower levels have any sort of law officers, it's them. In an ideal world, they'd be trained for protection and service. In practice, each officer household pays for the upkeep of a set number of them to promote the general welfare. Most are badly trained brutes with clubs."

"Are lower level rebellions common?" Aimee asked, thoughtfully.

"Not for most of Amut's captaincy," Belit answered. "But the rule of the Faceless started with one, or so they tell it. And now that he's gone, tensions are getting worse. People down here work without cessation, and most don't think the officer aristocracy cares for them anymore."

They walked for what seemed a long time, before turning into a side corridor that took them down dirty stairs and into an open square. "Wait here," Belit murmured to the two of them, and walked further into the crowd. For a few moments, Elias and Aimee stood alone, off to the side, taking in the surrounding scenery.

The square was the confluence of four corridors. At its center, a small dais held an empty, moss-covered fountain. People moved through. Most were workers of various sorts, dressed in homespun, threadbare clothes or the occasional dirty uniform. In contrast to the riotous, impractical fashions of the upper levels, there was a practicality on display that was both uniform, and jarringly diverse. Elias saw clothing styles from a dozen different countries, and faces in as many different shades.

The main unifying trait was that most of them were shorter than the people up above by a few inches.

He glimpsed Belit talking to a man by the fountain. Trying to read the room with his mystically enhanced senses mostly just produced a headache. Still, he couldn't shake the feeling of being followed, or watched. Early in his time with the order, he'd done brief stints as a bodyguard for guild officials. Working security in any sort of crowd like this was a nightmare.

"This doesn't add up," Aimee murmured next to him. Her back rested against the cold wall panel, arms folded across her chest, legs crossed.

"Which bit?" Elias asked. His head still hurt.

"Any of it," she answered. "I don't know if this Oracle is a practitioner of some sort of divination magic, to be fair, but if she is... the aristocracy blatantly disbelieving her existence doesn't make any sense. Divination is a known, mystic science. It's not always reliable, but it's *known*."

"Never run up against anti-intellectualism before?" Elias asked. For some reason, the thought that someone as educated as Aimee de Laurent hadn't encountered such a thing seemed... odd.

Aimee waved a dismissive hand. "This isn't the streets of Havensreach's lower district or some hinterland port that nobody goes to, though," she said. "It's a living, breathing skyship society. Contempt for knowledge kills people in places like this."

Elias frowned, remembering his old masters. "The order makes use of spies spreading false information to weaken the defenses of their enemies ahead of invasion." Lies, he remembered, were one of their favorite tools.

"Contempt for knowledge kills people everywhere."

Aimee gave him a sideways look. "That was blunt."

He read apprehension in her face. "I don't like remembering it either," he added.

She frowned and looked about to say something else, when Belit returned in the company of a shorter man in coveralls, a jaunty blue cap on his head and a ratty beard hanging precipitously from a thin chin.

"This is Ferret," Belit said in lower tones. "He's been good to my people in the information department, and he's trustworthy. We start with him."

Ferret was an inch shorter than Aimee, and Elias and Belit towered over him. Still, as he sized the tall, green-eyed man up, Elias had the sense that the man before him wasn't intimidated in the least. "Yeah," he said, and his accent was thicker than anyone on the upper levels. "But not here. Not here. Lily-pale-golden hair–" he gestured at Aimee "–and chisel-faced-green-eyes," he prodded Elias in the chest, "both stick out bad as ornamental doors on latrines. Too white. Too tall. Too *foreign*. Gotta find somewhere else to talk."

And with that, he started down one of the many corridors, pausing only to gesture over his shoulder. "Come on! Get you following, before my trust runs out."

Aimee and Elias exchanged a look of mutual confusion. Then a nod.

They followed.

After what seemed a long walk, Ferret closed the door behind them. They stood in a small room, the exterior of which had been drab and brown, but which inside was painted green. Elias turned, taking in the space around them. A prayer rug rested on the floor, threaded red and gold in beautiful, handmade designs. He knew art well enough to recognize quality. Between the rug and the gilded altar at the far end of the room, he was likely looking at the most expensive things whoever used this place owned.

"Yours?" Aimee asked, looking back at Ferret.

The informant shook his head. "This is the home of a woman I trust. Thick walls, and noise above, below, and to all sides without. Besides–" he flashed a small smile and gestured at the altar "–the gods are good at keeping secrets. A thousand gods, and a thousand, thousand ways to pray."

Belit smiled as well. "I told him you were foreign, but that you were trying to find the truth about what happened to the captain, and what's happening now that's making our people hurt."

Elias frowned. Something – a faint scent of magic – teased at his senses. But amidst the powerful enchantments that suffused the entirety of the behemoth, it was hard to pinpoint. It didn't feel strong enough to be dangerous.

"My name," Aimee started, "is Aimee, apprentice to–"

"–I know who you are," Ferret said. "Apprentice to Harkon Bright. Arrived on that beautiful silver skyship. We hear things, down below. We don't know *you*, but we know your teacher's legend. Elsewise even Belit's good word wouldn't be enough. Outsiders working with the top-levelers aren't trusted, down here. We also know Amut didn't die of just a sickness. Something *dark* is stirring in the shadows, foreigner. Outside our hull, and inside. We've heard stories of falling mountains and slain angels, of exile princes and sorceresses who split the sky."

Elias felt his heart pounding in his ears. Did Ferret know who *he* was? The man's eyes gave him no special attention, and he seemed at ease. It didn't seem likely that anyone would be calm and unconcerned if they thought the monster once called Azrael was in the room. Then it struck him. *Slain angels.*

The common story being told was that Azrael was *dead*. Elias tried not to let his relief show.

"Well," Aimee said, and Elias watched a calm, relaxed smile settle across her face. "That makes things a little simpler. I saw the glyph above his bed. A spell was cast that drained the life from your captain, and a powerful illusion masked it. The magic used was necromancy, and casting it would've required sufficient power as couldn't be done without taking the lives of others first. If the officer aristocrats had no inkling that this was coming, those first kills must have happened down here."

Elias smiled wryly despite himself. She hadn't exaggerated when they'd first been introduced to Viltas. Anyone that saw only beauty and not the diamond-sharp mind beneath was a fool.

Ferret closed his eyes for a moment, then looked at them with the expression of a person having his worst fears confirmed. "Yeah," he said, after a moment. "This... glyph, you call it. Can you show me?"

Aimee reached within her coat and produced a piece of paper, which she meticulously unfolded with long fingers. "It's hard to draw it correctly," she said. "The symbol carries power, and even without the spell behind it, causes discomfort to look at. I did it from memory."

Elias felt an involuntary chuckle slip out. Of course she had.

She held it up, jagged and dark, a stain upon the page. Ferret and Belit both winced when they saw it. "Put it away," the former said. "I know the mark. It's his."

"My teacher believes," Aimee said, putting the paper away, "that this is an imitator. Or perhaps a long-hidden apprentice."

"Pray it is," Ferret answered. "I hear many whispers. And many things I see myself. People have been going missing. The poorest. The weakest, at first. Then people who ask questions. Never in public places. Always alone."

Belit looked alarmed. "This is the first I've heard of this," she said. "Why?"

"You stopped coming down here," Ferret muttered, with hurt in his voice. "Not like we could reach you above."

"How many?" Aimee asked gently. "Do you know numbers?"

"Dozens before the captain died," Ferret said quietly. "More after. And there've been other whispers. Words we haven't heard in years: Grandfather. *Empty Sky.*"

Elias frowned. The phrase was familiar, but he couldn't say just why.

"No," Belit whispered. "They were wiped out. The last of them died ten years after the Faceless was slain."

"They were his followers," Ferret explained. "Or so our elders say. *The Children of the Empty Sky.* When *he* menaced *Iseult* and threatened to snuff one of the two hearts, they were his servants. The living ones, I mean. He never lacked for the dead."

"But you've seen no husks this time?" Elias asked.

"No," Ferret muttered. "But no corpses, either." His expression was wry and dark. "And no Amut, this time. No white knights to ride in and save the day."

"White knights?" Elias looked up. Another memory pricked at his thoughts, of his former master cursing in the dark, of old tapestries hidden in dank, forgotten rooms. Thinking about it made his head hurt.

"Long story," Belit answered. "Old. I'll tell you another time."

"Maybe sooner," Ferret said, standing. "But not from me. From *her*."

He looked at the altar, then back at the three of them. "The Oracle has agreed to see you."

He led them down, and this path quickly veered away from the busy, cosmopolitan squares and main byways of the center. They walked in silence for a time, and it gave Elias a chance to take stock of their surroundings. The interior of the ship was a massive patchwork of construction styles, cobbled together from what must have been a thousand cultures, some of which he had never seen before, and others he'd only heard of in old myths of the time before.

Wood paneling and hanging charms upon delicate threads sometimes lived beside harsh, rusted metal walls with doorways so narrow he had to walk through sideways. Here a door was paper and wood, there metal and blank. A window might be circular, square, rectangular, draped in slatted wooden shades, or dirty cloth curtains. He passed prayer strips etched in painted calligraphy, and sutras carved delicately into the hard, rusted faces of exposed steel beams.

"How far are we?" Aimee asked after what seemed near an hour. "From the square where we found you, I mean?"

"A quarter of a day below the surface," Ferret answered. "Perhaps half that from Her Lady's Chamber. An hour from the port wall and the open sky."

Aimee gave Belit a helpless look.

"Deep," Belit answered, "but not to the true depths or the cargo bays. Closer to portside, and not so far from the metadrive chamber."

"Why do you call it *Her Lady's Chamber*?" Elias asked.

Ferret flashed an amused grin over his shoulder. "Cuz that's where she lives, green-eyes."

"The Oracle?"

A caustic laugh escaped their guide. "Gods, no. Though that used to be her rightful place. No, not the Oracle; *Her. Iseult.*"

"She's *alive*?" Aimee asked, eyes popping.

Ferret looked back and forth between the two of them, then shook his head at Belit. "Foreigners. Land-born. They know nothing!"

"They'll learn," Belit said, amused. "Another story I'll tell you both, when we have a chance to go through the ship's ancient history. Suffice to say, to everyone other than the officers, this ship is a living, breathing thing. She has a soul, and it needs tending."

Elias didn't answer. He once again felt that rising of hairs on the back of his neck, as if they were being followed. Cursory checks, however, failed to reveal anyone, or anything.

They emerged into an intersection of five different corridors. The space was open, the ceiling high-vaulted and hexagonal. In the center was a decrepit old rock garden crowned with the pale skeleton of a bonsai tree.

It was so quiet that Elias could hear his own heart

hammering in his chest. There was nobody here.

"Ferret," Belit said, "what's this about?"

Their guide took a step forward, looking about with the nervous reticence of a possum considering a patch of unexpected light. "This is where I last met her, where she has been meeting the worthy for the past year. It's out of the way. Enforcers don't come here, and few others. A bit of old magic clings to it, you know? But something feels... wrong."

"Cold, like the captain's bedchamber," Aimee said. Whatever fear had gripped her, however, in the wake of her encounter in Amut's former chamber had fled her now, Elias could see. The portalmage's eyes were chips of blue flint, her face hard and determined. She sensed him looking at her and caught his gaze with a half-smile. "We didn't come all this way to run back empty-handed."

She took a step into the room proper, and the air before the tree flickered. Elias sensed the surge of magic, and impulse jerked him forward, putting him between Aimee and the rapidly forming, translucent figure of light that stood before them. He could make out the bottom half of a feminine face partially obscured by the hood of a ratty cloak. A blurry wisp of glimmering smoke trailed about the edges of the mystic projection.

Then Aimee was stepping around him, giving him a look somewhere between exasperation and surprise. "It's just a projection spell," she said.

"I'm sorry," Elias murmured, awkwardly. "Reflex."

Aimee's expression turned baffled.

"So you're the ones," the figure said, and her voice was surprisingly young, "drowning out the Song with your deafening fates."

"I brought them here," Belit said, stepping forward, hand resting upon the pommel of her longsword. Abruptly, the woman drew her steel, rested the point in the floor, and knelt before the projection. "Please, *Augress*," the title sounded formal, "I beg of you. They believe that Amut has been murdered, and troubling signs point to the return of the Faceless. The captain's chair sits empty, and three candidates bicker for its power." Her gold eyes blazed, pleading, in her dark face. "We need your aid, now more than ever. I beg you speak to them, with my honor as voucher."

Shocked into silence at the earnest display before him, Elias was lost for words.

The Oracle seemed likewise surprised. She paused, and in the line of her mouth, Elias detected something – regret perhaps, pain definitely. Then she spoke. "Poor warrior," she said, at last. "There is only so much that I can do. The lamps have been lit, the water has begun to run. The trials have started, and there is no stopping them. One will pass, or all will fall."

Belit's eyes widened in horror. Aimee stepped forward. "Please," she said. "I am Aimee de Laurent–"

"I know who you are," the Oracle fixed her gaze on Aimee. "Sky-splitter, Jester's niece."

"I must find Amut's killer," Aimee said. As Elias watched, the apprentice mage stood straight as a spear, fearless before the projection. "I know that divination is imprecise, but even blurry sight betters the vision of the blind. I implore you, *Augress*–" she used the title "–help us."

"You mistake me," the Oracle answered, and Elias heard a sadness in her voice. "Fate is neither a matter of vision nor of blindness. There is only the *Song*, sky-splitter. Only the grand symphony, and the notes without number within. *Iseult* hears, and so do I."

Abruptly the projection's hooded head turned. Elias knew why: he heard a sound down one of the corridors. Belit straightened beside him. They exchanged a look. The rasp of steel echoed in the half-light.

"You have been followed," the Oracle said, and her projection began to fade. "Save yourselves. Flee! Find me again!"

"Run, Ferret," Belit snapped.

Ferret stepped into the shadows behind them, and bolted.

"*Wait!*" Aimee shouted. Too late. She stood now in the midst of a dissolving image. Specks of light drifted to the floor, forming feathers of ice that melted snowlike, to nothing. Their eyes met. Hers were wide, frustrated, and afraid.

Belit elbowed him in the side. He turned in her direction. Three corridors branched from the space ahead of them. In the darkness of each, movement stirred. The half-light fired the edges of drawn swords.

"Draw your sword, *junk ritter*," Belit said. "Our foes are here."

They crept forward from three tunnels, moving with steps that made hardly a sound. A frigid fear preceded them, cloying like damp ice to the heart. Even the grace with which they moved was unnatural. Elias's eyes swept across them as they came. There was a rhythm and a rise and fall of tension in the muscles of living people, a cessation and resumption of movement never noticed until it was completely absent. Their perfect grace was disturbing. An instinctive part of him he couldn't name reacted with panicked revulsion. These killers were dead.

His hand closed on Oath of Aurum's hilt. The grip was hot to the touch, and the steel glowed white when he drew it, lit from within. He took a single step forward past Aimee. "Miss Laurent," he said, "forgive me, but this time I must *insist* you stand behind me."

"They're dead," the sorceress breathed. In her voice, he detected a rising terror.

"You've faced worse," Elias snapped back. She might be the only one here with the power to stop these things.

"Worse?" he heard her say, still in the thrall of her fear.

He risked a single glance over his shoulder at her wide-eyed, startled face. "You defeated Esric, didn't you?" He almost choked on the name. "You defeated me."

"Right," he heard her say, fortified. "Right."

He felt the flare of magic and heard words slip, practiced and sharp, from her lips. He had no idea what the spell was, and there was no time to think about it. The dead swordsmen leaped forward, and thought vanished. They were quick. The enchanted sword rang against an incoming blade. Shoulder to shoulder with Belit, Elias faced the dead. He tried to call on his speed, but his mind wouldn't focus. A sword was there, cutting in, he turned it aside, shifted his stance immediately to ward against another cut. The strikes were patient. Probing. Deft as willow reeds. And they never *stopped*.

Go ahead, Roland's voice rang mocking in his head. *Show them your power. See how quickly they turn on you.*

"Elias!" Belit shouted beside him. "Focus!"

Elias parried a second sword, a third, a fourth. The incoming strikes sped up. A wall of advancing steel pushed them back. The twist and crack of sinew and muscle pushed past its limits filled his ears. This close, he saw half-rotted faces with glowing eyes. Then their mouths started to move, and rasping voices filled the air.

"Where is my wife?" shrieked one.

"I'm so *cold*," whimpered another.

"Please, I can't see. Why are you doing this?"

"I can't breathe. I can't breathe. I can't breathe."

"Help me, *HELP ME!*"

The two warriors took a step back, giving ground as one. His nerves raked raw, his mind defying focus, Elias fought the urge to scream. The dead pressed in, the pace of their attacks increasing. Five blades now bore down on two, and it was all Elias could do to defend Belit's left and Aimee's front. An opening. The stink of rot and the flash of swords that needed no rest filled his senses. He needed an *opening*.

There *was* none.

Then two things happened. First, Aimee shouted "DOWN!" behind him. Elias dropped reflexively into a crouch, and the bloom of a powerful spell passed over his head, the tingling ripple of magic hitting his senses and making his hair stand on end. A wave of concussive flames hammered into their enemies in a semicircular arc expanding outwards. They staggered back.

Second, a scream sounded from the corridors behind them, and Vant, Vlana, Clutch, and Bjorn came charging into their midst, the former two wielding pairs of short shock-sticks, the latter two with a large boarding axe and a huge mace. Two of the dead were actively on fire. The others leaped to their feet. None of them had slowed down at all. Elias surged upward. Aimee grabbed his arm.

"I know you're holding back," she said. "Don't. We *need* you."

Then she was moving, her hands working through forms and a fresh spell on her lips.

Oath of Aurum blazed in his grip. The black knight tried to center his mind, but one of the dead was upon him. Steel rang on steel. He wound for a thrust. It shoved him aside and jackhammered its fist into his throat. "Help me," the dead man moaned. "Where is my child? Where is my child?"

Elias staggered from the blow, barely kept his balance. Pain rippled through his middle. *Go ahead*, the sliver of Roland within his mind sneered. *As if you could be anything without me.*

He parried again, but no counter was possible, as a second of the dead – this one actively blazing with Aimee's flames – set upon him. Pushed him back towards the dais. He glimpsed the rest of the fight. Vant and Vlana held their own against one of the dead, their four sticks scarcely blunting its darting cuts. Aimee summoned a shield spell, then thrust forward a punch that sent a blast of force into the center of another, sending it hurtling down the corridor whence it had come. Belit slipped under another's cut and buried her sword in its chest. The dead thing ignored its impalement and raked its blade at her face. She caught it on a steel gauntlet that wrapped her arm beneath her sleeve, and ripped her sword upwards, splitting the thing into two halves that still twitched and moved.

The next flurry of cuts nearly knocked him off his feet. Instead he rolled backwards and came up in a crouch, now separated from his friends. The dead came at him, repeating their begging pleas. He parried one, thrust in response. It was turned aside. Another counter came. Another. His arms ached and the force of the blows made his spine shake. He went down to one knee. Barely parried the next.

An indistinct, armored figure appeared behind his two assailants. Ragged-cloaked and translucent. An arrogant, bemused smile on the lower half of its face. A knight of the order. Behind it, the crew of *Elysium* and Belit fought for their lives.

As if you could be anything at all, the apparition said. *Without us.*

Something in Elias snapped. The blades came down again. His mind narrowed to a pinprick. A single thought filled his mind. *Speed.*

The steel rang against Oath of Aurum. Elias surged upwards, the world moving slowly as the spell suffused his limbs, made him *just quick enough*. He hammered the next counter aside, pressed his attack. They retreated, now. His blows came with grunts at first, then screams. The armored figure was gone, but the fear of it filled his mind. He hammered back in. The wind of his passing sword was a chorus of light-streaking whispers in the dark, until a blow turned aside the sword of one even as the second cut at his back. Elias dropped into a low crouch, caught the second strike high overhead in a hanging parry, whipped it away, and brought the glowing sword about in a perfect circle straight into the first's center of mass. The smell of burning flesh filled the air. The white sword blazed. Its light poured out of the animated corpse's eyes, and sheared through the dead man's flesh, leaving a severed, inert body in its wake.

Elias pivoted as the second assassin brought its sword back around, and offset its cut with a thrust down the centerline that put his point straight through its mouth. Light blazed from its eyes, and the dead thing fell silent and still.

Two of the dead remained. Clutch charged one, caught its cut on the haft of her axe. The twins rushed in underneath, and drove the points of their enchanted shock-sticks repeatedly into its middle, until the crackling charges ripped its mass apart. Even as it fell, it still screamed. Still tried to fight. Clutch had to hit it three times with her axe before it stopped moving.

A heartbeat later, and Aimee stood over the immobile form of their last foe, wisps of blue flames from a powerful spell dissipating about her slender fingers. "That," she breathed, "was a lot harder than it should've been."

"What the hell," Belit said, shaking in the sudden quiet, "were those things? I've heard stories about the walking dead. In none of them were they adept with swords, nor were they spewing nonsense at the people they attacked."

"It wasn't nonsense," Aimee said, and terror filled her voice. "It was the–" she gulped "–the cessation echo."

Elias closed his eyes. Of course. He knew the term. What he hadn't known was that the sword he bore would kill them so *quickly*.

Nor did he know *why*.

"Translation?" Belit asked, her voice settling.

The answer came from an unexpected place. Bjorn picked still-wiggling bits of gore from the large mace he'd brought as he spoke. "It means," he said, "their last thoughts. Newly animated dead sometimes carry the echo of the folk they were. These ones–" he gestured at the aftermath filling the room "–sound like they were just repeating their last thoughts before they died, over and over and over."

"Gods," Vant breathed. "What the *fuck*…"

Elias crossed the distance to reach the rest of the group just as Aimee turned to the three new arrivals, her tone somewhere between thankful and angry. "I *told* you," she said, "not to come with me. What are you *doing* here?"

"Hey, don't thank us or anything," Clutch said with a shrug. "Not like we saved your ass."

"That's not it," Aimee started.

"Then what *is* it?" Vlana demanded.

"Who is watching *Elysium*?" Aimee's eyes blazed, her expression fierce.

"We need to get out of here," Belit said.

Before any of their rescuers could answer that, the small room was suddenly sliced through with the beams of hooded lanterns and glow-globes contained in focused cylinders. Enforcers followed – near twenty of them, carrying heavy clubs. Behind them came breastplate-clad guards from the upper levels carrying spears and wearing short stabbing swords at their hips. And at the rear of them, armored head to foot in gold-gilded steel, a white-haired officer aristocrat who swept his eyes across the lot of them before drawing an ornate sword and fixing his gaze on Elias as he addressed the lot of them.

"Guardsmen, escort the *foreigners* back to the upper levels," Yaresh said, before gesturing at the enforcers. "Clean up this refuse and convey my orders to the commandant of this sublevel: the dead are aboard *Iseult*. This *entire level* must be punished and purged."

CHAPTER EIGHT
THE BELLIGERENT APPRENTICE

It would have been wise for Aimee to keep her temper in check until they were in private with the lord of the muster. Instead, her anger boiled up out of her as soon as the armored guardsmen finished escorting the group of them to the streets of the upper levels.

"Lord Yaresh," she said. The lord of the muster continued walking.

"Lord Yaresh!" she repeated.

"I will speak to your master, *apprentice*," Yaresh answered. In his voice was every lecturer that had ever blown aside her criticisms, every senior theorist ever to dismiss the magic of a *silly upper ring girl*, and more. She forgot her fear. She forgot position, status, or whatever absurd place this insufferable old bastard wanted her to keep to. Her vision tunneled and flashed red, and before anyone could stop her she had seized the officer aristocrat by the arm and spun him around. Perhaps from sheer surprise, he wheeled about, momentarily unsteady on his feet.

Aimee stepped directly into the old man's personal space and jabbed her finger into the center of his armored chest. "*No*, Lord Yaresh. I am Aimee de Laurent of Havensreach. You will speak to *me*."

Yaresh's eyes widened in a flash of anger, then his gaze narrowed, slit-like, and he stared her down, with that look she had seen so many powerful men wear: that *expected* anyone deemed lesser to simply cower. "Have a care, *girl*," he began. "You forget your position, and moreover, *mine*."

Aimee's blood pounded in her ears. She didn't move her hand. "No valid position exists that grants one man the right to massacre an entire level of people. I don't give a damn *who* you aspire to be. You're not purging *anyone*."

"Is that a threat?" Yaresh whispered. A guardsman reflexively moved towards her at this. Elias was suddenly beside her. The guard caught the look on his face and stopped like he'd hit a brick wall.

"Smart," she heard the green-eyed young man say.

"I'm not threatening you," Aimee said, deadpan. "I'm *informing* you. Every man has limits, Yaresh. Yours are staring you in the face. You have *no* right, and if you try, I'll snap that aristocratic pride over my knee and teach you why they call me *sky-splitter*."

Yaresh's face flashed red murder, but Aimee saw fear there as well. He took a step back, realized what he'd done, and fixed her with a hateful, water-boiling stare. "You arrogant, disrespectful *cunt*."

"She's right," Belit said, standing now at Aimee's other side. The warrior woman was slightly taller than the lord of the muster, and though her face was calmer, there was something burning in her golden eyes. Weary. Caged. "The Lord of the Muster may *execute* a purge, but only the captain may order one. You don't have that authority."

"When I require legal advice," Yaresh snapped, "I will consult the functionaries, not a glorified failure of a door sentry."

Belit looked as though the lord of the muster had struck her across the face – but rather than cowed, she seemed suddenly furious.

"What in the Maelstrom's Heart is going on here?" Rachim jogged down the streets towards them, a cadre of his own armed guards at his back. Despite his limp and his missing eye, their host projected a presence of fierce authority. Jogging beside him, wearing a hastily buckled sword, was Viltas's son, Vallus.

Yaresh turned. His lip curled. "Your *guests* have gone to the deeper levels without sanction, for the gods-only-know what reason. There they encountered a number of the walking dead, from which my men's arrival saved them. Now this uppity hellion has threatened me in the course of executing my duties."

The laugh – quick and caustic – ripped out of Aimee. "Hardly! We dealt with those walking corpses *ourselves*. Your trained guard dogs showed up *after* the fact, then you lost your mind and started talking about purges and genocides."

"Something that doesn't fall within his purview," Belit affirmed. "Not without express permission from the Officers' Council."

"Without an active captain," Yaresh protested, "threats to the welfare of the ship must be dealt with by those in the position to take action. I will *not* wait for permission from a committee before taking action to defend my people, my kin, my *home*, from the excesses of the rabble below." Now he stared at Belit, fury naked in his gaze.

"And I will not accept judgment from an up-jumped, glorified sentry who failed her *one job*, simply because of her lingering empathy for the people that produced her *whore mother*."

Aimee was momentarily robbed of further comment, her mouth hanging open. Belit's gold eyes had gone some strange combination of burning, frigid calm. Instead of backing down cowed, the commander of the Red Guard stepped directly into Yaresh's space and looked down into his eyes. "What happened to you, Lord Yaresh?" she said, her voice a cold whisper. "You were a hero, once. What horrible thing shriveled your heart and left this trembling, reactive, frightened man, afraid of those who have nothing? What turned you into such a coward?"

Yaresh's hand swept out automatically at the taller woman's face. Belit caught it in her grasp. "NO!" she shouted, and the sound was like thunder. "You may hold a position higher than mine, your purview may be broader, and heaven help me I may one day be responsible for your personal safety, but you *will not strike me!* Not now, *not ever!*"

Spears raised. Swords swept from scabbards. Out of the corner of Aimee's eye, Elias shifted his posture. She saw the glimmering blade of his enchanted steel slip one inch free of its scabbard. Behind her, her crewmates raised shock-sticks, axe, and mace. Rachim was shouting something, holding out his hands for calm even as nobody listened. Aimee felt the magic pulling at her fingers, itching to be let free, even as her mind grasped for the right words.

Then, thunder. A concussive *bang* erupted in the midst of them, physically pushing apart every man and woman standing in the upper-level street. The release of mystic power made Aimee dizzy, and for a moment she nearly lost her balance.

Harkon Bright caught her. He stood in the middle of the group, now, white hair like moonlight, gray eyes twin stars in his dark face. "That," he said quietly, "is enough."

"Belit," Aimee heard Vallus saying as the group walked towards the officers' hall. "Belit, please."

The commander of the Red Guard kept walking, her face fixed forward.

Violence in the street had been averted, but in a fit of rage, Yaresh had summoned the council of the officer aristocracy to call for a vote on the purge he wished to conduct. Now within the compound, the group followed Harkon and Rachim towards the still-closed doors. Every member present in the conflict below had been brought, in case there was need to testify.

As they stopped before the doors, Vallus caught up with Belit, and reached out, touching her arm. "Bel," he said, with jarring familiarity, "*please.*"

Belit turned, and her face was a mask of white rage. "What in the name of *Iseult*'s beating heart were you *doing* in the middle of that?"

Vallus paused as if he'd been struck across the face. In his thoughtful eyes, Aimee caught a glimpse of real hurt. "Rachim needed the assistance of my father's men–"

"That's not what I'm talking about," Belit continued, and there was something else in her voice, unlike what Aimee had seen thus far: a uniquely potent anger, as if she'd been personally, painfully hurt. "What in the name of the gods possessed you to wear a sword? Yaresh would've cut you to ribbons before you even got it free.

You're not a killer, Val. How could you be so *rash*?"

"Children," Rachim said over his shoulder. "Another time. Val, where's your father?"

"Deep in the records until first light," Vallus answered. "For the past two days. He's taken ill. I'll stand in his stead."

Rachim looked as though he'd just been told his guard dog had been replaced by a squitten. "Fine," he said. "Everyone follow my lead and for the love of the thousand gods, don't talk unless you're asked to. Understand?"

A seam of light split the great doors, and the group strode through as they opened. The daylight spilled through the high arched windows to coat the blue table with an iridescent glow. All around it, officers had gathered – in greater numbers than before – and the angry murmurings of hundreds filled the vast room with a storm of anger and malcontent.

Aimee watched innumerable eyes fix upon their small group as they walked, and a surprised functionary turned with alarm to regard them. "...And it seems his excellency Rachim *will* be here."

Aimee felt her jaw tighten and the red rage rise within her: the meeting had already begun.

"Yes," Rachim declared, striding into the room with Harkon by his side. "He will be, as will this council's moderator, Harkon Bright."

The functionary's eyes narrowed to slits. His hand raised to forestall objection, but Aimee couldn't help but notice that the gesture had the intensity of a religious rebuke directed at her teacher. "This meeting does not concern the debates of the candidates for captaincy. Harkon Bright's input is not needed."

"I don't know about that," Yaresh said, standing from his place at the blue table. "He may be needed to account for his use of sorcery to threaten senior members of the officer aristocracy. Let the foreign troublemaker stay."

Aimee felt her fists clench into knots of fury at her sides as the group was ushered in, stared at by faces that had a mere day or so earlier seemed at least receptive to their presence. Now the eyes were suspicious. Judgmental. Aimee kept her face carefully neutral, her posture proud. Social pressure was something she was an old hand at dealing with. It was amazing what being a contentious young woman at the academy had prepared her for.

Harkon, for his part, seemed as calm as she'd ever seen him. Her teacher waited, patiently, his arms folded across his chest and his eyes amused.

"The council is in session," the functionary declared. Those who were still standing took their seats, and a hush settled over the room.

"Yaresh, Lord of the Muster, has requested the floor," the functionary continued.

"Brothers and sisters," Yaresh began, and Aimee was immediately struck by how the cadence of his voice had changed. It was familial, now. Protective. Pained. "I bring news most dire: a wretched civil unrest has gripped the lower levels of *Iseult*. Our fair guests, themselves, were assaulted by some sort of revenant assassins–" here he paused, and Aimee wondered how he would couch the truth, "–created, doubtless, by some imitator necromancer lurking amongst the enlisted, or perhaps snuck aboard in Ishtier. It is my sworn duty to defend this vessel from such threats, but without Amut I must turn to you for authorization."

Sitting up until then, the lord of the muster rose from his chair, placing scarred hands upon the table. "I speak to you now not as a candidate for captaincy, nor as a master of men, but merely as a soldier who would protect his home: I call for a council vote. The entirety of sublevel 337 must be purged. The levels immediately above and below must receive full censure."

"Oh, that bastard," Vallus muttered to Aimee's left.

Belit was quiet, her hands balled into fists, jaw tight.

Loud muttering rippled around the edge of the blue table, loud enough to cover a breath of quick conversation amongst Aimee and those immediately near her.

"I didn't like anything I heard," she quickly said to Viltas's son, "but that sounded like it was about something very specific."

"I expected demands," Vallus said, bitter. "Not humility. I expected the entitled warrior, not the humble war-hero."

"Easier to refuse," Rachim agreed. "Harder to justify refusing."

"Only," Harkon mused, "if you were looking for a reason to meet rage with rage." And at this, Aimee's teacher held up a hand. The room quieted when officer aristocrats caught sight of the brown palm. The functionary glared at him, but nodded.

"I do not presume," Harkon said, "to gainsay the Lord of the Muster's understanding of his own home's strife. Yet I caution this council: to call for a vote when so few voices have been heard is an error, one Lord Yaresh doubtless makes in his passion to see *Iseult* defended."

Silence hung for a moment. Aimee glimpsed a twitch at the corner of Lord Yaresh's eye. Then someone – a midlevel officer – yelled "Purge!" And another slammed his fist on the table. "Vote!"

Aimee felt her heart sink, thinking of the numerous faces she'd passed below: diverse, harried, and hurried. Out of the corner of her eye she saw Belit's jaw clenched to the point of pain.

"Magister Bright has the right of it," came another interruption, soft but strong. Diara had broken her silence at the opposite end of the table. The Countess of Astronomers had lost none of her cold demeanor, yet the stare with which she fixed Yaresh made him hesitate. "These accusations are severe, and if true, a purge is the last course of action this council should authorize."

"I suppose," Yaresh said, spreading his hands wide and looking from right to left, "that we should simply wait to see if this enemy acts again? I respect the countess for her views, but one does not turn to a stargazer in war-time."

"Are we at war, Yaresh?" It was Pentus who spoke now. Behind the lord of the muster, the functionary ground his teeth. The duke of the midlevels had risen to stand as well. "Assassins lashing out at foreign travelers – while severe – is hardly an army in our midst."

The murmurings of the officer aristocrats were far less united, now. Aimee saw the ghost of a smile on the corner of Harkon's mouth.

"Did your excellency forget my warning that these killers were a necromancer's thralls?" Yaresh snapped. "When the dead walk, it is always war, and last I checked, neither you, nor the honorable countess were among those who fought the Faceless."

"Neither were you, Lord Yaresh," Vallus said beside Aimee. "But my father, Lord Viltas, was. He is home, as this transpires, and I stand in his stead. If we are to defer to expertise, then perhaps this council should hear the words of those who were actually attacked before it authorizes violence."

All eyes were on the young officer aristocrat now. Vallus looked nervous, momentarily wrong-footed, but he swallowed and kept talking. "Aimee de Laurent," he said. "Belit of the Red Guard," he faltered for a moment. "And Elias Leblanc."

All eyes were suddenly on the group. In the sudden silence, Clutch deadpanned, "Yeah, it's not like any of the *rest* of us were there too."

"Which begs the question," Yaresh said abruptly, "what were you doing in such low levels in the first place, and in the company of one who is compelled by law to maintain her neutrality in all political affairs?"

"When last I checked," Belit suddenly snapped back, "strolling through my old stomping grounds is hardly political, Lord Yaresh. I keep company with whom I wish, and I show them what I wish."

"Such as the oft-disproven Oracle in which you're rumored to place such faith?" Yaresh countered. Belit's eyes fixed on him, and Aimee suddenly feared that the woman would lunge across the space and put her hands around the old warrior's throat.

"Surely," Pentus interrupted from his space across the table, "accusing Commander Belit of belief in a known fabricated old skyfarer's tale is rather untoward, is it not?"

Belit fixed her gold eyes on the duke of the midlevels. "I don't need protection from *you*," she said. Then, turning to Yaresh, she countered: "What I believe is irrelevant to your desire to kill thousands of innocent people for the sake of convenience, Lord of the Muster. People – lest you forget – from whose midst I was upraised to my position by Amut, the Lion of Heaven *himself*. I take no part in the politics of the selection of our late captain's successor, but as commander of the Red Guard, my primary remaining duty in the absence of my charge is to the people of this ship. Your request is brutal and cruel. I will not support it, nor should any feeling person on this council."

Yaresh stared at her. The look on his face was somewhere between cold hate, and grudging respect. Out of the corner of her eye, Aimee glimpsed the ghost of a smile flicker across Diara's mouth.

Silence. Aimee saw her chance, and took it. "Honored council," she said, taking a step forward, remembering when she'd stood upon the podium before her graduating class, delivering a valediction. "If I may add some clarifying information, the Lord of the Muster does not lie: my companions and I were being guided by Belit to the lower levels, on our request. Myths have long been a fascination of mine, so leave that irrelevant detail to rest. Our attackers were undead. Advanced, graceful things. Terrible and perilous. What I ask this council to remember, however, is their own words. This subject is complex, but I will try to explain it as best I can. Recently animated dead frequently exhibit a magic side effect called *the cessation echo*. This is the remnant of their last thoughts in the moment of their death."

An uncomfortable look passed over the assembled officer aristocrats. Aimee took the opening and pressed. "Each of the foes we faced below exhibited this effect, repeated over and over and over, even as they attacked us." She stepped right to the edge of the table, and pressed her palms to it, leaning forward. Taking up space and forcing the officers nearest to make room for her. "Do you want to know what they said?" she asked. In the deafening quiet, she heard a man nearby her gulp.

"They were terrified," Aimee continued. "Mothers. Fathers. Ordinary workers, sisters, brothers. They repeated recollections of begging for their lives, not understanding what had happened to them."

"What is your point?" one of Yaresh's supporters – a hard-faced woman in gray – asked.

"The people Lord Yaresh wishes to purge are not faceless masses harboring your enemies," Aimee said. "They are their first, most vulnerable victims. If this council authorizes a purge, you will play right into their waiting, grateful hands."

A concerned murmur passed through the assembled officers. Aimee saw Harkon smile and give a small, approving nod. She breathed out, the sound hidden by the resurgent voices around her. Whatever else happened, they'd at least broken the lord of the muster's momentum.

"Enough debate," the functionary abruptly commanded, slamming his hand upon the table. "The request has been made, and now the council must respond. A vote will be held–" he regarded Harkon and Aimee with blunt dislike "–immediately."

Hours later, Aimee collapsed into a chair before one of the large windows on the upper floor of Rachim's villa. She closed her eyes, breathed out a long, exhausted sigh, and tried to make sense of the way everything had gone.

"For someone who just won a political victory, you're awfully somber," Harkon said. The vote had been close – too close – but they'd won. After what seemed like a long time, she turned her head and opened her eyes to look at her teacher. Harkon stood just past her, facing the windows with their view of the deep sky. It was later in the day, now. The sun was low in the skies. *Iseult* sailed between immense castles of cloud. Turning in her chair, she paused for a moment to stare. The skyfarers back home said that clouds were bigger in the deep sky... vast beyond imagining, bigger than any isle or continent. In their craziest stories, they said that things lived in them. Storm-Krakens and other myths.

"Sorry," she said, realizing that Harkon was looking at her now. "It just doesn't feel like a victory. The vote was too close. We didn't win by getting the whole council to repudiate Yaresh's insanity. We just made enough people feel indecisive. Victory would be the assembled realizing that they can do so much better than just... not killing."

"Welcome to politics," Harkon said. "Victory is never as clear cut or obvious as we would like. Believe it or not, you're doing well."

"It's not what I signed up for," Aimee said, regarding her teacher candidly.

"No?" Harkon shook his head, amused. "You persist in misunderstanding the complexities of the adventurous life you seek. Sometimes we are rebels. Sometimes we are politicians. Sometimes we are keepers of peace, and other times we are destroying it. We're explorers, troublemakers, dissidents."

"And when are we sorcerers, then?" Aimee asked, a small smile playing at the corner of her mouth.

"Always," Harkon answered. "You came up here to watch the jump, I assume?"

Aimee nodded. The cloud-castles drifting by were painted in an edging of royal purple and molten gold. The first time she'd seen *Iseult* make a portal jump, it had been from a grand viewing deck. She'd watched as the combined magic of four different magi distributed across the prow of the vessel had opened a beautiful, kaleidoscopic portal big enough to swallow the whole of *Iseult*. The sheer power of the magic had left her breathless – a trait the behemoth shared, as for the first hour after every jump, Aimee now knew, the ship had to run its metadrive cores at a lower intensity.

This time she was content to watch the jump from here.

"So the Oracle is real," Harkon said. He gave her a sideways look. "I had a feeling she was. These ships are older than their ruling castes, and Yaresh would not fear the rumor so much if he thought it was nothing."

"She is," Aimee said. "But she fled before we could get more than cryptic warnings out of her. Trials have started, she said. She called me sky-splitter, and spoke of fate like a symphony. Then the dead came, and she bid us run, while vanishing herself. It was like something out of the old stories from the prehistories. Nothing like what I read about divination at the academy." Her thoughts drifted briefly to the atlas stowed in her cabin aboard *Elysium*, and the jewel hidden beneath the floorboards of the room.

"I wish," she said after a moment, very quietly, "that the diamond were useable."

"Don't blame yourself," Harkon said. "None of us

expected it to go dormant after its encounter with Elias. And in any case, it might cause us more harm than not, were things otherwise. Sometimes the earning of a truth, and the worth it adds to the soul, is of greater value than whatever facts were sought to start with."

Aimee gave a single laugh. "Easy to say," she said, "for a man who already knows more than most. Or at least more than he ever actually shares."

Harkon chuckled, but beneath it there was an undertone of solemnity. The red and gold of sunset played off the moonlight of his hair, and highlighted the lines in his old face. "It's not just the things that have to be taught, Aimee," he said. "The order they're taught in matters just as much, in the long view. As for the Oracle... she's not a diviner. That's a magic for casting possible futures. It's long-term planning and deals in maybe, might be, and could've been. Diviners are some of the most miserable folk you'll ever meet. Divination doesn't deal with fate. That's something else altogether. If she can hear the music–" the old man shook his head, and for a moment, looked deeply sad "–that's something you're born with, and can never rid yourself of, no matter how hard you wish it."

Aimee turned in her chair to regard her teacher, opened her mouth to ask a hundred burning questions. Then Elias cleared his throat awkwardly behind them, and she nearly jumped – flustered – out of her skin. The tall man stood at the top of the stairs leading up to the landing they sat on. He'd shed his layers from earlier, down to a simple, loose-fitting white shirt unlaced at the neck, and the same snugly fitting black breeches and knee-high boots he'd worn to the lower levels. At a glance, it actually looked as if he'd been about to go bathe when something had interrupted him.

"Sorry to intrude," he said, apologetic. "But he asked to see you."

It was with a small amount of distracted embarrassment that Aimee now realized that the green-eyed swordsman hadn't come alone. She blinked twice, felt an irritated flush creep into her cheeks. Viltas stood just beside and behind Elias. She hadn't even noticed the lord shipman was there. She ran a hand over her tired face. Gods. She must not have been getting enough sleep. "It's fine," she said. Then, reflexively, she asked, "Are you alright?"

Elias frowned briefly, met her eyes, and opened his mouth to say something. Then, after a moment, simply said, "Don't worry. I'll keep."

He was gone down the stairs again, before she could inquire further. That was when she got her first real look at Viltas. The lord shipman looked exhausted and pale, but he shook his head when Harkon rose with concern. "It's nothing," he said. "Just a bit of a cold. I stayed up too late digging through the records, and on top of everything else going on these days, my constitution simply isn't what it used to be."

"Have you found anything?" Aimee's teacher asked.

"Nothing yet," Viltas said. "At least nothing concrete enough to report. But that's not why I'm here. My son told me everything that happened today, including what he could get out of Belit after... Which wasn't much. They're not as close as they used to be."

Aimee recalled Belit's rage at the risk Vallus had taken, and wondered just how true that was.

"Anyway," Viltas continued. "I thought... I didn't tell

you the full story of Amut's battle with the Faceless. I might be the only person on the ship who knows it like it happened. It seemed, given all that's transpiring, that I should be ashamed for not giving it to you all right at the start." His eyes burned in his tired face.

Aimee and her teacher exchanged a look. Harkon frowned, then nodded.

"We never knew where he came from," Viltas said with a tired sigh. "Never learned his true name, nor saw his real face. You must understand... even the powerful sorcerers on this ship, they have names and faces. Histories. Pasts. He was... He was a force of nature. Powerful in a way that defied concept. The greatest mages *Iseult* had would face him and shrivel to dead husks at a gesture, then rise as his servants. He came out of nowhere, and ruled the ship for a year."

"Those all track with the stories I have been told of him," Harkon said thoughtfully. "Understand that mages such as him are not unprecedented. Most mortal sorcerers reach a ceiling to their power and skill – but there are those few who live long enough, train hard enough, and through a combination of natural gifts and sheer will acquire an arcane might far beyond what most can dream of. The older they become, the more their power changes them. Until their original names become imbued with mystic potency. Then they take on monikers, mask their former identities, and cease to be what they were."

The old portalmage leaned forward, furrowing his brow and looking contemplatively at Viltas. "That the Faceless was such a sorcerer does not surprise me. What does is how Amut – by all accounts a normal man – managed to kill him."

"He had companions," Viltas said. "Myself, and seven others, and only we two survived. He had a magic sword." The lord shipman paused. "And he knew that the Faceless was not merely supported by his undying slaves, but by a cult of living people already ensconced within the ship."

Beware the Children of the Empty Sky. The Oracle's warning echoed in Aimee's mind. *Grandfather.*

Aimee's eyes widened. The implications of what he was saying hit her just a moment before he clarified. "I believe," Viltas said, "that perhaps one or two of these... acolytes may have survived, and are now attempting to *imitate* their former master's methods."

"The dead that we faced," Aimee countered, "weren't the sort of thing you see created by simplistic necromancy... They were graceful, fast." She spoke more easily about it now, than when she'd explained their encounter to Harkon in the aftermath of the vote.

"Agreed," Harkon murmured. "It's not amateur work."

"It's also been over twenty-five years – near thirty, since then," Viltas answered. "But apprentice or no, the important thing for you to know is that some of these people escaped." Here a look of profound guilt crossed his face. It took the lord shipman a few moments to summon up the courage for what he was about to say, and when he looked at them, Aimee saw something haunted in his kind eyes. "Amut killed the Faceless," Viltas said, "by ambush. We crept up on him in the metadrive chamber of *Iseult*, the very heart of the vessel. He was in the midst of some ritual, surrounded by silent, unmoving dead. In the years after, I never marked the importance of what he was doing – we smashed and destroyed his altar, burned his books, destroyed every last one of the undead bound to his will – but now? Now I wonder." He shook his head. "I'll try to remember it for you. So much of that horrible day is a blur. I remember a circle surrounded by nine robed figures before the core metadrive of the ship, bathed in its purple light. I remember chanting in a language I didn't understand. I remember a shadow that grew in the air, as the Faceless raised his arms to invoke something dark, ink-like. Mostly, I remember the smell."

Harkon's frown cut lines across his venerable face, and he leaned forward with laced fingers together. A master attempting to extract hints from the finest details. "What smell?"

Viltas shook his head, as if it made no sense to him that he should find his answer so unsettling. "Rain. Surrounded by corpses, in the heart of the metadrive chamber, all I could smell was *rain*."

He grunted, then coughed a few times. "That's the thing I remember best. That and the men who slipped away. We always worried that perhaps we'd erred by not pushing after them... but after today's vote, can you blame us? Men like Yaresh, they'd tear the whole ship apart, kill thousands, just to find the one wicked man in hiding."

"So that's why you never told anyone," Elias reflected. Aimee glanced over at the stairwell. The warrior had returned to the top of the stairs. "You didn't want to start purges," he said. "And the officer aristocracy proved today that just under half of them are more than willing."

Then, as Aimee watched, a sudden look of self-aware, awkward embarrassment crossed the black knight's pale face. "Sorry," he said after a moment. "It was too interesting to walk away from."

"Aye," Viltas said, regarding Elias over his shoulder. "That, and there was never much to tell that would've made sense to anyone hearing it."

A familiar rumble passed beneath their feet, and Aimee felt a sudden swell of magic energy – more familiar still – that drew her eyes to the window and brought her up and out of her seat. She rose in time to watch as the kaleidoscopic eye of the vast portal erupted in the heavens beyond *Iseult*'s bow. The play of innumerable colors painted the viewing deck with a collage of light, beautiful and intense. Aimee stepped close to the window as she felt the metadrive growl somewhere deep within the ship, and the behemoth lurched forward at full engine burn. Harkon and Elias stood beside her as the eye grew, swelling in the sky, until they passed through the amaranthine gate and into a heaven filled with different clouds.

"Where did we jump to?" Aimee asked out loud. It was darker here, but after a few moments, she made out lights amidst the cloud banks. Next came shadows, vast, and sprouting glimmering crowns of lamps without number. One of these passed near to them, and titanic engine vents blazed in her view as it passed. *Another behemoth*, she realized. Smaller than *Iseult*, but still the size of a small city.

Viltas rose from his seat, and Aimee heard a relieved smile in his voice, as he stepped up to the window to stare out at the ocean of skyships suspended in the twilight of the deep sky.

"Home," he said. "At long last. Welcome, my friends, to Flotilla Visramin."

CHAPTER NINE
Bitter Dreams and Better Men

Elias stood outside the training hall and stared across the vast expanse of Flotilla Visramin. In the daylight, it was a vision with no equal: a painting in the style of the early Impargnian masters spread out across a canvas of sky more vast and deep than any he had seen before. He leaned against the ledge outside the training hall, an ache in his shaking limbs. One day had passed since *Iseult* returned to her brother and sister ships, and a cloud of smaller vessels already fluttered back and forth between the behemoth and its kin in the heavens. In particular, they had flown alongside a second vessel, of the same size and similar appearance to *Iseult*. Closer than the others, as well. That ship hung suspended slightly lower in the sky, its upper decks in full view from where Elias stood. Peering across the distance, he couldn't help but notice that the gleaming finery of its top level seemed... shabby. As if it had recently fallen on difficult times.

"That," Belit said, stepping up behind him, "is *Tristan*. Our kin-ship, for as long as the two have been in the heavens, which is longer than the memory of any lineage."

Elias frowned, his eyes drawn to the battered spires of the other behemoth, so like *Iseult*, yet so painfully different. "How far back do those lineages go?" he asked. *What must it be like*, he wondered, *to have such a thing as a heritage?* Elias had only the name of a mother, and some painful memories that were more like open wounds than facts.

Belit folded her arms across her chest and frowned. "Depends on who you ask," she said. "The oldest lines of the officer aristocracy go back to when the guild supposedly first built these ships and crewed them with people who could stand to spend their entire lives in fiefs in the skies." She shrugged. "But those are all practically myth, and their descendants dote on them too much to make examining them critically a safe thing to do."

Elias's memory was pricked by the recollection of the days before Azrael had been sent to Port Providence. Of an old book over which Roland obsessed, of whose pages his apprentice had only ever been allowed a glance.

"People will kill to protect their favorite fables," Elias said.

Belit's eyes were sad for a moment, then she nodded her agreement. They had trained for several hours prior to this, but without touching on any topic other than the technicalities of their shared art. Nevertheless, when she next spoke, the question caught him off guard.

"What is the essence of our art, *junk ritter*?" she asked.

So immediate was it, that Roland's words came almost seamlessly from his mouth. "Aggression," he said. "Onslaught. Unrelenting destruction until victory is attained."

Immediately, he felt ill, the echo of Azrael's voice still in his ears.

Belit watched him quietly, thoughtfully… and with an expression that told him that here and now, she *knew*. "I thought so," she said quietly.

"It is…" Elias stumbled over his words. "I…" he fumbled, found nothing sufficient to defend himself. If the people of *Iseult* should learn the truth, if they should discover him…

"–please," he half whispered. "Don't tell anyone."

He wasn't sure what he'd expected: judgment, fear, shame. Instead, Belit laid a firm hand on his shoulder. "You are not them," she said. "That much is self-evident. More so for how ill at ease you are with their words in your mouth." Her brows drew together over her gold eyes. "Your crew knows?"

Elias nodded. "They spared me, when my rebellion put my life in their hands. They gave me a home, when I had none."

Belit watched him carefully. "Yet still you are alone."

Elias looked down. Malfenshir's condemnations about traitors echoed in his mind, before Elias had killed him. Roland's ancient book was in his head as well, for half a moment. Pages at which he had only glanced, in the hellish fever-dream that was his former life. "I am," he said, meeting Belit's eyes. "Those who break faith do not survive."

Belit nodded, accepting that, then the commander of the Red Guard squeezed his shoulder. "It is not aggression our art teaches. It is assertiveness. It is not hate that we must feel. It is passion. It is not prideful rage that fuels our limbs. It is the cold strength of a decisive mind."

"Why are you telling me this?" he asked.

"Because you have been broken," she answered.

"When we are broken, we fall back on what we know. For you, that means the lessons of your art." The expression on her face was protective. Fierce. Leonine. "Make sure they are the right ones."

She turned to go. "I have duties to attend to. Rest. Recover. And for the sake of the gods, forgive yourself. When next we speak, I have stories to tell you... and more questions to ask."

Elias stood there as she left. "Teacher," he said after a moment, around a small lump in his throat. "Thank you."

She stopped, considering for a moment, then looked over her shoulder at him. "Your skills were given to you by them, but remember, they do not own them. You do. I am no expert historian," she said, meeting his eyes. "But you should know... I don't believe you are the first to escape. Have hope. You own what you are. Never forget that."

Her footsteps echoed in his mind, long after she had gone.

Elysium sat at rest in the hangar of Rachim's villa, and Elias paused to look at her. The silver ship glowed in the sunlight from the open bay doors above. The landing platform was still damp from a flight through a morning cloud-bank, and the black knight's boots crunched on the rough surface. It was an odd thing to feel – longing for a place that wasn't quite your home. He had a room there. A place of retreat. Yet only two members of the crew were people with whom he had any sort of rapport.

He hoped at least one of them was available. The ramp up into the aft hold was dry, and the interior mostly empty. His room was in the belly of the ship, just off the main cargo hold. He considered retreating to that private space for a while, but the thought of staring at his old armor in the corner for an hour or so made him feel ill.

Instead, he followed the ghostly wisps of conversation up the stairs and down the long hallway to the common area. By the voices he heard, Harkon and Aimee weren't present, so he waited for a full minute, out of sight, trying to parse how to walk into a room full of people who didn't particularly like him.

"So she's studying now?" Vlana was saying.

"Aye," Bjorn answered. Elias heard the thump of a wood slat on the table. They were playing cards, then. "Hark gave her a whopping chunk of text to work through from one of his old books. He's taking a rest right now. Doesn't like to show it much, but he's straight out exhausted. Not exactly young anymore."

"Look who's talking," Vant quipped. "You were old when we were kids."

Elias stepped around the corner in time to see the old warrior cuff the engineer across the back of the head. "Can it, hull rat. I can still hoist both of you like grainsacks down the ramp, can't I?"

Vant and Vlana sat across from Bjorn. Childish grins split their faces, so alike and yet so different all at once, and the laugh they shared was more mirthful than any Elias had ever heard from either.

Then Vlana caught sight of him, and both laugh and smile fizzled and died on her face. She elbowed her brother in the shoulder. Vant coughed and looked at his sister before turning curious eyes to Elias. Whereas the look on Vlana's face then morphed to unabashed dislike, Vant's expression got suddenly neutral.

Bjorn didn't look up.

"Can we help you?" Vlana asked. Icy.

"Just came back from training," Elias answered. The words were awkward in his mouth, as leftover pride from a former life ran up against the discordant desire to not cause chaos on the ship.

"So you thought you'd eavesdrop?" Vlana pounced on his moment of silence. "Hark and Aimee aren't here, so why don't you just move along?"

"Vlana," Bjorn murmured. "That's enough."

The quartermaster's dark eyes narrowed, snapping from Elias to the big warrior who still had his back to the black knight. "Oh shush, Bjorn. I'm allowed a private card game with my family without the resident mass murderer feeling like he's entitled to a seat."

The words washed over Elias, a discombobulating wave. First it stunned. Then it unbalanced. Then came the pain and associated memories, since, of course, it was true. Elias took a breath to steady himself. He felt briefly nauseous, a tingling in his hands at the memory of blows meted out in unthinking response to commands, to doctrines he had followed while wearing the facsimile of another personality. His world tunneled, and when it came back into focus, Vant was speaking up. "Sis," he said. "That's a bit much."

"A bit *much*?" Vlana was on her feet now, her eyes wide and furious. "Alright, look, *both* of you. I love and respect Hark as much as everyone here, so I trust his judgment... But *that*–" she jerked a violent finger in Elias's direction "– is still responsible for the murder of countless thousands of people. He tried to kill all of us, wounded Harkon, and nearly succeeded in murdering *you*."

Bjorn's shoulders tensed at the reminder.

"Vlana," the new rebuke came from Clutch, who stood at the far doorway that led to the ship's bridge. "Let it fucking go. You got the same story as the rest of us: he's trying to make amends–"

"No, no no no, *no*," Vlana said, snapping. "He's a refugee hiding from crimes that there's *no making amends for*."

Clutch tensed. Vant looked away. Bjorn remained still.

"She's right," Elias said. Everyone stared at him now, uncertainty on their faces. "I am a refugee," he continued. "And there is no amending the things I've done. No making it right. I don't deserve the second chance you gave me."

A mixture of expressions stared back at him. Clutch's face was neutral. Vant looked pained. Vlana's face caught off guard. An old, dead pride tried to stir within Elias. *You can still command the attention of a room, at least.* But what was that worth?

"Which is why I have to try," he finished. "Or I'm shitting on it."

The common area was draped in a suffocating, awkward silence. Then Bjorn cleared his throat, addressing Vlana. "Your move, girl."

Elias couldn't tell if the old warrior was talking about the conversation, or the interrupted card game. He was no longer looking the black knight's way.

"Pardon me," the new voice came from one of Rachim's household servants, a slight man with simple robes and a nervous lilt in his voice at having interrupted the tense scene. "I... I was just given a message by the door guard. The deliverer said it was urgent."

"Give it here," Bjorn said with a sigh, rising finally from his seat. He held out a large, meaty hand for the thin envelope of parchment in the servant's hand. "Harkon's abed right now and his apprentice is hard at work. I'll hold it for them."

But the servant withdrew his missive with a shake of his head. "Forgive me–" he seemed unsure how to address the huge, old warrior "–sir, but it's not for your master, or his apprentice." He looked at Elias, offered the folded paper with its wax seal to the black knight, and cleared his throat awkwardly as Elias took it.

"It's for him."

Twenty minutes later, Elias stood at the doorway to a private garden, the missive in his hand. He was somewhere in the port district of the upper level, and something told him that whomever he was about to meet, this wasn't their actual home.

He glanced down a second time at the paper in his hand.

Swordsman,

Forgive my imposition, but certain troubling rumors have reached my ear, and I fear for the wellbeing of your crew, your master, and your cause. Word has reached me of your tremendous valor in the struggle against our enemies below. I would speak with you.

The letter was unsigned, and gave only the meeting place.

He pressed a gloved hand to the gate. It swung inward, and he sensed the faint ripple of magic. Elias's footfalls carried him down a tiled walkway over soft, moss-covered ground. It must have cost a fortune to install such land-like luxury here. He wondered at the expenses, the trades, the bartering, the brutal grunt work beneath all the hours and weeks of endless labor to enrich this microcosm in the midst of a forest of pale stone and gilded doorways. Moreover, Elias wondered, who owned it, and who was so well placed as to requisition its use for a clandestine meeting?

The answer came when he reached the end of the path, finding himself in a small, circular plot of grass, surrounded on all sides by blooming flowers of countless varieties – white roses and black orchids in particular. There waited a man the black knight recognized immediately, understated in a black and silver evening robe, his white hair pulled into an elaborate knot at the back of his head, and rings upon his long, delicate fingers.

"Welcome, swordsman," Pentus, duke of the midlevels said, with a white-toothed smile upon his face. "I am so glad you received my message."

Elias stood before the candidate for captaincy, at once acutely aware of every political lesson he'd ever had beaten into him, every warning about seeming, of appearance, of reputation and turn of phrase. Harkon Bright's moderation required the perception of neutrality between the three candidates. If Elias was seen in the private company of one of them–

"Had I known from whom it came," Elias said, "I would not have come. But you already knew that."

Pentus's smile turned cat-like. "I knew you were smart. I have known of Harkon Bright for some time, and he does not endure the company of fools or of the irrelevant.

Moreover, Yaresh would not hate you as he does if you were no one."

"Yaresh hates Belit," Elias corrected him. "Me only by proxy."

"So you confirm your meetings with her, then," Pentus said. "Thank you. I wondered if that was bluster or not."

Stupid mistake. Elias held back from cursing himself. He'd let these skills grow rusty in the past few months as he'd withdrawn from everything about him that had been tangled intimately with Azrael. Off balance and in the presence of a skilled manipulator, he opted to remain silent for the moment.

Pentus smiled, and he picked up a wine glass in a salute before drinking. "Ah, don't be like that. I am not your enemy, just a man who *knows* things, and who acknowledges that no person can be as black or white as their past portrays them." His eyes twinkled. "And I know there is more to you than what is suggested by your… impressive feats belowdecks."

He knew. Elias forced his heartbeat to steady, kept his face carefully neutral. "Did you ask me here to drop irrelevant hints," he replied at last, "or is this conversation to be of more substance? I have duties to attend to."

Pentus sighed, now a cat denied further chance to play a favored game. "Very well, I will get to the point: I am proposing an alliance, swordsman."

"Harkon Bright must remain neutral," Elias repeated.

"Agreed, and he should," Pentus said, holding up a hand. "But *you* are another matter entirely. There are rumors, swordsman, that have reached my ears. You train beside Belit in her archaic sword-style as a near equal. You're a *recent* addition to Harkon Bright's crew, and you're ever so cagey about your own past."

The duke of the midlevels' expression was knowing. "And I am not entirely ignorant of certain stories of recently fallen kingdoms, and the rumored death of an apprentice to the infamous Lord Roland. A death *some* believe may be exaggerated."

Elias met the probing stare with a practiced blank expression. "You have me at a disadvantage, Duke Pentus," he said. "I'm afraid I don't keep up on news of every dead warlord."

"Dammit boy," Pentus said, his veneer cracking. Beneath the calm exterior, Elias glimpsed something else – not ugly, as with Yaresh – but *fearful.* "How long will it be before the forces tearing this ship apart from within erupt into the open? I can *help* you."

Vlana's hateful eyes swam in Elias's vision. Vant's guilty, neutral expression, Bjorn's ambivalence. Harkon's distance. Aimee.

Aimee's smile. Without deception or ill-intent. Part of the crew.

"There is a place for you on this ship, if you want it."

His uncertainty dissipated, replaced with the bedrock of understanding. Perhaps the others didn't trust him, but Aimee did, and her teacher did. The rest, he might never earn... but as he had said less than an hour before...

I have to try.

"So long as I do... what?" Elias asked. "Betray my allies? Abandon their trust?" He took a single step forward. "Kill your enemies?"

The duke's expression paled. "I did not mean to ask murder of you–"

Elias felt the derisive snort come unbidden to his face.

"Of course not. It's never murder with men like you. Only justice, until it's someone else commanding the killers. With respect, your grace, the man you are looking for may be alive or dead, but he isn't in this room. I will see myself out."

"Please," Pentus said, as Elias turned to go. "Think about what I offer you: a fresh start – truly, away from people who know what you really are!"

Elias kept walking. He didn't see the furious, agonized look on Pentus's face – only discerned it from the anguished tones of the duke's voice as he screamed. "So long as a single soul knows the truth about who you are, you will *never know peace!*"

The black knight paused, the weight of the words settling on his shoulders. He let out a long, difficult breath. *Perhaps not, but I must try.*

"Good day, your grace," Elias said over his shoulder.

He left the way he had come.

CHAPTER TEN
THE PECULIAR MADNESS OF TWINS

Aimee had spent the first week on *Iseult* dressed in her professional best. With the exception of the excursion into the lower levels, the rule of thumb had been semi-formalwear, which meant high boots, her apprentice's badge, a freshly cleaned blouse, and hair put to order. A touch of makeup too, though a far cry from the effort put into high society events back home.

The past two days, by contrast, had been spent in extensive, rigorous study. Arrival back at the flotilla meant an eruption of trade and gossip between behemoths, and a temporary cessation of council meetings so that every officer aristocrat could see to their duties while the bridge crew directed affairs from the wheelhouse. Harkon had presented her the morning after their arrival with a fresh set of complicated form scrolls detailing a number of increasingly complex spells she was to commit to memory. Three combative: one for wind, one for flame, one for frost.

As a result, she'd hardly left her cabin, or the large segment of the cargo hold where she'd practiced the physically demanding forms over and over and over.

Her world was unwashed training clothes, sweat, aching muscles, and the precise mental repetition of the proper words until she heard them in her dreams. When she wasn't doing that, she was drilling in the patterns Bjorn had taught her with a shock-spear, not wanting to be caught unprepared again. She broke for meals, though she took them in her room half the time, and to demonstrate her progress to her teacher.

She lived on coffee and mystic theory.

On the morning of the third day, after falling out of bed and into a set of intensive calisthenics, she threw a robe over her shoulders and shuffled down the hall to get breakfast. The sounds of voices reached her before she got to the common area, and she saw Vlana leaning with her back against the wall, staring patiently at Rachim.

"Yeah, well," their host said, "all I'm saying is that my chef is heinously pretentious and easily offended. He takes it as a personal slight that you all haven't come to breakfast yet."

"What, lunch and dinner aren't enough?" Vlana asked, more amused than affronted. "Look, *Elysium* is home, alright? No matter how nice the villa is – and it is very nice – most of us are still more comfortable in our cabins."

"And Hark's had me training basically all day for the past two days," Aimee said sleepily, walking into the room and greeting the two with a wave. "The room I was offered is lovely, but I'm really not comfortable practicing my magic in your very nice house."

Rachim snorted. "I don't care about the room, Miss Laurent. But I'm starting to worry that my flustered chef may poison me in a fit of pique."

Both women laughed, and Aimee was still chuckling as she walked into the galley. Someone had already fired the stove to boil water, and soon a dark aroma was wafting up from her mug as she made up a plate of cured meat, buttered rolls, and cheese.

"Look," Vlana said as Aimee re-emerged. "I can talk to the others but–" she looked at Aimee and then shrugged, grinning at Rachim "–too late."

Rachim flashed her a one-eyed glare. Aimee grinned and answered around a mouthful of breakfast roll. "Phorry."

Rachim's glower turned to a begrudging smile after a moment. "That phrase, about how you can take the skyfarer out of the ship, but not the ship out of the skyfarer? It's wrong. You *can't* take a skyfarer out of their ship. I've tried."

"But we *do* appreciate the use of your landing space for our home," Vlana said sweetly.

"So where is everyone, anyway?" Aimee asked when her throat was clear. "Been cooped up with books for days, haven't kept pace."

"Hark is meeting with Viltas in my parlor," Rachim said. "More background information on the council – they've scheduled another vote in two days."

"Bjorn's gone for a run," Vlana said. "Haven't seen Elias yet–" she said his name with a subtle distaste "–Clutch is taking a nap on the bridge, and," she paused, "and I don't know *where* Vant is."

There was the tiniest ghost of a smile at the corner of the quartermaster's mouth that suddenly made Aimee suspicious. "Why don't I believe you right now?"

On reflection, the young sorceress at once realized,

she'd hardly seen the twins at all, the few times she'd left her studies in the past few days. Given her cloistering, that didn't mean a lot, but it counted for a little, given the two were more closely wed to the ship than anyone else other than Clutch.

Vlana's smile grew, and the hand she placed over her mouth didn't *quite* contain it.

Rachim frowned. "Oh, bugger all," he muttered. "Hark warned me about you twins."

"Oh relax," Vlana said to their host, nudging him in the shoulder with her elbow. "My brother and I are under strict orders to contain our shenanigans solely to the ship."

Rachim's expression turned from dubious to abruptly – and deeply – alarmed. "Which doesn't help if I'm *on your ship*."

Vlana's grin was feline. Any further comment from Aimee was disrupted by a piercing scream, followed by a stream of increasingly colorful curses erupting from the bridge in Clutch's voice, the well of profanity capped off by, "Vant, I'm going to pour meta-exhaust in your bunk!"

A half second later, a loud, burp-like fart sound ripped through the forward part of the ship, followed by a set of mewling chirps, followed by the pilot's groan. "Oh, sweet merciful *gods*."

Aimee and Rachim both turned to Vlana, who was starting towards the bridge while trying to contain her laughter. "Looks like Clutch found her!"

Realization dawned in Aimee's head as she followed at a jog, connecting the sounds to her recollections and culminating in a laughing choke. "You *didn't*."

"You're right," Vlana declared, "I didn't! C'mon, Aimee, I said I didn't know where my brother *was*, not that I didn't know what he was *doing*."

The bridge was chaos. The first thing Aimee noticed was the *smell*. A ripe, flatulent stink somewhere between rotten eggs and academy dormitory used gymsocks assaulted her senses, and she grasped the frame of the doorway to keep herself from doubling over.

"YOU!" Clutch screamed at Vlana before launching into a fresh stream of invective while the latter collapsed in a storm of giggles. "You and your godsdamned Kraken-loving cloud-fucking wind-fart hull rat brother did this!"

Something red flashed past Aimee, mewling and whipping through the air, every convulsion of its body leaving a loud fart sound in its wake.

"Did what?" Vlana said.

"That!" Clutch gestured. As Aimee wiped her eyes, she saw now that the pilot was covered from head to toe in a light, blotchy coating of ink. "Don't get coy with me! There is a fucking *squat* on my bridge!"

Aimee leaned against the door, furiously fanning at the air in front of her face to rid her sinuses of the stink. High over her head, the creature in question circled, the hair on its feline head and forelegs standing on end while its eight tentacles flexed with every propulsive fart of its air-bladder. It hissed and spit a wad of ink that hit Clutch on her clean shoulder. Aimee fought down a surge of rising laughter.

"Oh *gods*," Rachim swore as he caught up with them. "The *smell*…"

Holding her nose and stifling a smile, Aimee shot

Vlana a questioning look. "Where the hell did you find a squat?"

"Technically, my brother found it," Vlana said through a grin. "And the answer–" this she said sideways at Rachim's glare "–is *around*."

"What's relevant is not where you *found* it," Clutch snarled. "It's where you *put it*. Namely *on me, while I was sleeping!*"

"Look," said Vant, from the portal platform above the bridge, "you're the one who startled her by waking up with an ear-piercing shriek. They're normally very placid creatures, when people aren't screaming or swinging hatchets at them." The engineer's grin turned wicked. "Rather like me: I'm really nice until you drop me out of my hammock in the middle of nap time."

"Oh, for fuck's sake." Clutch put a hand on her forehead. "That was over a week ago!"

"The *last* time was over a week ago!" Vant snapped back. "You've been doing that for months!"

"How long was that thing on me, hull rat?" Clutch advanced towards the portal platform. "How long!?"

Above them, the squat made another flatulent noise and hissed, spitting a glob of ink towards the group of them. Aimee sidestepped it and freed her hands from her robe. Vant cackled, a mad conductor of a chaos orchestra. "Oh, I don't know, my chronometer is back in my bunk, and time is such a *fluid* concept–"

Clutch's eyes flashed dangerously. "How. Long."

"I mean it left and came back several times after I put it there," Vant said with an exasperated sigh. "But *cumulatively*? I'd say an hour, give or take."

Aimee fixed her eyes on their circling, gaseous guest,

breathed out her laughter, gestured upwards, and cast
the binding spell Harkon had taught her back in Port
Providence. Strips of light flashed into being, tying up
the struggling squidcat, which Aimee then slowly drew
towards her with an outstretched hand. It struggled
fiercely, its huge eyes yellow and angry. Aimee ran her
free hand over the fur on its head, then took note of the
yellow streaks down its rubbery flanks, and what they
meant.

"Um, Vant?" Aimee asked mildly.

"Wait," Vlana said. "Why was it *leaving*?"

"I don't know," Vant waved a dismissive hand. "She
kept going back into the cargo hold and I kept bringing
her back."

"Vant, what the fuck!" Clutch swore again.

Aimee sighed. "Am I the only one who understands
what these yellow stripes on her sides mean?" All eyes
at once turned to the sorceress as she gestured to the
colored bands on the squidcat's flanks.

"Yes?" Vant said.

"Oh *shit*," Vlana said.

"What did you *do*?" Clutch demanded of the engineer.

For a second time, further conversation was interrupted
by a series of shouts from the cargo bay, and this time it
was the voices of Elias and Bjorn.

Aimee sighed, and, still holding the squidcat in its
bindings, started towards the hold. "He brought a squat
aboard," she said over her shoulder. "A *pregnant* squat.
Looks like Elias and Bjorn just found the babies."

Aimee was halfway through the door to the cargo hold
when a rubbery, down-furred squitten hit her in the face.

It bounced off, squeaked loudly, then farted off into the center of the open space, where another *twelve* of the creatures were rushing this way and that, a chorus of mewing sounds and flatulent noises filling the air.

In the center of the chaos were Bjorn and Elias. Bjorn was soaked with sweat through his shirt from his long run. Elias... wasn't wearing a shirt at all. Aimee took a second, realized she was staring, then shook her head. It didn't matter how distracting the sight was. She had flying squittens to catch. Yes. Focus.

Elias caught sight of her and turned. One of the squittens was sitting on his head. Another had planted itself on his shoulder. The tall, shirtless man fixed her with a resigned, helpless look, before clearing his throat. "I'm assuming there's some sort of reason for this?"

The squitten on his shoulder squeaked and nipped at his ear. He winced slightly and gave a lopsided, helpless smile. "And, ah, maybe a way these things could be *moved*?"

A larger squitten was in the process of burrowing into Bjorn's beard. The big, old warrior was trying to discourage the creature even as he winced painfully at its claws tugging on his facial hair. "No, little bugger. *No*. Dammit, quit the mewling! There's no food in there."

The spell that was on her lips died with Aimee's composure. The laugh burst out of her, compulsive and helpless, and she sank to her knees just past the doorway to the cargo hold, laughing until tears leaked out the corners of her eyes. The others caught up a half second later to find her curled up on the floor in the gut-clutching throes of laughter, and Bjorn and Elias no less inundated with squeaking, flying squidcats.

"Laugh it up, girl," she heard Bjorn grumble. "Very helpful."

"At least they haven't inked us yet," Elias deadpanned. "May as well let it burrow. I think it likes you."

Aimee got to her feet as Clutch caught up with the rest of them. "Naturally," she growled, "they didn't ink either of *them*."

"You didn't tell me it was expecting a litter!" Vlana hissed at her brother.

"I didn't *know*!" Vant fired back. "I just thought she really liked the cargo hold!"

"Alright," Aimee said, not quite suppressing her giggles. "Keeping the mother bound is taking up a bit of effort, but if the rest of you can herd them this way, maybe I can expand the binding spell to gather the rest of them together, then we... Gods, I don't know, what do we *do* with them?"

"Keep them?" Elias asked.

"Not gonna happen," Clutch said.

"Yeah, wasn't exactly my plan..." Vant said.

"Hey," Elias fired back with surprising passion. "They didn't choose this. You brought them here. You can't just get rid of them because you think they're inconvenient."

A half-second's awkward silence hung after that, broken only by the sound of squitten flatulence. Then Bjorn grumbled, "Projecting much?"

"Technically not *my* choice," Vlana muttered.

"Gods," Aimee snapped. "*Enough!*"

"May I first state–" Rachim used the silence to interject "–that *none* of those things will be entering my house? Because that's a definitive."

"No no no! I am talking now!" Aimee shouted. The

room fell silent, and all eyes were on the sorceress, one hand still maintaining her binding spell. "I'll ungag the mother and use her to get her litter into one of the spare cabins. I'm going to need the rest of you to help corral them so they don't go flying to gods-know-where, spraying ink all over every little thing. Alright?"

A chorus of nods followed. Then Elias started moving first to heed her. Rachim chuckled just behind her. "Good commanding voice," he said. "I approve."

She might have reminded their host that his approval wasn't something she needed – was tempted, in the mood she found herself in – but that wouldn't have been productive. Instead, Aimee flashed him a sweet smile and said in her perkiest voice. "Thank you! Learned it from my mum."

Then she adjusted the spell with a slight twitch of her fingers. The mother let out a loud, chirping mew, and twelve squittens *surged* towards Aimee. The apprentice portalmage barely had time to gulp, then she broke into a run. It was amazing how long the central corridor of *Elysium* looked, when she was at a full sprint with a horde of tiny flying feline cephalopods on her heels. She heard noises behind her, shouts and cries of dismay, but at this point she was functionally beyond their help. Her running dash took her full tilt towards one of the unused cabins in the central corridor, and she almost overshot it, skidding to a halt on her bare feet in front of the doorway. Her free hand fumbled with the handle, then whipped it open, flinging the mother through the opening and throwing herself out of the way. "Have fun with your babies!" she said, and barely dodged as the mass of farting squittens shot past her and into the doorway. Then she heaved the door shut, and took a few seconds to breathe before letting out a nervous, relieved laugh.

When she looked up, a single squitten stared her in the face. Brown-furred, red-bladdered, with yellow eyes like its mother, and a mangy bald spot on its forehead. It cocked its head, then started to turn back down the hall. "Oh no," Aimee said, pushing herself off the door as she caught a glimpse of where the little creature was looking. "No no no no, don't you *dare*!"

She didn't even think to use the binding-spell. Her hand shot out reflexively as it let out a burping sound and shot back down the hallway towards a cabin.

Her cabin.

She launched herself after it, screaming "Shit!" as she rushed through the doorway, her head filled with images of all her things covered in ink. Instead, she found an unnervingly quiet interior in the same training- and study-induced state of utter disarray she'd left it in. Pausing just inside the doorway, she tightened her robe about her waist and took a few tentative steps, peering around.

"Wonderful," she muttered. "And the gold-bullion question is: 'Where in this mess are you hiding?'"

A squeak sounded behind her. She turned. The squitten was perched above her doorframe. Off to the side, on her desk, a familiar ironwood box had been opened, and in its tentacles, the creature clutched the glimmering Axiom Diamond. Aimee froze. Her breathing slowed, and she held up her hands. The last thing – *the last thing* – she needed was for a renegade squitten to run roughshod all over the ship in a panic, stashing the priceless, dangerous truth-stone in some tiny bolthole, or gods forbid, *off* the ship. If the little thing decided to take off, she was in for a lot more than a few hours' frustration.

"Alright, little squitten," she murmured, flexing her fingers. "A lot of people died, and a lot of horrible things happened before we got our hands on that priceless, truth-telling gem. So how about you let it go?"

As she uttered the last words, the creature turned its head, issued a ripping blast of wind, and shot out through the door. Aimee lunged after it, only to let out a shout of dismay as Elias skidded to a stop in the doorway, right in her path. She let out a squawk, too late to stop her jump. She crashed into him at full leap as the diamond fell between them, and had half a second to realize they were both touching the stone before she felt a familiar wrenching in her gut, and the world turned white.

They stood upon a broad, mirror surface, surrounded by an endless ocean of sunset sky. It took Aimee a few moments to orient herself. The Axiom Diamond had been dormant, unresponsive, since it had stripped the mental control of the Eternal Order from Elias in Port Providence a month and a half ago, and when she had joined her mind to the stone then, it had addressed her directly, suspended above a facsimile of the cavern in which she'd found it.

Last time there had been warnings, explanations. No apparitions greeted her this time. Only the empty sky... and Elias. The young man stood a few feet from her, staring about. "No—" she heard him say with rising panic. "Not again. *Not again!*"

"*Forgive me,*" the voice echoed all around them, familiar and pained. "*It is hard... to speak in this place.*"

Aimee turned in a circle. Elias took a step back on the rippling surface. Aimee compulsively grabbed his hand. "Elias," she said. "You're all right. You're *all right.*" He gripped her palm, closed his eyes. She felt the panic rolling off him in waves. "It's not going to happen again," she said, drawing close, clutching his hand as her other palm reached up to touch his face. "It's not going to happen again because there's nothing left to rip away. This is you. Do you understand me? *This is the real you.*"

His eyes opened, meeting hers. Fear – panic – receded just slightly. He nodded without speaking.

"And you both must see," the voice echoed, all around them. Aimee turned, still gripping his hand, and watched as a vision of blurred figures warred across the sky, a chaotic mass of churning violence in which she glimpsed the uniforms of officer aristocrats and their enforcers pitted against the defiant masses of the enlisted. The shades of *Iseult*'s people hacked each other to pieces, and from behind where they stood, a terrible wind rose from a keening wail into a deafening roar. A sudden fear seized her, primal and wild. The sunset dimmed as an impossible darkness surged from behind where they stood, and the wind blasted every shadow, aristocrat and enlisted alike, into screaming tufts of mist.

Aimee's breath came in ragged gasps. She didn't want to look.

"You must," the diamond answered.

"I can't!" Her voice sounded shrill in her ears.

"You can," she heard Elias say. She glanced up at him, afraid as she. Again, the small nod. Fortified, Aimee turned her eyes to the darkness that rose behind them, and stared into the dark heart of a vast, terrible storm that stained the heavens black. Before the darkness, a lone lion reared its head back, and roared.

"*HE COMES WITH THE STORM,*" the diamond thundered in her head.

Abruptly, Aimee was back in her cabin, gasping for breath. Her eyes squeezed shut, standing on her feet. Her heartbeat hammered in her ears. Her left hand was wrapped in a viselike grip around the Axiom Diamond. Then several more facts registered to her senses: first, Elias was leaning with his back pressed against the frame of her cabin doorway, the diamond wrapped in her fist pressed against his chest. Second, her right hand was clutching his. Third, she was standing very, *very* close to him. His forehead was pressed against hers, their breathing slowing in a synced, even rhythm. His other hand was braced against the other side of the frame, behind her. For a moment, she did nothing at all. Her mind – already spun about by the feverish terror of the vision – was suddenly able to focus only on her own intense physical awareness of the man she'd crashed into. Slowly, she opened her eyes. Elias's face was *inches* from her own. His expression was quietly intent, and his green eyes watched her with a cautious uncertainty.

"Are you alright?" he asked, after a moment. The sound was like a static shock up her spine.

"Fine," Aimee answered. Her face was flushed. Her throat was dry. Her voice sounded *considerably* higher than she'd have liked. "Sorry. That. That was. That–"

"–was unexpected," he completed.

"Yes." She stuttered at the word several more times than she needed to.

The sound of someone clearing their throat cut across

Aimee's thoughts, and turning, she saw Bjorn standing less than two feet away. The two of them abruptly separated – practically *leaped* apart – and Elias held up his hands like a suspected burglar. Whatever spell – strange, unfathomable, impossible – had held sway was broken. Aimee opened her mouth and "It's-not-what-it-looks-like!" came tearing out.

And what does it look like? her mind asked. *Shut up,* she mentally snapped back.

"That," Bjorn started, "is none of my business. Clutch caught your stray, though. And–" the big man's eyes caught sight of the glowing diamond in Aimee's hand. Whatever suspicion had been present was wiped from his face in a heartbeat. "–And that hasn't glowed since Port Providence."

Aimee swallowed, self-consciously tightening her robe about her waist, glad of the change of topic. Glad of being able to think of something – anything – else. Back to work. Eyes on the prize. The vision was fresh in her mind. "The squitten got it loose," she said, "and we both ended up touching it. Get Harkon. Now."

By the time her teacher returned, Aimee was fully clothed and considerably more comfortable with the state of the universe. Though, as the group gathered in the common area and she caught a glance from Elias where he stood by the window, she absently reflected that comfort – while not the wrong word – wasn't exactly the right one, either.

Harkon looked tired. If she had to hazard a guess, Aimee would've assumed that he hadn't slept all night. It was impressive, then, that through the exhaustion lines on his face and over the wrinkles on his dark, steepled hands, a keen amusement still lurked in the way he asked his first question.

"Really, Vant?" he asked. "Squittens?"

The engineer – in the end – hadn't escaped the ink himself. A large blotchy patch covered his left shoulder. He looked at it irritably. Leaning against the back wall, Clutch rolled her eyes. She'd since changed her clothes, but a dash of ink still discolored her blue hair. "Go right ahead," she growled at him. "Complain. I dare you."

"I didn't know she was gonna have a litter," Vant said.

"Neither of us did," Vlana said with an apologetic sigh that wasn't entirely genuine. "But it was funny."

"You've lived on ships too long," Bjorn muttered with an amused shake of his head.

"Says the man who lives on a ship," Vant quipped back.

"Only for the last third of my life," the old warrior answered.

"More pertinent is the vision Aimee just relayed to us," Harkon said, dismissing the argument with a wave. It was just the group of them now, Rachim having returned to his villa. On the table in the center of the room, the Axiom Diamond sat on a small pillow, its glow still present, but much fainter.

"They come with the storms," Elias said, one elbow resting against the edge of the window as he stared out into Rachim's hangar. The comment was more to himself than anyone else. Aimee looked his way a moment longer. This second encounter with the Axiom had left him deeply shaken.

She turned back to find Harkon watching her in thoughtful silence, and felt her face grow warm for just a moment before she shook her head. This was ridiculous.

"You're thinking of what Viltas told us," she said to her teacher. "Aren't you?"

The words played again through her mind, and she suppressed a shudder. *"Surrounded by corpses, in the heart of the metadrive chamber, all I could smell was rain."*

Harkon nodded. "Indeed. It would seem to lend credence to Lord Viltas's theory that our enemy was tapping into a greater menace than itself."

"Care to let the rest of us in on the secret?" Clutch asked. "I mean, fun as this is, listening to the three of you being all cryptic and such."

"Viltas warned us that the necromancer the late Captain Amut faced was operating in conjunction with some sort of cult," Harkon explained. "A cult that the lord shipman believes preceded him, having older roots on *Iseult* than the dark sorcerer they wound up following. He told us that when the monster was killed, it was in the middle of a ritual in *Iseult*'s core metadrive chamber, involving sacrifices to *something* lurking beyond what seems to be a small portal, something that he said smelled of rain. The Oracle also said to beware the Children of the Empty Sky."

Aimee wrapped her arms around her chest, seeking to dissuade herself from feeling a sudden, deep cold. "What he described sounded like Esric... that thing I faced in the bowels of the *Iron Hulk*'s own metadrive chamber," she said after a moment. Out of the corner of her eye, Elias physically winced. The monster of which she spoke had kept him in thrall for almost sixteen years, keeping him as the obedient, murderous warlord Azrael, servant of the Eternal Order.

"That's not its name," Elias said, not looking back at

any of them. "Just a bloody coat it liked to wear."

"I thought the diamond refracted truth back at you," Bjorn mused, looking at the faintly pulsing jewel thoughtfully. "Wasn't that what it did to him?"

Elias didn't respond to the reference, but Aimee saw his shoulders tense.

"Allegedly," Vlana said.

"That's *one* thing it does, or can do," Aimee said, cutting the former off before more damage could be done. Inwardly, she made a note that she and the quartermaster – her first friend aboard *Elysium* – were going to have a difficult talk, soon. "But to be honest, I'm not sure if that's the proper takeaway. All indications are that the Axiom is somehow sentient, or at least is close to it. It bestows its 'blessing' on individuals it chooses through some sort of test, and it works by a set of rules we don't fully understand yet." She paused, chewed on her lower lip for a moment. "What concerns me," she said next, "is its first statement: that it was difficult for it to speak to us, given where we currently are. What does *that* mean?"

"The jewel doesn't like behemoths?" Bjorn offered.

"Unlikely," Harkon said.

"Maybe the enchantments keeping *Iseult* together inhibit it somehow?" Vlana asked, flashing her brother a questioning look. But Vant shook his head.

"Not how metadrives work. Even ancient ones made the old way still have chaos dampeners on them to keep everything else on the ship working."

"The villa we're in? What sort of magical defenses does Rachim have in place?" Bjorn murmured.

"Wait," Clutch said. "What if you're all thinking about this wrong? What if it's not the ship the jewel is on – what if it's where we are in the sky?"

Vlana's brows drew together. "Alright, pilot, what do you mean?"

"We're way *way* out on the far reaches of the Dragon Road," Clutch said. "I've been checking the stars every night to mark our positions. They're just casual measurements I do as a part of my evening ritual, so there's a bit of a margin for error... but when we returned to Visramen, I noticed that we were way out on the far edge of the Tarragon Arch." The pilot took a calming breath. "And that means we're one jump or portal mishap away from the Tempest Crescent."

A silence settled over the common room. Elias had turned to look back at the rest of them, and Aimee caught his eyes. There was something knowing, and fearful, in his expression.

"I've... heard stories," she said after a moment. "Legends of ships disappearing, and of something beyond the crescent's edge that makes navigation almost impossible–"

"They're not stories," Vlana said quietly. She barely suppressed a shudder.

"It's still a *long* way away under normal engine power," Vant said. "The Arch is within one jump of the crescent, but that's not exactly next door."

"In portal terms it is," Aimee said. "In magical terms, one jump isn't very far at all." She shook her head. "What in the world is the flotilla doing this far out from civilization?"

"The Arch is still a frequent trade route," Harkon said. "It's fairly safe, and a sufficiently out-of-the-way place to conduct their own business before the ships begin their long circuit back along the trade routes. But yes, Aimee is right. Mystically speaking, it is... close. And while the crescent, and the maelstrom beyond, is years away under normal power, its reach is long enough to stir up trade winds and drive odd phenomena outwards that are felt even in the spheres of the Empire and the Republic." He paused. "And throughout the Unclaimed."

"Gods," Vant said, sitting down. "We've never been out this far before."

"I have," Harkon said quietly. "And further, a long, long time ago. If that is where we are, then the warning the diamond conveys must concern the maelstrom. And that–" he paused "–I have never directly seen."

"I have," Elias said, quietly. All eyes in the room now turned to him, which seemed to make him immediately uncomfortable.

"When?" The question came from Bjorn, and the old warrior's face wore a different look: sad, tired.

"I was... very young," Elias said. His eyes acquired a faraway look. Detached. Thoughtful. His brows drew together. "My former master brought me, and two of his other apprentices there. My memory of it is fuzzy. It was before he started using Esric to control me. I think the order sees the edge of the storm as sacred." He swallowed awkwardly. "We were taken in a ship, and left in our cabins for the night that we flew close to one of the storm's wall. That night, we all had... dreams."

The muscles in his neck tightened as he spoke. "And in the morning, one of them was completely mad. The other had torn his own eyes out. The storm is horrible for everyone, but for people with my abilities..." He shook his head. "We hear things, and see things, there."

"I've seen it too," Clutch said. The pilot wore a wry expression. "My first gig. Less than legal. We cut through the crescent as a shortcut. Got too close and then got the hell out. Nothing so dramatic as that happened, but... one of my copilots was never quite the same again. He lost his shit after I left the crew. Fell apart at the seams. A year later I found out he'd eaten his own knife."

"So the warning seems clear enough," Bjorn grunted. "Don't fucking go there."

"Perhaps a better translation would be: don't let whatever is behind this *take* us there."

Harkon stood up. "Do not tell anyone of the Axiom's role in this. Our possession of the diamond is still our secret, and that knowledge would only complicate everything we're trying to do here. However, I think the next step is clear. Clutch, I want you to redo those star-chart readings with Vlana double-checking your maps. Vant, you, Elias, myself, and Aimee will be paying Viltas a visit to see if we can't get access to the metadrive chamber of *Iseult*. It is possible – however unlikely – that there might be some answers as to the deeper mysteries therein. We have to try."

As he spoke, Aimee glimpsed Vant slowly inching his way out of the room. Harkon stopped him in his tracks. "Did you miss what I said?"

The engineer cursed under his breath, then stood at attention. "No sir."

Harkon smirked. "When we return, you will relieve Bjorn from watching over the squats, and ensure that no more of them escape. Do you understand? You brought them aboard, now you get to take care of them."

Clutch's grin was extremely smug. Vant stuck his tongue out at her.

"You've got your jobs," Harkon said. "Jump to them."

As the room started to empty, Aimee walked over to where Elias stood, still staring with a look of trepidation and unease at the diamond. For a moment, she debated whether she would say anything at all, given what had happened... but human concern won out over deeper confusions, and she nudged his shoulder. "Hey," she said quietly. "I meant what I said in there before. It can't hurt you."

Elias stirred, her words drawing him up from the depths of his thoughts. He blinked twice, as if seeing her for the first time. "What? No, sorry... I was just thinking about what we saw in there. A piece Harkon didn't talk about. It's eating at me."

"Which part?" Aimee asked.

"The lion," Elias answered. "There was a lion, roaring before the storm."

"They called Amut the Lion of Heaven," Aimee affirmed, "but–"

"–But he's dead," Elias finished. "So who, or what, was it supposed to represent?"

Aimee paused. "All I can think of at this juncture," she said, "is one of the candidates for captaincy... but I'm not sure the thought comforts me much."

She reached down and lifted the gem. It glowed slightly brighter when it touched her fingers, but no vision came this time.

She wasn't honestly sure if that was comforting, either.

CHAPTER ELEVEN
TWO HEARTS

Elias stood in his room, staring at the ghost that lurked on the wooden rack. The black armor he'd worn as Azrael, edged in gold, rested there, staring back at him like some sort of monstrous cage that he had escaped, but not actually managed to leave.

It was also the single best suit of armor he owned. He stared at it, weighing the value against the risk, both to his soul, and to everyone around him, were the gold and the black to walk forth again.

"I can't get away from you," he whispered in the dim half-light of his spartan cabin. His fists clenched by his side until they hurt. "But I don't have to use you." He paused. "Not yet."

In place of the familiar enchanted steel, he donned the makeshift hodgepodge of leather and linked mail that had sufficed in the interim since he acquired it in Ishtier. It fit awkwardly, unsized for him. The previous owner had been thicker around the middle, he thought, and weaker about the chest and shoulders. There was a mirror on the far wall, and he took his measure after tightening his sword belt about his waist. Azrael had been created, molded with specific intentions in mind. Always clean-shaven, long-haired and princely, trained to wear an arrogant smirk that disarmed as much as it frightened.

It was a comfort, then, that an altogether different man stared back. The ghost of what would eventually be a decent beard was starting to cover his jawline. His shorter hair was ill-behaved, and his expression was weary and worn. Even his eyes were different – still the same green, but more fearful, he thought, than arrogant. The image of a tired, beaten-down man stared back at Elias, dressed in badly fitting armor and clutching the gilded hilt of a dead prince's sword as though it were some sort of lifeline. This, then, was what Elias Leblanc looked like? It was the antithesis of princely.

A small smile curled at the corner of Elias's mouth. "Good," he said with more anger than he intended. "Stay dead, you unfathomable bastard."

In the smile, something familiar flashed, and for a fraction of a second, the dark apparition of the knight he'd seen in his battle-fever haze in the bowels of *Iseult* stared back, smirking, wearing Azrael's face.

"As if you could ever kill me."

The sound of a breaking mirror filled his ears, and it took Elias a handful of panting, terrified seconds to realize that he'd driven his fist into the reflective glass.

"Everything alright in there?" The voice was Aimee's, just outside the door. Elias looked at his hand. Blood stained his knuckles. He wiped them clean, then tied a strip of cloth around his hand before thrusting it into his glove. Then he turned and opened the door. "No," he said, emerging. "Can we go?"

"They're waiting outside," Aimee said, giving him

an odd look, before she glanced over her shoulder, then up to him with a seriousness in her blue eyes that would accept no argument. Pentus's paranoia-stoking comments echoed in his mind, mingling painfully with the confusing and dizzying memory of standing nose to nose with the sorceress in the doorframe of her cabin less than an hour earlier.

"I'm shaken," he said. He didn't say by what. He wasn't entirely sure. "But I am all here. Lead on."

She frowned with a look that said a more in-depth conversation was coming, then nodded and headed for the lowered bay ramp. It was a relief, he decided, not to have to meet that look anymore, for the moment. Again, he didn't trouble himself over why: the road down which such thoughts led was dangerous, and – he suspected – not just to himself.

Viltas, Rachim, and Vallus awaited them outside Rachim's villa. Elias noted at first glance that the lord shipman looked healthier than the last time he'd seen him, which was a source of relief. They could little afford for allies to fall ill at this juncture, and the ship had already lost one captain to necromancy masquerading as a disease.

Beside the lord shipman stood his son Vallus, looking somehow thoughtful and awkward all at once. Elias took his measure as they approached. He had the attitude of a man that had grown up in the shadow of a hero of whom he was forever falling short in the eyes of others. His face was softer than his father's, kinder, and whereas the lord shipman's gaze was worn and reserved, Vallus's brown eyes were open and attentive.

Azrael would've considered him an easy kill. Elias realized that so would many others, which made him wonder just how well the boy knew it himself.

Then he saw what Vallus was looking at. Also joining the group, approaching even as the *Elysium* party walked out through the doors, was Belit. And this time, she wore her full panoply of crimson armor and cloak, her helm tucked under her arm, and her longsword lashed to her hip. She walked, fierce and serene, stopping short and giving the group of them an approving nod with her dark, solemn face at their arrival.

Vallus looked as though he'd just seen the sun rise. Elias felt a small half-smile slip up one side of his mouth. So that was it, then. Perhaps he wasn't the wisest man in the world, and had only been free to be himself for a few weeks, but years of training in reading others had left him able to identify adoration when he saw it.

Belit spared the lord shipman's son a brief glance, in which lay a host of conflicting emotions. Then Harkon was speaking, and he had to pay attention.

"Lady Belit," the old portalmage said, "I hope that this assistance does not compromise the perception of your neutrality?"

Belit smiled. "The proper response to that, Magister Bright, is to ask 'in the eyes of whom?' The council's vote has made it clear that doing anything at all risks having my reputation compromised. Lord Viltas tells me that this concerns the menace behind the death of my late captain. If that is so, none may question my involvement." She paused. "If my reputation was worth more to me than performing my duties, it would be paper thin, and of no value."

Harkon smiled. "I knew I liked you. Regardless, I am grateful. I think between the lot of you, we have more than sufficient authority to gain entrance to the chamber, yes?"

"You would hope," Rachim chuckled, "but the Maiden's Chamber is sacred to both our highborn and low, and obstinacy is a bitch. Let's get moving."

The most obvious benefit of moving in an official capacity was the ability of the group to use more direct transportation methods. Their guides led them down the main thoroughfare of the upper levels, over glistening streets lined by the fine, stoneworked architecture that encrusted the entirety of the behemoth's back, and straight to a gilded elevator. It stood at the edge of a rail-lined, massive spiral aperture in the middle of a large square filled with aides, servants, household majordomos, and black-robed functionaries scurrying across the space in the fulfillment of their duties.

Somewhere high above them, the belly of another behemoth blotted out the view of the sky. Elias glimpsed a thousand bits of decaying, hodgepodge scaffolding, swarming with dirty people operating in what was probably the most dangerous, poverty-ridden part of their ship.

"Really," Elias heard a white-armored armsman say as he walked past them, "must overflights happen during the day? It's like watching a crazy man expose himself in the midlevel corridors. Filth."

He watched Belit's eyes flash with barely suppressed anger, then the lot of them were in the elevator, and the door was closing, before a hiss sounded and they began their descent. The window of the elevator was open to the interior of the vast bore, and a wind whipped past them as it slowly traveled below. The entire interior wall was a combination spiral roadway leading ever downward, and the host to numerous dwellings that faced outwards into the dank hole. Ladders clustered off makeshift scaffolds once they passed below the first three levels, and workers and enlisted rushed here and there on errands without number.

"You said that the chamber was sacred," Aimee said, raising her voice to be heard above the keening wind. "What do you mean?"

"That," Rachim began, "is a bit of a complicated thing to explain. Best to say that *Iseult*'s metadrives are its heart, that its heart is older than the memory of anyone else on this ship, and that people revere what's ancient."

"Also," Vallus said with a slight laugh, "Rachim is not known for his grasp of sentimentality." He smiled over his shoulder at the sorceress. "When people say this ship is alive, they're not joking."

Elias's brow furrowed. "The name," he said. "It's from an old legend, isn't it?"

"Very good," Vallus said, turning his curious gaze to the green-eyed knight. "You know your romances."

Elias paused, leery for a moment of how he should answer. "Required reading," he said.

"Wait." This time it was Vant who spoke up. The engineer's eyes widened with amazement and youthful fascination. "Are you saying what I think you are? Because I think you're saying that *Iseult*'s metadrive is one of the *ancient* ones. Before the process of synthetic inception was invented."

"Well, I don't know much about *that*," Vallus said, "but

I know my legends. They say that the ship was born from the grief of the maiden who bears her name, and her death, so that others might survive to sail the heavens."

"Oh my *gods*," Vant said. "I didn't think any of them were still in use."

"Care to explain further?" Aimee asked. "For those of us not educated on the finer points of metadrive engineering?"

"Sorry," Vant murmured. "Modern metadrives are ignited by a process called synthetic inception. A spark of the infinite is ignited in the core, and it boils into a raging manifestation of the first prime; raw magic churning in perpetuity, seeking the outlet that skyship systems then channel into power. It… didn't always used to be that way. A long, long time ago, it was only possible to create a metadrive by way of the sacrifice of mystically potent human lives."

"Dig deep enough into any history," Viltas mused, "and you find a font of limitless ugliness."

"That's not the legend," Belit said quietly. "At least, that's not how they tell it below."

The elevator came to a stop midway down the vast aperture, and suddenly began moving inward, sliding along a rail that held their compartment hanging in open air. All around them was the massive interior corridor of *Iseult* with the layered cake of all her mismatched levels visible in cross-section beneath them.

Elias caught sight of something out of the corner of his eye, and shifted to the far edge of the elevator, squinting until he saw the familiar uniforms of the enforcers walking the catwalks far below. Something struck him immediately.

"There are twice as many enforcers," he murmured, "than when we came down here before."

"The tradeoff," Rachim growled, "to staving off Yaresh's purge. He couldn't use his armsmen, but since he's still in charge of the ship's security, he can use his extant position to command the commanders below him to increase their personnel. Every lord below the upper levels has been ordered to double their complement of enforcers to 'keep the peace.'" The one-eyed man frowned. "Most of those brighter uniforms were doled out in the past three days, after maybe a day's worth of training."

"That's a lot of untrained men with weapons and newfound power," Elias murmured. The frown twisted his expression as he watched a man with a club take an idle swipe at a woman hurrying past with a basket. When you wanted to repress a people, hiring the vicious and destitute among them to exercise brutality over their fellows was a brilliant way to get the job done.

The tactic was disgustingly familiar: Lord Roland had taught him how to use it. His jaw clenched, and his bandaged hand balled into a fist at his side.

"Aye," Viltas said quietly. "He couldn't deliver a purge, but he could see that people beneath him were suitably brutalized. He sees this as his *duty*."

"In the hands of the wrong person," Harkon said, "duty is a dangerous word."

"Heads up," Vallus said, breaking into the conversation and pointing ahead. "We're nearly there."

The elevator let them out at the edge of a vast, bronze wall covered thickly with strips of parchment paper, and stained and tarnished by the innumerable filths that inevitably filled the interior of a city-ship this large, and this old. Still, by squinting, Elias thought that he could make out the outline of a set of images, moving left to right in lines over the large face beneath the countless bits of paper. They depicted war, loss, and something else, nearly obscured by the black burn mark of what seemed to have been some sort of explosion, a long time ago. The wall had a gentle curve, and it wasn't until he stepped back that Elias realized that the entire chamber was in the shape of a vast, metallic heart.

Viltas took the lead, with Harkon, Aimee, and Vant at the fore. Rachim followed, and Belit fell into step beside Elias, as the latter kept his eyes about him. A pair of gray-armored guards with shock-spears and large rifles waited before a large door at the base, and at the group's approach, one tilted back the visor of his utilitarian helmet to address them. "Entrance into Her Lady's Chamber is strictly regulated. Have you proper clearance to pass?"

"As lord shipman," Viltas said calmly, "I do. With us as well is Lord Rachim, and Belit of the Red Guard. Our errand is of–" he paused "–governmental concern. We will not interfere in the performing of the engineering workers' duties."

The guard took their measure, then gestured to his partner behind him. The guard pressed the palm of his armored hand to the door, and a brief glow flooded across it, before the doors opened slowly outward. Within, a soft purple light glimmered. "Proceed," the guard said. "Disturb nothing within this sacred space."

The walls of the chamber must have served as a barrier, keeping the overwhelming energy of the room from affecting the mystic senses of every mage on the ship, because the moment they stepped into the room, Elias nearly had to stop to catch his breath as a wave of dizzying power washed over him. They entered onto a long walkway that stretched from one end of a large, diamond-shaped chamber to the other. Suspended by an intricate series of cables, six long, translucent cylinders rose in a semi-circle, each the height of a large man, and filled with swirling, purple light.

"Subsidiary cores," Vant breathed, just ahead of them. "Oh *gods*," he said. "This setup *is* old..."

And there, in the center of the half circle, was another, larger core, crowning a pyramid dais of silver and platinum. The light within it was deeper, a gossamer, churning purple flame. Of all the cores, this one struck Elias the most, and immediately. Attendant to the power, an emotional weight seemed to emanate from it, beautiful, ancient, consisting of mingled desperate hope and deep sadness.

"Allow me to introduce to you," Belit said with a tremendous warmth in her voice, "at long last, and truly, *Iseult* herself."

In the warm glow of the chorus of lights, Elias glimpsed the faces of Harkon and Aimee. The face of the former was reverent and quiet... the latter was lit with wondrous awe for the beauty around her. "She's *beautiful*," Aimee breathed.

Viltas stepped forward, and pointed to a central platform near the center of the vast chamber, circular, etched with a number of arcane symbols, and edged by several upraised workstations of levers and switches. Elias knew a metadrive control-station where he saw one. "That," Viltas said, "is where we saw him performing his ritual, all those years ago. It's since been cleaned more times than can be counted, but perhaps the eyes of a true magister can determine something of value. This is what Amut protected. Perhaps it is also what he died for."

A tall man in a long gray coat approached the group. His shoulders had a rank insignia that marked him as someone of authority, and his balding pate was set with a number of decorative gemstones, as was popular with certain members of the officer aristocracy. "Lord Rachim," he said after a moment. "Lord Shipman Viltas... How may I help you?"

"This is Harkon Bright," Rachim said, gesturing to the old portalmage. "He's been promised a tour of the metadrive chamber whilst the council prepares for its next vote. I told him that you and your *expert* crew could answer any questions his people have about the illustrious maiden's history. Hark, this is Chief Engineer Hephus, tender of the cores, and notable eccentric. He's trustworthy."

The engineer's heavily lidded eyes slid from Rachim to the rest of them. They settled on each person in turn, seeming to take their measure with a hefty dose of analytical paranoia. Elias was starting to wonder if the man would actually refuse when he flashed a small smile, and said, "I am at your service."

Harkon nodded, and gestured for Aimee to follow him. "Vant," he said quietly. "Talk to the good engineer, I assume you have your questions ready?"

It was like watching an over-eager child straining at the grip his mother had on the cuff of his shirt. Vant's grin was boyish and infectious. "Had them even before you thought to tell me to compile them. Goodman, my name is Vant, engineer of the skyship *Elysium*. I have *so many questions.*"

Hephus's expression changed slightly from indifference to one of bemused alarm as Vlana's brother *descended* on him, but in short order the man was occupied, and Harkon was speaking to the group of them quietly. "Aimee and I will perform a tacit examination of the room. Elias, please stand watch. I would prefer that we weren't interrupted, if possible. If you sense anything... off, tell me."

"You have my word," Elias answered, then resigned himself to standing with Belit near the central platform as the others spread out to their work.

"So you clearly know a different version of the story than the rest of them," Elias said after a moment. He hadn't forgotten where his teacher had suddenly left her corrective rebuke hanging earlier on the way, and it had gnawed at him since.

Belit's eyes didn't leave their casual task of observing the room as the others began their investigation. "You were educated, were you not? What do you know of the legendary lovers, Iseult and her Tristan?"

Having his question answered with a question caught Elias off guard, and he paused to consider the shelves of literature he'd been made to memorize, at least in amounts sufficient to produce anecdotes when needed. "There are hundreds of versions," he answered, after a moment. "But in most of them, Tristan was a warrior, and Iseult a princess betrothed to his liege. He forsook his duty to be with her, and perished in the war that followed. When she learned her lover had died, Iseult took her own life in grief."

"She was no shrinking princess," Belit said quietly. "At least, not the woman from whose name this ship derives. She was a great sorceress, who loved a magister just as wise. But their people's home was dying, so she and her lover gave up their mortal lives to offer up their souls as the core metadrives of the ships that now bear their names, and who have always flown close and cared for one another's affairs. Iseult, and her Tristan."

Elias's eyes widened, and his gaze was drawn once more to the central core. "You mean–"

"I do," Belit said, nodding her head with a quiet, warm smile. "When we speak of the heart of *Iseult*, of the ship as if she possesses a soul, it is no hyperbole. Legend and time may have distorted the original tale, but what remains of a hero to whom every soul on this ship owes their life burns bright before you. That is why this chamber feels like a martyr's temple, and why the outer walls are encrusted with the loving prayers of countless thousands over the generations, covering up the gilded mirror that tells her story: this ship is alive, *junk ritter*, and her beating heart glows eternal before you."

It seemed absurd that he had not guessed it before, the way people had talked. Insane, that he had failed to see the plain reality, thinking it little more than some religious turn of phrase. Yet there she was, brilliant and bright, and shedding her amaranthine glow on the chamber.

The crime of the Faceless was even darker than he had at first thought: the dark necromancer that Amut had defeated had attempted to strike at the very soul of the ship, and unmake the sacrifice that permitted it to fly.

"I was told, long ago," he answered at last, "that the behemoths were made by the guilds, and that the societies upon them simply grew as a byproduct of the necessities of trade."

"The guilds love their lies," Belit answered. "Especially those that line their pockets."

"Your version of the myth doesn't exactly sound like the origins of a trade ship," Elias acknowledged.

"Funny, that," Belit said under her breath.

"And the white knights?" Elias asked, more quietly now. "The sword? There is much you haven't told me." As he spoke softly, they watched Aimee and Harkon walking a slow circuit around the core metadrive, whilst Vant stood on the platform, talking animatedly with Hephus while Viltas, Vallus, and Rachim spoke in hushed tones. Vallus briefly glanced their way, and Belit averted her gaze.

"That's a different story, but yes, I did promise." A wan smile curled at the corner of her mouth. "The officer aristocracy holds it as pure myth, but I know better. As it goes, long before the Faceless, a dark warrior menaced *Iseult*, and sought to poison her heart. The officers could not catch him, and he nearly slew the captain... but then–" a look of serenity crossed her face "–white knights came from the deep sky and killed him, before vanishing once more into the clouds. That is where the story ends for most, but not for me. I first heard it from my mother, and then again from my predecessor as commander of the Red Guard. According to our *private* traditions, one among these heroes remained behind for a brief time, to advise the captain of *Iseult*, and to train a group of warriors not merely to defend him, but to protect the ship, should our enemies return. This hero passed the secrets of the blade that you and I share down to the first commander of the Red Guard, and thus, teacher to student, they have been passed down ever since, along with the principles, the virtues, for which those secrets stand."

Over the course of the story, Elias had felt his breathing nearly stop in his chest as he waited upon every word, his feverish mind working furiously over the implications of every sentence.

Belit seemed to have caught on. "Do you understand me now, Elias Leblanc, when I say that I do not believe you are the first to escape?"

Elias was quiet for longer than he thought was appropriate. His mouth tasted dry, and he felt a dizziness settling over him. His hand had started gripping Oath of Aurum's hilt, and his mind was reeling. The memory of Roland's ancient book flashed through his mind, as did certain things his former master had once said of his desire for the Axiom Diamond.

"With this jewel in our possession, there will be no foe beyond our reach, no enemy we cannot find."

The grip of the sword was warm in his hand. "And the blade?" he asked, almost afraid to hear the answer.

"That I am sketchier on," she said. "Save that it fits – identically – the description I was once given of another. I don't know if you have come by the grandmaster's blade by accident, or if it is simply a copy, but…"

Her words fell short as Aimee jogged up to them, her expression intense and animated. "We found something. I think both of you should see this."

She led them past where Vant and the others were talking and towards the upraised, central metadrive core. The closer they walked to it, the more the feelings he'd first felt emanating from the ancient metadrive became almost overpowering. It took Elias a moment to adjust as they drew closer. More than the dizzying sensation of the emotions he felt in tune with its ambient mystic power, a confusion rose in him. This wasn't the first time he'd stood in the presence of something ancient, built from the sacrifice of lives. He suspected, deep down, that the vast metadrives that powered the Eternal Order's iron hulks were built off the sacrifice of many, *many* lives. He had never felt such grief and presence when standing before it.

Then again, he hadn't been permitted to feel much at all, whilst he was still in the order's thrall.

"Viltas was right," Aimee said. "This chamber was meticulously scrubbed clean over and over in the years since. Very little evidence of the original ritual work remains, and we didn't find anything other than an echo, but there *is* something more recent that bears observing."

She led them around the edge of the chamber, to a place where Harkon knelt near the wall, his hand outstretched and pressed against the metallic surface.

When they reached him, Harkon drew back his hand, and a ripple passed across the surface of the metal as he spoke a single, soft word of magic.

Scratched into the base of the wall was a symbol that made Elias's heart freeze and his throat go dry: a ring of nine stars, jaggedly etched, but clear to one who recognized what it stood for.

"I don't understand," Belit said after a moment. "That's not a symbol I'm familiar with."

Elias looked from left to right, suddenly *terrified* of what might happen if anyone other than the three around him heard what he was about to say. "I do," he said. "It's the symbol of the Eternal Order."

He took a step back, swallowed. A panic was rising in his chest. "Hide it," he murmured. "Please."

Harkon gestured again with his hand, and spoke another word. The image was once more concealed by whatever magic had hidden it. "There are others," he said, "marking every other corner in the room. I believe they were put there recently."

The old portalmage fixed him with a look, thoughtful, intense, and unreadable. "Magister," Elias said through a dry throat. "You cannot think–"

"I know you didn't," Harkon murmured. "Aside from the insanity of the gesture, I trust you. But it evokes troubling questions."

"Nobody on this ship knows the truth about you," Aimee said, putting a hand on his shoulder. She turned her eyes back to the blank patch. "What worries me is why they're there in the first place. What do they mark? Each is hidden behind a simple – but potent – illusion spell, and each marks a drive, while not actually containing any enchantment of its own. These things aren't easy to damage. For all their finicky nature, it takes a lot of physical or magical force to actually damage one. Otherwise they could hardly last as long as they have."

"You have to tell Hephus," Belit said.

"I will," Harkon said, then he looked at Elias again. "Is there precedence for this, among the order? It seems... odd, more overt, than they might do."

Elias fought through the fog of fear churning in his brain to answer. He stuttered for a moment at first. "No," he finally said. "That's just it, this is... this is too direct.

My former master, and cohorts, would ream any of their fellows for marking a target so obviously. They would use an innocuous symbol, previously decided on amidst those performing the task. Overtness and directness is for shock and awe, when they throw caution to the wind and rely on force."

"An imitator?" Aimee asked.

"A poor one, if that," Elias said. "But it is possible."

He racked his mind, thinking of the order's prior outreach operations, seeding enemy territories with friendly agents who might one day strike when it was warranted. He frowned.

"I will see that the chief engineer is informed," Harkon said, rising. "These symbols bear no special enchantment of their own. So far as I can tell they are scratchings without mystic potency. Only the magic that conceals them is present, which is what concerns me."

"Harkon," Elias said as the old mage turned to go. "That's not everything."

The eyes of all three were on him now. Belit's expression was reserved, Aimee's was worried. Harkon watched him with a steady, unblinking gaze.

"Since we came here I've seen visions of members of the order twice. Indistinct, reaching out to me. I don't know why. I thought at first that it was paranoia, or latent memory, but now..." He shook his head. "Now I'm not so sure."

And should the truth about me become known, he thought, *everything you are striving for will crumble to dust.*

Harkon looked at him for a moment, then asked a single question. "Waking visions?"

"Both times," Elias confirmed. "And my sword, when

it met the dead, it burned the enchantment from them. Left them burned-out corpses."

The old portalmage frowned. "Aimee already told me about the former. As for the latter… tell me if you have another. But no others." He glanced at Belit. "I presume she knows?"

"What your bodyguard was," the tall woman said, "doesn't interest me. Only what he is now, and what he may yet be."

Elias closed his eyes. Nodded.

"On that we agree then, Belit," Harkon Bright answered, then turned to his apprentice. "Come. It's time to make a relevant report."

Once more, the two glorified bodyguards stood alone. Elias watched as the two mages returned to the group and began a conversation that rapidly turned animated and agitated at once. *You didn't tell them everything*, a little voice whispered in the back of his mind. About Yaresh. About Pentus. About the men that had tried to threaten and buy him.

No point, he answered his own little voice. A warning of potential mystic threat was relevant. The grudges or fears of others was not.

"For a man who dreads as much as you do," Belit said, "you have good people in your corner. Less fear, *junk ritter*, and more mindfulness."

"Thank you for speaking in my favor," Elias said quietly. "But if the truth were to become known?"

"Less fear," Belit said, putting a hand on his shoulder. "More *mindfulness*."

From across the room, Harkon gestured for them to approach. "You said you were born near here," Elias said, the memory rising as they did what they were bid. "Who was your mother?"

Belit laughed lightly. "An eccentric," she said. "A dreamer and a bit of a mystic who loved lore and learning, but never thought much of turning either into power. One day she loved a man who lost her, and brought me into the world. Who she was isn't as important," she said, "as who she was to me."

The memory of his own mother, distant and faint, passed through Elias's mind. *Noble and brave. Gentle and kind.* This time something else emerged. In tune with his footfalls, he heard the echo of an old lullaby. It wasn't until he reached the rest of the group that he realized he was actually humming the melody under his breath. "I can understand that," he said.

"The guard will be doubled," Hephus said. "And I will have my engineers look into it. Were they evenly spaced?"

"No," Aimee said. "Randomly scratched. No unifying mathematical principles behind it, or mystic symbology. They could be marking the chamber's exterior for attack. Perhaps readying to breach the core room."

"It is possible," Hephus admitted. "But the walls aren't easy to breach."

"Unless you've got a horde of the dead at your beck and call," Rachim growled.

"You weren't here when they were last a problem for us," Viltas murmured. "And you've never seen a proper plague of them. Double the guard, and make sure there are sorcerers out there among them."

This seemed to move the chief engineer. "It will be done, Lord Shipman," he said. "Now if I may, your presence is beginning to distract and alarm my staff. The Lady runs best when her tenders are mindful of their duties."

"That's our cue to go," Rachim said, with a wry smile. "Our welcome has been overstayed."

The wall with all its plastered parchment notes stood out above Elias as they left, a wind from within the vast interior of the ship stirring the thousands of missives, prayers and devotions as feathers upon the breeze. How many were answered, he wondered. How many fell upon the deaf ears of a ship-soul consumed with keeping its people in the endless sky?

He wasn't sure which answer to that question he preferred.

It was only as they stepped out onto the broad platform before the vast interior of the hull that they noticed their elevator no longer waited for them, but was – in fact – returning. It came to a stop where it had disgorged them before, and the gilded doors opened, revealing a hurried messenger. "I am looking for Lord Rachim, and Harkon Bright."

"You have found them," Rachim said, stepping forward and sizing up the newcomer. "You're one of Pentus's men. What does the duke of the midlevels want?"

The messenger, catching his breath, composed his face into a broad flash of friendliness. "I am here, on behalf of his grace, to present Magister Bright, his host, and his entire crew with invitations to a Grand Ball, to be held in the Star-Dome three days hence. It is my master's opinion that there has been too much chaos, pain, and suffering of late, and that if there is to be debate, it should at least take place in the midst of finery, joy, and light."

It was *not* what Elias had been expecting.

Harkon, however, smiled, amused. "Tell your master," he said, "that my crew and I will be happy to attend."

At the surprised looks from those around him, the old portalmage's smile deepened. "I hope you packed fine clothes."

CHAPTER TWELVE
WHAT KINGS AND CAPTAINS DREAD

Aimee stood in a side room off the main Council Hall, with all three candidates, Elias, Harkon, and their host. She stood still, her hands folded patiently behind her back, as Yaresh screamed.

The council had just had yet another vote, and it hadn't gone as the lord of the muster wished.

"A *tie*," he declared. "Unheard of. How could it be a tie? This is insane and impossible."

"I assure you," Harkon said, calm, level. "It is no deception. I took the count, took it again, and the functionaries – who do not care for me – checked also. It is a tie, three ways. There is no mistake."

Yaresh looked like he'd just swallowed a mug of steaming bile. For a moment he fought for his voice, only to be interrupted by Diara before he could start ranting again. "Then we shall simply have to wait until another vote can be scheduled. The officers have their duties, and we must not keep them away from their tasks. The bridge crew will hold the wheelhouse in the meantime, as they have done."

"Do not interrupt me, woman," Yaresh snapped.

"Forgive me," Diara said with practiced calm. "You were not saying anything of value."

Yaresh's face went white with rage. "I will not sit here and suffer disrespect from this craven mystic who has no grasp of the fundamental realities my people face!"

"That mystic is your fellow aspirant," Rachim growled. "You'll bloody behave yourself."

A slight stirring drew Aimee's attention to her left. At Yaresh's last outburst, Elias had taken an involuntary – or was it? – step forward, and now stood watching the lord of the muster with a level, blank expression that was somehow terrifying to meet.

"I am content to wait, if that is what must be done," Diara said. "Perhaps the good duke of the midlevels is right, and a night beneath the stars will ease the contentiousness between the officers."

"Or," Pentus said, flushed, and looking suddenly determined in a way that made Aimee nervous, "I could disrupt all of this with an announcement I've been considering for some time. I shall attempt the ancient Trials of Captaincy."

Silence. Yaresh and Diara both stared in shock at the Duke of the Mid-Levels.

"That's absurd," Yaresh said. "No captain has done such in three hundred years."

"But it isn't without precedent, is it?" Pentus said, smiling. "I shall attempt them. There is no law stating that I can't, and we have need of someone, I think, whom *Iseult* herself deems worthy of her high seat, have we not?"

Before the other two could argue with him, the duke of the midlevels stepped out of the side room, and walked out to address the council. Aimee heard the announcement from a distance as Yaresh stormed after him.

"That's the second time I've heard these trials referenced," Aimee said. "Someone explain that to me, because I haven't been brought up to speed on that one."

To her surprise, it was Diara who spoke. "The council didn't always choose the captain. Once – the last time being three hundred years ago – those who sat the chair were expected to complete a series of trials, with the ship herself believed to be a sort of mystic judge of it all. On at least one occasion these trials were completed by one who didn't realize he was going through them. They have changed with time, but generally there were five.

"A prospective captain who would win by way of trials had to complete the following tasks: defend the ship from threats external; guide the ship by starlight alone; cross the ivory bridge in the midst of a storm; and show mercy to a hated foe. Those who completed the first four could then attempt the fifth: prove their worth by touching the heart of the core metadrive and come away unburnt."

The Countess of Astronomers gave a wan smile. "Needless to say, few were ever able to succeed, so rather than see its finest sons and daughters killing themselves in the effort to earn the approval of *Iseult*, they instituted their current system of voting for their captain from amidst their own ranks."

"I am surprised," Harkon said, "that Yaresh so strenuously objected. Such prophetic position would surely impart the sort of gloss he wants."

"I'm not," Aimee said with a shake of her head. "Yaresh isn't actually brave. He's an angry brute who fears tests of genuine worth. For all his disdain of politics, they're the only chance he has at winning."

"Truly," Diara murmured with a sardonic smile, "I am moved by your impartiality."

"Don't make the mistake of assuming he's not brave," Elias said, suddenly and quietly. "Arrogant. Selfish. Feeling entitled to a power he believes is his... but he is not a coward. If pushed, he'll fight."

The council exploded into an eruption of voices in the wake of Pentus's announcement. "Better get moving," Rachim grunted. Harkon agreed with a nod, and they crossed a floor filled with rising uniforms, jabbing fingers, and raised voices.

"ASSEMBLED COUNCIL, HEED ME!" Harkon thundered, so loud that Aimee nearly lost her balance from the shock of it. The room quieted, and turned to the suddenly authoritative face of the mage who meddled. "I confess," he said, "that I am not learned on this particular subject, and that I suspect it falls outside the purview of the task you set for me, so I will defer to Lord Rachim. But before you dissolve to your duties, I implore you do so peaceably."

As he stepped back, Rachim stepped forward. "Well, that was a damn fool thing to do. Still, there *are* ancient protocols for this. As Pentus has declared this as his intent, those upon *Iseult* are bound not to oppose his attempts to pass these trials. The eyes of the gods and the heart of *Iseult* are watching us, and watching him, the poor bastard. As of now, you are all bound to this requirement, I remind you."

A murmur of grudging assent passed through the assembled, and the roar of argument died down. Aimee breathed out and exchanged a look with her companions. The lull in the chaos was broken by the sounds of the vast doors to the hall slamming shut.

Yaresh had stormed out.

Frost. Flame. Wind. As they walked back to *Elysium*, Belit talking with Rachim up ahead, Aimee made use of the time to run through the gestures and the words in her mind, repeating them over and over as if doing so would soothe the raw shudders raking over her nerves. Her sense of relief at who the tie in votes had kept out of power was overridden by an overpowering awareness of just how bad the split amongst the officer aristocracy was.

Frost. Flame. Wind. She forced her mind to focus and her heart to steady. They were no closer to finding Amut's killer. No nearer to knowing where the cult was hiding, or who might be among them. A chorus of menaces seemed to play at the edge of her thoughts, threatening to drown out her ability to *do*.

"Are you alright?" Elias asked quietly. The young man had fallen into stride beside her. His leather and chain didn't fit well, and their time since Port Providence had worn him down, on reflection. He'd lost some weight, and his face was thinner. The prideful look he'd had as Azrael was gone, and with it, so much of the arrogance that he seemed an utterly different person.

She wrestled for a long moment with whether to admit her frustration, then simply repeated what he had said to her a day or two ago in the doorway to his cabin.

Honesty won.

"No," she said. "The council was split three ways between two politicians and a militaristic ass. It's hard for me to forget that. Maybe a year ago I might have thought it normal, but I've *seen* war now."

The man beside her said, very quietly, "I'm sorry."

She glanced his way, uncertain of how to respond. It hadn't struck her until just then that she hadn't even thought to ask for an apology, or thought of things in such a way as to consider that one might be necessary. After a few difficult seconds spent sussing out how she was to respond, she paused, then said, "The man who did that is dead. Don't you dare apologize to me, Elias Leblanc."

He watched her in unreadable silence for measured seconds, then his brows drew together over his green eyes. His mouth opened twice as if to summon a response, but none came.

Instead, as they drew close to Rachim's estate, Belit's hand closed on her shoulder, pulling her to a stop as the others forged ahead. Turning, she watched as the swordswoman shook her head and held a finger up to her lips. Eventually the sounds of the rest of the group receded. She caught Harkon's eye, and her teacher said nothing, giving a faint approving nod before continuing.

"We have a visitor," Belit said in low tones, and both Aimee and Elias turned in time to see the slight form of Ferret slipping from the shadows.

"Come quickly. The Oracle hasn't forgotten you, and she's sent me to find you."

Ferret led them quickly down the side street by which they'd come, until he reached a seemingly innocuous place in the wall, where he stopped. "I had to come by some complex ways to find you," he said. "Old, secret passages running between the top levels and the lower ones, predating the officer aristocracy, the functionaries, and the whole mess of them. Only she knows, since only she has the unbroken memory to recall them."

At this, he held out his hands and pressed them against the stone. There was a grinding noise that echoed beneath their feet, and Aimee felt the familiar tug in her gut as magic was released. A hidden door.

A passage, lit by fading, flickering lamps opened up before them, and Ferret beckoned for them to follow. "She's been watching you," he said. "But the evil threatening *Iseult* drains her, makes communicating harder. It took her days after our encounter to sufficiently recover to contact me." The downleveler looked deeply worried. "I've never seen her this sapped of strength. She won't be able to talk for long, but I can get you to where she's manifesting."

"You see why I held you back," Belit said, though now that they were apparently getting closer, she looked more afraid than sure of herself. Beads of sweat stood out on her brow, and her hand flexed occasionally beside the hilt of her sword.

This time, they entered a confluence of two other passages. The distant sound of wind through worn exterior paneling could be heard somewhere, and cobwebs rippled in an unseen breeze over their heads.

And in the center of the space, semi-translucent and surrounded with a halo of light, was the same figure they'd previously seen in the bowels of *Iseult*. This time, when she turned, Aimee glimpsed more of the face beneath the cowl, and took an involuntary step back. The features were youthful, beautiful even. But the eyes were immense. Luminous. Pupils swollen to the edge of the iris and filled with stars.

"Forgive my long silence," she said, in a voice that echoed from far away. "This is not easy. Heed what I say, please, and do not ignore the signs."

"Augress," Aimee finally said. "I have so many questions. The symbols of the Eternal Order are scratched on the inner wall of the metadrive chamber. Lord Yaresh condemns any who heed you. The Faceless remains elusive, and I have been warned of storms, and those they bring."

"You have a little while," the Oracle answered. Her gaze was now fixed on Aimee. "Ask."

"Who killed Amut?" Aimee asked. "Who is this necromancer? Imitator or echo?"

"Neither," the Oracle answered, and her face was pained. "The Faceless himself yet lives. I have felt his presence, diminished, but here."

Somehow Aimee had known it. Dreaded it, yet understood on a fundamental level that this was what they were contending with. "The cult..." she started.

"More dangerous, and numerous, by far," the Oracle said. "Older, with an origin that is hidden from me, but I know their name. Beware the Children of the Empty Sky, sky-splitter. Beware the Grandfather. They have been plotting their vengeance for longer than the history of some kingdoms."

"Revenge for what?" Elias asked. There was an earnest, worried look on his face. Aimee remembered what he'd said in the metadrive chamber. Visions.

"For what not?" the Oracle answered, and the weight of her tone was heavy with grief. "The rank and file turn because they are desperate. And how not? Those beneath the officer aristocracy live lives of rigid servitude and eternally blunted ambition. In their dogma, they mourn for their beginning. But in their day to day, they hunger for the pound of flesh denied to them by justice."

"My mother once said that the officer aristocracy would have to learn," Belit said, "or they would be their own undoing."

"Yet you serve them," the Oracle replied.

"I served *Amut*," Belit said with quiet verve. "And I serve *Iseult*."

"My pardons," the Oracle answered. "But you will only perform those tasks to your full ability when you stop living in denial. The trials have begun, Belit, and the time is nigh for choices."

"There has to be more than that," Aimee pleaded. "The Children of the Empty Sky, the Faceless. Who is Grandfather? How could they hide for so long? And *where* are they hiding?"

"The song reveals only so much," the Oracle answered. "And the nearer we draw to the Tempest Crescent, the harder that music is to hear. This is by their design, I suspect. In the shadow of the storm, we are all blind and deaf. Expect more powerful undead. Expect them to strike when their attack will bring the greatest despair. Expect storms. As to *where* they are," the Oracle paused, "look for them in the shadows cast by the brightest light. Among the richest and the poorest, but above all else in those who have lost so much that oblivion seems preferable."

"Why," Elias suddenly, desperately demanded, "do I see visions of a black knight even when waking? Why are the symbols of my old masters etched into the walls of the metadrive chamber? What in all the hells does the Eternal Order have to do with *Iseult*?"

Slowly, the Oracle turned her gaze towards the one-time black knight, and cocked her head to the side as she looked at him. "Three deafening fates before me, discordant melodies in the song that drown out what is with what might be. Forgive the riddles, Elias Leblanc, but sometimes there is no straightforward way to articulate the truth. You are not the first time the order has come here, and they do not forgive. So great is their hatred that even the echo of their memory will lash out at one who betrayed their trust. As to the chamber–" the cowled head shook, regretful "–the heart of *Iseult* is beyond my sight. It is too bright, its place in the song too indistinct. I hear *because* of *Iseult*'s beating heart, but you cannot see the inside of your own head. As to Grandfather, I don't know. Beware the shadow behind the shadow," the Oracle said. "The monster that monsters fear."

A flicker passed across the projection. Ferret stirred beside Belit. "She's weakening," he pleaded. "Augress, you mustn't tax yourself. The ship still needs you."

"I have strength enough," the Oracle said with difficulty. "To say my proper farewells. I am glad to have met you, Aimee de Laurent, sky-splitter. Elias Leblanc, knight upon the White Path. This ship will not forget your service. Skyfarers remember."

"Please," Belit said suddenly, stepping impulsively forward. "Augress, I don't know what to do. Vallus thrusts himself daily into dangers to which he is not equal, and I do not have the heart to watch him die. My people are suffering by the day, and I do not know how to protect them."

"Yes, you do," the Oracle said, and her voice was full of rebuke. "You have *always* known, since the very beginning. But you will only see when you stop ignoring the plain truth, and do what must be *done*."

And with that, before another question could be asked or answer given, the glimmering spell projection flickered and vanished, leaving the four of them alone at the confluence of two dim, uncertain passages.

Aimee finished giving the report to Harkon two hours later. The two of them were alone, in the small room that served as his private library aboard *Elysium*. Her teacher paused, considering the full length of the story with his contemplative eyes.

"Sky-splitter has a fine ring to it," he said at last, in his unhelpful way. "What is your view of this?"

"She's no charlatan," Aimee said. "That much has been clear since the first time we saw her. The sort of magic necessary to maintain a projection like that is powerful, and the toll it took from her physically was obvious. The passages likewise made me think. Everything we were told about the behemoths growing up, that they were trade ships built by the guild for the sole furtherance of trade... I'm starting to have my doubts. My uncle always said they were older than the guilds claimed, by far."

The memory of her uncle made Aimee smile. Jester de Laurent had been one of her closest relatives as a little girl, had been the one who inspired her to make her career as a portalmage traveling the drifting lands on a skyship. His death in an explosion when she was still little had only solidified the desire.

"The Children of the Empty Sky," Harkon considered,

rolling the words around in his mouth as if trying them. "Whoever they are, they're unique to *Iseult*. That's not the name of any apocalyptic movement I've ever encountered or read about in all my years exploring. Her warnings are cryptic, but there's useful information. Grandfather, as well."

"We know that the cult is recruiting from among the destitute and desperate," Aimee affirmed. "And the nihilistic. We know they're not offering hope. And we know that the Faceless is still – somehow – alive. It gives us more of a sense of what we're stacked against than what we can actually use, but that's better than before. As to Grandfather," she sighed. "I have no idea what she's talking about."

"Worry about details as they become relevant," Harkon said. "Your spells. How are they coming?"

"Frost, flame and wind?" Aimee answered. "I'm ready to demonstrate them at any time. Didn't figure it was safe to do that in the library, though."

"Good," Harkon said. "Good. Because the time has come to give you the next one, and it's taken on a greater urgency with our friend's warning. I spoke with Elias, about what his sword did to the assassins you faced deep within the ship. The effects closely mirror those of something I am going to teach you: something whose gestures and words combine elements of all three that I had you memorize and perfect. Frost to focus, wind to direct, flame to burn. Fetch your notebook and form-scroll. It's time for you to learn not only to destroy the dead, but to repel necromancy itself. This will be difficult, as it relies not only on proper gesture and phrasing, neither of which is easy, but also upon will and strength of heart. Are you ready?"

Aimee's grin spread from ear to ear and her fingertips tingled at the thought of the challenge. No more being left unready in the face of a sort of enemy for which she had no ideal spells, she now scented the thrill of possibility, and the advantage of a fresh card added to her deck.

"Born that way," she answered.

CHAPTER THIRTEEN
AN IMPENDING FETE

Somehow the prospect of Pentus's upcoming fete was more unnerving than being shot at. As Elias looked over the trunk that contained his few meagre possessions, it struck him how ridiculous that actually was. Shipboard fatigues. A handful of pants and simple shirts. Books he'd found for cheaper than expected. An atlas – why was he staring at the atlas when he needed to find something proper in which to not shame his crewmates in a few days?

Behind him, the mirror was a fractured kaleidoscope from his previously vented fury. His knuckles hadn't healed yet. He could have asked either Harkon or Aimee to mend them, but somehow that didn't seem right. No more right than telling them of Yaresh or Pentus's suspicions. Those were his to carry. They didn't need the extra complication, especially when the ship on which they traveled seemed ready to fly apart.

Unfortunately, it also left Elias with no immediate confidants. Even as Azrael, he had possessed a few of those. His fellow knights of the Eternal Order. Lord Roland on one occasion. Esric – monster that he was – had served as a twisted sort of adviser. It seemed absurd that some part of Elias should actually *miss* the people that had abused, twisted, and used him for sixteen years of his life. And yet.

Noble and brave. Gentle and kind. A melody played in his deepest thoughts whose words he didn't know, and whose origin he could barely place, but for a mother that had once hummed it in echo. His fist balled as he addressed the emptiness of his cabin. "Dammit," he whispered. "I need *more* than that."

He closed his eyes, breathed in and out. White Path. *Junk ritter.* Azrael had been little more than a pastiche of a person, a facsimile of a personality stitched together from the remnants of the Elias whom Roland's monsters had inadvertently broken. And now? Chasms. Good intentions. Chasms.

Elias forced himself to breathe in and out. In and out. One hand rested on his sword. Belit's words came back to him. *When we break, what remains is what we know.*

His art. He had to make sure that the lessons he drew from it were the right ones. Chasm. A shaking threatened his hands as the screaming faces of former allies-turned-enemies rose from the abyss. Betrayal. Murder. Death. Disgrace. The void was big, and he stood at its edge. *What will you do?* The mocking voice came back. This time, the face it wore was that of Malfenshir, who lay dead by Elias's own hand, beneath a thousand feet of crumbled mountain. *How long before you succumb to the pit?*

The even breaths slowed, and a final cessation of tension in Elias's limbs came, though his hands didn't quite cease their trembling. "If you're trying to scare me," he whispered out loud, "you'll have to do better than the face of an enemy I already killed. It's a hole. I will do what you *do* with holes: fill it up."

He dressed in something simple, buckled his sword about his waist, and left the ship for Rachim's villa.

This early in the morning, the space was mainly abuzz with hired staff. Elias understood that their host employed considerably fewer than most people of his station. He stopped to examine the art he'd first admired awkwardly when they'd come to the villa. The painting in question was of a whirling storm seething around a single point of light; staring more closely, he saw a tiny skyship in the center, illuminated by the eye of the hurricane. Within the storm were writhing, indistinct shapes.

"The eye of the maelstrom," Rachim said, walking up. "Painted by Vierus of Albatross. I took it off an art thief who had murdered the original owner when I was a younger, bolder man. There was no one to give it back to, so I kept it as a dual reminder of how there's always light in the storms, and always storms waiting to break. Also to remind myself that expensive things shouldn't be sold just because they can be."

That made Elias laugh. The contagious chuckle spread to their host, and Rachim grinned. "You looked like you could use the laugh."

"Appreciate it," Elias said. His own voice was cracked and hoarse. "But what I actually need is apparently an outfit. I've got a coat, but little else."

Rachim sized him up, considering. "Well, you're damn near a head taller than me, so I somehow doubt you'll fit anything that I own, but I think we can figure something out for you. Your shipmates up yet?"

"Bjorn guards Harkon," Elias said, "if that's what you mean. My time is my own."

"Good," Rachim said with a nod. "Come on, kid, I'll take you to a proper tailor."

By the time they came back, both the villa and *Elysium* were buzzing with activity. It took Elias a few moments of glancing around the main foyer just inside from the landing platform where the skyship rested to realize that workers were furiously cleaning ink stains off the exterior doors. There was the sound of a loud bang, and Bjorn and Rachim's seneschal rushed past the doorway holding large nets. "That way," the big warrior yelled. "No, no, the fat one! It went *that* way!"

A loud curse exploded from outside, and Elias – still standing and observing with a sort of morbid fascination – watched as Vant stormed after the seneschal and Bjorn, completely covered in ink. "CLUTCH!" he screamed. "WHEREVER YOU ARE, THIS ISN'T FUCKING FUNNY!"

Elias was still holding the large parchment bag that held the results of his excursion to the tailor with Rachim. Despite the door between himself and the complete mess outside, he reflexively held the bag a little closer. "Perhaps it's best I wait before going back," he mused out loud.

"Oh by all means." The voice that spoke next was Clutch's, and turning, Elias caught sight of the pilot sitting – more sprawling, really – in one of Rachim's large leather chairs, a bottle of something red and expensive open in her hand as she refilled her glass and sniffed the rim. "These are the best seats to enjoy the show."

Rachim flashed a small, amused smile. "Do I want to know how the squittens got loose again?"

Clutch shook her head. "You do not," she said, an indulgent, wicked smirk on her face. "I hear that a number of them may have been surreptitiously placed in Vant's bed and closet while he was napping."

Elias and Rachim both reflexively winced at the same time. Clutch's grin only widened as she held up her cup. "Gentlemen, a toast to me: the queen bitch of the heavens. Cross me and I will destroy you."

"I don't want to know the year of that bottle, do I?" Rachim deadpanned.

"I mean, I can tell you," Clutch chuckled. "But that won't make it less than half drunk. Hark pays me well, I'll repay you."

Elias watched for another moment as the others ran past the door. A squitten shot past, larger than the last time he'd seen any of the ones from the litter. Bjorn and the seneschal charged after it. Vant rushed on their heels. The servants kept up their furious scrubbing.

For once, it seemed as though getting involved was... not a good idea. "...Got any more glasses?" Elias asked.

And *that* caught the pilot off guard. She blinked at him twice, then shrugged. "Fuck, why not? Pull up a seat, pretty boy. You drinking too, one-eye?"

"Might as well," Rachim said.

They sat in a trio of chairs, drinking a dizzying red, while the chaos continued outside. Elias had never been much of a drinker – his drunken near-suicide in Ishtier aside. During his time with the order he was loath to compromise his senses or cloud his mind. A head that wasn't clear got you killed. If not on the field, then by a rival who knew your drinking habits and your poison of pleasure.

And that was how Aimee and Vlana found them a short time later, as Elias was realizing that his tolerance for alcohol was downright abysmal. He looked up as the sorceress and the quartermaster emerged, carrying bags of their own. The two women stopped just short of the doorway and – like Rachim and Elias before them – took their time assessing the even more chaotic progression happening outside the doors.

It was Aimee who spoke up first. "Well, that didn't take long."

Elias was the first one to start laughing. He hadn't expected that, nor did he expect the explosive force of the full-body cackle ripping out of him to knock him out of his chair, but all at once, his ass was on the floor. Through the haze of his vision, he saw Aimee and Vlana staring at him as if he'd sprouted a second, tentacled head. Their expressions just made the absurdity of it funnier, and his laughter louder.

"Oh my gods," Aimee said. "Are you *drunk*?"

"That is the most disturbing thing I have ever seen," Vlana said, almost to herself.

"Yes," Elias heard Clutch say with smug satisfaction. "Yes, he is."

Rachim let out a snicker, far from sober himself. "Fucking lightweight. If I threw you off the ship you'd float away. How come Hark's bodyguard can't hold his port?"

Elias planted a hand on the table, pushing himself up into a standing position. "Excuse you," he said, "but this body is a finely tuned combative machine that subsists on self-loathing. There are costs to being this beautiful, one-eye. Piss off."

Clutch burst out into a mad eruption of laughter, nearly falling out of her chair herself. "The dam is broken!" she declared. "He started cursing! You may now all hail your queen and *bow*."

"What did you *do*?" Vlana demanded, not *entirely* able to keep the amusement from her own face.

"I don't actually know," Rachim said around a chuckle. "And since it so far hasn't meant a bigger mess for my house, I basically don't care. Cheers." He drank again. Elias considered his glass, then put it down.

"No!" Clutch snapped at him. "Noooooo. You cannot chicken out on us now! The performance isn't done yet!"

"You put the squittens in his closet," Vlana guessed.

"*Someone* did," Clutch said. "But I have no idea who."

At Vlana's expression of widening horror, Clutch mouthed, "Less talking. More bowing."

A whoop of victory erupted from outside, and they heard Vant start making vindictive cheering noises before he and Bjorn made their way back into *Elysium* with the squitten in question in a net.

"Give us another few moments," Aimee said, "and we should be good to go back."

"I will be remaining here," Clutch replied to this, raising her glass. "Until this bottle is finished. I started it, and like so many other things in my life, I have a moral obligation to end it."

"Yeah," Elias answered with a shake of his head. "Best I... not. I'll head back to the ship."

"And still my fantastic charity is ignored," Rachim replied. "I promise, the beds in my estate won't *bite* you."

Aimee laughed as she walked towards the door beside Vlana, her boots clicking audibly on the stone floor. Elias smiled despite himself as he followed. "Not going to bed, Rachim. I sleep more comfortably on the floor anyway."

The two women he was walking behind both flashed him an odd look. He let it go. Neither of them knew about how Azrael had never been comfortable, not even in the bed of a king. Not since Elias was broken the first time by sleeping on a cold stone floor.

As they crossed the landing platform, he took stock of the people frantically cleaning up the mess, simply absorbing the sensation of having his mind addled. He didn't much enjoy it. "What's in the bag?" Aimee asked as they approached the ramp.

Elias glanced down at the wrapped parchment paper around his new acquisitions. "Goodwill from Rachim."

"That sounds ominous," Vlana said.

"Mostly just expensive," Elias replied with a small smile. "Though it looks like you made similar outings."

"Yes, well," Aimee replied, in a tone that was at once mildly irritated and oddly self-satisfied, "I've never once shown up at a grand ball and failed to impress, I'm not about to start now."

It was as they ascended the ramp that Elias saw Harkon for the first time that day. The old portalmage looked tired, as if he hadn't slept well the previous night. There were dark circles under his eyes, and he fixed his gaze on the black knight walking behind the two women. "Elias," he said. "We need to talk."

The old mage took a few moments to assess the state of affairs – the blankets on the floor, the broken mirror – and said, "Is this typical?"

Elias dropped his parcel on the mattress and gave a

candid shrug. "Not to sound flippant, sir," he answered, "but it hasn't been long enough to establish what typical *is*."

Harkon flashed a small, wry smile. "Fair enough. But now the heart of the question: how much of this state of affairs is because of your visions?"

Elias appreciated the blunt honesty of the question. "I started sleeping on the floor again after the fight against the dead. Tried the bed before, but it didn't take."

"And the mirror?" Harkon asked.

"Saw my old self the other day," Elias answered. "It was hard not to punch him."

Harkon cocked his head to the side. "Are they getting worse?"

And if he told the truth, what would be the consequence? Yaresh's paranoid, angry face floated before Elias's eyes. The implications of what the truth might do, if the trust so carefully cultivated this past month evaporated, hung pendulum-like over his soul.

But if he lied about it... Azrael's smirk rippled through his thoughts.

"Yes," he said. His voice sounded dull, coming out of his mouth. Far away and detached. "Perhaps one night out of every three, now, I see it. The face changes every now and again, though it seems particularly fond of mine."

"What does it demand of you?" Harkon asked. "Or does it say nothing?"

"Mockery, mostly," Elias answered. "If there's a plot at work other than to make me lose sleep, I can't suss it out. No orders. No imploring. It seems content to chip away at my sense of calm, not that there was much of that to begin with."

Harkon nodded slowly, then looked him in the eyes. "I have been remiss," he said. "And distant, and I am sorry."

Elias looked down. "Sir, with respect, you don't have to apologize–"

"But I do," the older portalmage said. "I took you on – yes, at my apprentice's insistence – but also because you earned it, and I have hardly spoken with you since. I gave you a second chance, yet no guidance in helping you find what you must do with it. I told you I knew your mother, yet I have told you nothing of her since you came to live on my ship. And as you have been targeted by this echo of some horror deep within *Iseult*, I have, again, done nothing."

The old mage's eyes looked haunted as he spoke. Elias had never seen him appear so tired. "I am in no position," he said, "to ask for more than what you have given."

"But that's just *it*," Harkon said. "Becoming a whole person, learning who you *are*, that can't happen so long as you live in this shadow of guilt that tells you you're worth less than normal people simply because you have blood on your hands. Aimee told me of what happened with the Oracle, and your training with Belit has given your soul a new lease on life, but I would be no friend to you if I didn't tell you that whatever path you're on, whatever destiny is calling you, *you don't have to follow it*. And if you do, make sure it's for the right reasons, not because you believe that destroying yourself will somehow atone."

Elias was silent, momentarily unable to muster an answer. When at last he had one, it was in a voice cracking from alcohol and tiredness. "Why are you telling me this now?"

Harkon took a long, deep sigh, and the wave of his

own pain seemed to recede slightly. "Because you chose to be on this ship, but that is not the same as choosing to leap headfirst and eyes open into the dangers we face, as the rest of my crew, and my apprentice, have done. I want you to understand that becoming the person you wish to be, recovering yourself... it shouldn't be the justification by which anyone manipulates you into becoming their weapon or tool. You can be good only when you are free."

The words rolled over him, even as Pentus's offer replayed again in his mind discordantly with Roland's one-time benediction when the slap of a sword upon his shoulder had rendered him Lord Azrael. He remembered one of the first kind things Aimee had said to him, as he'd faced a final choice within the Axiom Diamond's vision not so long ago.

"The truth will set you free."

Make sure your lessons are the right ones.

After a long moment, Elias breathed in, trying to think clearly through the muddying haze of the wine, and answered. "Don't compare yourself to Lord Roland, sir," he said finally. "Not even by implication. You are nothing alike. My answer, sir, is that ever since I first encountered the Axiom, everything I have done has been my choice. That has... carried its own difficulties. I don't always know which way is right, or whether I am making a terrible mistake, but even those choices are mine. I am not your unthinking weapon."

Harkon watched him quietly. Then he slowly nodded his head. "Thank you, Elias," he said. "My conscience needed desperately to hear that."

"I understand," Elias answered.

"I am afraid," Harkon said then, "that something is coming that will catch us all off-guard. My suspicions are as yet indistinct. I will tell Aimee of them soon... but in the event that something happens that separates us..." His eyes suddenly seized Elias's own with their frighteningly intense stare. "Protect them. All of them. *Especially* her."

Elias was suddenly worried. He turned his head slightly, narrowing his eyes. "Sir?"

Harkon shook his head, seeming to master himself. "Don't overthink it, Elias. I simply... needed to know the truth, and now that I have it, I can rest easier, and return to work. Remember what I said, and be always mindful. Thank you, my boy."

The gentle click of Elias's door behind him echoed in the room after the portalmage departed. Glancing at the fractured mirror, he breathed out a sigh that felt almost normal. Then he dropped his satchel on the bed and opened it to examine the custom-tailored clothing within. Green and black edged with a hint of gold thread stared back at him. It was dissonant, to find joy in something as simple as this, when he'd once commanded vast wealth.

But, of course, it hadn't really been his. This was Elias Leblanc's, not Azrael's.

It was such a small difference.

It was *everything*.

CHAPTER FOURTEEN
BENEATH THE LANDLESS STARS

Getting ready for a ball had once been such an act of
rote repetition that Aimee could have gone through
the motions completely without thought. Years being
educated in the finer points of Havensreach's high society
by her mother; years of charm school after that, in the
effort to placate familial sensibilities enough to get her
access to the Academy of Mystic Sciences. She'd learned
to dance, speak well, walk right, and when wearing a
proper gown, turn heads with just the right look.

None of that was helping her cope with the fact that
she was monstrously, deeply nervous. She stood in her
cabin, considering the minutiae of her appearance,
and everything seemed *just* off by such amounts that
the whole picture failed to satisfy. And that annoyed
her. She raised a hand to check how she'd done up
her hair. Wrong? No, it fit with the way the gown fit
– not immodest, but very figure-hugging. Something
else. Some tiny critical piece was missing that would
have ordinarily tied the whole ensemble together. She
shouldn't have cared, but whenever this happened, a
thousand suggestions from her mother rippled through

her head and threatened to make her insane.

Straightening from finishing her makeup, she turned around, examining the flowing folds of form-flattering blue silk that matched her eyes. Apprentice's chain about her neck, with the badge just above a neckline neither immodest nor conservative, gold hair up, and something... something. *What?*

The knock at her cabin door nearly made her jump out of her skin. She took a moment to calm nerves that really shouldn't have been so ravaged, then fetched her things as Bjorn spoke without. "Hark says it's time to go. Best hurry up."

Just Bjorn then. The nerves lessened a little, and once she'd fetched her things, and stepped out the door, she paused in the hallway. A lot of things were riding on tonight: peace between political factions, information that could be divined by knowing or impressing the right people. Yet some part of her didn't respond to those stakes. She'd faced demons and armies and come out the other side. It made no sense for her to feel the butterflies tonight. Ignoring it dutifully, then, she made her way down the hall to the cargo bay where Vlana and Clutch were waiting, the two having bargained themselves out of ship duty, the former by way of a deal with Bjorn, the latter by way of a promise of food without the cost of having to be excessively social.

Clutch was dressed in the long slacks and buttondown uniform of her guild dress-blacks. Vlana wore the burnt copper gown she'd acquired on their earlier outing. The former let out a whistle as Aimee appeared at the top of the stairs, the latter waved excitedly. Just beyond them, Harkon waited, dressed in his gray and purple robes. Ever the sorcerer, teacher, and portalmage, even on the most formal of nights. His magister's chain hung around his neck, a reminder of what Aimee would one day attain herself. *Someday,* she thought, with optimism.

Elias was nowhere to be seen. She spent a few moments glancing about for him, before Harkon spoke up. "He went ahead."

"Hmm?" Aimee said, a little wrong-footed. "Oh, no, I was just–" *just what?* "–just curious."

"It was on Rachim's request," Harkon said. "Something about his presence lending weight to Yaresh's arrival."

"Poor man," Aimee said.

"You look stunning, Miss Laurent," her teacher said, then, smiling at the others, looked past them to Bjorn and said, "We'll see you soon."

"Don't get too drunk," Bjorn said with a chuckle and a smile. Then, to Clutch, he said, "If you bring someone… or several someones, back, don't use the ship, alright? Rachim offered us rooms. Use those."

"You are *no* fun," Clutch snorted as the group headed down the ramp.

The Dome Beneath the Stars was located further back down the top level of *Iseult*'s hull, not far from Amut's former residence. The fete was to take place as the sun set, and the sky had not disappointed. The railcar they took was on one of two tracks that ran the length of the district, and from out of the main, marble-lined window, they could see a beautiful eruption of gold, purple and the first hints of moonlit silver explode across the heavens, refracting off the surfaces of the other behemoths like gemstones. She walked beside her teacher, with Vlana and Clutch coming behind, and they were ushered from the railcar across sunset-painted cobbles towards the dome's exterior doors, which were open inward, guarded by a pair of Pentus's armsmen, a single functionary standing watch beside them. Names were given, and they were ushered through into a space that nearly stole her breath.

From outside, the dome had seemed nondescript, a multifaceted half-sphere with a silvery glint to it that caught whatever color the sky threw at it. Inside, Aimee found herself at the top of a staircase wide enough for five people to walk down shoulder to shoulder without overcrowding half of it, above a vast ballroom with a tiled floor polished to near-mirror sheen. Her senses came alive with the tease of potent magic in use, and raising her eyes, she looked upon circular walls lined with gleaming, diamond-like lamps, and a chandelier that was a hovering conjuration of multicolored starlight, a living constellation in constant motion. Up overhead, the sunset was a glorious splash of color slowly giving way to innumerable stars glimmering in the eternal sky, kept from being blotted out by the ambient light of yet another layer of enchantment.

"Now *that*," she said quietly, "is impressive."

"Wow," Vlana murmured. "I... Wow."

"My friends," Clutch said, fetching a glass of wine from a passing tray. "It has truly been an honor, but my solemn duty to engage in depravity is calling. Don't get into trouble in a way that keeps me from my usual portside activities, understand?"

Harkon's face creased with amusement. "Please refrain from destroying any relationships tonight, Clutch. I don't need angry husbands coming to my ship."

"They won't," the pilot said with a laugh. "Bjorn's

making me use Rachim's house, remember?"

"What's the goal tonight?" Aimee asked her teacher as they descended the stairs.

"Well," Harkon said, still looking amused. "First, do no further harm to the political situation if we can avoid it. If this can cool heads sufficiently to let virtue prevail, we let it. Second, watch for prominent players we may have missed before. Voices whispering in ears, notable social presences."

"And third?" she asked, as they reached the bottom of the stairs. A sea of fantastically dressed officer aristocrats spread out before them, and at the far end, she glimpsed a live band composed of strings, several gracefully curving horns, a flute, and two shredders with glimmering strings made of light. That was rather different from what she thought this crowd might have appreciated.

"Third," Harkon said, turning and laying a hand on her shoulder. "*Enjoy* yourself. Since leaving home we've faced violence, terror, murder, and intrigue. There is no shame in relaxing. Go. Have a fine night."

Being set loose was only unsettling for a few minutes before Aimee re-found her balance. She selected a white wine from one of the trays and started making her way around the room. Two conversations with young men and women of the upper levels later, and she had a better feel for the rules of the social game into which she had been thrust.

Courtship in the upper levels of *Iseult* was as intricate a game as anywhere else, and the ship – even its officer class – was so diverse, so much a melting pot, that the upper crust was both wildly conservative about their own, private traditions, and shockingly liberal in what they considered acceptable.

As she walked away from a brief jaunt around the dance floor with a red-uniformed midshipman with gold rings on his fingers and a swaggering smile, she wondered about what the people she'd gone to school with would have thought of this. Two sorts of soirees had been in Aimee's social appointment book back at home. The first kind were formal high society functions that she came to by way of family. Those had rules upon rules of formal etiquette. The second kind were the private parties wealthy kids in her social spheres had thrown – those had rules as well, but they were far more cavalier and risqué. It was at the latter sort that she'd met several of her serious boyfriends. It was there that she'd made a number of bad mistakes, both with her own heart, and the hearts of others.

Having talked to several young men and young women, and having learned principally about regional irritations with a plague on *Tristan* that was currently stifling travel and trade, she started looking for people she knew, and that was when she saw Belit.

The commander of the Red Guard wasn't wearing armor. Aimee wasn't sure why that surprised her. The warrior wore a gold gown tailored for her, and fitting her dark skin and gold eyes to perfection, yet still she seemed dissonant standing there, and it took Aimee a moment to realize that this was because she stood alone. Wherever she stepped, the crowd naturally parted about her, taking note. The commander's social presence had a physical element that made most step back, for fear of being in a space that was inviolate.

She caught sight of Aimee and smiled approvingly with a nod of her head. Grinning, Aimee strode up to her. "You look amazing, commander," she said.

"It is not my usual, I confess," Belit said warmly, "but once in a while, when occasion provides the opportunity, I am glad to take advantage. Are you here with your crew?"

"Some of them," Aimee answered. "The sociable ones, in any case. You?"

The swordswoman scanned the crowd, and spoke more quietly. "I'm here on Pentus's invitation, giving several of my people a night off to enjoy themselves. I think it's working. As for myself…" She shook her head with a light, self-deprecating laugh. "I am content to observe. To just see and be seen. My life is complicated enough without worrying about attachments."

Aimee nodded slowly, but couldn't help follow the woman's gaze across the floor to where Viltas's son stood talking with one of Pentus's subordinates. Vallus was dressed in gray and green, his boyishly handsome face relatively unornamented, and his kind eyes alight with the conversation he was having.

"Would it be rude," Aimee finally said, "if I asked you what the story with young Lord Vallus is? I don't mean to pry, but the two of you seem very fond of each other."

Belit's smile was wry. "Ah, unfair," she said. "When we were younger, he liked to escape the higher levels and explore the rest of *Iseult*, and I was always getting into trouble. We became friends from different worlds, and briefly… more. But then I was taken on by the Red Guard, and relationships for those who guard the captain are… dangerous. I ended it, and I do not think he has forgiven me. Vallus is a dreamer. He sees the best in people, even unto denial of their worst qualities, and he believes there is no obstacle sufficient devotion cannot overcome. He is a rare man, to have survived as long as he has in politics while remaining that way."

Aimee smiled softly. Her own amorous history was a patchwork of errors, passions, and silly mistakes, but for all that, as she regarded the woman before her, she knew she was recognizing the real thing. "You don't hide your feelings well," she said quietly.

Belit gave a single, amused laugh. "There is no need. Reality is what it is. We are who we are. I'm sure you know something of that."

That caught her just a little off guard. "Hmm?" she said. "Oh, no. Honestly, my own history is mostly knowing what I wanted and going and getting it. I didn't leave anything unfinished behind me, though my last boyfriend might disagree." His name was Tad, short for Tadreth. They'd dated in her final year at the academy, and for a brief time been the proverbial *it* couple of her graduating class. The breakup hadn't been perfect, but from the start she'd been clear with him about her goals in life.

Apparently he'd harbored the thought that he could change her mind. He'd been wrong.

Belit's brow furrowed as if momentarily surprised. "Not exactly what I meant, but... ah, here comes our mutual friend."

"What?" Aimee turned. Elias Leblanc descended the stairs. She'd seen him dressed up before, of course, at the reception for Amut's funeral, but this was different. He'd cleaned up. He wore a long coat of black and green, with minor accents of gold thread. Beneath was a black shirt and an ascot of burgundy silk at his neck. Black breeches, and knee-high boots polished to mirror shine. He'd trimmed his beard down and his short hair was wavy and well managed.

Oh. Aimee's brows drew together in consternation. Her mouth hung briefly open before she remembered to close it. That was different.

He paused at the middle of the stairwell, his left hand resting on the pommel of the sword he still wore, and his green eyes swept the room with a disarming self-consciousness. Aimee shifted from foot to foot, at once acutely aware of her own physical senses. She pursed her lips.

"He cleans up well," Belit said, a slightly smug amusement in her voice. Aimee shot the other woman an arched eyebrow, catching the faintest of insinuations. She was about to raise an objection to the unsaid implication, but found herself pausing and thinking instead. "Well," she said. "He's always been handsome, so it's not really–"

She turned back to her previous line of sight. Elias had spotted her across the crowd. His green eyes met hers, and turning towards her, he *smiled*.

"–Surprising–" she coughed awkwardly "–is it?"

She'd never seen that smile before. Broad. Honest. Wide and intelligent and boyish. She felt her forehead tense in consternation. Her face flushed, and her heart pounded in her ears.

He gave a nod of his head and started towards them. Aimee's composure all at once found itself fighting a losing tactical action against a rising swell of stomach butterflies. She didn't have time to process all of her reactions, or the sudden and abrupt response, every bit as intense as it had been in her cabin doorway a few days ago... but one thought passed through her mind as she tried to settle herself: that smile was going to be a *problem*.

As he wove through the crowd towards them, her head suddenly started ringing with quotes from dozens of old romantic etiquette books her old charm school teachers had made her read. Outdated and boorish, but somehow – inexplicably – now running roughshod through her head. *"A proper Lady,"* went one of the obnoxious snippets, *"always lets the gentleman speak first."*

And for some unfathomable reason, doing the exact opposite of the script suddenly seemed very important.

Instead she walked towards him, and let herself smile. It came much more readily than she'd expected. Bold. She had to be the opposite of what the books suggested. *Why?* Never mind that. "Elias Leblanc," she chided. "It is *entirely* unfair of you to hide that level of composed spitshine from me up until now."

He was caught off-guard by that. A small part of her reveled in the triumph.

"Thank Rachim," he said, with a small smile after glancing down in response to her gesture. "He insisted I go to a tailor, else I might shame him with my sackcloth and rags." Before she could counter, he looked up at her again and said, "You look lovely."

Dammit. She laughed to toss off the sudden swell of nerves and hopefully suppress the flush she felt in her cheeks. The confusing implications of *that* reaction were too much to unpack. Instead, she offered him her arm and stepped up beside him. "Well," she said, with a clearing of her throat to brush off the butterflies, "if you're going to be like that, then I must *insist* you accompany me. Someone has to protect your innocence."

Elias responded seamlessly, almost reflexively. Her hand came to rest on his upper arm. That was a mistake. "Such a gentleman," she covered with a bright smile. "Yes, I can't let you out of my sights. The women here will devour you alive."

He flashed a sideways smile at her, full of a mirth and warmth that seemed to drive aside the pain and uncertainty she was used to seeing, even if just a little. "Miss Laurent," he said, mockingly formal, "I appreciate your concern, but I'm far from helpless."

She raised her eyebrows, cocking her head to the side. Not so shrinking and unassuming then, eh? This was fun. "Oh no, *Miss Laurent* is what my teachers called me, and my mother when she was angry. Aimee. Always. Yes?"

"Aimee," he agreed. She bit her lip. Letting him say that had been a mistake.

Three more steps, and they were with Belit again.

"Teacher," Elias said with a polite nod of his head and a smile.

"*Junk ritter*," Belit said approvingly. "You've been appropriated."

"Excuse me," Aimee said, "I am saving him from the perils of the room."

"Clearly," Belit said, a smile still playing across her face. "I commend your wealth of virtue," she teased. "And self-knowledge."

"I don't mind," Elias answered smoothly. "I wouldn't say I'm helpless, but it's an awfully big room, and a great many people, and there are a great many things I am having to relearn." Again, the warm, amused smile.

"Besides, she's been in my corner longer than anyone else in my life."

Something about the way he said the words made her pause. The complete candor. Aimee wasn't certain for a moment whether to feel honored or as if her heart would break. "I could not be otherwise," she said, and wondered at the vehemence of her sincerity.

He looked at her again, level gaze intent. She averted her eyes and instead reached up to correct an imperfection in how his ascot was arranged. "Hold still," she murmured. "And don't fuss."

She didn't have to look up at him again – thank the gods – because the lights abruptly dimmed, save for those at the top of the staircase, as Pentus appeared in the company of a cadre of white-clad bodyguards, his hands spread wide like a conductor, quelling the mass murmuring of the crowd before beginning a grand orchestral movement. The duke of the midlevels was resplendent in red, his white hair knotted behind his painted face, and elaborate silver threadwork spiraling across his velvet coat and black gloves. At length, the crowd quieted, and the three of them watched as their host addressed his captive audience.

"In my birth land," he began, "we have a saying: let no unkindness pass between those who break bread and dance together. *Iseult* is my adopted home, and I have found its hospitality no less fervent than my birthplace. Aristocrat, enlisted, lifelong native or recent immigrant, we are, all of us alike, souls bound to the infinite heavens by our blessed Maiden as she sails the skies. The guild holds our mandate, yes, and the houses of trade blow the winds upon which we fly, but *Iseult* is our *home*, and in the wake of our dear captain's loss we find ourselves divided. It has been said, I know, that I intend this night as advertisement for my candidacy to take our departed Amut's place. Let me correct this presumption on two fronts: first, that our captain can *be* replaced. And second, that I would buy your love with feasts. No such ploy. This night, my brothers and sisters, is *yours*. Revel, dance, drink, and find solace in one another once again, beneath our landless stars."

A chorus of cheers broke out from among the assembled crowd. Aimee allowed herself a small clap. The speech hadn't been that bad, honestly, though some of the motives were paper thin. *This is not a bribe, here, enjoy it.*

Right.

"If I may have a moment?" Elias said, then added, "Wait here," before stepping away. The orchestra struck up a tune once more, and the crowd began to move towards the edges of the room to give their fellows space to dance freely.

"How exactly can I protect you if you walk away?" Aimee teased him.

"A moment only!" Elias promised, bowing and smiling with a hint of mischief before he slipped into the masses.

"He's temperamental," Belit mused.

"Two people at any given time," she said. Then, looking at the other woman, said "You know, yes?"

A solemn nod followed, then Belit said, "Yes, but you've got it wrong. There's only one man in there, and the memory of wrongs done."

"Belit," a voice said, and turning, Aimee saw Vallus standing before them. A small smile was on his face as he offered his hand.

The commander of the Red Guard looked completely caught off guard. "Val," she said.

"Please," Viltas's son said earnestly. "Don't mistake this for duplicity on my part. I don't want to talk you out of anything. But if I didn't ask you to dance tonight, I would never forgive myself."

Momentarily at a loss for words, Belit watched the eyes of the young diplomat, then, at length, the veneer of cool composure cracked for just a moment, revealing the smallest of girlish grins. "Very well, young man," she said with a faint, teasing formality, "I will humor you. I expect your best, however. It's been years since we taught each other. Show me no rust."

Vallus grinned as if he'd found the key to the legendary treasures of the Varengard Library. "You have my word, Bel. I shall not disappoint."

Hand in hand, the two stepped into the whirling mass of dancers, and Belit shot a look behind where the sorceress stood. "This is your fault, *junk ritter*," she said. "I will not forget."

Aimee looked back, and there Elias stood, his hands clasped behind his back, and a supremely satisfied smile on his face. "I hope not, teacher."

Dancers swirled past them like tufts of multicolored cloud beneath the dimmed lights. Elias stood beside her, watching as the couple spun away into the crowd. "Sneaky," Aimee remarked.

"Impulsive," Elias agreed. "Perhaps nothing will come of it, but it was *right there*. Just a little push, and something rather nice happens."

Aimee gave him a sideways smile, remembering how he'd spoken of training and impulses tied up with imperatives for which he no longer had any use. "Finding a better use for that social training, are we?"

He smiled as he watched the pair dancing. "I was taught to read people so I could manipulate or kill them," he said. "I like this better." Then, looking back at her, he seemed to remember something, and produced a small blue budded rose from somewhere, and gently slipped the stem into her hair behind her ear. "Forgive me," he said. "It seemed appropriate."

Bold. The impulse boiled up from her, and she stepped in front of him, extending her hand. "Elias Leblanc, if you're going to go and talk like that, I am afraid I must *insist* that you dance with me. For your own protection."

The warmth of his smile reached his eyes, and his calloused hand closed over her fingers as he gave a gentle bow at the waist. "Who am I," he said, "to refuse such a demand?"

Mine, she selfishly thought, without regard to how it sounded in her mind. *At least for the next little while.*

His other hand came to rest on her hip, and suddenly they were off, spinning through the dancers. "Any luck reading the room?" he asked. A reference, she at once remembered, to the reception after Amut's funeral, when the two of them had identified the major power players with whom they now contended.

"As it happens, yes," Aimee said. She liked that he remembered. "Of the people in this room, perhaps half actively support one of the three candidates, and of these, Diara and Pentus together command a smaller share each than Yaresh, though together it is bigger."

They turned, and his hand left her hip to turn her.

She stepped deftly, then moved back into hold. "Diara is *slightly* more popular than Pentus, but nobody will admit it."

"And the other half?" Elias asked. There was an amused look in his eyes.

"Debauched and bored," Aimee said. "Afraid because they know somebody killed their captain, and glad to have a night of distraction."

A wry look briefly crossed his handsome face as they turned again, footwork in sync, steps sure and careful mirrors across the marble tiles. "I can't say I blame them," he said. "It feels as if we know almost less now than when we started."

The slight break in his eyes, the look of guilt over perceived failures opening a door to so much worse, pulled a reply out of her, reflexive. She didn't realize that she was touching his face until she'd already done it. "We know the monster's name," she said, "if not the mask he wears, and the names of his servants. We've saved lives, even if it wasn't all of them. We've blunted the ambitions of a would-be dictator, and found allies and friends in a strange place."

His eyes closed at her touch, and she felt him take a deep breath, as if all the pieces of the broken man were straining to keep themselves together. "Elias," she said quietly. "We've had wins. More wins than losses, so far. So please, take them, and don't blame yourself. More than a few were because of you."

They'd stopped dancing, and moved just off to the side as she'd spoken. Out of the corner of her eye, she glimpsed a reflection of the two of them in a mirror panel on the wall. The flower that he had placed in her hair added the smallest accent to her outfit, the one that had been missing at the start of the night.

Perfect.

The lights had further dimmed, and a silver light from above lined his face like the moon from behind a cloud. Then he glanced up, and her gaze followed.

Looking up, Aimee saw a wild starscape spread out above them: a limitless field of diamonds in a whirling mass of black silk. *Iseult* had positioned itself so as not to be beneath any of the other behemoths in the flotilla, and now they had an unhindered view of stars without number in the vast night sky. She sucked in a breath at the unfurling majesty of it, the beauty, and allowed herself to be captivated. This was what she'd set out for, in part, cast herself on the winds of the infinite skies. This vision: surpassing in its loveliness. There was no way to see stars like this at home.

"I wish," Elias said quietly, face inches from her own, "that I had been able to appreciate sights like this the last time I saw them."

Aimee turned her head to look up at him, and gave his hand a squeeze. They were still in hold, and *very* close. "Appreciate them now."

He tilted his head down at her as they stood together under a thousand jewels in a glimmering black. Their eyes met, and all of her previous assurances that this was nothing seemed to melt. No platitude came forth, only a burning, intense look, and three words said quietly enough that only she could hear.

"I will remember."

Her hands slipped from the hold to the lapel of his coat. A whirl of talk was happening around her, but it was mostly drowned out by the sudden intensity of her focus on the tiny details. There were flecks of darker green in his eyes, and a hint of dark circles about them. Why had she never noticed that before? *The last time I was this close,* she remembered, *I wasn't thinking.*

You're not thinking now, her mind chided her. But in a sudden flash, she didn't care. She didn't know what was about to happen, but quietly, she mused, part of her *really* wanted to.

"Aimee!"

Vlana's words cut across her thoughts, and the world slammed back into focus. Aimee and Elias leaped apart. Abruptly, a part of her was suddenly cognizant of the social dynamics aboard *Elysium*, and she tried to muster a mental defense against an assailment of accusatory questions... but it wasn't what Vlana said. No sooner had she arrived than the words from her mouth shattered the mood and cut through Aimee with sudden fear.

"Aimee, Elias," Vlana said, out of breath. "Harkon is *gone.*"

Elias's hand suddenly gripped her shoulder. "What's that?" he said, quietly, urgently. Aimee followed his long arm, pointing to a place outside the dome, where sudden bursts of multicolored light were flashing across the night sky at irregular intervals. The fear that had just seized Aimee surged as amidst the intermittent flashes, a familiar, cyclopean eye of light erupted, then flashed closed again with a concussive force that shook the deck beneath their feet. Another followed, and louder. The music stopped, and everyone was now looking at the explosive light show in the sky. "We need to find cover, *right now,*" Aimee said, pulling both of them along with her. "And find Clutch. It's a portal storm. This is about to get very, *very* bad."

They didn't get to the doorway before another random portal exploded into the heavens, much closer this time, ripping across the sky and silhouetting another behemoth. The ship rocked visibly in the sky. The deafening concussive crash came a half second later, and high above their heads, Aimee watched as a crack zigzagged down the center of the dome. A large piece of glass shook loose, split apart. A hail of knives rained down. Without thinking she lunged forward. Her hands whipped through the gestures of the shield spell, widening it, thickening it, and with the releasing word a glimmering disc of translucent force flashed from one end of the room to the other, catching the fragments. The force of the spell's size and scale drove her to her knees and she grunted with the strain.

"Don't just stand there!" she shouted at the people nearest to her. "Clear the dome! Get out, *now!*"

She caught sight of the others running towards her. The crack in the dome had destabilized the entire roof of the structure, and it groaned, now, with the strain of its own collapsing weight. She forced herself onto one knee – thank the gods she'd chosen a dress she could move in – and tried to push the shield up. She almost had it. The room was emptying of people. Yaresh shouted at a far wall and ushered people through doors. She glimpsed Pentus at the top of the stairwell, looking over his shoulder before fleeing after someone, shouting, "Wait!"

She just had to hold it up for a few more seconds. Let the last of the stragglers out. A fraction remained. More pieces shook loose, striking her spell. She felt the impact jar through her limbs, and shouted in defiance and pain.

High overhead, another crash sounded. Aimee's face drained of color as the fresh eye of a new, *massive* portal tore open right overhead and swallowed the sky. She heard someone shout her name, had just enough time to feel the first hint of terror.

The blast hammered down at them, and the whole dome *shattered*. Aimee screamed as a rain of debris smashed into her shield, covered it, overwhelmed it. She felt her fingers tingle as the magic started to give way and death hammered down. *No*.

An arm seized her around the waist. She felt a surge of magic, and Elias was moving, blindingly fast, carrying her and Vlana at once. Massive glass shards exploded all around them.

They skidded to a stop in the street. People fled in every direction, order replaced with chaos. Vlana staggered, and Elias caught his balance on a lamppost as he stopped. All Aimee could do was stare upwards, at the still-blazing portal in the skies. They felt a shift beneath their feet, and tension groaned along the spine of the ship as its rear engines blasted to full burn. The wheelhouse was attempting to pull the behemoth away from the portal, she realized. The strain of the blazing engines against its pull set the entire ship to groaning in the black, and at the stern end, Aimee could see an apocalyptic glow as the exhaust vents blasted the full power of its multiple metadrives into the heavens. Aimee watched, helpless in the moment to affect the tremendous forces warring against one another in the sky. "Come on," she pleaded, hands balled into fists as the fierce wind tore her hair loose. *Why isn't the portal closing?*

"It shouldn't still be open!" she shouted over her shoulder at the others. "Portal storm apertures don't last this long!"

Slowly the direction was reversing. The ship was pulling away. "We need to get back to *Elysium*!" Vlana screamed. Across the streets, Clutch came running towards them. "Get your asses back to the villa, *now!* Wait, where's Hark?"

Before anyone could answer, the entire ship shook and the sound of a muffled detonation sounded somewhere deep under their feet. Aimee felt the whole vessel lurch, and looking sternward again, watched as the glow of the exhaust vents suddenly dulled. A moment before pulling away, with an oddly quiet creak, *Iseult* began to fall towards the portal.

"Clutch is right," Aimee shouted. "Run! If we're outside when the ship goes through that thing, we might never be found!"

They fled. Across city streets, as the baleful glowing eye painted everything a kaleidoscope of reds and purples. The fitful roar of the struggling engines filled Aimee's ears as they tore over the streets towards the nearest building they could find. She felt the thrum of terrible interdimensional magics overpowering her ability to sense anything else. Elias reached the door and tore it open with a surge of strength. "GET INSIDE!" he screamed. Aimee looked over her shoulder as the rear of the ship entered the portal. A wall of blazing chaos-light surged up the street behind them. She dove through the door after all the others and landed on her back. Her hands furiously filled the doorway with a shield spell. The light washed over their sanctuary, and everything was noise. She held onto her spell with every ounce of will, as the chaos outside fought to get in. Her teeth set. Sweat stained the back of her neck, and she strained.

I am a portalmage.

I am a portalmage.

I AM A PORTALMAGE!

The last thing Aimee remembered was screaming against the black.

She was in a place that was dark and cold. A dim awareness of rushing sights and sounds came to her, visions in an ocean of mist. Her mind reeled in the fog of her senses, unable to form coherent thoughts. Somewhere under it all, she heard a faint music.

"You are alright," she heard a voice say, and turning, Aimee beheld the Oracle, resplendent in a nimbus of light. "This is a place between. You remember your dimensional principles."

"In a portal," Aimee replied, half to herself, "time behaves differently."

"And you are behind a shield spell, not within the safety of a skyship with its chaos dampeners," the Oracle answered. "In a few moments, it will end, but I can reach you here. Now. Your teacher is in terrible danger. All of you are, and it falls to you to save them all."

In the distance, Aimee heard yelling. She turned, and a figure of mist faded from view.

"*I'm sorry,*" a familiar voice wept from the misty form of a cloaked figure at the edge of the bed. "*I am so sorry, I had no choice.*"

"*You...*" the bedridden figure croaked. "*You let... him...*"

"Not fast enough, Amut. Not fast enough."

"Aimee," the Oracle's voice was growing fainter. "He is here! Hold on. Hold on!"

Her teacher's face formed in the mist. Harkon seemed to see her, and she heard his voice echoing from far away, only every few words legible. *"...Never ended... Mask of flesh!"*

Aimee swept her hand towards the apparition. It dissolved, and in its place suddenly rose a towering, robed figure. Its cowled head turned towards her, an empty darkness in place of a face fixed upon her, and a sepulchral, hissing voice rasped at her in the darkness. "WHERE IS THE LION?"

Nothing again. Then a tiny ray of light. Slow, creeping awareness of her own body. She heard her breathing coming in a slow, even rhythm. The light became a warm glow. Then coalesced into a fire burning in a hearth. She blinked several times. Warm bedclothes. A canopied bed frame around her. Slowly, she stirred, only to wince at the familiar sensation of overclocking exhaustion.

It took her a few more moments to muster the energy to move again, and she sat up. She wore full-length pajamas, warm and comfortable, and a cursory touch told her that her hair was in the same disheveled state it had been when she fled the dome. The logs in the hearth snapped beneath the flames.

In a chair on the other side of the room, slumped against the wall, was Elias. He was still dressed in his Grand Ball outfit, though his left arm was tucked inside his coat, wrapped in a sling. There were bandages on his face, and his right hand had a death-grip on the hilt of his drawn sword resting across his lap. A faint glow emanated from the blade. His eyes were closed, and his chest rose and fell with the lilt of a light sleep.

When she cleared her throat, he opened his eyes. His eyes fixed on her, and a series of emotions passed through them, too quick to read. "I promise," he started to say. "All I did was carry you back–"

She was slightly taken aback at the bluntness of the concern. *It's fine*, she meant to say, but when she opened her mouth, the sound was a croak that immediately degenerated into a coughing fit. Instead she rasped, "Water."

He was by her side quickly, handing her a glass. Once her throat was soothed and she could talk again, she sank back. "Gods," she murmured, closing her eyes. "Alright, so we're clearly at Rachim's. Yes?"

"We are," he replied.

"How long?" she asked.

"Better part of a day," Elias said. He straightened back up, putting the glass on a bedside table. "Your spell held just long enough, and when we came out the other side, we brought you here. Rachim had access only to chirurgery, so it was mostly about making sure you got water in you and were still breathing." He sighed. The sound was labored. Weighted. "Others weren't so lucky."

He looked down at her for a moment, silhouetted by the firelight. There was an unease, a reservation in his eyes.

"You're not telling me everything," she said, gentle, but blunt. "Please. I know the danger of a portal storm, and if it's been a day, Clutch will have done her calculations. She's too smart not to. Where are we?"

Elias looked back at her. His expression assessed her for a moment, and she was struck by how often she'd seen that look on men's faces before they told her she needed to rest first, calm first, eat first, get her head on straight, settle her nerves, do literally anything but hear the truth when she wanted to hear it.

"We're in the Tempest Crescent," he said, unflinchingly honest. "And as soon as you think you can move on your own, we need you: Harkon is still missing."

CHAPTER FIFTEEN
DEEPER INTO NIGHT

"You should wait longer," Bjorn grunted. "This is too quick."

"I can't, you heard what Vant said," Elias answered, buckling his sword about his waist. "The explosion was deep within *Iseult*. Combined with what we've heard from the downlevelers, that means the metadrive chamber. We're going, before things get worse."

It was a small group of them. Vant, Aimee, Elias. Belit and Rachim. In the twenty-four hours since the portal had thrown them into the Tempest Crescent, the ship had already started to fracture. There was havoc below, he was hearing. Pentus hadn't been seen since he fled the Grand Ball. Diara was struggling with her fellow astronomers to help the wheelhouse put *Iseult* back on course but – a quick communication Rachim had been sent revealed – they couldn't do that until they knew what had happened in the metadrive chamber, and communication with it had been lost.

And Yaresh was only concerned with rallying his armsmen – and those officers who would listen – to maintain the ironclad security of the upper level.

Elias grabbed one of the packs that the older warrior had assembled from *Elysium*'s emergency supplies, testing his left arm, feeling functional again after Aimee had mended the broken bone. It was still tender, but it would have to do. "We're going."

A small smile creased the corner of Bjorn's mouth as Elias shouldered his pack and headed towards the ramp. "Elias," he said, and that made the young knight stop. Bjorn seldom – if ever – used his name. He turned his head, watching the old mercenary he'd once nearly killed, and since fought beside, standing in the dark behind him.

"I don't know if the others'll come around. They're stubborn, see? Been hurt. We all come from bad places of one sort or another. So... I'm sorry, for not seeing at the outset that you're no different than the rest of us. So you fucking take care of yourself out there, aye boy? No more walking to the edge. No more knives in your hand. You're one of us."

A wave of emotion washed over Elias. He swallowed, unsure of how to process it. There was no answer in the well of his mind, save the echo of a simple lullaby and the repetition of six words. *Noble and brave. Gentle and kind.*

"Thank you," he said. "For everything."

Then he headed down the ramp and through the main foyer of Rachim's home. As he crossed the landing pad, he caught a glimpse of the cold stars in the skies. The last time he'd been here, it had been as a shivering child. Evil memories crept across his mind like cold fingers in the dark. His hand reflexively gripped the hilt of his sword. How many other children without number were about to be exposed to what he'd seen in the cold darkness of his nightmares?

None, he thought resolutely. *Not if I have any say in it.*

He was the last one to get there. Just outside the doorway to the streets, Aimee stood with Rachim examining a map. Vant was dressed in his leathers, his shock-sticks hanging from his hip. Rachim was wearing mail and a breastplate, and for the first time since Elias had seen him, carried a gilded black hammer at his waist and a heavy matchlock on his opposite hip.

Aimee herself wore her field gear: blue coat, knee-high boots, and fingerless gloves. Her hair was pulled away from her face, and the expression she wore – though tired – was like steel. "We can't rely on the railcars," she said.

"No," Rachim said. "According to my sources they're down between here and the midship aperture. But obviously there's still power below, or we'd be in for a hell of a worse time."

To fall forever. The fate of skyships that dropped from the heavens was the stuff of terrifying stories, as was the eternal dark that waited below. Even mentioning it on an airborne vessel was considered taboo.

"What's the status of the streets?" Elias asked, stepping into the conversation. The others looked at him, and this time he received a chorus of nods. Fear made allies of the suspicious very quickly. *"It's only your strength they value,"* that niggling, vicious voice whispered in his mind. Elias didn't dignify it with an answer.

"So far, aside from cleanup efforts and rescue efforts, clean," Rachim answered. "Not as much rubble as feared, either. They build most structures on the upper levels squat and broad for a reason." He turned back to Aimee. "But if we can reach the aperture on foot, a working railcar should be findable. Belit sent word that we'd find her and her people there, as well."

"Then let's get moving," Aimee said, seeming to square her shoulders and push aside her weariness. As Elias watched, she stepped into the role of leader, and took the reins firmly in hand. *Good,* he thought. *Hold them tight, and we may yet weather this.*

It was not the first time that Elias had walked through the ruins of a once-wealthy city. The crumbled, battered fronts, scarred buildings, and blasted statues were all nauseatingly familiar sights, and conjured the ghostly specter not only of burned and blasted Port Providence, but of other times, earlier, when he had walked beside Lord Roland through shattered neighborhoods as the accounters took their blood-money measurements. *"This is the natural order,"* his old teacher's words echoed in his mind. *"The weak grow decadent and fat, and exercise their forceful decree, but inevitably, nature seeks a redressing of balance, and we, enforcers of its law of strength, come to collect what is due. This is the way of the world, writ in purest form."*

Elias stepped over the smashed face of a statue, and through the hazy memory of evil men and their evil words. *My one-time master,* he thought. *How utterly wrong you were.*

It was not the first time Elias had seen this, but it was the first time he had nothing to do with it.

It took clambering over a few rubble piles to reach the first stop in their route, but when they arrived at the aperture's edge, Belit awaited them. Her red armor had sustained a few scars, and her face bore signs of recent magical healing, but she looked resolute, and whole, if tired. Next to her was her second-in-command, Hakat.

The barrel-chested, bald-pated warrior wore a similar longsword to his superiors, and his armor was a darker shade of red. He favored the group with a nod as they approached.

"I don't know what we're going to find down there," Belit said candidly. "But I *do* know that there have been violent scuffles in the area. A servant fleeing upwards from the lower levels just after we came through the portal said that she'd heard the sounds of gunfire and weapons clashing, a short time before the explosion. I choose to believe the chamber hasn't fallen. If it had, more would have certainly gone wrong than has. Are you ready?"

"Born that way," Aimee said with a fierce energy. "Rachim has brought ten of his best armsmen–" She gestured to the armed, armor-clad men with their short-swords and flame-projectors who were walking behind their host. "Elias you know, and Vant has metadrive expertise, in the event that people down there are dead."

"The gods save us," Belit said, "if that is the case. Come. *Iseult* is in need."

The elevator still worked, but they only got halfway down its path before it let them out at an earlier stop, and a quick glance at the ceiling above showed them why. Beyond the catwalk onto which the group stepped, the rail high above had been physically blasted apart, and its tangled wreckage hung out into the cavernous interior of the ship, shedding sparks into the darkness. As Elias watched, he saw the lights constantly flickering on and off on some levels, and utterly shut down on others. It was worse, then, than Rachim had thought. Much worse.

"Shit," Aimee swore.

"I know the way from here," Belit said. "Follow."

The walk was long and arduous, past apartments that had emptied, store fronts ravaged by explosions, and dark windows from which Elias occasionally saw frightened eyes peeking past threadbare curtains. One or two glances told him everything he needed to know: these people had seen recent violence.

When they turned a corner and came into sight of the great wall of the metadrive chamber, he glimpsed the first real sign of the aftermath. There were corpses all around the foot of the wall with its innumerable prayer notes. When they reached the first, Elias paused to kneel and examine a black-robed figure that had been carrying a makeshift cudgel made of a long broom-haft capped by an unstable power source from a shock-stick. The dead man wore a crude mask that was supposed to seem like an opaque face, and stripping it off, Elias stared into the dead grimace of an utterly ordinary, half-starved, gaunt man.

Well-fed, well-treated people who felt they had a wealth of options weren't likely to join apocalypse cults. This man had been killed by some sort of high-powered magical discharge that had put a hole the size of two fists through the center of his chest. As the others fanned out, he rose and walked to examine another, much the same as the last, and another still.

"Eyes open," he said to the others. "There's either a sorcerer inside, or someone packing some impressive firepower."

Aimee rose from where she'd inspected another corpse. "It looks as though they threw themselves at the chamber," she said. "Probably in waves, given how many of them there are… and the people within boarded themselves up."

Elias followed the aim of her hand to where the doors they'd passed through mere days before were now more barricade than entryway. "So then," he answered, "the question is who's in there now, and will they talk to us?"

"I heard the downlevelers were rioting," an armsman said behind them.

"Trashing their own living space," another affirmed. "Maybe Yaresh was right about bringing order to this wretched place."

"Shut up, both of you," Rachim snapped. "These corpses are cultists, you damned fools."

"Don't. Move."

Elias slowly looked in the direction the new voice had come from. A figure approached from the far end of the wall, dressed in the dirty, stained uniform of one of the enlisted. There was soot on his brown face, and in his hands he held a large, chrome-plated weapon that glowed at the end of an aperture mangled by its last discharge. Elias's eyes widened. He knew *exactly* what that thing was.

"Put that damn thing down, Enlisted," the second armsman snapped and leveled his shock-spear at the newcomer.

"I wouldn't point that at him," Elias said, flashing the armsman a look that stopped him in his tracks. "That's a mystic force projector." All eyes were suddenly on Elias, who held up his hands to show their lack of weapons. "It looks homemade, which says a few things about the genius of the man carrying it. It also needs to recharge for at least twenty seconds between each shot," he said.

"But one shot," the newcomer said, "will obliterate the target and everything else within a fifteen-foot radius. So I repeat. Don't. Move. There are more of us, and we hold this chamber. You're not touching the Maiden's Heart."

"Dammit boy," Rachim snapped, "do you not understand that we're here to help you?"

"No," Belit said, in a tone that shut down further argument. "He doesn't. Look at him, Lord Rachim – no, really, look at him. He's half-starved and looks like he's been fighting for days. Tell your frightened warriors to lower their weapons. This man isn't our enemy."

She stepped more fully into the light cast from the cracks in the barricade. "Do you know who I am?" she asked.

The young man hesitated, then nodded. "Belit of the Red Guard."

"That I am," she said, her arms spread wide. "And this is Aimee de Laurent of the skyship *Elysium* and her companions. You don't have to give up your weapon. Just lower it and let us come inside. We're here to help. Can you tell us what happened?"

"Don't fully know," the man said after a second, though he seemed to relax, just a little. "We saw the explosion from three levels down. Purple fire belched out of every hole, and the power was cut to our entire level. Enforcers started going nuts, confining people to their quarters. Didn't work. Then we heard the shouting and the screaming and cut loose. Got up here in time to find them–" he gestured at the corpses "–throwing themselves at the doorways. Killed a bunch of 'em, then it became clear no help was coming, so we–" he paused again "– used some of the spare bits they've got inside to put together a few of these. A warning: there are fifty of us. We've already restored a measure of power to some of the lower levels, and kept more of these robed bastards from slipping in. Any funny business, and you're all gonna fry."

"No funny business," Aimee said, with a shake of her head as she stepped forward.

"I'm a metadrive engineer," Vant said. "Whatever's happened in there, if I can get a look at it, I may be able to help."

Elias spoke up last, adding his voice with a question nobody else had asked. "What's your name?"

The enlisted man looked between the group of them, then slowly lowered his weapon. "There's seven more of these trained on you right now. The armsmen and the aristocrat stay out here, where maybe they can help fend off another attack, if they're sincere. The rest of you... you can come in, but only if you can *fix* this mess." At the last he looked at Elias. "My name is Jerich. Junior sanitation."

"You have my word," Belit said, as an aperture appeared in the barricade, many organized hands quickly moving debris to allow entry into the interior of the chamber. "We will do our utmost to fix this."

As the group slipped through the entryway one by one, Elias heard the same, bewildered armsman say to himself, "they told us the lower levels were rioting."

Jerich rolled his eyes. "Sure they did," he grunted as Elias walked past him. "That's what they always say."

The interior of the metadrive chamber was chaos. The purple lights of the main core and its secondary supports still filled the room, but all around the floor, wires were twisted, cables smashed and frayed. A great shower of sparks occasionally disgorged itself from somewhere high above, and it was looking in that direction that showed Elias what had happened to lay *Iseult* so terribly low.

The first secondary metadrive core of *Iseult* had been completely destroyed. The translucent cylinder was smashed open midway up its length, acrid smoke still leaking from its now-dark interior. Whatever had destroyed it had shifted the entire thing in its frame, and it now sat, a leaning, broken pillar capped with mangled wires and ruined enchantments, forcing its burden on the remaining cores in the semicircle. Each of these gave off an uncomfortable heat that Elias recognized all too well as being a sign that the entire chamber was dangerously destabilized.

The group was immediately greeted by a host of hungry faces of a dozen different shades. Dirty enlisted uniforms were worn, or, in several cases, stained nightclothes or off-duty casual clothing. Makeshift weapons were in evidence: tools repurposed for defense mostly, including several shock-sticks homemade from spare parts... But here and there Elias saw a sword, mace, or truncheon taken from a foolish enforcer. Along the far wall, behind *Iseult*'s prime metadrive core, a number of bodies had been laid in state. Elias felt his heart sink: a large number of them wore the uniforms of *Iseult*'s metadrive attendants and engineers.

"My gods," Belit said as they stepped fully into the chamber. "What happened here?"

"I'll let the chief explain," Jerich said. "He's over there. We've done what we could, but we're not sure how much longer he's going to last."

No, Elias thought. They were led forward, through a parting crowd of determined, tired faces, to where Chief Engineer Hephus lay at the foot of *Iseult*'s prime metadrive core. The soul of the Maiden herself. His back was propped up against the base of the platinum pyramid, and there were blankets over his legs, but the bindings about his middle were stained a red that bordered on black, and his face was the color of ash and milk. Only by the steady rise and fall of his chest did Elias discern that he was still alive. Aimee walked past them without thinking, jogging to the engineer's side. On the opposite side, one of his subordinates was holding his hand, trying to get his superior to drink some water from a battered tin flask.

"I promise," Aimee said with quiet certainty to the other man. "I have some skill at healing magic. I won't hurt him. Just let me look."

Hephus stirred as she crouched beside him, and his eyes slowly opened. "Should've," he croaked past dry lips, "should've... seen them coming. Didn't... didn't think they were that... desperate."

"It's alright, chief," the junior engineer said. "It wasn't your fault. It wasn't your fault."

"He was worse when we found him," Jerich explained. "Don't think the initial explosion did this to him... but there's only so much we could do with makeshift bandages and boiled moonshine." The bitterness in his voice was palpable.

"Not your fault either," the junior engineer said, through a lump in his throat. "They snuck some sort of makeshift bomb in here, a null-stone attached to a small charge. It destabilized the interior of the secondary core.

Started a chain reaction that would've taken more of them out. Chief Hephus jumped in. He climbed up the damn thing and manually severed the secondary core from the rest of them before it could do any more damage. He was on the way down when it... went off."

"Just... wasn't fast enough," Hephus breathed. "Too slow. Too old."

Aimee looked up at them, and Elias saw something in her face that he hadn't before: a deep, sudden pain. "Gods," she said quietly, "this is... I can't..."

"Please," the junior officer pleaded, "you said you know healing magic."

"The wound has to be properly stitched, cleaned," Aimee's voice shook. "I can... I can ease his pain, I think... but the internal damage is... it's beyond my skill."

Vant moved forward, knelt in front of the trio where they stood. Elias closed his eyes. He'd seen this before, on too many battlefields to count, and his mind took him there even as the others struggled to catch up with the implications. Healing magic, at least the basic kind, such as that Aimee knew, required chirurgery to make sure the wound was properly cleaned and stitched and everything was in its proper place, before it could accelerate the healing process. If Hephus had been hit by a powerful mystic blast to the gut, and it had gone untreated for the better part of a day...

That he was alive now was something of a miracle.

"Hephus," Vant said, and Elias recognized a gentleness in the engineer's voice that he'd never heard before. "I am Vant of the Engineers' Guild. I can finish the work. Pick up where you left off, and keep *Iseult*'s sacred heart beating, but I need to know as much of what you know as you can tell me. Are there *any* plans in this room to which I can return? Or schematics I can rely on? Tell me. Help me save the heart of your ship."

Hephus closed his eyes. Nodded slowly. Then, with great effort, he lifted a shaking hand and pointed to a central control station. "Under floor panels. Bastards demanded them. Never gave in. Use them. Use *him*." He lifted his apprentice's hand, then said to the junior, "No more secrets. They're here. They're... *beneath*. Should've *seen*."

His eyes bulged and his body convulsed. Then a terrible rattle shuddered out of the chief engineer. His head thudded back against the pedestal, and his eyes stared sightlessly up at the still-beating heart of the ship he served.

"Chief Hephus," the junior engineer murmured. "Chief Hephus. *Chief Hephus!*"

Two of the enlisted reached out and began to pull the younger man away from the corpse of his mentor. Aimee slowly rose to her feet, a new, terrible weight evident on her face when she looked at Elias, and then the others.

"Do your job," the young knight said. "His troubles are over."

"Alright, you heard the man!" Vant snapped. "Get those floorboards up under that central control station! We've got minutes, not hours!" Abruptly *Elysium*'s engineer gestured at Hephus's junior. "What's your name?"

"Nubin," the man said, barely keeping his composure. "Junior engineer, first class. I... I don't have my tattoos yet."

"And the other engineers?" Vant said. Elias detected a falling hope in his tone. The black knight looked behind the heart of *Iseult*, to the far wall, where rows of corpses were laid in state.

"Over there," Nubin said, gesturing in the same direction Elias had looked. "The robed freaks hit hard and fast, slit as many of their throats as they could, before our backup arrived."

"Of *course* they did," Vant grunted. "Fine, then it's you and me, and Jerich and the other people he brought who put together those damn weapons."

"Sir," Nubin objected, "Jerich and his companions are *enlisted*, they're not *trained*–"

Elias had never seen Vant wheel around so fast, or look so angry. The engineer's hand fisted itself in Nubin's coat collar and pulled his face down so they could speak eye to eye. "You have no choice, you arrogant prick! All your other engineers are *dead*. You have *me*, and a number of fucking *geniuses* that built powerful crowd control weapons with *spare parts*. Now follow my damn orders and *teach* them!"

Nubin's eyes flashed to Belit, and the commander of the Red Guard crossed her arms and nodded. "Do as the man says. Now."

As conversation and activity exploded around him, Elias knelt beside the corpse of the engineer, reached out, and closed his eyes.

Next to him, Aimee took a few seconds to gather herself. He caught sight of a shaking in her hands fading as her steel will reasserted itself. "Next time," she breathed, "next time I won't fail."

"You didn't," Elias replied. "Don't carry his weight. Let it go." Straightening, he fixed her with a level stare. "What's next?"

Aimee took a hard breath, and he watched as her face passed from frightened and grieving to hardened and focused. "We find out how they got in here," she said. "And if those damn symbols had anything to do with it. I'll start at one end, you start at the other. We'll meet in the middle."

They walked in opposite directions. It had been so long since Elias had used his magic in any complex way that calling the powers to mind felt sluggish, uneven. That was to be expected, of course. A muscle that went unused atrophied. Still, he had some spells for truthful sight, though none of them were as strong as what Harkon had effortlessly used. Kneeling near one of the spaces where Harkon had later indicated one of the hastily scratched symbols of the Eternal Order, Elias took a breath, reached for his power.

His head *exploded* with pain, with noise, and with discordant music. He was aware of lurching back from the wall, clutching the side of his skull with his left hand. Abruptly his vision of the room began to fall away, bisected by a tear in reality, behind which indistinct white and black shapes battled, slicing each other to ribbons and leaving streaks of red across his waking sight.

Through the chaos walked Lord Azrael, resplendent in his black and gold armor, his mocking face contemptuous and predatory. "You wretched, contemptible *worm*," his own voice snarled in his head. "No. You will *not* take what is mine from me. You will *not* restore power to this ship. You will *LISTEN TO ME*."

Elias's head felt as though it would split apart. He dropped to one knee, dimly aware of his own scream. People were moving, elsewhere, running towards him. Elias felt his right hand move against his will to grip his enchanted sword. Smoke obscured his vision, enclosing him in a darkness where he faced the dark mirror reflection of himself, and it thrust its hand into his chest. In the twin pits of Azrael's eyes, Elias glimpsed a thousand flashing images. Elias's hands were both gripping his sword as Azrael manipulated his movements. "Kill them, worm. As your master commanded you to. Kill them all."

"NO!" Elias's hands stopped moving. The sword heated in his hands.

"I am *you*," Azrael snarled back. "Do as I command." The face contorted in fury. "To have waited so long, to have patiently bided my time in the darkness, restively awaiting my revenge, and to be sent *you*? A mewling coward ashamed of what he is? IT IS GALLING."

Realization struck him at the words. "You," Elias snarled back, "are not me."

A flash, and for just a moment, Azrael's face was replaced with the leer of a rotting visage, little more than a desiccated skull fixed in a rictus scream. "Mayhap not, but you have been the slave to powerful magic before. The weakness is within you, aftereffects of whomever ruled you before." The image's face was suddenly Esric's, and its command echoed through his head like a hammer blow. "COMPLY."

The shock of the all-too-familiar word ripped through him. Elias felt his eyes flash wide, and a jolt shot from his feet to his forehead. The sword blazed white hot in his hands. "I," he heard himself say, "don't do that anymore."

He twisted free as the specter grasped at his thoughts and raked its hate across his mind, and with a shout of defiance, drove Oath of Aurum through the center of the awkwardly scratched symbol.

There was a scream, keening in his mind, then a crackle of light, and a small discharge of mystic energy that sent sparks flying across the floor.

The vision receded, but only a little. The specter still roared at the edge of Elias's mind, and he could now see the chamber again. People were moving away from him or running towards him. He heard screams, saw people pointing at him fearfully.

"Don't move!" shouted one of the men, bringing a mystic force projector to bear.

"Elias!" Aimee shouted, pushing her way through the crowd. "What the hell are you–"

"Destroy the symbols!" Elias shouted back. "Every one of them. I'll explain later, there's no time!"

"Wait," Belit said, as one of Jerich's people aimed the powerful mystic weapon at Elias. "Lower your weapon, he's not your enemy."

Elias staggered along the perimeter of the wall as the specter screamed in his mind, and began ramming the point of his sword through each, marking their intervals by sight. Each one released a small burst of light and a shower of sparks, then the voice faded further. Soon Aimee was beside him, sweeping away the illusions with repeatedly uttered spells, blasting the marks away with summoned, precision flame.

When it was done, thirteen black, burnt-out symbols clearly marked the walls in a semicircle that mirrored the metadrive cores of *Iseult*.

Elias sagged to the floor and dropped his sword, pressing his hands to an aching scalp.

"What happened?" Aimee said, kneeling beside him.

"*Junk ritter*," he heard Belit say. "You started screaming, then you looked as though you would turn on the people around us."

Elias let his head fall back against the wall. The voice was silent. After a few labored breaths, he answered in a croak. "I saw it again, the vision that wore my face. Tried to use Esric's last vestiges of control to force me to do its will. Wanted me to kill you all."

He closed his eyes. The thought of what he'd nearly done, the revelation, began to sink in. Palpable shame came in its wake, dragging his limbs down with a terrible weight. "It almost worked. It happened when I tried to use my powers. Not safe for me to do it. Not here."

Vant rallied the workers back around the broken core. As the three of them watched, they slowly detached the large cylinder from its base and lowered it to the side, before Vant began directing with broad gestures and commands. Elias reflected, as he watched and caught his breath, that *Elysium*'s engineer really was an underrated genius.

After what seemed both too little and too much time, Vant gave the command to connect two massive cables to a makeshift box hastily assembled, then stood back as the men started screwing them into place. "We built a subsidiary node," Vant said as the three stepped up to stand beside him. "It doesn't replace the lost subsidiary core, but it does... help take the burden off the other ones, hopefully causing less degradation to the grid, and letting power flow through the whole ship. I mean, so long as it works."

"And if it doesn't?" Belit asked.

"Well, either nothing happens," Vant said, "or it explodes and we all go the way of Hephus. But let's be optimistic, shall we?"

Elias stared at the box as the cables were attached. There was a loud *crack*, and purple light flared from within it. Then – slowly – the furious glow of the other cores receded, just slightly. Somewhere without, they heard the sounds of ship functions coming back to life.

Someone called from the doorway, "It worked! It worked!"

They jogged after the call, across the battered floor of the room, through the aperture in the barricade, and out onto the platform that overlooked the cavernous vastness of the ship's interior. One by one, in a cascading wave, the lights on the lower levels glimmered, and flicked back on. They weren't as strong as before, Elias noted, but he felt the swell of relief ripple up from him. Aimee physically leaped and pumped her fist into the air. Belit laughed, and Hakat grinned. Behind them, a wave of cheers erupted from Rachim's armsmen and the host of enlisted that had guarded, and now saved, the heart of *Iseult*.

Even given what he'd just endured, nearly caused, Elias felt his own face breaking into a wild smile at the relief that surged through the assembled people. "We did it," he breathed. Turning, he grinned at Vant. "You did it. You fucking *genius*."

Vant grinned back, crossing his arms across his chest as Nubin and the others surrounded him with cheers and whooping cries of victory. "Course I did," he said. "Hark doesn't pay me to drop the ball when it matters."

"And not a moment too soon," Rachim grunted, nodding his head past the group to where another, smaller group of people were approaching on foot.

Vallus jogged towards them, accompanied by three of his father's armsmen. The diplomat's face was soot-stained, and he had a cut on his forehead that had been recently bandaged, but looked otherwise none the worse for wear. The relief on Belit's face at the sight of him was palpable.

"Lord Rachim," he said, out of breath. "Miss de Laurent... Where is Harkon? We need him at the Council Hall now."

"What in the damned Maelstrom's Heart is going on?" Rachim asked. "Hark is... Hark has been missing since the portal storm. Slow down. Tell me exactly what's happened?"

"The lot of you need to get up there immediately," Vallus said, "before the whole council finds out: Pentus is dead."

CHAPTER SIXTEEN
WHAT WALKS IN SHADOWS

Less than an hour later, Aimee stood in the heart of the Council Hall, before the vast expanse of the blue table, and tried to reconcile everything that she knew about what this space was for – and the number of times she had stood within it, hearing powder-faced officer aristocrats argue with one another – with the dissonance of the horror before her eyes.

Pentus's corpse was spreadeagled across the center of the blue table. He wore the clothes in which he'd hosted his Grand Ball – his political masterstroke – little over a day ago. That was well, for were it not for the Duke of the Midlevel's garments, Aimee wouldn't have recognized him. His shirt had been slit down the center, and his coat was open, leaving his chest bare. His eyes were open in his frozen, rictus scream of a face, and his entire body desiccated and prematurely aged, every moment of life ripped from him. The sorceress swallowed. It hadn't been quick.

And whoever did it left a final message.

In the center of his chest, burned into the dead flesh, was the same symbol as had been scratched into the walls of the metadrive chamber far below. The nine Stars of the Eternal Order.

Across from her, Elias stared at the same mark on the dead man's chest. His hand gripped his sword, white-knuckled, at his side, and his face had lost nearly all of its color.

"This is how you found him?" Aimee asked.

"One of Diara's astronomers, actually," Viltas said from beside Elias. The lord shipman had an angry vigor about him, no longer looking ill. Crisis had a way of revitalizing people, and adrenaline was damn near magic itself, Aimee reflected.

"The poor man was in a bloody panic when he found me. I figured we had only a brief window to get to the bottom of this before Yaresh learned of it and made a move. He has only one opponent, now, and a corpse to use to stack blame. The truth could be buried in a matter of hours."

Aimee leaned forward over the table, going over everything her teacher – dammit, where was he? – had had her read on necromancy since they'd first learned what they were up against. She hadn't had the chance to inspect Amut's body, had only had a glance at his bedchamber, but this was still familiar. Amut's death had been slow, as the life was drained from him bit by bit under the auspices of a deadly illness. This was a similar thing, but done with far greater haste, directness, and sheer malice. It was the act, not of a hesitant, quiet-working sorcerer, but of a powerful mage become bold and proactive. Extrapolating from that, and where they were finding the body…

"Yaresh is wrong," Aimee said. The suspicion had been

growing in her for some time, and there was no denying it, now. "The Faceless hasn't been hiding amongst the downlevelers. He's been lurking amongst the officer aristocracy, and using the cult below to funnel strength to himself. In return, he creates undead killers to serve their ends... As to those," she faltered. "I don't know."

Grandfather. She didn't have any answers to that, either.

"That," Rachim grunted, "is going to be a hard thing for the council to swallow."

Aimee leaned forward, inspecting the body. She formed and released a spell of detection, very minor, to seek the shape of the magic that had been cast here. The ritual in Amut's bedroom had been immense, long-term, with too many parts for her to attempt to canvas at once... but this had the feel of a single – if potent – spell. Pentus's chest collapsed slightly inward as she released the magic, and a series of glowing glyphs appeared above the corpse.

Viltas's eyebrows raised in surprise. "I didn't know you could do that," he said, impressed.

"Fairly basic academy spell," Aimee murmured as she pulled out a small notepad and started jotting down notes. "One of the first things we learned was how to identify hostile magic. I'll be able to look these up as soon as I get back to *Elysium* – though I can tell you that this is... very advanced, very dark work."

"We need to act quickly," Viltas said to Rachim.

This is something whoever did this couldn't likely have done a mere few days... hell, weeks ago, Aimee thought. Not only were they facing a powerful necromancer that had completely managed to play those around it for fools, but it was growing more powerful by the second. Hephus's last words echoed through her mind. *Beneath.*

"And do what?" Rachim answered. "Hide the corpse? We can't keep this from the council. I'm sure that astronomer has already told Diara."

"Well," Viltas admitted, "it is... *hypothetically* possible that he hasn't been permitted to yet."

"Father!" Vallus said with anger in his voice.

Aimee was still lost in her thoughts. The Faceless came from above, clearly, and the cult had its roots somewhere deep in *Iseult*'s lower levels. Pentus had been caught off guard. She looked over her shoulder towards the door, tracing potential lines of trajectory across the vast room. At range? No. Whoever had done this had struck quickly, and violently, and had grabbed Pentus physically, with a great deal of strength. They hadn't been weak, whoever they were.

"The accusations are going to start flying," Viltas warned. "So quickly that we won't be able to keep the council functioning as a democratic body. Yaresh will seize power. He'll find some patsy to blame quickly, and by their execution and trial, build himself the coalition to take control."

She pushed aside Pentus's coat as the others argued. There, the shoulder had been broken, and the bruising was shaped like the palm of a sizable hand. Up close. Personal. Hateful. She glanced down at the glyphs she'd written down as the spell had dissipated. One was the same as that which she'd seen over Amut's bed. The other two symbolized expansion, quickening. A third she didn't recognize, but the basics were becoming clearer. Necromancy required life-energy, and this spell would've needed a not insignificant amount... and *Iseult* had just been through a day of chaos, wherein it was much easier to kill without being caught.

"He'd need an ideal target, first," Rachim said. "You sound like you have someone in mind. Care to share, Vil?"

"On that I..." Viltas shook his head. "I admit, I don't know."

"I do," Elias said, breaking silence for the first time since they were brought to the corpse. His eyes were haunted as he raised them to look at Aimee. "Yaresh already suspects my training. There will be stories going about, about the things I did during the portal storm, and just now in the metadrive chamber." He swallowed. "I'm the perfect target. An outsider with abilities most can't explain, and that many fear. It won't matter that I can't perform necromancy. Most people don't *know* that. Yaresh is going to pin this on me."

"The symbol," Aimee nodded, as the reality of it sank in. She wanted to reassure him, but he was also dead right.

"That makes no sense," Rachim began. "What are you–"

"I marched under that symbol," Elias said, "not long ago. Please. Don't ask me to tell you more. Suffice to say I was a different person, and now the man I was is a danger to your whole cause."

Viltas's expression paled. Rachim took a step back. Aimee's mind was running a thousand possibilities per second. *Dammit, Elias. Why did you tell them that?*

"We'd best prepare for accusations, then," Rachim said slowly.

"How long do we have?" Viltas asked.

Aimee took a step forward as they talked, summoned a spell to her mind, and whipped her fingers through the requisite gestures. Then, before the others could object, she aimed her finger at the symbol, and burned it, the precision flames crisping and warping the mark on the dead man's chest until it was gone. Two more spells followed: frost to cool the mark, then wind to blow away the scent.

The others stared at her in shocked silence. "Elias couldn't have made that mark," she said. "He has been with my crew nonstop since the night of the Grand Ball. Whoever put that symbol there did it to frame him. To bog us down in another fight that just distracts from finding and dealing with our real enemies. So I'm not playing the game. I have everything I'm going to get from this corpse. Let them find it as it is, and obsess over meaningless shit."

"Our laws," Viltas breathed.

"I'm not from here," Aimee said, looking Viltas in the eye. "And with Harkon gone, *Elysium*'s crew are *my* people. Nobody is imprisoning them, jailing them, laying any bunk accusations at their feet. And if Yaresh tries?" The white hot anger surged inside her. "He'll find out why Harkon Bright chose me as his apprentice."

Then she turned. "We're going. Let them find the body and come to their own conclusions."

They were climbing the ramp up into the hold of *Elysium* when Elias spoke to her. "You shouldn't have done that," he said.

"No," Aimee shook her head. "I shouldn't have waited as long as I did to *do* it. Rachim and Viltas both got a good look at that symbol, and Vallus too." She ran an irritated hand through her hair. "In the name of all the gods, Elias, *why* did you tell them the truth about yourself?"

That caught him slightly off balance. "The accusations were coming," he said. "I needed to make sure that none of you were caught unprepared."

Oh, that was rich. "The time for that warning would've been in the privacy of this ship, amongst the crew, first, not in front of three of our biggest allies who now have every reason to doubt our sincerity!"

"And you think destroying evidence in their full view will help with that?" Elias's temper finally appeared. She saw a flash of anger deep in the green eyes. "You had no right," he snapped. "No right to presume to shield me from–"

"From *what*?" Aimee cut him off, stepped directly into his personal space. "From an accusation over something you didn't do? Please, by all means, tell me how it would help us at all to have you tied up in some sort of mock trial while our enemies laugh at us and the ship goes to hell? What possible purpose could that serve?" The man that had emerged from the ashes of Lord Azrael had proven intriguing, kind, and altogether different from what she had expected a month ago, but a fire was blazing in Aimee's chest. Right now this obnoxious virtue streak was infuriating.

"You don't know–" he started again.

"Oh, *do not* go there with me," Aimee cut him off again, face flushed, voice raised. "Do not presume to give me that same stupid speech I've gotten every day since I was a girl. I know damned well exactly what I'm doing, and you will not give me a paternalistic lecture on–"

"YOU DON'T KNOW THAT I DIDN'T DO IT!" Elias thundered.

Silence. Slowly, Aimee became aware that the crew

of *Elysium* – sans Vant, who still helped in the metadrive chamber below – were standing around, watching the two of them in careful, alarmed silence. It took her half a minute to recover her voice.

"Don't be ridiculous," she started.

"I'm not," Elias said, and mingled with the anger there was a deep pain. "I've been having those visions for weeks. In the heart of the metadrive chamber that thing nearly took control of me. The closer it came to it, the less awareness I had of what was happening around me. You don't know that it hasn't taken control of my mind once before already."

Silence, again. "You've been with me the whole time," Aimee said.

"You were unconscious for a day," Elias said.

"You waited by my side," she retorted. "Your arm was in a fucking sling."

"Did the others keep continuous eyes on me?" Elias asked, and now his eyes swept the room, pained. Fearful. "Can any of you guarantee that at no point during my vigil I slipped out? I'm quiet as hell, when I want to be. And I don't remember the whole of that time. I slept for a good chunk of it."

Aimee was silent. Her mouth opened once or twice to object. A more reasonable response refused to manifest, so at last she fell back on what she felt on a fundamental level to be true: "I don't believe it. I *won't* believe it."

Elias looked down, and when he looked back at her there was a maddening frustration on his face mixed with something else. "Dammit, Aimee," he swore.

"You couldn't have done it," another voice, female, said, and Aimee – and every other person in the room –

turned to find themselves staring at the person who hated Elias most: Vlana. "Bjorn and I kept a rotating watch over the ways in and out of the villa for the entire time Aimee was unconscious. We didn't know what might be coming, so we were very thorough."

The quartermaster folded her arms across her chest and fixed Elias with a level stare. "I don't like you. I think you'll bring death and horror to this ship, one day... but you never left Aimee's room. Wouldn't. After she woke up, one of us was with you straight through from then till now. You didn't do it."

Then she paused, and looked at Aimee. "Now can someone tell me what he didn't do? All I know is he'd have had to leave the ship for it, and that categorically did not happen."

"Pentus is dead," Aimee said. "Murdered by the Faceless. I'm certain of it. He burned the symbol of the Eternal Order into the corpse's chest – Elias believes he did this to frame him for it, and then he told them about himself."

She stepped away from him, and gestured at the space between them in emphatic, futile fury.

"Well," Clutch said. "That was... not smart."

"Then Aimee burned the symbol off the corpse's chest," Elias countered.

"Aaaaaaand it got worse," the pilot sighed.

Bjorn pinched the bridge of his nose and closed his eyes, muttering, "It's like there are two of him. Two Harkons."

"Alright, alright," Clutch said, holding up her hands to forestall further argument, "let's take a step back and recoup. First, the power's back on, clearly, so the trip below was a success?"

"The cult destroyed a subsidiary metadrive core," Aimee said with a nod. "Vant managed to reroute power to reduce the strain on the remaining ones. It restored functionality to a lot of the ship, and it'll hold for a while, but *Iseult*'s engines aren't going to be as strong as they were before. He's still down there, doing everything he can, then he'll rejoin us."

"That's my genius brother," Vlana said with a quiet, fierce warmth.

"We've redone our math," Clutch said. "We're definitely in the Tempest Crescent... and it looks like, from what one of Rachim's people said, *Tristan* is too. From what I hear, though, they're even worse off than we are. A small supply ship has already been sent over to make contact, but I guess communications from that way are garbled and don't make much sense."

"Lord Yaresh is still trying to bring order to the upper levels," Vlana said, crossing her arms with a sigh. "Talk to enough servants and you get a pretty clear picture. The working people on the top levels are scared to death. The sort of language our Lord of the Muster is using is all purges, and death-to-the-filth-from-below. Most of them have families there. They're terrified."

And all that rage would soon be vented at – more than likely – one of their own. "Alright," Aimee said, organizing her thoughts. "Here's where we are: Yaresh hasn't made his move yet. Vant is down below in the chamber, and Belit's second-in-command Hakat is leading the chamber's defense. Belit herself is going to take the 'investigation' of Pentus's death into her own hands, since as commander of the Red Guard, she can argue that it should fall under her purview. As for us..."

She took a deep breath. The way they all looked at her, she was in command, a thought that terrified her.

"We have a few priorities: we need to make sure *Elysium* is ready to fly at a moment's notice. We need to start figuring out what the hell happened to Hark. We need sleep," she took a deep breath, "and I need to figure out what he was studying right before he vanished. Is that sufficient directions?"

One by one they nodded. "Relax," Clutch said with a smile as she walked past. "We've been at this long enough. We know our jobs."

"I'll do a top to bottom sweep," Vlana said, picking up her tools and signaling to Bjorn, "then it's crash time. Don't burn the oil too long, any of us. Rest is gonna count for a lot in the next few days."

Bjorn was the last to leave, and when he stood beside them he paused. "He'd be proud," was all he said.

"Thank you," Aimee said, smiling her best. "But don't talk about him in the past tense. We're going to find him. I know it."

Entertaining the alternative wasn't possible for her right now. She waited for a few moments as the footsteps receded into the distance. Then it was only her, Elias, and a whole lot of awkward silence.

"Aimee–" he started.

"Don't," she cut him off. "I'm still mad at you."

He stared at her, then objection settled into a look of resignation. That somehow only made her angrier, and before she knew it, the words were pouring out of her like blood from a wound. "How could you do that? What in the abyss is wrong with you?"

A pause followed. Then Elias simply said, "I was trying

to warn you, trying to protect you. I didn't think–"

"No," she said, and the pain in her own voice was tangible, burning. "Clearly you didn't. Elias, step back and consider the bigger picture: we are surrounded by enemies. There's a necromancer at large and a cult down below, and right now? They're winning. You do nobody any good rotting in a cell, and I can't have your self-destructive guilt threatening to take you out of the picture, do you understand?"

"Shortly before he vanished," Elias continued, "Harkon spoke to me… he asked me to protect you all, to–"

"You can't protect us if you're dead!" It was coming out of her now, full force. Her eyes were wet, her voice was cracking. Her fists clenched by her side. "You're an ace up our sleeve, a fucking member of this crew, and we can't have you taking yourself out of play, do you understand me?" She was shouting. "Dammit, Elias Leblanc, I need–" The words caught in her throat and she corrected herself. "We need you!"

Elias stood there, a wreck of a person, then nodded. "I'm sorry," he said at last. Then, "I feel responsible."

"You shouldn't," she started to say. "This has nothing to do with–"

"I'm not talking about my time as Azrael," he cut her off quietly. "A few days ago, I met with Pentus in some other aristocrat's private garden. I didn't know when I agreed to meet that it was with him. I thought, when I went, that it might have presented some new opportunity for us. Instead he needled me, having clearly heard rumors as to my abilities and past. He wanted me to ally with him. I refused, and walked away."

He looked down, then back up at her. "And now he is dead."

Aimee strove to wrap her mind about all of the implications of this. "Why didn't you tell us?"

"I thought – naively –" Elias answered "–that my departure was the end of it. As for the conversation, there was no need to burden you all with it. Harkon's position demanded neutrality."

Aimee hated to admit that with all her anger, but it wasn't wrong. "You can't hold yourself responsible for his death," she said. "Listen to your own advice. Don't carry his weight. Let it go."

She was one to talk. The dead engineer still hung heavy at the back of her thoughts. When this was done, she imagined a good, solid cry was coming.

But for her words, she was rewarded with a sad, rueful smile from the man across from her. "Yet here we are," he said.

In the honesty was a pain she recognized. "Here we are," she agreed.

It seemed to take her an eternity to walk the length of the ship to Harkon's cabin. Longer, it felt like, to bring herself to open the door and step inside. The private room of the mage who meddled was part study, part bedroom, part place of experimentation. Atlases were everywhere, and a small collection of books had been left out on the bed, presumably what he'd been reading before the Grand Ball. There, on an open page, she saw a strange diagram, and next to it scrawled the words "Soul," and "Bind." A separate book showed what appeared to be an organic crystal of some sort.

Aimee took a deep breath, and held back the tears.

There would be time later. She didn't tell herself when that would be. No false optimism could guide her actions now. She would not cry yet. She would not collapse into a fit of painful wallowing.

She would get to the bottom of this mess, solve the problem, and bring the monsters behind it *down*.

Pushing back her exhaustion, Aimee pulled up a chair before the books Harkon had been studying before he vanished.

"Alright, teacher," she murmured. "Show me what you found..."

CHAPTER SEVENTEEN
ASH AND BLOOD

Elias Leblanc dreamed terrible dreams. Pentus's corpse was slowly torn apart on the council table, remade as a nail-covered rack whose chains creaked and groaned in tune with the sounds of crunching bones. In the distance, the miserable echo of the specter loomed, wearing his own, empty-eyed face as a rictus mask of snarling flesh. He swept his sword at shadows that mocked and fled and danced, ever out of reach. Every time he spun or turned, the light cast by Oath of Aurum made new shadows that gnawed at his limbs and staggered his steps.

At the last, he stood upon a vast plane of dust and ash, and turning, beheld the ruins of a vast city of impossible beauty laid low. It was filled with the sounds of clamor, of ringing blades and crackling magic. His senses hummed, pulling him towards the noise, and with every footstep that took him nearer, the sounds grew more distinct.

He was nearly at the gates, when a high-pitched scream of a thousand voices tore outward, ripping through his mind. From the heart of the ruin, a beam of white light shot mournfully into the sky. A sword pierced a heart.

The storm roared at the edge of perception, and pale roses grew from a white chalice.

Silence. The simple warmth of a familiar cottage. His mother sat in an armchair, humming a familiar melody that made his heart ache. He raised his eyes to ones so like his own, and she smiled.

"My dear boy," he heard her say. *"You need to wake up."*

BANG.

His eyes opened. He lay on his back upon the hardwood floor of his cabin, bedclothes in a sweaty tangle about himself. His breath came in a slow rhythm, and the melody still played through his head.

And gods, *everything* hurt.

BANG. This time he started at the sound – a knock, hard, on his door – and staggered to his feet. "Elias!" the voice was Bjorn's. "Up! Gotta get to the Council Hall!"

That brought him immediately to consciousness, sharp and focused, if not articulate. "Mmm up!" he reflexively shouted back. "Gotta pants. Boots. Sword."

Silence followed, then Bjorn answered, "Whatever you need to do, kid."

Elias swore under his breath and started pulling on his clothes. Definitely not articulate.

By the time he arrived in Rachim's foyer, the others were all assembled, looking bleary-eyed and tired. Aimee had both hands folded over a mug, and despite the generally put-together appearance she projected, the hint of tiredness at the corners of her eyes told Elias that she'd barely slept last night.

"Alright, someone bring me up to speed?" Elias asked.

"Yaresh has called an emergency council meeting," Aimee said. "He tried to keep us out, but Rachim brought the hammer down, so we're going, but we have to do it *now*."

"And it's show-of-force time," Bjorn said. The big warrior was fully armed now, with his two-handed sword across his back. "There will be lots of armsmen there. The man is dangerously unstable, and looking to force the process."

"I didn't want it to come to this," Rachim agreed, "but I'm bringing my armsmen, too, and Viltas. Belit will hold her ground as custodian of the investigation into Pentus's death, and one of hers holds the metadrive chamber. We're well positioned, we just… don't know exactly what the madman is going to do yet."

"I need all hands for this," Aimee said, finishing off her mug, then sweeping her blue eyes around the assembled. "Is everyone ready?"

A series of nods. Elias tightened his sword belt and followed. He'd gone to bed sincerely fearing accusations of murder in the morning, but now there wasn't even time in which to feel any fear. His hand grasped Oath of Aurum's hilt. A familiar warmth flared in response.

It wasn't much, but it was something.

The doorway to the hall was ringed by Yaresh's security forces in their finery. The clouds shielded the sun outside the windows, and a cold, damp gray filled the heavens immediately about *Iseult*. As Elias beheld the wall of shock-spears, the head of their number stepped forward to address Rachim. "You dare bring armsmen to this council function?" he snarled.

"My men are here to counter your own," Rachim snapped back. He wore his armor this time, and despite his stooped, limping stature, commanded a presence that made the gilded officer pause.

"Lord Yaresh has commanded me to secure this hallowed building against any roughness, rioting, or factional uproar." Finding his courage, he added, "You were host to Harkon Bright, moderator of the deliberations over the elections to captaincy, but I do not see him."

"Harkon is among the missing in the aftermath of the portal storm," Aimee said, stepping forward. "As his apprentice and second, I am empowered to act in his stead."

Elias's eyebrows raised. Bold. The armsman looked down his nose at the blonde sorceress about whom many rumors had spread. Elias couldn't help but notice the hint of reservation on the man's face. Somewhere between fear and respect.

"You are Aimee de Laurent," he said. "Many from the Grand Ball owe you their lives. Our gratitude is beyond measure, but that does not entitle you to dictate terms to this council."

"Nor is Lord Yaresh's door-warden empowered to forbid me," Aimee quipped back in a dangerous tone.

Behind them, Rachim's men shifted to a defensive stance. As one, Yaresh's men tightened their grips on their weapons. The sergeant's hand fingered the hilt of his sword.

Elias stepped forward. "Surely then," he said quietly, "you've heard the rumors of me as well?"

The armsman turned. Elias was a few inches taller than him. The man assessed him, frowned. "Yes," he said after a moment. "He warned us. I know all about you."

The black knight let a small smile flicker across his face. "Do you?"

It took a moment for the two words to sink in. Elias watched the man come to the proper conclusions. When he did, his face drained of color.

"Sergeant!" Turning, Elias watched as Vallus approached from behind them. A host of his father's own men was at his back. Viltas's son had never looked more than boyish and innocent to the black knight's eyes, but in the moment his face was livid. "The Lord of the Muster has no right to keep lawful members or attendants of this council from entering the hall. In the name of the ship's charter I command you to open these doors that we may pass through. Rachim and I both hold voting seats, and my father is within. Stand aside, or by the beating heart of *Iseult*, full censure will be brought against both you and your master!"

The sergeant looked back and forth between the lot of them, then said to Vallus, "Count yourself fortunate, Vallus, that this council recognizes the votes of heroes' sons, even if they've never done anything of note themselves. Other than talk."

Then, grudgingly, he stepped aside, and two of his men began opening the immense doors.

Vallus walked straight past the man. "Thankfully I don't require the approval of bullies in uniforms."

The interior of the Council Hall hadn't changed much since the previous night, though Pentus's body had been since removed. The session had already started, Elias realized the moment they entered the room. A large number of officer aristocrats surrounded the blue table, and at either end sat the two remaining candidates for the captaincy. Likewise present, and still resplendent in her red armor, was Belit. Two of her Red Guardsmen flanked her.

Yaresh wore armor as well. A gilded suit of plate wrapped his physique, gray steel edged in lapis and crimson, and a curved blade hung from his right hip, its pommel bearing just enough signs of cleaning for Elias to feel certain that the lord of the muster knew how to use it. He barely spared them a glance as they entered, but what look he sent their way was angry and disapproving.

Diara sat, patiently, at the opposite end. Her calm, inscrutable face was as unreadable as ever, and she wore a uniform of dark blue, her hands folded upon the table before her. The Countess of Astronomers had several sheaves of parchment in front of her, but as they emerged into the room proper she rose. "Aimee de Laurent," she said, her stoic voice echoing in the room, "where is your teacher?"

"Absent, I am afraid," Aimee answered, stepping forward. "But I am empowered to act in his stead, if this council is willing." Only the faint twitch of one of her hands showed Elias just how nervous she was.

"That is not what was agreed upon–" Yaresh began.

"–But it is acceptable to me," Diara said. "I move that this council recognize Aimee de Laurent as valid stand-in for her teacher in his absence. I believe that the heroism she displayed in the midst of the portal storm demonstrates that she is more than qualified. At least half the people in this room owe her their lives."

"I move to second the honorable Countess's suggestion," Vallus said with a triumphant smile. "All in favor?"

Elias caught the head functionary's glare as a small majority chorus arose from the council. "Motion carried," the bureaucrat-priest agreed with obvious distaste.

"Very well," Yaresh said, rising. "With that bit of business out of the way, we can get to the heart of the issue: Countess Diara. By my position as Lord of the Muster and defender of *Iseult*, I formally accuse you of dereliction of duty, of collusion to commit murder, and of the unlawful killing of Pentus, Duke of the Midlevels. Answer these accusations which I lay at your feet, or prepare to face righteous justice on behalf of all of *Iseult*."

Elias stared, momentarily shocked into silence by the sudden turn.

That had not been what he expected.

"Lord Yaresh, forgive my bluntness," Viltas said from his seat, "but have you completely lost your mind?"

"Not at all," Yaresh said. "Pentus declared it his intention to attempt the trials of captaincy, and Diara vehemently disagreed. I have eyewitnesses to a vigorous argument between the two in the hours before he was found killed. Diara is a powerful sorceress in her own right. Perhaps she has made a study of the forbidden arts herself?"

"Now you accuse me of trafficking in necromancy?" Diara said, incredulous. "You know even less about me than you know about magic. My duties have kept me at the star-map nearly the entirety of the past days, striving to provide the wheelhouse with the forecasts they need to keep us alive."

"Clearly you had time to argue with your rival," Yaresh accused. "And come to think of it, he is not the first to fall. Hephus – our dear, late chief engineer – lies likewise dead, and the two of you often quarreled. Every opponent to cross your path in thirty years of your political rise has conveniently fallen just as your ambition waxed. I posit that stories of this *cult* are nothing more than paid agitators from among the unwashed below, seeking to destabilize us in preparation for her ascendency. That her *vision* is nothing more than a sorceress's hunger for ever more power."

Elias looked at the Countess of Astronomers, and remembered the sentiment Aimee had expressed of her when they'd first been brought up to speed on the candidates. *She must be everything to everyone, or they will have her be nothing at all.*

"Your proof?" Diara said in low, dangerous tones. She straightened, staring across the open space with a sharp look in her cold eyes. "So far all I hear is bluster and threats from a man who would clench this ship in a steel fist until he's crushed every ounce of dissent."

"One of my men witnessed your argument," he said, "and it was potent, deadly magic that killed Pentus, easily within your reach."

"You have no concept of the differences between necromancy and the divination and star-tracing I practice."

Yaresh spread his arms wide, laughing in a way that encouraged the other council members to do likewise. "Does a man need to be an expert in thievery before he may say that thievery is bad? Let us not split hairs, Countess."

"And you intend to back up this threat how?" Rachim spoke up. "If your only proof is an overheard conversation, that hardly warrants arrest."

"And a vote on captaincy has yet to produce a definitive winner," Aimee said. "You lack the authority to back up the accusation, Lord Yaresh."

A rumble of alternating agreement and objection rolled through the assembled officers. "And none of you," Yaresh said, "are empowered to refuse me this investigation."

"But I am," Belit said. "And I remind you that the investigation into Pentus's death falls under *my* authority. Should the countess come under suspicion in the course of that investigation, I will deal with the issue then."

"So," Yaresh said. "A full coalition of foreigners, downlevelers, activist officers, and one-time, two-bit heroes is what stands against justice for our ship, our society?"

His hand flashed dangerously close to his sword. Elias took a step forward. "You have a strange notion of gratitude, Lord Yaresh," he said. It was not his place to speak. Not his prerogative, but silence wasn't possible any more. His cold, relentless anger narrowed his focus to a pinprick as he stared at the lord of the muster. "You've been served by downlevelers, protected by activists, aided by heroes and saved at every turn by foreigners."

Yaresh fixed his gaze on Elias, and his voice lowered. "I do not need to be lectured by a foreign–" Something lurked, unuttered, and Elias knew what it was.

He met Yaresh's eyes and said simply, "Go ahead. Finish your sentence."

"–By a foreign criminal," the Muster Lord finished.

Not certain enough, then, Elias thought. "I'm not lecturing you," he said simply. "I'm using words. The things that civilized men use until one of them forgets to take his hand off his sword."

Yaresh's eyes narrowed. His face flushed. But his hand slipped slowly, reluctantly, away from his weapon. Then he fixed his eyes on Aimee. "Control your bodyguard."

"He's notoriously uncontrollable," she answered. "But if you wish to call for another vote, the prerogative is yours." Elias watched as the gamble was laid out by the young portalmage. To her credit, her expression betrayed none of the fear she must have been feeling. "Otherwise, I am afraid the issue must be left to lie."

Elias watched the lord of the muster's eyes sweep the assembled room. He almost imagined he could see the calculations happening. The consideration of faction and politics. Risky. The faces were too unreadable, their countenance by and large too reserved.

"A time will come when you do not find yourself with such convenient allies all around you, Aimee de Laurent," Yaresh said, stepping back. "This is not over."

"Spoken as a man who has never stared true evil in the face," Viltas murmured coldly.

"Should I find myself in such a position," Aimee replied, "what fool corners me will learn of their errors. For the moment, Lord Yaresh, I assure you, it is."

The rest was far less exciting. Arguments happened between various officers about where their armsmen should be sent to secure the upper levels. Another purge was suggested and shot down – there was not the manpower or means to execute it – and Viltas spoke of the status of *Tristan*: the ship was drifting further into the Tempest Crescent, and the vessel the lord shipman had arranged to send to *Iseult*'s twin had not reported back. The lights on the other behemoth were flickering oddly, and there was no word on the status of her crew.

They exited the long hallway to the hall onto the steps leading down to the streets. The sunlight was breaking through the clouds, but they still seemed more intense, oppressive than they'd appeared amongst the rest of the flotilla.

"We don't have a lot of time," Rachim grunted. "That was a temporary stopgap. He's been blunted, and enough people are worried by his stances that they won't vote for him, but give us a few more disasters, and we'll see how quickly the officers swing his way. And if he's blunted further?"

"The answer," Viltas said, "is to fix the underlying problems before he tries to seize power directly."

Somewhere far in the distance, thunder rumbled in the heavens. Viltas looked upwards, then said, "Miss Laurent… I don't suppose you and your bodyguard would mind walking with my son and me back to my residence? I would like to… talk, if I could."

Aimee exchanged a look with Elias. The black knight nodded. "It's fine," she said to Rachim. "We'll be back in a timely fashion."

Elias fell into step beside Vallus, just behind his father and Aimee, and just ahead of about twenty armsmen of quality who walked behind them. Looking about in the windswept streets of the top level, none of the officers he saw going here and there were doing so unarmed.

"Thank you for your words today," Vallus said beside him. Elias shot the young man a look. "I never thought to see Yaresh cowed."

Elias considered carefully how to answer that. "I merely reminded him of inalienable realities."

Vallus gave a small laugh. "Well spoken, for a bodyguard."

The black knight caught a glance from Aimee over her shoulder. "I had a classical education," he deadpanned.

"Have you had any luck finding your teacher?" Viltas asked earnestly.

As Elias watched, Aimee shook her head. "There hasn't been time to search. He was last seen by one of ours at the Grand Ball, just before the storm. I've heard no rumors since, and we've barely been keeping on our feet."

Viltas frowned as they turned into another side street and started towards one of the smaller estates spread out between other, more elaborate dwellings. The lord shipman gestured in the direction of what was apparently his home. "I heard... rumors," he said, "of some sort of sorcerous confrontation in Platform 325. The same from which our rescue ship departed to make contact with *Tristan*. I will ask my people there for more precise descriptions of what was seen and exactly when. Despite the population of working mages on this ship, most people are not terribly educated on the finer points of sorcery. I don't want to get your hopes up, Miss Laurent, but perhaps I can dig something useful up."

"The crew and I would be... very grateful," Aimee answered. Elias watched her fervently attempting to keep control over the spark of hope lit within her.

Another rumble of thunder passed overhead, and the skies began to darken quickly. "We need to get indoors," Elias said. "That's not a normal storm. In the crescent, squalls break off from the maelstrom and strike quickly."

It was more than that, however. The hairs were rising on the back of the black knight's neck as they neared

Viltas's home. Something in the air felt *wrong*. Breathing out and reaching for his rusty mystic senses, Elias felt a sudden surge of unease even as the recognition struck him: he'd last felt this the first time they met the Oracle, in the darkness of the ship's bowels. Necromancy had a very specific scent.

There was a flash of lightning and a rolling crack of thunder, and in the flickering shadows just up the street a figure was abruptly present. The rolling flicker of petering lightning revealed more shapes. Gaunt. Ragged. Makeshift weapons were in the hands of some. Others simply flexed blackened fingers as they approached. Elias heard one of the armsmen shout, and turning, saw a second group of them at their rear. Seven ahead, seven behind, and each of them more than a match for an ordinary soldier. "Get ready!" Elias shouted, and ripped Oath of Aurum free. The blade glowed white in his hands. It steamed faintly as the rain began to fall.

As one, the dead charged them. Aimee leaped forward, her shield spell slamming into place, a gossamer wall between the dead ahead and the startled living. Elias watched her physically wince as the first of them slammed its body into it.

No choice. Elias summoned his speed, and blurred forward, vaulting over the heads of the armsmen and into the oncoming press.

They were faster. Oath of Aurum's descending blade struck a sword that whipped through the air with no physical tells. He heard sinew snapping and bones straining past their limit. He struck again. It danced back. The head whipped about, and rotted eye sockets lit by a fell light fixed on him. A rasping laugh echoed from a decomposing mouth. "Fallen Angel, is that the best you have?"

He heard the shifting of feet behind him, barely managed to snap his sword about for a parry. He twisted, cut. His enemy wasn't there. Too fast. These undead were exponentially more powerful, quicker, and smarter than the last. Out of the corner of his eye, there again. He cut, pivoted, swept his sword at a blurry center of mass. It darted back, and steel rang on steel. From his left side, another lunged at him simultaneously. He hammered forward, pushing his first foe aside and making just enough space for the other to crash into a stone wall on the street-side. Its claws shattered granite.

If they could do that–

Elias pressed into the bind. The dead thing was stronger than him. It pushed harder. The black knight yielded to the pressure and wound his hilt outwards. It didn't notice that his point was in line with its face until the black knight – screaming – was already driving the glowing sword a foot through its mouth. Fire blazed. The corpse fell. Then he turned and rushed back towards the group. Stupid. He'd let himself get pulled away from the people who needed his protection. The second of the dead launched through the air at him. No time. He called on his strength and heelkicked it through the stone wall with a brick-shattering crunch. "I'm just getting started," he snarled.

Screams. The first of the dead slammed into the wall of shock-spears the armsmen had formed. Two of the crackling spearpoints punched through its body. In return, the lurching thing laughed. "Oh Viltas," it cackled. "As if these tawdry flesh-rags could ever stop my children."

Elias rushed back towards them as the thing pushed itself further forward on the spears and the crude splitting-maul in its fists set to rend the heads and bodies of the foremost armsmen like exploding wine-grapes. Red showered everywhere. Before he could reach them, another came at his flank. An axe descended, strong enough to shatter cobbles. Oath of Aurum sheared through its shaft as it dropped, and this time he was fast enough. The white sword exited the body, heat trailing red steam as the thing burnt out and dropped. He charged. A second of the dead had joined its companion, ripping and tearing. Five of Viltas's armsmen lay on the ground, dead or screaming as blood pulsed from open wounds. None of the spells Elias knew would spare the living in such close quarters. He surged forward anyway, nearly back with them.

Viltas shouted a warning. The thing Elias had kicked through a wall scrambled up the back of a decorative statue and leaped through the air, as another jumped from the opposite direction.

Elias saw Aimee twist. Her free hand flashed through the gestures of a spell as she aimed at one. He summoned his strength and leaped upwards straight into the trajectory of the other. His sword sheared through its center of mass, and burning chunks fell to the earth as he angled for a landing atop the wall.

The first of the dead from the other side of Aimee's shield spell cleared it, and slammed into him as he came down. He felt razor claws ripping at the mail and leathers he wore. The two of them hammered into the shrubbery of a decorative garden, and Elias nearly lost his breath. The rotting, hideous face loomed above him.

Behind it, he glimpsed the specter of his former self, smirking. He couldn't reach his sword, somewhere in the grass nearby.

"No magic sword," the dead thing snarled, "no victory for the little wretch. I wonder what I can do with *your* corpse?"

"There's so much more to me than you know," Elias said. No more bystanders to worry about now. He wrestled his hands free, slammed them into the dead thing's chest with all his strength. Magic flared beneath his fingers. Detonated upwards. The thing screamed and released him. Elias rolled, snatched up his sword, and split the monstrosity from crotch to neck.

He vaulted back over the wall in time to watch as Aimee's shield spell collapsed. But Viltas and Vallus were behind her, and five of the remaining armsmen.

The two of the dead that had set upon them were burnt, charred-out husks, and something was happening to the sorceress. Her hands trailed wisps of smoke, and a furious expression was on her face. *The spell,* he thought. *Harkon taught her a new spell.*

The moment the shield collapsed, Aimee's limbs swept through gestures of wind, flame, and frost, slammed into a focus point, and blasted a beam of iridescent light straight through the center of the foremost of the dead. It burned like tissue paper, as did the one behind. The remaining five charged forward. Elias hurtled into their midst. The world was light and shearing steel. Steam and falling rain. Claws, blades, leering eyes and ripping limbs filled his senses. He was hit. Repeatedly. His piecemeal armor was knocked loose. He felt something cut his face. *Focus on me!* his mind screamed. *Focus on me!*

Blood and burnt flesh fell like ash and rain.

He twisted as the last two tried to slip past. They blurred ahead of him at his companions. Elias chased. The remaining armsmen barred their way. The dead charged through them, lunged at Aimee, Vallus, and Viltas. Aimee's hands flashed. The spell shot out again as Elias launched himself at the other. The first exploded in a shower of ash and blood. Elias hewed at the second. The sword traced a shearing white line across his vision. It was just a hair faster. He heard it roaring Viltas's name. A shape moved in front of it. Vallus screamed, "FATHER!"

The sword cut through the dead thing, and it burned away. Overbalanced, Elias rolled. His shoulder slammed painfully down and he tumble-fell, bouncing across the stones of the street, landing on his back. The breath left him. His head struck something hard. The world grew indistinct and fuzzy.

Screams brought him back. He rolled. Blood in his eyes. His fingers tingled. Concussion. He knew the signs. He had to move. He snatched the enchanted sword from the ground. The heat of its blade had burnt away the blood that had stained it. It took him a moment to focus, and his vision finally landed on the source of the sound. Elias's heart froze, and his mouth dried. No. Too late. Not fast enough.

Viltas was on his knees in the street, Aimee immediately opposite the lord shipman. The screams came from the old man, cradling his son in his arms. Vallus's breath came in choking gasps, and across his chest, a horrible, bleeding gash had opened him up.

"Vallus," Viltas sobbed. Each time he screamed, the

sound hit Elias like another blow to the head. Everything was gray and red. Thunder rolled in the distance, and the rain poured ceaselessly from a weeping sky.

"Vallus!"

"VALLUS!"

CHAPTER EIGHTEEN
THE BLIND AND THE TRUE

The spell Harkon taught her – Radiance – to use against the dead had worked, but Aimee felt numb. Her footsteps carried her down the interior hall of Viltas's humbler dwelling. She stopped just short of the common area where the others were waiting, and leaned against the cool wood panels of the wall. Dimly, she was aware of the intricate patterns on the walls – swirls of ivy and lightning, intermingled and faded across the pitted, scarred surface. Despite being a prominent hero to many on *Iseult*, and an officer aristocrat of some positioning, Viltas didn't put much of his resources into enriching himself. Hephus. Her uncle. Countless dead at Port Providence. Possibly her teacher – no, she wouldn't think it – the list of dead weighing on her conscience was only growing.

Slowly, she made herself turn the corner. Viltas waited in his main foyer. He looked as if he'd lived a hundred years in a day. She ignored the others for a moment, making herself focus only on him.

Then she took a deep breath and said, "He will live."

Viltas breathed out, closed his eyes, and wept. Aimee felt her own eyes wetting, and let the relieved smile come. Today, at least, she'd managed to save *one*.

The next sign of relief she heard came from Belit. The commander of the Red Guard stood just behind the lord shipman, her hand in a viselike grip on his own. Her face relaxed visibly at the news, and she breathed out. "Thank you, Aimee de Laurent," she said. "How is he?"

Aimee folded her arms and leaned a tired shoulder against the wall. "Well, that's the other side of things," she said slowly. "The chirurgeon you called was able to work quickly enough for me to apply the healing spell... but the trauma was immense. If I had to guess, I wouldn't expect him to be awake again for at least a day. If you want him to make a full recovery, you won't let him get out of bed for a week. Minimum."

"It doesn't matter," Viltas shook his head. "Alive. Able to fully recover. These are the things that matter. I owe you a debt that cannot possibly be repaid."

"Can I see him?" Belit asked.

"Of course," Aimee said with a nod. "The chirurgeon still watches over him, and he's not awake, but you can sit with him. It might be good for him, honestly."

The tall swordswoman walked past her, after giving Viltas's hand a squeeze. "Thank you," she said again, as she passed Aimee, then her footsteps receded down the hallway behind them. Aimee allowed herself to become more aware of other people in the room. Bjorn had been summoned back, and Clutch had come with him. The old warrior still wore the armor he'd donned when they went to the Council Hall, and the pilot looked ready to take one of her long knives straight to someone's throat. Both were comforting sights.

Elias stood by the window, his head heavily bandaged. The black knight stared out into the rain as if by doing so he might freeze each drop. She'd done what she could for his injuries, but he needed rest. There was no substitute.

Before she could say anything, Viltas said, "This would have all been different, if Amut had only had legitimate children of his own."

Aimee looked up, drawn from her concern for her friend. It struck her that it had never occurred to her to ask as to the family of the late captain. "Had he no family?" she asked. "I was not aware that the captaincy could pass from parent to child."

"Not by default," the lord shipman said with a shake of his head. "But he was a good man. He'd have been a good father, and might have raised a suitable candidate to follow in his footsteps. But the only woman he ever loved was some downleveler girl. The officer aristocracy would never have had it, and when she died… it changed him. He became ever more set on reform, after that. Bettering their lives, chipping away at the privileges of his fellow officers. He slowed inexplicably, the past few years, but he might have succeeded, if he only had more time."

Viltas ran a hand through his graying hair and shook his head. "It's a sorry sight for folk like you to see, I'm sure. We were heroes, once. Now the rest of my old companions are dead, and here I am, trapped by the very social system I fought to reform." His voice turned bitter. "Waiting for my failures to kill me."

Aimee crossed her arms, reflected on the books she'd obsessively studied since Harkon vanished. The texts over which her teacher had pored, prior to his disappearance. One page on a tome concerning the nature of necromancy stood out in her mind, and the theoretical horrors of which it was capable.

"Before he disappeared," Aimee said, "my teacher was researching the lore around necromancy, and what a practitioner such as this Faceless might have been capable of. What I'm about to say doesn't leave this room... but I don't think he hides among the downlevelers. I think he hides among your peers: the officer aristocrats."

Viltas looked up at her, his tired eyes intent and thoughtful. "Do you?"

"He knew," Elias said. He stared out the window as he spoke, frowning at the rainstorm.

"I don't understand," Viltas said.

"When the Faceless spoke through his assassins," Elias said, "he called me *Fallen Angel*. Only three people on this ship know the significance of those words, and one of them is dead."

"You *can't* think that Belit–" Aimee began.

"I don't," Elias shook his head. "I've spent endless hours working closely with her. If she was any sort of mage I'd have smelled it."

"You can do that?" Viltas asked.

"Not always," the black knight answered. "But suppressing that sort of power into invisibility is... hard. The longer you're around someone doing it, the greater the chance they'll slip up."

"I had no idea," Viltas said. "But I don't know much about the Eternal Order."

"Most don't," Aimee covered quickly.

"Then I shall pry no further," the lord shipman said. "I should've said this in the hall when we stared at Pentus's corpse, so I'll say it now: you have more than proven your quality to me, over and over. Your secrets are your own."

A knock echoed at the door, abrupt, jarring. Viltas rose, waving off the armsman that emerged into the room at the sound. "Back to your post," he said simply. "I'm not so frail and afraid that I can't open my own door."

"You need to head back to *Elysium*," Aimee said to Elias after Viltas had left the room. "I patched up your head, but it's still going to take rest before you're fieldworthy again."

"It feels fine," Elias said, still not turning. "I've fought through worse. I'm durable."

"No, lad," Bjorn said, "you're *young*. And a demon is no longer force-patching your skull every time something cracks it. Those wounds'll add up before long. Listen to her, or I'll haul you back myself."

The black knight turned, and looked between the two of them. "You'd have to leave her without a bodyguard."

"Excuse you," Clutch said. "You forgetting that I put an axe through undead skulls myself just a few days ago? Don't sweat it, pretty boy. I'm not going anywhere."

A half second later, Viltas reemerged, and beside him was a young woman Aimee hadn't seen before – tanned, with wiry, dark hair bound up in an intricate series of knots at the back of her head, and dressed in midnight blue. It took her a second to mark the starlight symbol of the astronomers at her collar.

"Sorry to interrupt," Viltas said, "but this is First Lieutenant Haysha of the astronomers. She's come to speak with you, Aimee."

Haysha didn't waste a moment. "Miss Laurent," she said. "Forgive my intrusion, but I come on behalf of my liege, Countess Diara. She wants to speak with you immediately."

• • •

Bjorn did – in fact – insist on bringing Elias back to *Elysium*, so it was in Clutch's company that Aimee made her way towards the ivory-tinted dome where the astronomers worked under Diara's ceaseless supervision. They walked through the lingering after-drizzle of the passing squall. The streets were soaked, and Aimee had her hood up.

"My liege is grateful for your agreement," Haysha said as they walked. "She likewise wishes to convey her admiration for your work, both here, and in Port Providence. Rumors travel swiftly, and your teacher was not shy about his praise."

"Did she spare any for the daring, legendary pilot of *Elysium*, by any chance?" Clutch asked, giving the astronomer a sideways glance of obvious interest. "I'm asking for a friend."

Haysha shot Clutch an amused – not disinterested – glance in return. "She didn't, but I've heard stories, and appreciate the legends."

Aimee let out a small laugh. "You're shameless," she said.

"When you've seen the things I've seen," Clutch answered, "living in the moment is the only thing that makes any sort of sense."

Stepping into the dome was a jarring experience. Enchantments upon the ceiling high over their heads recast the space above them as a vast view of the night sky, with a thousand constellations. Aimee paused, momentarily arrested by the panorama. She'd seen similar star-maps – they had one in the academy back in Havensreach – but she'd never witnessed one this *big*. She racked her brain, trying to call to mind the names: they were far from her home, and the positions were all different. Still, she thought she recognized the Pillar and the Hatchet. Far to the aerial north was the Wheelwright of Stars and his grand chariot.

Out of the corner of her eye she watched Clutch throw a salute in its direction. At the questioning glance that followed, the pilot said, "All pilots salute the Wheelwright, Aimee. Gotta give credit to the ones who came before."

Up ahead, in the center of the dome, a control station crowned the rise of a cylindrical dais climbed by a set of milk-pale stairs. Its top was broad and flat, and dozens of astronomers moved here and there, chatting irritably as they examined old parchment maps, comparing them to the heavens. There was a general air of unease as the trio approached – even panic.

"What's got them all worked up?" Clutch asked, though something in her tone implied that she had suspicions.

"My liege will explain better than I can," Haysha said. "But in brief, we are losing our ability to properly read the constellations."

That brought Aimee's head swiveling from its observation of the platform to staring at Haysha as they walked. "What?"

"As I said," the astronomer answered, "my liege can explain better."

And there at the top of the stairs was Diara. She had yet to change from the uniform she'd donned for the aouncil meeting. The Countess of Astronomers stood over a central table that contained a vast atlas more detailed than any Aimee had ever seen – and more ancient, by the look of it. The older woman's eyes settled on her, and she gave Haysha a nod, before the other astronomer went back to her duties, sparing a small, coy smile for Clutch.

"Aimee de Laurent," Diara said. "I had hoped we might get to speak under better circumstances. Thank you for heeding my request. I know it appears... irregular."

The risk the countess took of delegitimizing her efforts towards the captaincy was not lost on Aimee. The council already distrusted the woman. If she was perceived as attempting to sway the moderator...

"These are clearly irregular times," Aimee answered.

"This has nothing to do with the captaincy," Diara answered. "Save by small proxy. I understand you have been looking into Captain Amut's murder, and I have heard that mere hours ago you were attacked by more of those monsters in the street."

"Both correct," Aimee said. "Rumors travel fast. We did not yet report what happened."

"Risky," the countess said with a shake of her head. "If those things can reach the upper levels, then–"

"I believe they *originated* on the upper levels, with respect," Aimee countered. "The belief that their master lurks among the downlevelers is a preposterous idea that only Yaresh believes. There are no secret passageways or quick byways near Viltas's residence. These things came from up here this time."

"Nonetheless, he will not wait, once word reaches him," Diara warned. "But that is not why I called you. For what it is worth, I believe you, because Yaresh was correct: Pentus and I argued less than an hour before he was killed. On the night of the portal storm. And ever since we came to this wretched Tempest Crescent, our ability to read the divinatory signs has diminished. Today it has dropped precipitously, and I fear that I know why."

At this, the countess gestured at a place at the edge of

her vast parchment map. Aimee followed the movement to where it stopped at what seemed almost a barrier of clouds drawn onto the page. "The storm dropped us much deeper into the crescent than we at first suspected," Diara continued. "I estimate we are less than three days' straight flight from the wall of the maelstrom."

The Axiom's warning flashed through Aimee's mind, and she recalled the vision. "What did you and Pentus argue about?" she asked. "Forgive my prying, but if that information can be used to dispel dangerous rumors, I would have you tell me."

Diara paused, assessed Aimee with a carefully neutral face, then sighed. "He came to me, raving like a lunatic, hours after the portal storm ended. I have known Pentus at least passingly since he first came to power as duke of the midlevels. He has always been eccentric, but this was... beyond madness. He claimed to have gone down to his fief after the clamor started, to assure himself that everything was in order. Then his words degenerated into nonsensical talk of secret rooms, and a man encased in crystal. He screamed about a corpse-throne and a black book, then he begged me to use my influence to immediately turn the ship around."

Corpse-thrones. Black books. Familiar motifs, at least, but it was the man encased in crystal that stuck in her head, calling to mind a page in one of her teacher's books. A spell she couldn't quite remember the name of. Hephus's last words echoed in her head. *Beneath.*

Where *was* Pentus's estate in comparison to the metadrive chamber?

"And you couldn't," Aimee said, urging Diara to continue.

"Even if I had that influence, no. *Tristan* has been falling deeper towards the storm since we arrived. The wheelhouse will not see our sister ship abandoned, and they are still trying to reestablish contact."

Aimee ran her hands through her hair. This was maddening. Every time she thought she understood who was in control of the ship, it seemed to change dramatically. "So, absent a captain," she said, "the ship is functionally ruled by the wheelhouse, while the council argues about who should be captain next, and each of these damned lord-officer-whatevers conducts their duties and their affairs as they see fit with no oversight?"

"It is rather a miracle," Diara said with a nod, "that we haven't destroyed ourselves yet."

"So after you talked," Aimee said, "he just… left?"

"I wish I could tell you something more profound or revealing," the countess answered wryly, "but other than the fact that he clearly seemed to believe he was being followed. Given that he was murdered shortly thereafter, that is hardly surprising." Diara shook her head then. "I believe that you have the potential to be every bit as skilled as your teacher. A mere few days ago you saved officer aristocrats and their entourages almost without number, and one of your own holds the metadrive chamber. I called you here because it has been made clear to me that those of us on *Iseult* who believe in a better future – however slim the chance – must start speaking with one another, and coordinating, or we are all lost."

Aimee fixed her eyes on the older sorceress, so accustomed to walking a razor's edge lest she offend too deeply or insufficiently. Then, carefully, she leaned forward, pressed her hands to the table, and said, "You want me to support your bid for the captaincy? Is that what you are saying?"

Diara met her stare unflinchingly, then said, "No."

It wasn't the answer Aimee had been expecting. "What?"

"You misunderstand my motivations," Diara said. "I put forth my name because the alternatives were a well-meaning dilettante who buys power, and a narrow-minded soldier longing for his next war. In truth I do not *care* who becomes captain, so long as it isn't Yaresh. I called you here to help you defeat the Faceless and this cult below."

"The only alternative," Aimee said in frustration, "is *you*."

And for just a moment, Diara looked away. "I am the only other candidate who has sought *election*," she said quietly. "But I think we both know that I am *not* the other *candidate*… there is another."

Aimee stared at her. A possibility flashed through her mind, one that she had never considered, which seemed absurdly outlandish.

"You see it, too," Diara said, nodding with a grim smile. "And I am coming to believe, so does *Iseult*."

Before Aimee could answer, a shudder passed beneath their feet, and the lights in the astronomy dome died.

A second later, the lights immediately around them, the control station at the heart of *Iseult*'s long-range navigation, flickered back on, casting all of them in a pale blue light. Clutch freed her knives. Diara started giving orders. "Protect the central control station!" she said. "Without it, *Iseult* is blind!"

Diara suddenly grasped her arm, turned her around. "Whatever happens," the countess said quickly, "I did everything I did for my people, for the ship. If my candidacy has failed, it must be her." She shook her head, and Aimee saw regret in her eyes. "Perhaps it should've been her to begin with. She has better claim than any. Go, look upon his face, and you will see."

"I will," Aimee said. "We'll fix this now, then we'll talk."

Aimee freed her fingers, turning in a circle as the astronomers jumped to follow the orders of their superior.

"Another attack on the metadrive?" Clutch asked.

"No," Aimee said with a shake of her head. "This was localized. Close by."

"Astute," said a voice just to Aimee's left, one of the astronomers whom she had neither met, nor recognized. With his left hand, he drove a shock-stick into one of the panels next to the main control panel. A shower of sparks exploded across the platform.

Diara turned, sweeping her hands through forms Aimee didn't recognize. Cold flames sparked in the air about her fingers. Aimee swept her hands high, summoning her binding spell, only for Clutch to shove her to the side. Aimee swore. A bolt of unstable mystic power exploded in the air where her head had been a second before. The astronomers shouted. Aimee pushed herself up on her hands in time to watch as Diara was forced to shift her hands into a defensive posture, deflecting another spell while the traitor astronomer cackled madly by the panel he'd destroyed. Then he lunged for the central console.

"Her eyes will burn!" he screamed. "Sightless she shall stagger into Grandfather's waiting arms! Rise, Children of the Empty Sky!"

Diara's hands flashed with coruscating light, and the traitor ignited. Fire blasted from his eyes and mouth, and a shriveled corpse fell to the floor.

Aimee had half a second to catch her breath, then a mass of black-clad cultists swarmed over the platform's edge, screaming, "Blind the eyes! Blind the eyes! Empty Sky! Empty Sky!"

"Defend the console!" Diara shouted. The astronomers hurtled themselves forward. Clutch slammed into a running cultist. Her knife darted in and came away red. The man dropped, twitching. Living, not dead. That made things easier. She froze a man solid with a bolt of frost and shattered him with a gust of wind. These, then, were the wretches that had tried to kill *Iseult*'s beating heart, whom the Faceless used as his living agents of murder and chaos. Who worshipped a thing that smelled of rain. Aimee felt a swell of terrible, overpowering rage. She stormed forward as they came. Her hands summoned combative spells sparking into the air around her.

"Was it one of you?" She ducked under a swiping knife and set fire to its wielder's face. Her booted foot stepped over his twitching body and she wind-blasted the man behind him into one of his compatriots. "Where is he?" she heard herself demanding. Cold. Furious. Another came at her. She froze his arm and shattered it at the elbow. Her scream carried above the uproar, hateful and loud. "WHERE IS HARKON BRIGHT?"

The fight raged around her. She tried to keep her back to the console, but the cultists were everywhere, swarming, lashing out viciously at anything that looked breakable. Their targets were the objects, not the people. Sorcerers. There were sorcerers among them. Unrefined.

Likely half-trained, but fighting to control the panel from swinging cudgels was nothing when two people could melt it at a distance.

She didn't have to look far. They climbed the steps behind their brethren, wearing rags and clutching profane talismans in gnarled fingers. A pair of hedge mages, likely reared on the mad scribblings of stolen form-scrolls. All skill. No theory. A bolt of fire was hurled at her, disjointed, barely contained. She sidestepped it. There was nothing so simultaneously incompetent and horrifically dangerous as a hedge mage that thought they knew something.

"Was it one of *you*?" she snarled. "Did your wretched cult come for my mentor?"

"Foreign *bitch*," the more forward of the two snapped back. "Soon all will know Grandfather's embrace. Your wealth and your teaching will not save you from him."

A crude blast of mystic force thundered up the steps at her. Aimee's hands swept up, formed a wedge, and split the chaotic spell down the middle. The sundered energy dissipated behind her. "Get a new line."

Her two enemies unleashed a barrage of crude, unstable mystic assaults. Aimee ducked, weaved, blocked, and cleared the last of them with a leap that brought her into direct, physical range. A spell lashed from her right, one from her left. She formed a wedge-shaped shield spell between the two of them. Caught the brunt of each. Then she summoned her frost, dissipated the barrier before they could react, and unleashed her magic on both hedge mages at once. "Enough!" she screamed. "I'm done with fear and beyond sick of dealing with amateur hour at the psychopath establishment. This is my arena, you incompetent fanatics. Out!"

Her hands flashed one more time, and a blast of wind ripped outward, shattering the two frozen mages into a thousand pieces of ice. She stood on the steps, breathing hard. Tingling from the expenditure of magic energy. Then she heard the cries coming from behind, and spun on her heel so fast she nearly fell off the stairway. She rushed upwards, clearing the steps two at a time.

Aimee reached the top just as the lights came on once more, the power restored. The platform was a charnel house. Dead cultists lay strewn across the floor along with over half the astronomers. She saw Clutch, covered in blood, but still standing, and breathed a momentary sigh of relief. A second glance. The central control panel was still intact.

Then she heard the wailing, and it took her a few seconds to recognize that it was Haysha weeping. "Blind!" she cried. "We are blinded!"

Aimee's mouth dried. Her hands felt like lead weights. The astronomer crouched at the base of the central control station. Cradled in her arms, unseeing eyes staring up at the starscape to which she'd dedicated the whole of her life, lay Diara.

The Countess of Astronomers was dead.

Aimee's footsteps carried her through the street. Behind her, the chaos of the dome was being managed. Clutch followed. Dimly, the apprentice portalmage processed the immediate aftermath of the countess's death. She knew what would happen next. Yaresh would make a direct play for the captaincy. It would take him perhaps two days to gather everything he needed. But there would be no more council meetings. No further moderation.

Her footsteps carried her through the streets. She had succeeded. She had failed. In one day she had saved a single life, and lost so many others. Viltas's armsmen. So many of the astronomers. Diara herself.

Yet amidst the terrible weight of a pressing failure, there was also a sudden, visceral clarity. *Iseult* could not survive what was coming without a captain. That captain could not be Yaresh, and now Diara was gone, which meant it could only be one other.

"Where are we going?" Clutch asked. "You're headed in the opposite direction of *Elysium*."

"I just have one thing to do," Aimee said. "A suspicion to confirm. It will only take a few moments."

"Still not an answer to the question," the pilot said, though her voice had lost most of its snark.

"Amut's compound," Aimee said. "There is something I have to see. That I have to know."

Look upon his face, Diara's voice echoed in her mind. *And you will see.*

The black estate emerged from the curtain of rain. Its glossy walls wept rivulets of pouring water, and its stately windows were cold and dark. Aimee climbed the steps. The main doors yielded to her at a simple spell, and she stepped across the threshold into the interior of the late captain's residence.

This would've been different, Viltas said in her mind, *if he'd had any legitimate children.*

How could she have been so blind?

Her boots echoed across the hardwood floor, past furniture now draped in pale white sheets that made them seem as ghosts in the darkness. A flash of lightning painted the edges of the interior white for just a moment, and Aimee walked as if in a dream towards the great hearth that dominated the room. Over it, still covered by a shroud, was a barely visible portrait of the former captain.

"Seriously?" Clutch said. "You came here to look at his painting?"

The Oracle's words flashed through her head. *The trials have begun. The time has come for choices.*

There is one other they would follow.

There was a black cord hanging from the shroud. Aimee clasped it in her hands.

…the only woman he ever loved was some downleveler girl…

"…My mother loved a man who lost her…"

She pulled the cord as hard as she could, and the shroud fell away, revealing the visage of Captain Amut. Behind Aimee, Clutch swore as she belatedly realized what Aimee should have seen from the beginning. "Holy shit."

The resemblance wasn't perfect: Amut's face had been squarer, his expression more reserved. His eyebrows were thicker than the slender ones of his daughter's face. Yet the dark skin, the warmth of disposition – captured by a superb painter – was unmistakable, and the gold eyes of the late captain were the twins of ones that Aimee knew all too well.

Aimee stood beneath the portrait of Captain Amut, and stared into the face he had given – along with so much else – to his daughter, Belit.

CHAPTER NINETEEN
A Breath before the Night

It was the better part of a day before the aching in Elias's head subsided. The healing magic had done its work, but for that span, he'd been forced to wait in his cabin aboard *Elysium*. The leather and mail were mostly repaired, rings knitted back together and leather stitched where it had been torn or battered. The repair work was supposed to be a focal point for calming his nerves.

By the time he was done, it hadn't worked at all. And as word rolled in of what had happened since he'd returned with Bjorn to *Elysium*, it became so much worse. Diara, and half the astronomers, dead. The council in shambles. The officer aristocrats fled to their duty-stations and their estates, abandoning even the pretext of fulfilling their task of selecting a captain. All the while, *Tristan* flew deeper into the crescent, and *Iseult* pursued. Finally, Elias gave up trying to cloister himself, and ventured out into the ship just in time to hear Aimee talking down the hallway in the common area.

He climbed the steps, still dizzy. It wasn't just the blow to the head. He hadn't used his own magic with this sort of regularity in well over a month now, and, like any muscle, when it went unworked, the endurance faded first. He staggered a little. Hiding had been the game since they came to *Iseult*, with a handful of exceptions when his powers were necessary... but it seemed that wasn't going to be an option any more. If he wanted to be useful, to make a difference, anything less than his best would not suffice.

He stepped into the common room and found the rest of the crew seated. Aimee and Clutch had cleaned up and gotten at least a little rest. He felt a small pang of relief, again, that neither of them were injured.

They stopped when he entered the room, and an awkward silence settled. Then, to his surprise, Vlana spoke up. "Heard what you did out there. How's your head?"

"Still sore," Elias answered, quietly, "but better. I'm good to go, once I know what we're doing. Bjorn filled me in, at least on Diara."

"The question is," Vant said, "what now?" The engineer had returned from the metadrive chamber earlier that morning. "We've got, what, a day before Yaresh storms the wheelhouse?"

"Maybe a little more," Rachim said. "The wheelhouse is well guarded, and taking it by force won't win him any allies, but I don't know that he'll much care any longer. *Iseult* is headed for the maelstrom, and he can argue that pursuing *Tristan* is a suicide mission. He wouldn't be wrong, even if there are a lot of people on our sister ship."

"Do we stop him?" Bjorn asked. "Does that make sense any more? The ship needs a captain, and–"

"And the ship is already *choosing* one," Aimee cut him off. "We just didn't see it before, though the signs were obvious. The trials of captaincy are already being put forth, by the ship's Oracle." She gave a small smile, rueful for how long it had taken her to see the obvious. "It's Belit. She's a proven leader, adored by downlevelers, respected by many of the officer aristocracy, and–" she looked at Elias "–she is Amut's illegitimate daughter."

As the truth washed over Elias, all the disparate parts, only seen piecemeal since they arrived on *Iseult*, fell into place. It had been Amut, after all, that had first chosen her to join the Red Guard. It seemed insane that he'd never guessed at it. *You were distracted*, he reminded himself. *By many, many things*.

"So that's your play," he said. "Throw Yaresh down and put Belit on the throne?"

"No," Aimee said, shaking her head, then pausing. "Well, not entirely. I plan to stop Yaresh. He's benefitted enough from all this insanity to make me suspicious that he isn't at least allowing it to happen."

"Yaresh is no sorcerer," Rachim murmured.

"I don't think he needs to be," Aimee countered. "Everything I've read in Harkon's books suggests that a necromancer as powerful as the Faceless might have been able to survive the destruction of his original body. I believe, in fact, that he has been inhabiting someone on the upper levels of *Iseult*."

"He can speak through any of his thralls," Elias added. "And when I last faced them, he called me..." He paused, Rachim didn't know. "...He called me by a title that only a few people on *Iseult* – three, to be precise – might recognize the significance of. Yaresh is one of those people."

"He has seemed energized by every unfolding of death and chaos that's happened on this ship," Vant acknowledged.

"It's possible," Rachim admitted. "Enough that we can't discount it."

"Then we convince Belit to finish the trials," Aimee said. "And then, hopefully, we save the ship, and *Tristan*."

"Do we even know what's happening over there?" Vlana asked.

"Last I heard, madness," Rachim grunted. "There was a plague gripping the ship when we arrived back at the flotilla… They were trying to quarantine the lower levels, but it wasn't looking good. Viltas had a smaller ship sent over shortly after the portal storm, but they never returned and there have been no communications."

"We may have to leave them to their fates," Clutch said. Elias looked at the pilot in surprise. The others did likewise.

"Why?" he asked.

"In the astronomy dome," Clutch said, "those cultists – the Children of the Empty Sky. Most of what they were saying was rambling, apocalyptic nonsense… but I heard one of the sorcerers Aimee killed talking about bringing the ship to the waiting arms of Grandfather."

The pilot wrapped her arms around her middle and suppressed a shudder. It struck Elias that this was the first time he'd ever seen Clutch look afraid. "Look," the pilot · said. "I'm not advocating for leaving countless innocents to their deaths… but I've flown through the crescent before, and I know that name. A half-mad skyfarer we picked up in a lifeboat on that trip whispered it, and that whisper was enough to make a crew of hard-nosed salvagers–" Elias noted she used the word very deliberately "–damn near piss themselves and abandon both the treasure they sought and the mission they were on." She looked at each of them. "Whatever that thing is out there that they're worshipping, it's not just a story, and I'm not in a hurry to learn what degree of real it is."

"The Oracle mentioned it too," Elias recalled. "And Viltas said the thing the Faceless was communing with back when Amut killed him smelled of rain."

Clutch shook her head. "We've gotta get control of this ship back, then turn it the hell around."

"First we have to talk to Belit," Aimee said. "Then we gather what allies we've got, and we move first thing tomorrow." She fixed Clutch with an understanding, but unyielding look. "We'll worry about things outside the ship once we have the ability to do something about them."

Elias had met Belit dozens of times before, but this was different. He and Aimee walked through the ominously quiet streets towards the agreed-upon meeting place: the training hall of the Red Guard. They found the room empty, its lamps extinguished, and only the intermittent light that pierced the thick clouds outside poured through the windows.

In a training circle in the center of the room, she stood, a sharp longsword in her hand as over and over she repeated the basic overhand cuts every student of their shared art was required to know. With every descent of the blade and every snapping rise, the keening wind of the edge splitting the air echoed in the cavernous room.

She addressed them before either had a chance to speak. "There is an old legend," she said, "that in the ancient times, before we came to the Drifting Lands, a space such as this could not be left empty without a light on to drive the demons away."

She paused, and turned to regard the two of them. "I first came here as a ten year-old girl, and my first teacher taught me that absent a light, a practitioner of the art, training in somber focus, would suffice. Since that day, this room has never once been empty. When the guard is not performing their duties or sleeping, they train. Now all of them are on assignment, and only I remain to keep the demons out."

"Do you know why we're here?" Aimee asked.

"I suspect," Belit said, "that you want my help against Yaresh in his inevitable coup. But if Diara is dead, and the council will not meet, I suspect the wheelhouse will not resist him. My duty is to defend the captain... If Yaresh claims the seat, I fear I will have to become your enemy."

"Yaresh is not captain yet," Aimee said.

"There is no other to oppose him," Belit said.

"There is, teacher," Elias said. "You."

Belit stopped. The look on her face was a mixture of emotions – fear, apprehension, and pain... but not, Elias noted, surprise. "You cannot ask me that," she said.

"The Oracle has already asked you," Aimee said. "Twice now, in our presence."

When Belit averted her eyes, Aimee's own expression turned surprised. "And you knew it, didn't you?"

Belit sheathed her sword. "The suggestion has been made more than once," she murmured. "At first it was a handful of officers in Amut's company. He was... a reformer. When I was chosen from the downlevelers to serve in his Red Guard, many whispered it was because I was being groomed for command. But there have been no trials in a long time, and the council selects its rulers. They would never suffer one from the lower levels to sit in his seat… a foreign hero was an indignity galling enough to them. As I climbed the ranks, my own men began to murmur it. I bid them stop. Power was never my aim. Only excellence, and service."

"Belit," Aimee started to say. "It must be you."

"Why?" The commander turned and stared at them, anger and pain apparent on her face. "Because I am the most useful of allies you possess? Because I am respected? Because I wield a sword? None of these things make me fit for the role of guiding *Iseult* through the heavens! None of them make me the worthiest guardian of her people, her traditions, her…" Her voice faltered, filled with a deep and raging self-doubt which Elias knew too well. "…her heart."

Aimee's face froze.

"I am no expert on this ship," Elias said quietly, "on her traditions, or her rich history, but I know a few things about leadership, if only the traits that render a person unfit for it. Your doubt is all the proof I need, teacher, to know that your heart is humble enough to sit in the chair. You have the sort of courage people follow, and the benevolence of spirit that inspires them to greatness."

That stopped her for a moment. Belit closed her eyes and swore under her breath with the vehemence of one that had faced those sorts of statements before. "The council would never recognize me."

"We're past that," Aimee said, recovering. "The trials are already happening, commander. You're the one they were laid out for. You're the only one who can truly complete them, I think, which is why Yaresh fears you… and I believe you are the only one whom the council *would* accept, after all this. You are Captain Amut's daughter."

The words hit the commander hard, and she stared at Aimee for a long moment, before breathing out, and saying – at last – "So, you know."

Elias opened his mouth, and Belit gave him a pointed look. "I'm no squitten-eyed shop-girl, *junk ritter*," she said with a sad smile. "Yes. I knew. We seldom spoke of it, but I long ago guessed. How could I not?" The slightest bitterness crept into her voice. "A thousand downleveler children he might have noticed, might have punished for attempted robbery, and the one he spares happens by chance to share his face, his eyes? I'd have been a fool not to realize, and in time, I did."

"Why didn't you put your name forth for the captaincy?" Aimee asked.

Belit sighed, helplessly. "Do you not listen, sorceress? My life was defined by where I came from, and I have spent it proving that my skill, my virtue, and not my blood earned what I had accomplished. To fall back upon an accident of birth to justify a claim at a power that I am not even sure I am equal to? Unthinkable. I earn what I am, Aimee de Laurent. No one can take that from me." Her tone carried a weight of mingled pains: abandonment, pride, bitterness, and a complex affection deeper than words could express. "Not even my father."

Elias took a breath. The answer was clear, then, even if she did not yet see it. "Then do as you always have, teacher," he said quietly. "The trials are not a given, and neither is the captaincy. Pass them, by your skill and virtue," he pressed. "And earn it."

Belit fell silent for a long time. She stared at him in frustration, then with an affectionate exasperation, then she let out a long sigh. "You're far too clever for your own good, *junk ritter*."

"It's why we keep him around," Aimee said. The approving smile on her face was feline.

"I will need a little time," Belit said, "to alert my inner circle. I assume you mean to move on him tomorrow?"

"With every ally we can," Aimee said.

In his mind, Elias was thinking about every able-bodied soul that could be lost putting a stop to Yaresh. It was a disastrous military gambit, tactically. But if they won–

"Then I will come to you tonight," she said. "At Rachim's villa, no later than midnight. Be waiting for me."

"We will," Elias said. "You have my word."

As they turned to go, Belit spoke one last time. "I fear you may have doomed us both, *junk ritter*. But perhaps that is not so bad."

Elias paused before they slipped out the door. There seemed no point, now, in being anything less than candid. "I've been living on borrowed time for months," he said with a grin. "Choosing where you die is a novelty."

They spent the rest of the day preparing. Rachim went to rally up the allies that remained to him amongst the council. Vant made sure *Elysium* was still skyworthy, Vlana redid an inventory of their supplies. Plans were laid out. Paper got involved. Math.

When that was over, Elias found himself alone in the main bay, and – for once in his life – in the midst of what was essentially a military plan he was neither leading, nor taking the lead on preparing. It was dissonant, not being the one to make the hard choices. It was not that he craved the position, and if asked, would have refused it. The memories of choices he'd made as Azrael in Port Providence were fresh, and painful, and if there was one thing of which he was certain, it was that he never wished to be a mercenary or soldier ever again.

But it still left him feeling uncertain, and with a profound sense of not knowing what to *do* with himself. Alone, the sound of his breath filled the cavernous bay of the small ship that was his adopted home. He wondered, idly, if Belit's story had originated from the same white knights as her branch of the art they shared. He wondered at a dim memory of Roland's old book, with its depictions of roses and chalices, of the visions from his dreams, and a simple, faded stone statue in Port Providence, at whose feet Azrael had collapsed, only for Elias to arise.

Knight upon the White Path, the Oracle had called him.

Perhaps it didn't need to be as complicated as any of those things. Perhaps it was as simple as Belit had said: one practitioner, one light to keep the demons at bay.

He drew Oath of Aurum. The blade was warm. Its white lantern-light pushed back the shadows.

"More literal than you meant, I think," he said out loud.

"Talking to yourself isn't healthy," Aimee said. Turning, he saw her standing at the entry to the main hallway that spanned the spine of the ship. The light from the common area framed her silhouette, firing the edge of her blonde hair. Elias squinted as he turned. Sometimes Aimee was hard to look at directly.

"Still getting to know myself," he quipped back. "There's no knowing without conversation."

"You know," she said thoughtfully, "I actually can't judge you for that one."

He smirked, sheathing his sword. "It's a night for firsts."

She laughed, the sound light – a little nervous – then recovered. "Come on, Elias Leblanc," she beckoned for him to follow. "The crew is sharing a drink in the common room. We're already one less. It shouldn't be two."

The common room was dimly lit. Enough that outside the big window, the skyline above the lip of the landing pad could be seen. Thick clouds had gathered, and another squall approached. A chill went through Elias at the sight of it. He remembered the terrors carried by the storms that spun free from the maelstrom. The whispers and magic they carried. It was an unnatural place, never fully mapped save the sheer breadth of its edge. The legends said that it was over a thousand years old, the extant penance the thousand gods had meted out upon humanity for the hubris of long-destroyed Varengard.

It was an old story, and not one that he remembered well, but the Eternal Order considered the storm sacred for a reason.

"And there they are," Bjorn said, producing a flask. "Sit, kids. Hark would bust our asses if we didn't throw one back for him on the eve of battle…" At the uneasy looks from the others, he added, "…wherever he is."

He raised his flask. "To Hark." Small glasses sat on the table, already poured. They each lifted theirs in turn. It smelled like wine – not expensive, sweet. Elias drank, echoing the words of the others. "To Harkon Bright."

"Never seen storms like this," Vant said. "And I've flown a lot of places. Never thought home would bring me so near."

The word *home* had a weight to it just then, Elias thought. The others caught it.

"Where is that, anyway?" Clutch asked, thoughtfully. "Don't think we've ever asked that question, have we? In all the times we've drunk before we were supposed to die. What's home, when it's not here?"

"Questions like that don't get answered without the flask," Bjorn said. "Guess we're not doing any bullshit before we just jump right into the tradition, are we?"

"It's simple," Vlana said, and she nodded her chin in Elias and Aimee's direction. "Answer and drink. We learn a bit more about each other. We taste the same swill. We remember that we're crew."

"My spirits aren't *swill*," Bjorn objected.

"Whatever, old-timer," Clutch said. "You start."

They sat around the table in the dim room. Outside, thunder crackled through distant clouds. The silence had unsettled Elias the last time he came to the Tempest Crescent, and it unsettled him now.

Bjorn's fingers wrapped around the dented flash. "Before here?" he said. "Home was a farm on Skellig." Red-eyed, he took a drink then passed it right. "It's gone, now."

Next was Vant. "Home," the engineer said, "has only ever been a hammock hanging over a metadrive core." Short words. Abrupt, but there was a fondness in them, rare for the engineer to show to anything. He drank, pounded his chest, and passed the flask to Vlana.

The quartermaster contemplated the table in front of her. Thunder rumbled far away. "The nest," she said. "On some other behemoth where Vant and I were born years ago. It was small, and there were maybe three dozen other orphans to share it with. At night it got cold, but sometimes I think that it wasn't so bad." She drank too, then passed it on. Her face squinted up at the bitterness.

"The Navigator's Loft," Clutch said with simple affection. "Where I was raised. You could always see the stars." Short in her words, she drank the dark liquor, then passed the flask to Aimee.

The sorceress looked exhausted. Her blue eyes played over the metal thing in her hand. As Elias watched, a fondness, a soft light, kindled in their depths at the sparking of some good memory. "The upper ring of Havensreach," she finally said. "The library, with its old book smell. And–" she shook her head "–the rose gardens. They always smelled like spring."

She drank. Elias almost didn't notice that it was passing into his hands. For a moment he was completely silent. What was he to say himself? The metal turned over in his hands as a series of answers ranging from the cynical to the macabre played through his mind. The word *home* seemed ludicrous, coming from his mouth. He had only the distant recollection of a place that some part of him wasn't even sure had existed. A place. A person. More than either, a melody that sometimes found itself on his lips. It seemed an insufficient answer, but at least it was true.

"A song," Elias said simply. He drank the dark burn without blinking. "Home is a song."

Outside the thunder rolled on and on, into the night.

CHAPTER TWENTY
THE RED SUN RISES

In the pre-dawn dark, Aimee stood in Harkon's quarters. The dim light of the glow-globes played off his abandoned notes, his books, the possessions he counted as sacred. She'd dressed for battle. Boots. Pants. The blue coat she'd worn from Havensreach and through a war. She'd bound her hair up behind her head and slid leather fingerless gloves over her hands. Her fingers flexed in the darkness. She was an apprentice, alone now. Possibly orphaned. Fists clenched. No. She was the sky-splitter. Aimee de Laurent. She had destroyed demons and torn down mountains. She had quested across the sky and plucked truth from the heart of darkness. With a shaking, forceful breath, she buried the fear, the doubt, anything that kept her from acting, and searching and fighting. She would neither cry, nor throw herself on the mercies of her enemies.

She would find who had done this, and she would *bring them down*.

"Yaresh," she murmured under her breath. "We're coming for you."

Then she started down the hallway to rejoin her

companions. It was time to pick a fight.

The crew of *Elysium* waited for her in Rachim's foyer. She heard them talking as she approached, ghost-voices echoing long before she saw them. She paused for a second, just out of sight, and took their measure. Bjorn had a hard, murderous look on his face, quieter than she'd ever seen him. The twins wore matching leather armor, and Vant had his shock-sticks hanging from his hips. Elias stood alone, off to the side, with his repaired secondhand leather and mail. He picked up a curved, single-edged messer from the table before him, and belted it over his left shoulder.

Rachim leaned over a large map on a table, speaking to a number of his guards. "Yaresh has his own armsmen, and – in theory – authority over a proportion of those men sworn by other officer aristocrats to his service. I suspect we can rely on several of them to refuse, especially with the ship being in the state that it is. One of ours holds the metadrive chamber, which gives us leverage... But the *key*–"

Her feet impulsively guided her forward, and Aimee stepped into the light, finishing their host's sentence. "–is getting Yaresh."

Conversation ceased. All eyes were upon her.

From the far end of the room, Belit stepped into the light as well. She no longer wore her red plate. In its place, munitions grade steel of plain gray swathed her from neck to foot. Her broad-bladed longsword was belted at her hip, plain and razor sharp. "I pray," she said, "that you leave him to me."

Aimee looked at her, and felt the small object in her pocket, her insurance, if it worked. "No promises."

Especially, she thought, *if he's hosting a necromancer I'm not sure I'm equal to facing.*

Fortunately, she reflected, she wasn't alone.

The dim red of pre-dawn painted the skies as they left Rachim's villa. The wheelhouse stood out at the prow, visible by its running lamps against the fading stars. A thin layer of fog played through the streets, passing wisp-like around them as they walked. Aimee, Rachim, and Belit were in the lead, and as they passed, the apprentice portalmage caught glimpses of lights in windows, seen for only a moment before curtains were hastily closed. When Aimee had been in primary school, she'd learned about a period in Havensreach's history where the city had been ruled by a runaway chancellor-turned-dictator. She'd asked her father how such a man could seize power when so many in the city, highborn and low, despised him.

Most people don't like conflict, her father had told her. *Not when it stands before them and they stand to lose the many fineries of a comfortable life.*

She'd always wondered what she would've done. Despite her fear as they walked through the streets, she also felt a small sense of relief: now she knew.

They reached the base of the wheelhouse tower first. It seemed strange to Aimee that she'd been aboard *Iseult* this long without seeing the thrumming mind of the ship. The tower was nondescript. Ivory-colored, with simplistic doors crowning a small semicircle of steps at its base. It was flanked by two equally tall black spires at the foremost corners of the massive behemoth, and connected to both by one seamless white bridge, pale in the darkness.

"The last time I was here," Belit murmured, "Amut was still captain, and I stood watch over him."

"Austere," Elias remarked.

"The finery of officer aristocracy has not yet infected everything sacred in our home," Rachim said. Then he turned and addressed his men. "Fan out. Semicircle at the base of the stairs. We'll force him to answer us before he makes for his objective. At the very least, he won't be able to go around us."

And then they waited. This close to the prow of the skyship, the wind of its passage through the heavens was a dull roar rather than a distant groan. Of their allies, Viltas alone had not joined them, still watching over his unconscious son. He'd sent his remaining armsmen, however, and they joined Rachim's men at the base of the steps, arrayed and armored, armed with shock-spears, and two mystic energy projectors, more refined versions of the weapons the enlisted had assembled down below in defense of their home. Behind Belit was Hakat, her second-in-command, and three more members of her Red Guard.

After what seemed too long, the cold and the silence both started to creep into Aimee's mind. Had they misjudged their opponents? Was Yaresh trying another tactic? Had the council perhaps been assembled without their knowledge? The questions rose like a bile in the back of her throat. She'd triumphed in Port Providence, but that had been as much luck as it had been skill. She'd had her teacher to help her, and Elias had betrayed his former masters in order to do the right thing?

What if she'd gambled everything, and guessed wrong?

Then Elias shifted, his hand going to his sword. The gold chasing on the hilt caught the light of the slowly rising sun, and he inclined his head towards the central thoroughfare that spanned the spine of *Iseult*. "They're here."

Aimee squinted through the morning dim half-light… but it was the sound she caught first. Rhythmic. A steady, intermittent thump of many feet drummed on the streets in unison.

"That," she heard Vlana murmur, "sounds like a *lot* of boots."

Aimee saw the points of their shock-spears first. They glinted in the red dawn light. From the pale fog they emerged, a wall of beige uniforms, lightly armored, with ranks in perfect order stretching out behind them.

And in the lead, unafraid to be seen, clad in his gilded, ornate steel and bearing a naked sword in a gauntleted hand, the authoritarian himself. His helm was crested with feathers, and his cold eyes fixed upon them with murderous intent. He reached the square and raised a clenched fist. The ranks of his small army – still bigger than their own – came to an orderly halt.

Yaresh.

Silence. The would-be captain stepped forward, and his voice rang out across the space. "Rachim!" he shouted. "I confess, I never thought you would take your suicide-pact politics this far! *Iseult* sits at the edge of oblivion! Will you not let me *save* her?"

"I've never seen a man more giddy at the suffering of his ship!" Rachim shouted back. "You're not taking the wheelhouse, Yaresh. Even if you do, I doubt the chair will have you. *Iseult* is already in the process of choosing her own!"

That cut close to the heart. Yaresh's face twitched as

Aimee watched, and he took several steps towards the line of armsmen at the base of the stairs. "Pentus is dead," he said. "Diara is dead. Only I remain. Only I am worthy."

"And isn't it strange," Aimee shouted across the space, "that at every step of the way, the people opposed to you have met their deaths at the hands of cultists, undead, and convenient *accidents*."

She saw the faces of the men behind him shift, glancing left to right. So he *had* cloistered his armsmen against contesting ideals. Not well, apparently.

"Your task is done, little girl," Yaresh snapped at her. "The council you were here to moderate has abdicated its sacred duty. You cannot moderate this. Crawl back to your foreign silver skyship and weep over your coward master. I have a home to save."

The fury in Aimee's chest exploded. She stepped forward impulsively, ambient sorcery sparking in the air around her hands and eyes. "I didn't come here to moderate you, Yaresh. I came here to put you the hell down."

"The sorceress seeks my death!" Yaresh shouted. "You all heard it! This is a contest for power between our people and the foreign influence of meddling outsiders with *no* respect for our sovereignty, our culture, our very safety! You wish to know whom I stand against, people of *Iseult*?" He shouted at the assembled. "It is her!"

"NO."

The declaration rang across the square. Aimee nearly took a step back at the force of the words, and by the time she'd identified their source, Belit had already descended the steps and entered the square beyond the line of Rachim's men. Her gold eyes stared down the lord of the muster as her armored feet trod over the cobbles, stopping a few feet from where her opponent stood.

"Belit," Yaresh said after a moment, and for the first time, Aimee caught a hint of fear. "You overstep your place."

"Wrong," the lioness answered. "Captain Amut raised me from nothing to the command of the Red Guard. I've been from one end of this ship to the other. I have lived as a downleveler, an officer aristocrat, and everything inbetween. I am the daughter of Amut, Lion of Heaven, and the Oracle herself laid the trials of captaincy at my feet. *Iseult* is my home, my duty, my burden."

Her sword rang free, the cold steel painted red by the light of the rising dawn. "You stand against me, Lord of the Muster."

A murmur passed through Yaresh's men. Their confidence wavered. *They don't want to fight her,* Aimee realized. *Diara was right: there is only one on this ship whom everyone will follow.*

Yaresh took a step forward, and his words were filled with the fury of wounded pride. "You have no authority to oppose me."

"I have every authority," Belit replied, dark face fierce. "You stand accused of sedition, of conspiracy to murder, of collaboration with our enemies. Of tyranny by force over all those beneath you, and now of mutiny. As commander of the Red Guard, I order you to stand down."

The lord of the muster's eyes were wide. Aimee watched the assembled armsmen behind him hesitating. Beside her, she heard Elias muttering under his breath. "If he breaks, they break."

Yaresh watched Belit in silence for what seemed an eternity, then he let out a furious, humiliated shout of rage, and lunged at her. His ornate sword snapped out at her head. He still knew how to move. His strength had not yet abandoned him to age.

Belit's sword descended. She hammered into his cut, controlled his sword, and snaked her arm around his own blade to grip her gray steel halfway up its length. Her hips rotated. The lord of the muster's sword was levered out of his grasp and sent skittering across the street. His gauntleted fist rose to strike her unvisored face, and with a triumphant shout, she pulled his bodyweight through the punch. The lord of the muster let out a shout of dismay and shock as Belit flipped him through the air and body-slammed the entirety of his armored weight into the cobbles. Yaresh landed on his back, his breath leaving him with an explosive cry. Belit crouched over him, sword still held in two hands, its point hovering inches from his eye.

"This is over!" she shouted. "Yield!"

A quivering series of chokes and gasps escaped from the downed man, as the assembled men and women in the square stared on. Then Aimee heard a small, choking reply. "I yield."

Belit drove her knee harder into Yaresh's hip. Something had broken when he went down. He let out a cry of pain. "So they can hear you. Command your men to stand down," the swordswoman pressed.

"I yield!" Yaresh screamed. "Throw down your weapons!" he shouted at his men. "I YIELD!"

A chorus of clattering sounds echoed through the square as hundreds of warriors let their armaments fall to the streets. The sun was up now, and its red rays filled the square with a brilliant light, painting the ivory tower of the wheelhouse in crimson and gold. Belit had disarmed Yaresh's uprising, without spilling a single drop of blood.

Aimee let out a breath she didn't know she'd been holding.

It was over.

The interior of the Council Hall was dark and cold. They stood before the blue table, and in his own personal seat, Yaresh sat, stripped of his armor and bound hand and foot. In a semicircle, they surrounded him: Belit, Aimee, Elias, Rachim, Viltas. Behind them stood Bjorn, and the rest of the *Elysium* crew. Haysha, new Countess of Astronomers, stood by as well, her cold anger chilling the air.

"And now," Rachim said, his voice a low growl, "we will have answers."

Yaresh slowly raised angry, dejected eyes to stare at them. "I owe you nothing."

"Every one of your political opponents and enemies has died," Viltas said. He looked tired again, Aimee thought, ravaged by the recent near-death of his son, and there was an intense, fierce dislike in his face. "You were always Amut's most stringent opponent, when it came to his reforms for the downlevelers."

"Don't think to lecture me," Yaresh snapped, "washed-up wreck of a former hero: I remember the dominion of the Faceless as well as you."

Something snapped in Viltas, and the lord shipman exploded, slamming his hands into the arms of Yaresh's chair. "No!" he screamed. "You will not profane his memory by association! Not in the presence of those who have opposed your authoritarian insanity! You, who spit on the idea of reform, who have truncheon-bearing brutes brutalizing our people below! You will not profane the heroism of my companions by association! While we fought the Faceless, you sat in your ancestral mansion and cowered in fear!"

For the first time in the brief span that Aimee had known him, Yaresh's expression showed a hint of something near to shame.

"Pentus," Belit said. "Diara. Amut. Answer."

"I didn't kill Pentus," Yaresh said. The force of Belit's throw had left him shaken, probably dislocated a joint or two. He was in obvious pain. "Nor did I kill Diara."

He looked at Aimee, as if seeming to sense her next question. "Nor do I know what became of your master. But he–" the defeated lord of the muster inclined his head towards Elias "–is Eternal Order, so you will forgive me if your cries of virtue seem empty to me."

"You're one of only a handful who knows of my former allegiance," Elias said, bluntly. "Something the Faceless has used against me."

Yaresh looked back and forth between them all, and then his face split as he started laughing. "Oh... oh gods," he said around his laughter. "You think it's me."

"Have a care how lightly you treat this," Viltas said dangerously. "My son still lies abed from the wounds received at the hands of the dead. You are the obvious candidate."

"If I were truly a necromancer," Yaresh snapped, "do you fools think any of you would be alive right now?"

"We could be at this for hours," Bjorn snarled. "Around and around."

"Then let's end it," Aimee said. The insurance was in her pocket, the tool she'd brought with her to suss out the truth. She pulled the small satchel from inside her blue coat, and produced the glimmering Axiom Diamond. A collective gasp echoed from around them.

"What," Viltas breathed, "is that?"

"The means," Aimee said, and before anyone else could object, she pressed it to the center of Yaresh's forehead, hoping it would still work this close to the maelstrom.

The world faded. Aimee braced herself for the visions of before, the complexity that had come when she'd had the truth of Elias Leblanc revealed to her... but instead, she simply heard the familiar voice in her head, its words thick with strain.

"You don't ask small favors, do you, hero?"

And in a storm of images, sights, sounds, and whirling recollections, she came to know Yaresh, soldier, politician, coward, warrior. A man who aspired to greatness, yet choked over and over, or mistook the signs when the opportunity for virtue lay before him.

The callow boy, resentful of others' glories.

The bitter teenager, given wealth and stature, and not a slice of wisdom.

The angry man, hiding in terror from the shadow of a monster beyond him, then shamefully cringing from the impossible shade cast by the hero that defeated it.

She saw failure. She saw double deals. She saw planned political killings, and innocents left to die when it didn't suit the lord of the muster's aims to save them. She saw neglect, fear, nationalism, and authoritarian ambition.

But she did not see the blood of Diara, of Pentus, of even Amut, on the lord of the muster's mind. And across the darkness of his pathetic, mediocre life, only the fear of the Faceless cast its shadow.

When she pulled back, in the empty cold of the Council Hall, before the blue table, it took her a moment to summon any words at all. She'd taken the measure of the man named Yaresh, looking for the darkness of a dread lord, and had instead found nothing at all.

"Aimee?" Elias's voice brought her back to the now. Yaresh stared up at her, his eyes wide, tears of shame leaking down his face. In place of the terrible would-be conqueror was nothing more than an old man, broken and pathetic.

"He didn't do it," she said, feeling a mingled panic and despair rise within her. "It's not him."

She was still struggling with the revelation, with the utter dead end her plan had led them to, when the far door to the chamber burst open, and Belit's second, Hakat, came running towards them. At the same time, there was a loud crash without, and the floor beneath them shook.

"Commander!" he shouted across the room to the swordswoman. "The wheelhouse sends word! Raiding ships have been spotted astern, closing fast. We're under attack!"

CHAPTER TWENTY-ONE
THE HELPFUL STRANGER

If there was one thing Elias understood well, it was war. They sprinted out into the street in time to see a tower further down explode into flames as a cluster of three ships loomed against the risen sun. Their make was hodgepodge, mismatched sets of broken pieces bolted together and powered by unstable metadrives that sent flaring bursts of light from their exhaust ports at irregular intervals.

"Oh hell," Elias heard Clutch say behind him. "Crescent raiders."

He shot a look over his shoulder at her in time for Aimee to snap, "Clarification please?"

"I told you," Clutch answered. "People who fly in the crescent for too long start to lose their minds. Crescent raiders are the worst of the lot. Even bog-standard pirates fear these freaks. The storm *does* things to them, twists their minds and bodies. My old crew called them the storm-crazed."

"And a big, juicy behemoth is too big a prize to pass up," Vlana said.

"They'll be coming for plunder," Clutch said, and there

was genuine fear in her eyes. "For raw supplies, and more than any of that, for slaves."

"Send word to the wheelhouse, and every officer aristocrat on the ship," Belit said, sending Rachim and Hakat running. "Call up the armsmen and get people on the guns."

"Clutch," Aimee said.

"Already on it," the pilot said. "No way in hell I'm fighting this war in the street. Bjorn, I need you on guns! Aimee, we're gonna need you on the bridge, come on!"

Aimee nodded. She still looked shaken from Yaresh. From the revelation that the authoritarian lord of the muster hadn't been responsible for the political killings and cult activities from which he had benefitted. The handful of words she'd had a chance to say still had Elias's head swimming.

"You said the storm twisted these people," he said to Clutch. "How fast are they? How strong?"

The pilot fixed him with a look that held no exaggerations. "Pretty damn. They'll be dropping men on the deck. Precision. Violence. Shock and awe."

"Go," Elias said to the others. He knew where he was needed, then. "Get those damn things away from us. I'll stay here, where my skills count for something."

Belit looked at him as she turned, ready to organize the defense of the ship. "It will take us time to organize a defense."

"How long?" Elias asked. The ships were getting closer now. Blasts of mystic energy raked across the sky.

"Ten minutes for us to get into the air," Aimee replied.

"Half that for me," Belit said. "Yaresh's men are still armored. They will defend their home." The commander of the Red Guard looked at the ships again. Elias did the mental calculations. *They'll be here, putting killers on the top level by then.*

"Get moving," he said. "I'll buy you the time."

"They'll know," Aimee said. Worry was written across her face.

Belit grabbed his arm. "People are already starting to suspect. If you do this, *junk ritter*, the secret will be out. Yaresh's accusation that you're Eternal Order will hold weight. I can't ask you to do this."

"We don't have a choice," Elias replied. "Besides, don't the stories speak of white knights coming to save the ship in its darkest hour?" He flashed his bravest smile. "Maybe I'll give them a few more legends to tell."

A small smile quirked up the side of Belit's face. Aimee just watched him with a piercing intensity. Finally, the commander of the Red Guard nodded. "I'll find you in the streets, student. Fight well."

Then she was gone. Elias looked at the sorceress who had saved his life. "Time to fly," he said.

"Your head hasn't fully recovered," she accused.

"And you're still tired," he fired back. "No breaks today."

"Dammit Elias," she swore.

"Aimee!" Clutch screamed.

"They need you more," Elias said, trying with every ounce of will he had to get her to follow her crew. "Go. Get skyward. Shoot down those ships. Save the day."

She looked as though she would strike him across the face, then she did something else entirely: threw herself forward, and wrapped him in a fierce embrace. When she broke away she hesitated for just a moment, as if fighting some deeper impulse, fiercer still.

"Go," he interrupted it. They were out of time.

"Don't die," she swore at him. Then she too was gone, following her crew.

The first of the raiders was overhead now. Elias saw a flash of light in its interior, and cables descended. They were coming. The black knight drew his sword alone in the square, and reached for his power. The blade glowed white in his hands. The first of several misshapen figures vaulted streetward.

Elias summoned his speed and exploded forward, a blur of shimmering steel.

War he understood.

The first of the raiders landed in the street a second before Elias reached the base of the rope. He had half a breath to assess a hulking figure draped in rags and piecemeal armor, large goggles bolted over its eyes, before it raised a black hatchet as thick as a splitting maul, and hewed straight into his path. He pivoted, stepped beneath the range of the chop, and swept his sword across its center of mass.

An arm of glimmering steel blocked his strike. Gods, it was fast. Elias felt the ripple of wild, chaotic magic infused into its body. He called on his strength and endurance – just in time, as before he could get his weapon free, the raider hammered him in the center of his chest with the butt of its axe.

Elias staggered back. His powers spared him the worst, but without his plate, the hit had cost him. In the brief moment it took him to recover, four more of the raiders dropped to the street. Each was a different mishmash of flesh and armaments. Blades sprouted from arms, ritual scars criss-crossed heads set with metallic plates. The scent of ambient magic teased at his senses, infusing his enemies with something not unlike his own powers. The five surged forward. Elias had been successful: he was their target now.

He leaped as they came, over their heads and turning as he summoned another spell. A gout of white flames surged from his fingers, upwards at the aperture in the base of the ship. There was a small concussive burst, and the burning remnants of the ropes fell coiling to the streets. He landed. They rushed him, feet pounding the street in thunderous slams. *Like my powers*, he realized. *But always on. Imperfect.*

All power. All rage. All destruction. No thought. Elias grinned, took his sword in two hands, and streaked towards the oncoming force.

The white sword struck an arm-blade. In the instant of contact, a second fist rose to strike him. He pivoted away from the blow to bring it up short, jumped, and gripped his sword with a gloved hand halfway up its length. The steel was hot to the touch, yet it did not burn him. Screaming, he drove the point like a spear straight through the raider's throat.

Another came behind him. He kicked off the ground, drove the screaming body of the dying foe backwards and followed as it toppled. The swipe of a jagged-edged sword passed just over his head as he descended. He turned the fall into a roll and surged out the other side, whipping the sword around in a screaming cut straight through the next raider. White, glowing steel sheared through flesh, bolted steel, and bone. Elias exploded through the collapsing halves of the dead man. He turned, skidding to a stop further down the street as the three remaining raiders rushed to catch up. "Next?"

They came at him from different angles now. No more fortunate mistakes. Cunning, then. Elias backpedaled, turned aside a huge, swiping greatsword, the same giant splitting axe as before, and a pair of barbed maces that splintered stone where they struck. He checked blows, sought openings, dodged, jumped back, vaulted, hammered, pressed and chased.

Still they came. The ships streaked overhead in a second pass, and Elias was forced to summon a shield spell of his own as a fresh burst of mystic fire rained down through the streets. A blast cored the side of a private residence. Exploding glass and masonry sprayed across the street. As Elias lowered his shield spell the first of them crashed into him, heedless of the debris that struck its back in the midst of the charge. The axe cut down. Elias caught it overhead reflexively. Mistake. The force drove him to his knees, and only the imbuing power of his magic kept his skeleton from shattering under the force of the blow.

He took his left hand off the grip of the sword, slammed it into the center of the raider's chest, and unleashed the biggest lightning bolt he could summon. A crackling, flesh-crisping surge of summoned magic blasted a palm-sized hole through the middle of its chest and struck the next in line behind in the shoulder. The next raider spun from the impact and staggered forward, off balance. Elias heaved the corpse into the path of the running raider's legs. Exploding stone rained around them. The storm-crazed stumbled again, caught himself on one hand, and lashed out with one barbed mace at Elias's legs.

The black knight leaped over the strike and drove his glowing sword through the top of the monster's skull and into the street. He heaved himself up as the last one came. The greatsword descended. Elias sidestepped it in a blur, poured strength into his limbs and, screaming, heel-kicked the monster in the face. A loud *cracking* shockwave echoed through the street as its neck snapped from the force of the blow.

Elias stood, panting in the aftermath of the carnage. A handful of people were in the streets, staring at him with a combination of shock, fear... and for the first time he could remember in his life... *awe*.

"Who are you?" one of them – a little boy clutching his mother's leg – asked.

Elias looked back, momentarily unable to answer. His lips moved. It took him a second to find his words, then he simply said, "Just a helpful stranger. Get back inside."

He staggered. His head still hurt. The raiders' ships made a keening, wailing noise as they flew overhead. A second set of blasts tore up a street further towards the prow and back near the wheelhouse. Elias heard the sounds of screams and clashing blades.

He pulled his sword free, and ran towards the sounds of chaos.

He found them at the base of the wheelhouse. A second pass had dropped more of the storm-crazed attackers into the square, and corpses lay in their wake. Yet around the base of the ivory structure, a cluster of armsmen battled. In the flashing press, he glimpsed Belit shouting orders, watched her second, Hakat, charge at one of the killers as it snatched a man by the leg and bashed his head against the rocks until it spilt red in every direction. Three shock-spears struck it at once, sending jolts of lightning through its body. Handled.

He shot forward. Two of the storm-crazed dashed into his path. One strike came upward from the left, another downward from the right. Elias darted in deep, pressing his thumb to the flat of the sword just above the cross, caught the rising blow on the lead edge of his blade, flicked the strike away in time to catch the second with the rotating back edge. Speed. As both weapons flashed in opposite directions, he swept the sword in a horizontal thwart-strike over his head, right, then around in a perfect arc to the left. Another. Another. Oath of Aurum slashed four arcs through the air, trailing streaks of white and red.

The two storm-crazed fell carved at his feet. A group of panicked functionaries ran past him, darting towards the wheelhouse. A roar reached his ears, and turning, he saw one of the raiding ships flying low over the tops of the behemoth's towers. Its mystic batteries flared with light.

Then a sorcerous blast of tremendous power burst through the air, and a beam of blue light struck the raider amidships. Punched through its fuselage. The vessel shuddered, and its own batteries ignited. Ash and rubble rained down onto the bloodstained streets as the wreckage of the main body spun away from *Iseult*. A second flare of light erupted as its metadrive detonated with a concussive bang.

A roaring cheer went up from the fighters in the square, as the swept-wing, silver profile of *Elysium* streaked across the sky. At once, the remaining two raiding ships were no longer focusing their attention on *Iseult*.

Turning, Elias watched as Belit cut the legs from beneath one of the raiders, dashed out of the way of its falling strike, and opened its throat with the point of her sword. Then she turned to a pair of officers behind her and screamed her orders. "Raise the platforms!"

A rumble passed beneath their feet, and one of the remaining storm-crazed was knocked back as a section of the street beneath it slid aside, and a large mystic battery rose. One of the two officers Belit had addressed vaulted into a seat at its back and gripped the controls. The coruscating power of *Iseult*'s metadrives arced up through the weapon, and it released a blast of purple light upwards with a loud *whump*.

More ether-cannons rose, the street sliding away, and men rushed to man them. One of the functionaries cowered behind Belit, screaming something incoherent about guild regulations.

Further down the square, one of the storm-crazed seized a man by the hair and dragged him back down the street. *Slaves*, Clutch had said.

Elias charged. His innate magic wasn't as powerful as Aimee's. The great spells were beyond him, but he had a lifetime of precision training. Training he'd feared ever since he was freed from the yoke of those who had made him. Belit's words rang through his head as he put on a burst of speed and aimed his magic for the line of rope that connected the storm-crazed to its netted prisoner. *You own what you are. Never forget that.*

He fired a precision bolt of flame. It split the cord. The netted man fell behind his dragger, and the storm-crazed spun to see who had robbed it. It shifted its feet and lunged towards him. A sword snapped out in a downward slice. Elias skidded to a stop as the blade came, set his feet and sidestepped, dropping a cut across the centerline and straight into the angle of the incoming attack. The opposing sword was blasted off to the side, and Elias stepped in. The point of his sword pierced the storm-crazed just above the collarbone and burst out behind the base of its skull. It dropped, gurgling.

A second volley of weaponsfire from *Iseult* ripped across the sky as *Elysium* turned in an arc. The second of the raider ships came apart, and painted the sky a red stain of fire and light. The third vessel swept high, arced upward, then turned back towards the behemoth.

Elysium flared low over the buildings atop *Iseult*, and Elias watched as a massive, blazing version of Aimee's shield spell caught the incoming blast of weaponsfire meant for the wheelhouse. The silver skyship moved in the air like a pirouetting ballet dancer, and its batteries blazed white. The last raider detonated with a blast that filled the sky with incandescent light.

Elias grinned as his eyes turned upwards. *Wherever you are, Harkon Bright,* he thought. *Be proud.*

He turned. The last of the storm-crazed in the square had fallen, and a cheer rose from the assembled armsmen. At the base of the wheelhouse, Belit wore a smile of relief. Elias watched as her guard relaxed.

The functionary behind her rose and darted forward. Elias saw a knife flash in his hand as his face contorted with hate. Too far. He'd run too far. All he could do was lurch forward, screaming, "TEACHER! BEHIND YOU!"

He ran, as fast as he could. Not fast enough. Too far.

It didn't matter. The warning made Belit shift. The thrust of the knife raked off the back of her breastplate instead of the gaps beneath the arm. She caught the arm, twisted it until the knife clattered to the ground, and hammered the pommel of her longsword into his face. The bureaucrat-priest screamed as his nose broke, and he dropped to the street.

By the time Elias reached them, the functionary was face-down. Hakat's boot kept his arm twisted behind his back and a forest of blades surrounded him. "Assassin," the Red Guardsman snarled. "We have you."

Struggling against the boot, blood from his broken nose pouring down his face, the functionary snarled, "It doesn't matter what you have, guardsman. The guild will never accept that bastard-born bitch as captain of *Iseult*. Better that we all perish in Grandfather's arms. The Children of the Empty Sky will not be denied."

Belit and Elias exchanged a glance as he came to a stop.

The raiders had been beaten, their skyships destroyed. Yaresh had fallen, and at long last, they had a member of the cult, alive, as their prisoner.

CHAPTER TWENTY-TWO
THE CHILDREN OF THE EMPTY SKY

Aimee ran through the halls. The damage was worse than it looked from *Elysium*'s bridge. Only three raiders, and a delay in getting *Iseult*'s defenses up and running, and the upper level had seemed a pockmarked painting, or some sort of sculpture peppered with burn marks.

The hallway she'd once jogged down to first see the Council Hall was littered with broken glass. The roof had been blasted in at one place, and she had to go around a healer crouched over a dying woman coughing out the last red threads of her life. No time. She couldn't stop. Not when there was a chance to get to the bottom of this mess once and for all. *Forgive me*, she thought. *Forgive me for walking by as you died.*

She came up short of the door to find Elias and Belit waiting there. The door was open slightly, and Aimee could hear conversation within. First, however, the tangible relief to see both of them alive, and apparently uninjured. She let out a breath. "Well," she said to the green-eyed young man by the door. "I see you managed not to get maimed." A grin split her face.

"Not for lack of their trying," Elias answered. Then he added, "Nice spell work."

"Rachim said you took one of the cultists prisoner?" she asked.

"Aye," Belit said. "He's a functionary. The rest of the bureaucrat-priests, conspicuously, have fled the top levels. Suddenly the cult's seeming ability to be nearly anywhere at all on *Iseult* makes more sense."

"The Axiom," Aimee said, fingering the priceless jewel still in her pocket.

"No," Belit shook her head. "Wait. Viltas is grilling him. They've got him angry. Indignant. Soon they're going to mention your mentor. When that happens, walk in slowly. It will throw him off, and he's already barely emotionally balanced."

Amut's daughter let out a long sigh. "The functionaries... their origins aren't on *Iseult*. They were originally guild representatives, generations ago, responsible for streamlining our relationship with the great trade houses, and over time they integrated themselves into our political processes. Became representatives of the aspects of government that never changed from captain to captain. They are not accustomed to being questioned. That is our advantage now. If you use the diamond, it will be said that sorcery was used to force the words from him. It worked against Yaresh, but not here."

Aimee regarded the warrior woman, considered her words, then let the Axiom slip back into her pocket. It grated, when the direct method was available to her, not to use it... but Belit was also right. "Do you think that all the functionaries have been compromised?" she asked.

"I think it is possible," Belit answered. "That so many have fled is deeply concerning. At the least, compromising them would have made it much, much easier for downleveler members of the cult to hide. The functionaries control much of the record-keeping aboard the ship." Her gauntleted fist clenched.

Aimee leaned close to the small crack in the door, and listened.

"None of you ever cared for Amut," Viltas said. His voice was a low growl. "You obstructed his efforts at reform at every possible juncture. Yet still his popularity never slipped. Is that, then, why you threw yourself into the insanity of these Children?"

"You know nothing of the great society this ship once constituted," Aimee heard the functionary reply. "It was a seamless, beautiful organ in the grand body of the guild. Harmonious. It remembered its purpose, in service to its true masters. Its people did not bow to the archaic wills of an outdated Oracle. Better it die than become the tool of a foreign upstart and his bastard bitch of a downleveler daughter."

She heard footsteps, as if Viltas's boots were bringing him closer to the prisoner. "Is that what you told Harkon Bright?"

Aimee pulled the door open, and walked slowly through the room towards the place where the prisoner was held, before the blue table as Yaresh had been mere hours before. Aimee's boot heels clicked on the stone, and she freed her hands, fixing her eyes on the man that had tried to kill Belit. He was much like the others of his order: shaven-headed, pale, with a small glyph beneath his eye that marked him as a member of the functionaries. He turned at the sound of her approach, and though his face didn't waver in its hate, she saw him gulp.

"Where is my teacher?" Aimee said, her voice deathly quiet.

"I do not have to answer the bitch's questions." He averted his eyes. "She holds no dominion over me."

Until that moment, at every juncture of her interactions with these people, save her confrontation with Yaresh, Aimee had maintained something at least close to calm. Yet the slow turning away of his face, the subtle twitching at the corner of his jaw, the strange combination of obvious fear and smug self-confidence, struck a deep, personal nerve. Before anyone could stop her, she surged forward. Her hands slammed down on the arm of the chair, and the harsh thunder of her voice filled the room. Magic sparked and flashed in the air around her, and she felt a burning heat around her eyes as fire colored the edges of her vision.

"ANSWER THE QUESTION."

The functionary screamed and reeled back in his chair. When he tried to look away, she grabbed his face in her fingers and jerked his head back to meet his eyes with hers. "You're right," she snarled. "You're not dealing with another officer aristocrat, or enlisted, or even one of your own precious functionaries. You're dealing with the frightening, uncouth, disrespectful foreigner now. And you know what happened to my teacher."

Her left hand flicked through the gestures of a minor spell, and a single tongue of blue fire appeared just above her right index finger. "Tell me what you know. Everything. Or this foreigner finds out at what temperature that glyph burns off your skin."

"He froze himself!" the functionary screamed.

An image flashed through Aimee's memory: a crystalline structure sketched in one of Harkon's books. "I need more than that," she said.

"I'm not a sorcerer!" the terrified functionary snapped back. "I only know that the dead brought him to us encased in a block of golden ice, and their master said that when he confronted him, he froze solid rather than fall before his magic! We kept him hidden!"

"Where?" Aimee pressed. The tongue of flame in her hand blazed.

The functionary looked at her fearfully, back and forth between the flame, and her eyes. "Where our master lies, until Grandfather takes us all… In the rot beneath her heart."

Viltas stepped up behind her. "You will take us there," he said. "And show us everything. Or I will allow her to do whatever she wants to you."

Breathing quickly, still in a state of panic, the would-be assassin looked back and forth between them. Then, after a silence that hung in the air for a long time, he closed his eyes and nodded.

The war party of Aimee, Viltas, Belit, Elias, Hakat, and fifteen or so of Viltas's armsmen made its way down, through the aperture, past scenes of destruction and death. As they slipped away from the top levels, Aimee took a look over her shoulder. The sky darkened again, with clouds blacker than those she'd seen before. The air held a faint thrum of magic, previously absent.

"The clouds are different," she said, as they left the daylight behind.

"We're close to the maelstrom now," Elias said. He held

the manacles of their prisoner. "Less than a day's distance from its outer wall, I'd guess."

"Then we're running out of time," Belit said, tightening her armor. She cast an uncomfortable glance Viltas's way. Vallus's father had donned light armor that hung off him somewhat awkwardly, and an old sword hung at his hip.

"You shouldn't be coming with us," Belit said. "It's been years since you fought."

"My son is still abed because of the actions of this cult," Viltas said, "and their monstrous ally is the foe Amut and I sacrificed so much to destroy. I'm going, Belit."

"He does know more about the Faceless than anyone else," Elias added.

"Very well," Belit said after a moment's reluctant silence. "Stay to the back."

They'd sent warning ahead to the metadrive chamber. Jerich met them outside. "They say Yaresh is no longer in charge, up above," he said when he saw them.

"Relieved," Belit confirmed. "He will not be captain, nor does he currently command the muster."

"They also say," Jerich said, "that Belit the Red is captain." There was a nervousness in his face, Aimee saw, barely masked by a defensive stoicism.

The expression on Belit's face was a combination of exhaustion and apprehensive gratitude. "Not yet," she said simply. "But she will try."

"Many below pray she will succeed," Jerich said.

"We think we know where the cultists have been coming from," Aimee said. "But we need access to her heart."

Jerich nodded, and led them through the doorway. The purple glow of the metadrive cores played off the cables, the wires, the consoles and the burnt, defaced symbols they'd destroyed a mere few days ago. This was the third time Aimee had stood in this chamber, but this time, her attention wasn't on the gorgeous, ancient cores of *Iseult*'s beating heart, but on the floor. Hephus's last words played through her head. *Beneath*.

Nubin met them. His confidence had increased since the last time Aimee had seen him. He walked with purpose, an expression cognizant of the weight on his shoulders. Not arrogant, either. That was good.

"What's going on?" he asked.

"When the cult attacked this chamber," Aimee said, "where did they come from?"

Nubin's face fell, a look of shame emerging. "I don't actually know. I was outside when they struck within, and by then everything was chaos. While they assaulted us with numbers from without, there were only a handful of them. I heard Hephus's last words, as you did... and we haven't been able to search the chamber from top to bottom yet for secret passages."

"You won't have to," Elias said, and nudged the prisoner forward. The functionary looked around, dejected. "He's one of them," the black knight finished.

The man raised his bitter, dark eyes to regard the group. Then, after a moment, he started shuffling towards a place just behind the blasted, no longer functional subsidiary core. "They will kill me for showing you this," he said.

"Don't touch anything," Viltas said. "Show us."

The cultist threw the lord shipman a fearful look, then indicated a blank space on the outer wall. "There."

"I see nothing," Hakat said.

"You wouldn't," the cultist answered, disgusted. "Can't

hear the voice, can you? As uneducated as you are brick-dumb."

"Magic, then," Aimee said, nodding. Stepping closer, she felt the faintest scent of it, unnoticed before because of the overwhelming power of the metadrive cores. Harkon's lesson about illusions from Port Providence echoed through her head. *The most powerful illusions play off the expectations of the one watching.*

She expected to see plain, unmarked wall. There were spells that could be used here for dispelling, but they had another tool available to them that had already proven itself adept at destroying powerful enchantments.

"Elias," she said. "Your sword. Put it through that section of wall."

The black knight looked at her. "Are you sure?"

Aimee nodded. "It destroyed the order symbols along the walls without issue. I believe that one of its powers may be the breaking of magic. Do it."

Slowly, Elias stepped forward. He drew his sword, and the blade glowed a warm white in the dim light of the chamber. She saw his brow twitch, and his eyes closed. "I can hear him," he murmured. "Fainter than before... but still here."

"Yes," the cultist sneered. "He reaches out to those that are his. And you, Elias, cannot deny what you are."

"No," Belit said softly. "But others cannot define that for you when you own it."

Elias took two steps forward, and rammed the point of his sword through the blank space of the wall with a sudden, forceful shout. The piercing blade shattered the ancient enchantments holding the illusion in place. The magic fizzled, sparked, and collapsed with a thunderclap.

Aimee smiled. She'd been right.

Before them now, in place of a space of unmarked wall, was an aperture in the steel, one that seemed almost to be the remnant of some old rip in metal. Beyond, a tunnel bored outward. Aimee summoned a globe of light, and stepped up beside the black knight, who now took one hand off his blade to grasp the functionary by his manacles.

"I didn't..." the cultist said with gulping, surprised fear "...I thought–"

"That the whispers would seize control of me the moment I came within their range?" Elias answered. "I know. Now lead on. I believe your cold master and I have a reckoning due below."

Sniveling, cringing, his last option seemingly exhausted, the functionary started downwards. Aimee and Elias followed, and the others came behind. The walls closed in around them.

The tunnel was old, made of great pipes lashed together piecemeal, improved upon haphazardly over the course of decades, centuries even. The steps were uneven divots incised into the floor. There were scratches on the wall. Profane blasphemies that Aimee only half recognized from Harkon's texts. Every so often a half-spent glow-globe or faint torch guttered in the dark, but by and large, Aimee's summoned light source and the glow of Oath of Aurum were their only illumination. Just ahead of them, the functionary whimpered as he walked.

"Forgive me, master," he wailed. "Prophet of Grandfather, Ninth Star Once-Extinguished. Whom even the Faceless heeds. Forgive me, I have failed you."

"Can you still hear the whispers?" Aimee asked.

There was the faintest mark of sweat on her companion's brow. "They're getting louder," he said. "But at least I know where they're coming from now. It's easier to say no to something wicked when you know it's not coming from inside your heart."

Abruptly the tunnel turned, and a large room opened up before them. It was old, Aimee realized immediately, perhaps an ancient storeroom long forgotten by the crew of the ship. The ceiling was high and vaulted, and light came from a number of candles, guttering on pedestals splattered with melting wax collected and reused, over and over.

But it wasn't the light that set Aimee's blood to freezing, nor the strange shadows it cast across the blasphemy-scrawled walls. It was the smell. The moment they stepped through the doorway, the scent of blood, bile, piss, and shit assaulted her senses. A simple glance downward told her why: the room was a charnel house, carpeted thick with fresh corpses.

"By the thousand gods," she heard Belit say behind her.

They were functionaries. Enlisted. Downlevelers, officer aristocrats. They wore threadbare robes over common-stitched clothing and a handful were in elaborate finery. Their bodies lay at random across the floor, and a terrible silence filled the room. She crouched to examine one, then, seeing the mode of its death, raised her eyes to see the same gruesome pattern repeated over and over. Blood poured from opened necks, and everywhere, knives were clutched in the death-grips of dead hands.

"They slit their throats," Aimee said. "All of them. All

at once. Why?"

"Too late," the cultist they'd brought with them exclaimed. "Too late too late too late too late too late…"

When Aimee looked up, she saw Elias's face fixated on something at the far end of the room. His eyes were wide, the expression pale and nerveless. "…Him."

Before them lay a throne, lashed together of bone and broken steel. It crouched, vulture-like, upon a dais of black stone, as if crammed into a space that didn't well fit it, and upon the jagged, rust-coated chair sat a mummified, motionless corpse armored from head to foot in faded, weathered plate armor. A leering, eyeless skull stared in agony from the helm, and the same nine stars were stamped upon the battered breastplate.

The cult had killed themselves revering the armored remains of a knight of the Eternal Order.

And Harkon was nowhere to be found.

Aimee turned, wheeling on the cultist. "Liar!" she snapped, in rage and in pain. "Where is my teacher?"

"I don't know!" the cultist whimpered. "He was here, when last I was!"

"Fan out," Belit said. The armsmen obeyed. "Check to see if anyone lives."

Elias walked forward through the corpses, until he reached the base of the dais. A small number of dust-coated effects lay at its feet, surrounded with devotional gifts, like worshipped relics. The black knight knelt and began digging through these furiously, all at once, until he rose, holding a yellowed book with cracked and torn pages that had to be as old as the body before them. When he opened it, a small cloud of dust filled the air.

"Is there anything there that makes sense of this?"

Hakat called out from the entryway to the door.

"I don't understand," Aimee murmured. Everything about this was wrong. Only faint magic emanated from the corpse upon the throne. Despite the elaborate evidence of worship, all indications were that the body was nothing more than a dusty, venerated idol. Whatever malice had once animated the dead man, it was long gone. "This thing couldn't command them. It's dead."

Elias pored through the book, his hands turning the pages as his eyes devoured the writing.

"Maybe they just... found the dead man," Hakat said, "and started worshiping it? No one said these cultists were smart..."

"No," Elias said. Silence. All eyes slowly turned to the green-eyed man holding the book in his hand. "This is... is his journal. He was a knight of the order, on a long-range mission, planted here centuries ago. His job..." the young man's eyes widened with horror "...was to infiltrate and corrupt the functionaries and the downlevelers... to build a religion that venerated the order's principles, and could be lying in wait, one day, for any other member of the order to take advantage of, when needed. It was a social experiment."

A chill crept down Aimee's back. She looked once more at the dead knight. Closer, now, she saw signs of damage to the armor. A place where powerful magic had rent the once enchanted steel. Another place where a sword had delivered a wound, possibly fatal. "This... this is nothing like what you describe."

"He died without finishing," Elias said. "His notes get more sporadic. Someone discovered what he was doing. He was put to flight before he could finish his plans, and had to abandon his followers. His last writings speak of someone calling out to the true enemy; he describes fleeing deep into the ship, being hunted, and then..." He trailed off. "Then it ends."

Belit and Hakat exchanged a look of wonder, then the woman said "...'and white knights came from the deep sky, to vanquish evil.'"

"You're wrong," the cultist sneered. "He died so that Grandfather could find us, and lead us to his waiting arms."

Aimee turned to stare at the far wall. Above the door where they had entered, a horrible effigy spread across the metal and stone: black, multi-tentacled, and massive. Something old, vast beyond comprehension, too hideous to describe. It was crude, but familiar enough that finally, an old myth from Aimee's childhood sparked with recognition.

"A Storm-Kraken," she breathed. "When their founder died, the remnants of the cult were left half-finished, their ideology incomplete... and they began worshipping a Storm-Kraken. Monsters – more ancient than any human civilization. They're supposed to be pure myth, older than memory, cunning, immense, devourers of skyships, even ones as big as *Iseult*."

"Grandfather waits," the cultist giggled. "We have already taken *Tristan*, and now *Iseult* shall follow her lover, into Grandfather's longing arms."

"There's one thing I don't understand," Elias said. He still held the book. A look of deep worry was on his face. "What does any of this have to do with the Faceless?"

An ear-piercing, keening shriek filled Aimee's ears, and a bolt of black energy flashed across the room. It shot past Aimee, Belit, even the cultist, and struck Elias full in the chest. The black knight's eyes widened, and his face froze in a soundless scream as the force of the surprise attack lifted him off his feet and hammered him into the far wall, where he sank to the floor. The white sword clattered from his hands to the ground. Aimee couldn't tell if he was alive or dead. She heard herself scream his name. He didn't rise.

She spun to find the source, only to watch in horror as one by one, the corpses of the suicided cultists pulled themselves from the floor, knives in their hands and a fell light in their eyes.

And amidst them, one hand raised like the conductor of a grand symphony, was Viltas. The lord shipman's eyes had changed, their kind, clever gaze turned a rotting corpse-white. Aimee felt the back of her mouth go dry. The power that emanated from him now was dizzying, oily slick, and profane. It was as if she glimpsed the tip of some terrible, vast structure jutting from the fathomless depths of a bleak swamp.

"That's enough," Viltas said, and now his voice was different: at once deep and hoarse. "Be quick about it and die, will you? I have lives without number to end, and I'm on an accelerated schedule."

Aimee's shield spell slammed into being as the first of the dead rushed forward. It stopped in its tracks. She pushed back, then let it fade, and unleashed the spell Harkon had taught her. A beam of pulsing white light burnt the first corpse, and the one behind it, to ash. Belit leaped into action, Hakat by her side. Viltas's armsmen were frozen at once in confusion and horror. Aimee saw two pulled to the ground, screaming, as ripping knives found openings in armor and punched through exposed faces.

"Viltas!" she shouted.

"Sorry." The lord shipman's neck popped unnaturally and his face twisted into a mirthless expression. "The lord shipman isn't here any more. For a long time I was forced to act as an influence only, nudging, pushing. It's taken a long time to siphon enough death to take complete control of him, but with these wretches finished, I can act without his interference. You must admit, the symmetry of using the last of Amut's companions to undo his victory is apt and proper."

His hand flashed and a second bolt of black energy flared across the room. Aimee summoned a shield spell. It split like a fractured window when the spell hit, and her feet were driven back across the floor. The corpse looked down at her from its throne. "You spoke to them through it," she said. "Manipulated their faith to suit your ends."

"Is that what passes for cleverness in the Academies of Havensreach these days?" the Faceless answered through Viltas's mouth. "Yes, girl, I spoke through its corpse, and its lingering essence helped, though there is so little of him left now. Your teacher made you adept at stating the obvious."

A knife-wielding corpse came at her from behind. Aimee twisted, loosed a gust of wind that sent him hurtling across the room, all while maintaining her shield spell. Another tried to grab her. She sank to one knee. Radiance required two hands. She caught him with another gust as he lurched over her, and propelled him head over heel into another just beyond.

"Dammit!" she screamed at her companions. "Keep these things off me!"

Belit had gotten herself free from the first of the dead she'd brought down. "Viltas!" she screamed, running towards them. "Fight him! This isn't you!"

The necromancer wearing the hero's skin pivoted, made a gesture, and the air between his hand and the would-be captain *rippled*. Belit flew backwards into Hakat. The two of them went down. "Correct," he said. "But Viltas was pliable. Eager for change... and Amut's reforms were slow. I didn't have to push hard."

It was an opening. Aimee let her shield spell drop, spun her hands through the motions of Radiance, and unleashed the beam of white light straight at the necromancer's center of mass.

Viltas's body snapped back towards her so quickly she heard tendons creak and muscle-fibers snap. With a gesture, he swept one of his dead into the spell's path. It burned to ash. "Tsk," he replied. "After the fight your teacher put up, I expected better."

His counterattack was another contemptuous gesture. Aimee felt the incoming power, saw the ripple of air. She let herself fall back, and pulled a trick she'd last used in Port Providence: she wove a spell of blooming flames as she dropped, and unleashed it with a hard kick of her feet.

The ripple of magic surged overhead. Put a ringing dent into the metal wall ten feet behind her. And the Faceless swore in frustration as fire erupted upwards at him from below. Aimee rolled to the side, came up in a crouch, and loosed a spear of ice at his chest. The Faceless clenched Viltas's fist and the projectile shattered in the air between them. There was a burn up the side of his face, black and red and angry. "More ruthless by far, though," he said. "He, at least, thought he could save my poor host. You don't seem to care."

Aimee unleashed the Radiance again, her fury rising. This time it was stronger, brighter. The Faceless backpedaled, tried to deflect it, but the edge of the spell lashed across his shoulder, and the face of the lord shipman contorted in agony.

"You said yourself," Aimee said, readying another spell. "He's not here anymore." She loosed an even brighter beam of light. "Where. Is. My. TEACHER?"

The black energy tore forth from the Faceless in response. The two pulsing bursts of magic crashed into one another, exploding in a shower of solidifying shards that tore up the floor and blasted two nearby walking corpses to dust. Aimee was lifted off her feet by the backlash, felt an impact so hard the air went out of her lungs. She slammed into the floor in front of the corpse-throne. Her world swam, and she gasped for breath.

"Oh, your little amber-dragonfly-master is aboard *Tristan* by now. Food for Grandfather," the Faceless replied. He stalked lazily towards her. She couldn't see Hakat or Belit anymore. Behind him, the necromancer's last victims and newest thralls were moving quickly. All fifteen of the armsmen were dead. "It's a simple ritual," the necromancer continued. "Grandfather is old, and cunning, and doesn't much care for worshippers or those who would use him… but he is always hungry for the agony, the lifeforce released in the moment of death. Oh – he'll consume most of it when *Iseult* dies, but there will be plenty for me to snatch up. Enough to leave this body and flee this wretched firmament. I won't be as mighty as I was in the ancient days, before the storm, before Varengard and its degenerate, modern descendants... but I remember the time before the Drifting Lands. Before the guild claimed humanity's lifeboats as their trade ships. I have seen wars. Madness. I have seen empires rise and fall... and I have sensed what is coming. Better to flee the Eternal Sky altogether, than be made a slave when dead gods rise."

Aimee's hands swept up. Her mind was murky. Her breath was uneven. This thing was so far beyond her league it was laughable, but she had to do something. She had to try. She called up the spell of Radiance. The beam of light was weaker. Its light danced off Viltas's rot-pale eyes as the Faceless summoned a shield spell of its own, and slowly pushed back against her spell. "Spirited," he said as he slowly pressed the barrier down against her, the dissipating beam making sparks of refracting light against it. "But the world doesn't care. Goodbye, little mage–"

Viltas's body suddenly, violently convulsed. His chest split, and the glowing white point of Oath of Aurum punched through him, steaming blood. The necromancer's mouth opened and closed. "Impossible..." it croaked "... took him out..."

Behind the possessed hero, Belit stood, her face set, her golden, leonine eyes filled with fury, defiance, and agonizing grief. "Forgive me, Viltas," she said, and twisted the sword.

Realization dawned in the white eyes, and Aimee heard the necromancer curse. "Royalty. Dammit. Should've... remembered."

His head jerked back. The shield spell died. Aimee's

beam of light smashed into the necromancer as she pushed her hands forward with every ounce of willpower and training she had. Light vomited from Viltas's eyes, mouth, from his wound. She saw the terrible, writhing effigy of a translucent figure surround him, cling to his flesh. It fixed hateful eyes upon her... Then with a release of tremendous mystic force and a cacophonous bang, it ceased to be.

Aimee rolled onto her side, aching. Head clearing. She blinked. No concussion. Her breath recovered. She rolled onto her belly, pushed herself on her arms, and stumble-dashed across the blood-slick floor to where the black knight lay. Reaching him she dropped to her knees and checked his pulse. Strong. His eyes were closed, his breathing steady. She closed her eyes, breathed out the relief of a deep, frightening pain leaving her chest. Her fingers fisted against his armor.

"Elias," she half-sobbed. "Elias!"

Green eyes opened. He blinked. His gaze settled on her in recognition, then realization, and genuine surprise. "I'm not dead?"

A choking laugh escaped her, half euphoric. Half relieved. "No, you're not. Thank the gods. Can you stand?"

"I think so," he said, taking her hand and pulling himself into a sitting position. "Viltas?" he asked.

"Not long now," Belit said, behind them.

Relief turned to grief, as Aimee turned. The swordswoman knelt on the floor. The lord shipman's head was cradled in her lap, his face pale, his breathing irregular and rattling. "Forgive me, Viltas," Belit whispered. "Forgive me."

The lord shipman stirred. He coughed, and blood leaked out the corner of his mouth. Aimee moved to his other side. Elias followed. "There is nothing to forgive," Viltas whispered, weak. "He's gone. After all these years. I never thought I would be myself again."

"Can you help him?" Belit asked. The would-be captain's eyes were wet at their corners, grief naked upon her dark face.

Aimee looked down at the wound, red and pulsing, in the center of the old hero's chest. That, plus the damage done by the wicked thing that had inhabited him for so long, the spell he'd been hit with, his advanced age...

"I'm sorry," Aimee said.

"It's alright," Viltas whispered. "It's alright. After everything. This is better."

Abruptly he reached out and seized Aimee's arm. "Harkon," he said, "is in the metadrive chamber of *Tristan*. The Faceless knew his power would act as a beacon, to lure Grandfather out. The ship is already dead. So sorry. I should've fought... harder. Too old. Too slow. Too angry. I don't think the gods will take me."

"There are a thousand of them," Belit said quietly. "You'll not arrive as a beggar."

Aimee closed her eyes, suddenly dizzy at the implications. Her teacher was alive... but in so much more danger than she'd ever guessed. But Viltas wasn't done. His grip on her arm tightened. "He sent the other dead away. A last mission, to wake the others... there are many more in the depths. You have to stop them. They will try to take the wheelhouse. Aimee... I've seen things. Things in his mind. He did not lie. Something is coming, something worse. He was... afraid. Be... ready."

He shuddered. "Viltas," Belit pleaded.

"Take care of Vallus," the lord shipman said. He clutched Belit's arm. "Tell him I am proud. And sorry."

"I will," Belit said. "On my word of honor."

Viltas's eyes closed. His body relaxed. "I will tell your father what you've become."

A shudder passed through him, and the last of Amut's companions was gone.

Aimee slowly rose. There was no time to grieve, nor even to process anything more than the information most relevant to now. They sailed into the arms of a monster, and her teacher – though alive – was in mortal peril. She looked about. Of the war party that had entered the cult chamber, only the three of them remained alive. Hakat's body lay a short distance away, pierced by a dozen cuts.

"I have to get to the wheelhouse," Belit said, rising. "They have to be warned. And the metadrive chamber has to be protected. I need your help, Aimee. You and your crew."

Aimee stared helplessly back at the warrior woman. "You heard him," she said. "Harkon is aboard *Tristan*, in its metadrive chamber. I have to go. I have to save him."

There was a sudden discharge of magic energy behind them, and turning, Aimee watched as Elias pulled the glowing blade of Oath of Aurum from the center of the dead knight's corpse. "That takes care of any echo of him that might remain," the black knight said. The look in his eyes was tired, but resolute. "Belit is right," he said. "You're needed here. You're a portalmage, you know how to fight these things. When she takes the wheelhouse, she'll need you."

Aimee felt the frustration tear at her. The dual obligations. "Harkon–"

"I owe him a debt too," Elias said. "Let me repay it. I'll take *Elysium*, and one or two others to *Tristan*, and bring him back."

•

CHAPTER TWENTY-THREE
NOBLE AND BRAVE, GENTLE AND KIND

He'd never gone into battle feeling worse. The necromancer's attack had hit him harder than Malfenshir's sword, than any weapon or fist that had ever gotten past his defenses. What had followed had been darkness that was broken only when he'd awoken to find himself staring up at Aimee's worried face. Now his head ached, his body was shaky and his skin tingled as if a tight piece of clothing had been suddenly ripped away.

He stood on the bridge of *Elysium*, one hand clutching Oath of Aurum to fortify himself, and remembered that people were counting on him. He knew necromancy well enough to understand that the hit had been from a spell designed to simply end up draining every ounce of his essence away.

What he didn't understand is why it hadn't killed him.

Rachim handed him a pile of papers. "These are the maps of *Tristan*," he said with a grunt. "They weren't easy to come by. You'll want to make your landing somewhere amidships, not on the top level, if you're going to have a chance of reaching its core metadrive chamber quickly. Don't get diverted. As you've more than likely seen, every behemoth is unique, and each is a complete nightmare of tunnels, corridors, and side passages… but this bay here–" he pointed to a spot on the ship's flank "–will help you reach it quickly."

"That's why I'm going," Vant said, doing a final check aboard the bridge. "Past a certain point, a grid is a grid is a grid. Show me a power conduit, and I can find my way to the damn chamber." The engineer had a fierce look on his face as he rolled up the proffered maps and stuffed them under his arm. "Take *my* boss hostage to feed to some sort of sky-horror? I'll get him back, you abominable sons of bitches. You fucking *watch* me."

Clutch flipped a number of switches, checking the wheel and her pilot station one last time before she looked over her shoulder at Elias. "Good to go," she said. "Just say the word."

Behind Elias, Bjorn had donned his armor once more, and was decked out in weapons. "Ready," he grunted. "Time to bring him home."

"One more thing," Aimee said, striding onto the bridge. She'd recovered somewhat from her battle with the Faceless, but there was an unsettled, rattled look on her pale face. The blue eyes were shaken in a way they'd never seemed before. She gestured, and two of Rachim's armsmen dropped one of the mystic energy projectors onto the bridge. "We know from reports in the downlevels that these things can destroy the dead. Best if whomever goes aboard *Tristan* with you also has the ability to fight back without being overwhelmed."

Elias nodded. "Thank you," he said, turning towards her. "And thank you for trusting me."

"I was the first," she replied, the ghost of a smile on her

face. "Not about to stop now."

"Be fast," Rachim said. "*Tristan* will hit the wall of the maelstrom in three hours. If *Iseult* doesn't pull short before then, we may never get out."

"That's the idea," Elias answered. "Vlana staying behind too?"

"Yes," Aimee said. "Her skills will be useful in the wheelhouse. And that leaves two of us here."

Vant jogged past, headed down to the engine room. A few moments later there was a rumble, and Elias felt the thrum of *Elysium*'s metadrive awakening.

"Time to fly," he said.

"Bring him back," Aimee said.

"I promise," Elias answered. She nodded, and started down the hall with Rachim.

"Aimee," he said after her. She turned, looking over her shoulder.

"Don't die," he said.

She smiled, then the door to the bridge closed. A few seconds later the communication came up to the bridge. "We're off."

Clutch turned the wheel, and Elias felt the deck shift beneath him as the silver bird rose into the heavens.

The vision beyond the landing pad arrested the breath in his lungs. Finally visible, past the running lights of *Elysium* and the idle fog and light clouds that surrounded her top levels, was a vast, unending wall of black storm clouds riddled with flashes bigger than a behemoth. It was a small comfort to Elias that the gasps heard from the rest of the bridge weren't his.

"I've heard the stories," Bjorn said behind him, "but they don't come close to the real thing. It's... huge."

Elias knew only an ancient verse that he'd heard Roland murmur in the darkness of that ship as a frightened boy, all those years ago. It came to his lips unbidden.

"Day to night
Hope to fright
The Righteous scarred
Forever marred
Within the maelstrom."

Bjorn gave him a sideways look.

"My former master," Elias said, "was obsessed with this place."

"This is the closest I've ever been," Clutch murmured as she urged the ship forward. "And the last time I wasn't flying towards it."

In the distance, looking small before the vastness of the wall of the storm, another set of lights could be seen – engine trails – flaring from the rear of an immense ship hurtling full throttle towards a place that haunted skyfarers' nightmares.

Tristan.

"There she is," Elias said. "Go."

"Already on it," Clutch said. "Vant, hard burn."

The rumble became a roar, and *Elysium* shot forward through the sky, rippling through the heavens towards the wall of the storm.

A moment later the wind hit them. Clutch grabbed the wheel, bracing the vessel against the sudden force that made its whole length shudder. "Abyss take it all," she snapped, then hit several switches. "Stabilizers are gonna be working overtime in this damn hurricane. Alright, hold on to your pants, kids. This is gonna be a rough flight."

Elias had just enough time to grab a nearby brass railing for support before the ship started shaking violently up and down. Bjorn let out a wild laugh as they shuddered and bucked, and Elias heard Clutch whooping and hollering as she moved the wheel with the deft skill of a master painter.

Through the viewport ahead, *Tristan*'s lights grew brighter. A pelting, vicious rain began to fall. The ship was in exponentially worse shape than *Iseult*. The lamps on the upper deck were mostly doused, the towers shattered and broken, interspersed with perforated domes and blasted top-level architecture.

"Gods," Bjorn breathed. "Damn thing looks like a warzone."

"It's what *Iseult* almost was," Elias said, as they approached. He picked up one of the exterior maps Vant had put down, quickly trying to identify the bay Rachim had mentioned. There. He found it. Pulling himself forward, he showed it to Clutch. "There. We need to find *this spot* to put down. Rear-facing!"

He saw Clutch's eyes dart across the sky as they neared the other behemoth. "That one?" she shouted, gesturing with her hand to a dimly lit aperture halfway down the side of the exterior hull.

"That's the one!" Elias shouted.

"You *do* realize that will have us flying backwards," she deadpanned, "into this horrible wind?"

Elias flashed his best grin.

"Yeah, that's what I thought. And for future reference? That grin only works on Aimee. I got my pretty-boy immunizations a long time ago. Now hold on, kids, or you might just end up pasted to the ceiling."

Elias managed to grab another rail, then the whole ship spun. His already-aching head thundered with the pulse of blood through his ears, and he held on for dear life as the direction of the ship abruptly reversed. "Hang on!" he heard the pilot shout.

He saw the walls of the bay suddenly close around them as the ship shot backwards through the aperture. Clutch's fingers flew over the controls and the ship came to an abrupt, complete stop. There was a loud thump as the landing gear came down, and the ship settled.

"Go," Clutch said over her shoulder. "I'll hold down the fort, but I can only do that for so long. You get Hark, and you bring him back."

Elias and Bjorn jogged down the spine of the ship. The bay door slammed down, and Vant caught up with them, the mystic energy projector now in his hands. They dashed into a dark landing bay lit by the still-glowing exhaust vents of *Elysium*'s engines and the flickering overhead lamps.

Elias drew his sword. The blade glowed in the darkness. He stretched out with his senses, reaching for the familiar pull that a metadrive exerted on anyone with magic abilities.

He and Vant turned at the same moment, towards a battered doorway at the far end of the bay. Here and there blood was splattered across the floor in abstract patterns, or palm-printed onto the walls. "That way," the engineer confirmed, then they were moving.

The lights were intermittent, at best. The darkness of the savaged ship's interior emphasized the half-sounds of the remaining systems fighting to maintain their functioning. Somewhere far away, the indistinct echoes of what might have been voices or groaning supports wailed in the shadows. Elias struggled to fortify himself against the oppressive fear that hung in the air like a stink. A plague, the rumors had said. Then the dead must have risen. When the end came to *Tristan*'s people, it must have been quick, explosive, and violent.

They pushed deeper still. Around a corner were signs of struggle. The burn marks of shock-spears and flame lances against the walls. They stepped over the remains of a man physically torn apart as if all four limbs had been tugged in opposite directions until he burst.

They turned another corner. Bjorn prayed behind him, though Elias didn't know the name of the gods he invoked.

At once they emerged onto the edge of a grand promenade, not unlike the walkway that spanned the vast cargo apertures in the middle of *Iseult*. Yet no consistency of warm, life-evidencing lamps glimmered here, and the doorways to the top level had been violently wrenched asunder, and their mechanisms still spitting a shower of sparks into the darkness below. From high overhead, a flash of lightning painted the ruined interior of the immense chamber a chilling silver. The light danced off broken railings, ruined living quarters, ruptured doorways and fractured, bent columns. *Noble and brave*, Elias repeated in his mind. *Gentle and kind.*

"There!" Vant said. Turning, Elias followed his arm to the source of a faint glow, perhaps a mile away. *Tristan*'s metadrive chamber was the twin of *Iseult*'s: built of a beautiful bronze, its structure like that of a vast heart.

Or at least, it had been once. Some tremendous force had torn the wall open, as if from some giant's ripping dagger strike, and the purple light from within bled out into the immediate vicinity. It flickered, irregular and indistinct. "Two hearts," Vant breathed.

"And one of them dying," Bjorn said.

A mad determination seized Elias as he leaned out over the rail to see. He couldn't see the core itself, but by the light, it still worked. Still lived.

"Dying isn't dead," Elias said, and straightened. "Come on. There's still time."

He took two steps forward, and another flash of lightning from high above painted the walkways on both sides of the vast aperture silver again. Silver, and alight with thousands of stars.

No. Elias's heart nearly stopped. Not stars. Eyes.

They stood silently upon the gangways. They stared from the other sides of ruptured doorways. They crouched at the edges of rails and stepped softly from within the darkness of lightless corridors. Blood splattered them, leaked from the wounds that had slain them. Faces of a thousand varieties, unified in the pallor of their rotting ends.

Tristan's crew. Undead. All of them. And all of them locked hungry eyes on the three men that had just stepped into their ship.

"Oh," Vant swallowed to his left. "So that's where they all went."

A unified sound of mingled wailing, whimpering, and screaming surged around them, and Elias readied his sword. The warmth of the glowing steel was a comfort in his aching hands, and the flow of adrenaline quieted some of the pain in his head. "Get ready," he said, and summoned his speed. "I'm going to make a path."

CHAPTER TWENTY-FOUR
AT MAELSTROM'S EDGE

"Viltas," Rachim swore. "How in the name of all the gods could I not have seen it?"

"Don't berate yourself," Aimee answered as they walked swiftly through his villa, past armsmen preparing. She was shaken, still recovering from her duel with the Faceless down below, but there was no time to evidence weakness or let herself rest. Everything now depended on the desperate. "Even his own son didn't know."

Near the doorway they stopped. Vlana armed herself, and Aimee flung her fingers several times through the Radiance gestures, as if so doing would drive the ache from her limbs and quiet the raging swell of fear that surged through her. Fear for her friends. For her teacher. For *Iseult*. For Elias.

Somewhere further down that list, she was sure, concern for herself had to lie.

"Are the other officers going to help?" Vlana asked.

"The messages I sent aren't getting returned," Rachim said, checking the edge of his sword. "And I just received word of a number of smaller ships departing, about an hour ago. I can't say how many of them exactly, but it seems a fair bet that at least a small portion of the officer aristocracy is cutting and running rather than staying here."

"And the portalmages?" Aimee asked.

"The two still alive are with Haysha and the remaining astronomers," Rachim said. "But they're doing everything they can to get the ship's navigation back up and working. They won't be any help going forward."

"Hey," Aimee deadpanned. "It's not like we've had to do everything ourselves up until now in any case."

"You don't." She turned. Vallus stood in the doorway. He was pale, still weak from the healing and his injuries before. "And you don't need to worry about the officers or their armsmen. Not so long as you have weapons."

As he said this, Belit emerged from the next room, having cleaned the blood from her armor. She stopped at the sight of Viltas's son, orphaned less than an hour before. "Val," she said.

"I already know," Vallus said. A spasm of grief crossed his face. "A mutual friend brought me word."

And from just behind him stepped the familiar figure of the downleveler in service to the Oracle, Ferret. "That's the thing about us enlisted," he said. "We hear everything that happens. I needed to know that the son wasn't the father. Now I do... so I got this young diplomat an audience, and let him speak."

Belit's eyes widened, as Aimee watched an understanding sink in.

"The people of *Iseult* have no love for the functionaries, or their guild masters," Vallus said. "And they didn't care for the three candidates for captain, all of whom argued for how they would better serve its ruling caste... but they remember Amut. They remember that he tried to serve them... and they will follow you. All you have to do is arm them."

Rachim's eyebrow cocked over his one good eye. "The other officer aristocrats will see that as naked rebellion."

Silence. Aimee and Vlana exchanged a look.

Belit's eyes closed. She breathed out... then she opened them. "Then rebellion it is. Are you still with me, Rachim?"

That wasn't what their host was expecting. He stared at her for a longer moment, then looked at Aimee.

"Don't look at me," Aimee said. "Harkon stirs trouble wherever he goes. I'm absolutely behind this."

The older man paused, then shook his head with a sigh. "How many did you get?"

Ferret's eyes sparkled. "The question isn't how many people I got you, it's how many weapons can you get them."

Rachim's eyebrows shot up. "Well, I suppose I'm a rebel, then. Count me in."

"The Faceless is gone," Belit said, "but most of the cult he allied himself with have been raised as the dead in his service. With their master gone, they're functioning on their last order, which is to drive *Iseult* straight into the storm. We have to secure the wheelhouse and the metadrive chamber, and ensure that they're not able to compromise our ability to power or fly the ship."

"Jerich holds the chamber," Ferret said, "and he's not about to vacate. I've got several thousand waiting just below the surface, and that's without counting those currently organizing beneath our feet. If the dead want to take *Iseult*, they'll find themselves with a hell of a fight on their hands."

Belit smiled. "Rachim, between what we confiscated from Yaresh and the combined armories owned by Pentus and Diara's estates there should be enough to spread around a large chunk of hardware. Val, go with him. Get on it."

"You're the boss," *Elysium*'s host replied.

"Thanks for not commanding me back to bed," Vallus deadpanned with mild amusement.

"You wouldn't listen anyway," Belit said, then she turned to Aimee and Vlana. "The two of you come with me. We're headed to the wheelhouse."

They stepped out into the fringes of a horrible storm. Lightning flashed in the distance and thunder tore across the heavens in its wake. The crackle of mystic energy played at Aimee's senses, wild and chaotic. This close to the maelstrom, it followed, she had to beware the third prime of magic: things do not always happen as people understand they should.

Never had she been in a place where her magic going awry was more likely, or less convenient. And now here she was, the mystic muscle behind what had started as moderation in the democratic selection process of a new captain, and was ending as an out-and-out revolt. Belit drew her sword, and set her eyes on the ivory tower of the wheelhouse, visible above the other buildings, a white spike against the black wall of the immense storm. Then she started walking, and Aimee and Vlana followed.

What was the ancient phrase her uncle had been so fond of? *Go big or go home.*

They were midway there when the pelting rain began to fall. It drove at them almost vertically, and the street tilted as a vast wind buffeted *Iseult*'s flank. They were crossing into the storm's outer perimeter. Up ahead a light gleamed atop the tower, and the bridge that connected it to the two other corner towers swayed in the wind.

They fought their way to the base of the tower, and that was when Aimee saw the state of the guards. Freshly dead. Their weapons scattered. The remains of several destroyed undead lay at the foot of the steps.

Behind the slain sentries, the doors to the wheelhouse had been wrenched open, and stairs wound up into the darkness. A scream echoed from somewhere high above.

Belit snatched up the shock-spears from the two fallen guards, and tossed one to Vlana. "Keep hitting them," she said. "Like you and your brother did when you came to our aid below. Remember, if you don't have powerful magic, there's only one way to bring these things down: catastrophic structural damage. They can't fight if they can't move."

Vlana looked down at the weapon in her hands and swallowed. "I hate these things," Aimee heard her mutter, but then she held it in a not unfamiliar grip. "Ready."

Aimee flexed her fingers. "Let me lead," she said. "And keep the damn things off my back."

The three women stepped into the darkness. A winding staircase of carved stone ascended before them. Aimee started up, first walking, then jogging, summoning a small light to illuminate their way.

Nothing came. No further screams issued from the tower's apex. At length they crested a length of stairway and stepped through a pair of double doors. Above their heads, Aimee glimpsed gold words etched into the stone and metal.

"Wise must be the mind Her heart sustains."

On the other side of the doorway, a scene of ruin

waited. *Iseult*'s wheelhouse – what in newer ships might be called the bridge – was beautiful. A flash of lightning illuminated a stone chair, throne-like, upon a central dais surrounded by a room in a half circle. An immense navigation table of exquisite crystal was splattered with blood, and a dead pilot slumped over the large black wood wheel that steered the ship through the heavens.

All around them, the slaughtered remnants of Amut's once-faithful bridgecrew lay in bloody tatters. Belit stepped through the door behind her, took in the horrors, and closed her eyes for just a moment to steady herself. "I knew them," she said quietly. "I knew them, and when they needed me, I was not here."

"You destroyed the Faceless," Aimee said. "It would be worse if you hadn't. The question now is, what do we do?"

Belit looked around, keeping her shock-spear in hand. Aimee saw no trace of the dead, nor was there time to tell which of the corpses had been most recently slain. Most were barely recognizable, their uniforms splattered with red and faces mutilated.

"You're *Elysium*'s navigator, right?" Belit asked Vlana.

"And quartermaster," she answered. "But yes. Clutch and I split the duties."

"Alright," Belit said. "Quickest explanation I can muster: the astronomers' dome handles long-range navigation, but the crystal table over there is for direct, short-range work. It responds to touch. I need to know precisely how quickly we're headed into the maelstrom's wall. Aimee, see if you can get the communication tube to the metadrive chamber working. I'm going to need to give them very specific orders in a few minutes."

"Understood," Aimee said, and moved to a series of

tubes and mouthpieces, each connected to a set of labeled switches. Gods, there were a lot of them.

As she worked, she saw Belit approach the wheel with trepidation in her eyes. "Sorry, pilot," she said. "Your shift has ended, and I can't let you fly us into hell."

She shifted the corpse, and it suddenly spun, bashing the swordswoman across the face so hard that she crashed to the floor.

Turning, the glowing eyes of the undead pilot blazed as it repeated the same phrase over and over again. "They killed me. Kill their hope. Kill their hope. Kill their hope. Kill their hope."

And roaring the Faceless's last command, muscles straining, the corpse began pulling at the wheel until the timbers groaned.

No time for Radiance. She didn't have the space. She might incinerate the wheel as well, or blast other delicate controls on the wheelhouse. Instead, Aimee vaulted over the control tubes, and blasted the undead pilot with a gust of wind. The corpse held onto the wheel with one hand. It snarled. She wove her hands through the gestures of the spell again. It let go, lunged forward, and kicked her in the chest. Aimee's breath left her. She staggered back. It advanced, swiped with a limb, forcing her to dodge. No breath, no voice. No voice, no magic. Belit rolled on the floor, groaning.

Aimee croaked for breath. Vlana vaulted up onto the table behind her and jabbed over her shoulder with the shock-spear. The jolt sent a blast of lightning through the corpse, pausing it for just a second as every limb twitched. Aimee sucked in a breath of air, wove another wind spell, and delivered it at the end of an uppercut to the dead thing's jaw, as hard as she possibly could.

The walking corpse hurtled backwards across the room and slammed into the far wall. It rose, unfazed.

"Gods, I hate these things," Aimee croaked.

"So use the damn undead-killing spell Harkon taught you!" Vlana yelled. Belit rose. She'd lost her spear, and now drew her sword. The steel glinted in the darkness.

"Not in here!" Aimee answered. "It could fry half the instruments!"

"Dammit!" Vlana swore.

"Remember what I said!" Belit shouted as the undead rushed them.

Aimee popped her neck, remembering. "Catastrophic structural damage."

They came together at the foot of the stone throne. Vlana's shock-spear set it shuddering again. Belit's sword rose and fell, over and over. Aimee fell back on one of the most basic self-defense spells taught to first years at the academy: she hardened her fists with an infusion of mystic power, and laid into the walking corpse like a wet punching bag. They drove it back. Belit's sword sent a limb splattering to the floor. Vlana jabbed it again, sending it shuddering backwards, with its back to the door and the stairway down. Aimee pivoted back as it set its legs to rush again. Finally, the space she needed, with nothing sensitive behind it.

Her hands flashed as it lunged, and the brilliant Radiance beam blasted it to ash before surging out the doorway, away from the controls.

Breathing hard, Belit rushed to the wheel. "Back to your positions!"

Aimee dashed for the tubes and switches. Vlana's fingers flew over the crystal table's surface. Lights flashed into being in the air just above her hands.

Blood had stained the switches and labels of the communication tubes, but after a few seconds of searching, Aimee found the one she wanted, flipped the switch to open the line, and said, "Metadrive chamber? This is Aimee de Laurent in the wheelhouse."

An agonizingly long moment followed, then the familiar voice of Jerich came back. "We haven't heard from the wheelhouse for hours, what's going on up there?"

"Everyone's dead," Aimee snapped back. "Belit has taken the wheel, and she's got orders."

She looked over her shoulder at where the tall woman held the wheel, straining as she acquired a feel for the contraption.

"What were your orders again?"

"Vlana, I need those numbers!" Belit said.

The quartermaster's eyes flicked across the lights displayed before her. "No autoquill," she muttered. "Gods, I'm not used to this. Alright, give me a second. We're on a direct course towards the maelstrom's outer storm-wall. *Tristan* is ahead of us, and moving slower. I give it an hour until those winds make turning this thing almost impossible!"

Belit's expression was grim. "Tell them I need them to reverse thrust and get ready for a hard port turn. We'll need stabilizers to keep from rolling, especially in this damned wind."

Aimee pulled the tube. "Reverse thrust, ready for port turn, ready stabilizers, it's getting really damn windy out there!"

"Understood," Jerich's voice came back, clipped. "Also, Nubin wants me to tell you that we just got a shipment of weapons courtesy of Rachim. We're getting reports that Pentus's old estate is completely overrun, and there are dead things coming up from below. Why are you in the wheelhouse?"

"That is a long story," Aimee fired back. "For now I'll leave it at 'the bridge crew is dead and you shouldn't worry because we absolutely know what we're doing.'"

Silence. Then came "What?"

"Yeah," Aimee said. "That's what we said. Will keep in touch. More weapons should be coming soon."

"Comforting."

"Isn't it?" Aimee replied, then ended the communique before glancing over at a vaguely horrified look on Belit's face. A half second later they felt the whole ship shudder under their feet as the engines reversed. Belit's arms strained as she pulled the wheel, and slowly, the immense behemoth began to turn.

CHAPTER TWENTY-FIVE
AMBER IN THE HEART OF BRONZE

Elias sank into the violence. The white sword split the trunk of a dead man. Ash and embers trailed in his wake. He moved forward, deliberately slow, carved another, and another. They sheared down the catwalk, and when Elias fell back, Vant stepped in, and the mystic energy projector let out a loud *whump*, blasting a channel down the center of the walkway. Elias lunged, stepping over corpses blasted near to paste, and into an advancing tide of glowing eyes and ripping limbs.

They careened down the catwalk, running, fighting, dodging. The black knight sent a blooming gout of fire tearing across the edge of the rail, sending a cluster of the dead hurtling into the abyss below. Closer, he glimpsed the heart of *Tristan* glowing. He dropped as a raking limb lashed across the space above him and put the glowing sword through its center of mass. Light exploded from its mouth and eyes as it burned away. He dashed forward. These dead were less individually powerful than the assassins the Faceless had sent against them, but there were more of them, by far. They came, needing no strategy where sheer numbers sufficed.

The three men hurtled down the interior promenade. Bjorn split one from neck to crotch. Vant dashed and shot. Elias kept the pressure on. The sword rose and fell, again and again. Bodies split and burned. His blood pounded in his ears, and the ingrained, rote repetition propelled him forward, until they burst onto the open platform just before the battered, broken bronze heart of the chamber. Here the purple light bled forth from the tremendous rent in the thick metal walls, torn by a force that dizzied Elias to imagine.

"An explosion," Vant said, as if reading his thoughts. "If I had to guess, they overloaded and destroyed the subsidiary cores, and the backlash ripped the chamber open."

Elias turned. The dead were holding back from them, now. Wherever the light of the core shone, the dead held back like shadows fleeing the sun. Ironically, the only place they were likely safe from relentless attack was the unstable heart of the dying ship. At least it was where they had to go.

"They're staying away from the heart," Bjorn said, flicking gore from his two-handed blade. "Is it the magic?"

"Maybe," Vant said, "but let's not burn time worrying about the why, yeah? We gotta get in there."

They emerged into a macabre twin of *Iseult*'s heart. A nightmare of shattered controls, broken cables, and obliterated subsidiary cores greeted them. The central control station was a blackened mass of twisted wires and shattered consoles. The corpses of the engineers were scattered around the room in multiple parts, flesh burnt away and screaming skeletons frozen in positions of agony.

"Well," Vant breathed, as they stepped through the wreckage. "*Iseult* got off easy."

There was so much magic in the air that Elias felt dizzy. He pressed a hand to his forehead, trying to steady himself against the fresh assault on his perception. It was like trying to see through fog, and he swayed on his feet, caught himself on a piece of wreckage, and muttered, "Not yet." He caught his breath and looked around. "Where's Harkon?"

Bjorn grabbed his shoulder, and pointed.

The source of the purple light in the chamber was the primary metadrive core of *Tristan*, sitting atop its platinum pyramid, somehow still blazing in defiance of the destruction surrounding it. The twin heart to *Iseult* shone, the churning magic energy within so bright it was hard to look at.

But it wasn't the core that Bjorn was pointing at. Lashed to its base by steel cables was a large, coffin-sized cyst of golden crystal, and within it was the silhouette of a man, his hands clasped as if in the culmination of a spell.

Harkon Bright.

Elias stumble-dashed towards him, almost fell on his face before he reached the pyramid's base. Up close, the crystal was clear, and within, Harkon's face was in an oddly serene look of repose.

"Is he dead?" Vant asked, giving voice to their shared fear.

"No," Elias said, peering closer. The storm of spilt sorcery clouding his senses made it harder to tell for sure, but there were clues. The moment his fingers brushed the crystal, he felt the energy like a static shock. His knowledge of magical theory wasn't as strong as Aimee's, nor of her exponentially more powerful master, but in a flash he understood what he was looking at.

"I don't know how he did it," Elias said, "but this is the crystalized energy of a powerful necromantic spell. He must've seen it coming, and somehow managed to trade death for a sort of mystic slumber. That's powerful magic, and I have no idea how to undo it."

"Then we take him back," Bjorn said. "Maybe Aimee can. I know Hark. He wouldn't do this to himself if he didn't believe someone could get him out again."

"This is heavy," Elias said, assessing the man and his crystal prison before him. "And those undead are still swarming outside the chamber. I can't fight them and carry this."

Bjorn swore. "And once we get too far outside the damn chamber, they'll hit us. All at once."

"It was expected that these subsidiary cores would be replaced," Vant said. "Ideally, we shouldn't *have* to carry it. We just have to find one of the wheeled platforms they moved them on. I saw at least one back in *Iseult*. Start looking!"

They cast about in the flickering light, overturning wreckage. It was only a few moments before Bjorn called out. "Over here! Gonna be hard to push, unless you can get some power into the damn thing, but we might be able to swing it!"

"Let me look!" Vant jogged over to the blackened platform. The engineer crouched and started pushing bits and pieces of ruined equipment off it. "It'll run," he said, "but not fast. We'll still be fighting the damn things off while it crawls towards the loading bay. I don't know if we even *have* that kind of time."

Elias stared up at *Tristan*'s core. What was the legend again? Two hearts in two ships. Mythical lovers separated by death, sustaining their vessels through the eternal skies. *Tristan* was dying now, and there was no way that even its mighty, ancient heart could save it.

But it *could* still save *Iseult*.

Two hearts.

"Vant, wait!" he called over his shoulder. Both of the other two stopped. Elias looked back at them, a mad grin crossing his face. "How fast would it go if you hooked it up to *Tristan*'s core?"

"Pretty damn," the engineer answered, "until we ran out of cable... Wait."

Bjorn's eyebrows raised, and the two of them exchanged a look. Elias watched the comprehension sink in.

"You're a mad genius, Elias Leblanc," Vant said. "Alright, come on! Let's get this done!"

Removing the core ate up more time than they'd hoped, but Vant got the job done, and as they finished laying the priceless power source and the crystalized form of their leader onto the platform, the engineer jumped down and started fiddling with the wires. Beneath them, the core thrummed, encased in a steel shell that covered the translucent exterior for transport.

"For the record," Vant called up to Elias as the black knight took hold of one of the cables, "we're going to have to steer by leaning. I have no idea just how quick this thing is going to go, and there's always the risk that the influx of energy will make this platform's little engine, um, explode."

"The alternative is all of us dying!" Elias shouted back. "Are you ready?"

The engineer hopped up, looped his arm through one of the cables tying the core and the crystal-frozen Harkon together, then held up two sparking wires. "Hang on!"

A spark flared between the two ends, and the platform exploded forward. They burst through the battered remnants of the door and out onto the exterior platform, straight towards the edge of the abyss, sending a cluster of undead hurtling into the darkness. Elias grasped the cables and threw all his weight to his right side. "Lean right!"

All three of them cast themselves in the same direction. The super-charged platform arced, ran nearly to the edge of the rail, then turned violently inward. "Left!" Elias screamed, and they arced just short of smashing themselves into the far wall. "Center!" he screamed again, and they were shooting up the long, broad promenade by which they had come. Bjorn shouted something incoherent behind him, and Vant started laughing. They accelerated, moving faster the longer their line was straight. The dead parted before them, hammered out of the way, run over, smashed aside.

Then the entire ship started to tilt. It was hard to notice at first, but suddenly they were leaning simply to remain upright, and the core walls were beginning to roll.

"Well," Elias heard Vant say, "that took longer than anticipated. With the core disconnected, *Tristan* has no power, which means she's at the mercy of the abyss's pull and the storm's winds!"

"No auxiliaries?" Bjorn snapped.

"Not with the subsidiary cores destroyed!" Vant shouted. "We might want to get out of here *now*."

There. The corridor entry to the bay loomed ahead. "Get ready!" Elias shouted. "And *lean right!*"

They crashed through the doorway. The platform bashed into its edge. Elias held on. They careened off the corridor's far wall, bounced off the frame of the exit, and spinning, crashed into the landing bay. "Kill the power!" he shouted.

Vant lurched, hooked his legs into the cable to keep from falling, and pulled one of his shock-sticks, jamming it into the platform's engine. There was a loud bang, a discharge, and their propulsion died... but not their momentum.

The platform skidded across the floor towards the open bay door of *Elysium*, wobbled, slowed. Elias turned. The glimmering, hungry eyes of the dead appeared in the entryway to the corridor they'd come through. "Get the platform into the cargo hold!" he shouted, then leaped clear of the skidding contraption. Oath of Aurum flashed free and blazing, and he landed in a crouch before the charging horde. There was no more time to see if his friends had done it. He loosed concussive flames into the first mass of the dead, then carved the first to reach him in half. Then the second. The third. He kicked the body of the fourth, blasted the fifth, then had to give ground as ever more came rushing in.

More kept coming. He piled on speed. It made no difference. Blasts of magic kept them from overrunning his flanks only long enough for him to defend himself from upwards of four attacks at once. No matter how many he struck down, more pressed in. He could give no more ground. He hoped they'd made it to *Elysium*'s loading bay. He hadn't come here expecting to die, but the thought crossed his mind that there were worse ways.

Noble and brave, he thought. *Gentle and kind.*

Borrowed time. Make it count.

He was running out of strength. His arms ached. The hands gripping the sword were almost numb. One of them had hit him at some point. The steel darted across his vision, leaving streaks of white through the air. "Come on, you bastards," he breathed. "I can put another hundred of you down before this is over."

"ELIAS!" he heard Bjorn scream behind him. "DROP!"

He obeyed without thinking. A brilliant flare of light roared overhead and slammed into the press of running dead. An entire cluster of them splattered into red mist. He rolled onto his belly, surged up, and ran for the landing bay. Bjorn and Vant had loaded up the platform with its precious cargo, and as he dashed, the old warrior could be seen behind the glass of the rear gun turret, blasting concussive bursts of light into the rushing, undead remnants of *Tristan*'s crew. The floor lurched. The sky outside the bay door tilted. Elias ran, until the bay swelled in his vision and he hurled himself up over the ramp and onto the floor of the bay, gasping for breath. "Go!" he shouted. "I'm in!"

The ramp slammed up; *Elysium* rose from the floor and shot into the open air. The wind struck her, making the floor tilt so hard that Elias was nearly thrown against the cargo bay wall. He grabbed a rail to steady himself, sheathed his sword, and ran up the stairs and into the central corridor of the ship.

Halfway to the bridge he reached the common area with its large viewport, and what Elias saw froze him in place.

Tristan hadn't tilted because its core had been removed. *Elysium* was in the process of turning against the wind, giving them a sideways view of the behemoth. A vast limb, blacker than night, lashed across the entryway through which they'd just escaped. It was wider than the thickest tower, longer than a warship, and visible only by the light it defied to illuminate its ink-like surface. It took a full breath for Elias to make sense of what he was seeing, then another arm lashed up across the hull of the behemoth. Bits of surface construction exploded, estates and fine marble sloughing from the vessel in a torrent of collapsing buildings. Beyond the bow, something vast beyond measure, and incalculably dark, rose from within the storm.

Grandfather had come.

CHAPTER TWENTY-SIX
ONE-WOMAN ARMY

Aimee turned from the controls. *Iseult* swung, but not fast enough. Belit strained behind the wheel. Slowly, the black wall of raging storm moved in their view, and the sorceress held on to the rail before her, urging the ship beneath her to fight against the winds even as she prayed.

Rachim burst through the doorway with two more men behind him, and a storm of curses escaped his mouth at the sight of the bodies strewn across the bridge. "By her beating heart," he swore. "No survivors?"

"None," Vlana said from behind the crystal table, "and it's worse: I'm not sure if *Iseult* has the power to break free of this wind. Not with one core down and her crew fighting the dead on every damn floor!"

Abruptly the quartermaster paused as another light on the table flashed. "We're getting a communication from *Elysium*. They're alive!"

She pressed her finger to the blinking light, and the image of Elias Leblanc flashed into the center of the room. He looked battered, but not seriously hurt. Aimee felt a surge of relief flood through her.

"We've got Harkon, and we're coming in hard," he

said. "Grandfather is destroying *Tristan*. I'd wager we only have a little while before he realizes we took the Faceless's magic bait out of the ship and turns towards *Iseult*."

Again, a surge of relief flooded the young sorceress. Alive. Her teacher was alive.

"We're trying to turn away from the maelstrom," Aimee answered. "But with the winds and our previous speed, it's a struggle. Being one core down is making this a lot harder, as is Amut's bridge crew being dead."

"We actually have the solution to that!" Elias said, and his excitement was palpable. "We pulled the primary metadrive core out of *Tristan*, and we're bringing it back with us."

"You what?" Rachim exclaimed.

"Long story," the young man answered. "We can't land at your villa. There won't be room to get the core out."

"The nearest bay to the chamber is the starboard amidships aperture. It's adjacent to Pentus's estate," Rachim answered. "And it's completely overrun with the dead. They're fighting them down there, we'll have to find another–"

"No," Aimee interrupted. "It's their best shot. We don't have time to haul the core halfway across the ship, not when they can fly it in closer and get it to the chamber in time."

"We don't have the men to spare," Rachim said.

"But the wheelhouse does," Aimee said. Turning back to the image of Elias she said, "Tell Clutch to make for the starboard amidships bay near Pentus's estate. I'll meet you there."

Elias gave a nod and a half smile. "Hang on," he said. "We're coming in hot."

The image flickered and vanished.

Aimee picked up one of the shock-spears, grateful for the training Bjorn had briefly given her with it.

"You're out of your godsdamned mind," Rachim started.

"I didn't acquire my reputation by playing it safe," Aimee answered. "Belit, do you have things up here handled?"

"In as much as I can," the swordswoman answered. "The three of you," she snapped at Rachim and his men. "Make yourselves useful. Get the bodies away from the consoles so we can access the workstations. Rachim, help Vlana get the star-charts up and running. Once we have the power to get free of the wind, we're going to have to fly ourselves out using old-fashioned navigation."

Rachim grunted his disapproval, but he headed towards the crystal table, where he laid a map out across its surface, pointing to a specific route from the wheelhouse down to the bay in question. "This is the most direct route you can take," he said. "It's also compromised, and once you get there, all we really have is a perimeter keeping them from threatening the metadrive chamber. I still don't like this. You're one of our most valuable assets in this fight."

"Thanks," Aimee said. She memorized the route, then folded up the map and stuffed it in her coat. "And I know," she said over her shoulder. "I'm going where I'm needed."

Aimee de Laurent stalked through the raging wind and the pouring rain, blasted the door to the access corridor off its hinges, and dropped down into the darkness. The dead were waiting, but there was no longer a need to worry about shielding her companions, obsessing over the preservation of delicate instruments, or holding back for fear of what the people in power might do. As the first of the corpse-functionaries turned towards her, she blasted the entire corridor with a wind spell that sent it hurtling into its fellows, then summoned the Radiance, and unleashed hell. Bodies hurtled backwards, slammed into walls. She unleashed the spell again and again, then stalked forward through a cloud of embers and ash.

She turned, stepped out onto the edge of a winding staircase and glimpsed down the long shaft to its bottom, further down than she cared to think. Her target level was at its halfway point, she estimated. Aimee took a breath, tightened her grip on the shock-spear, stepped out onto the edge and held a spell in her mind to slow her fall, when the time was right. Then she jumped. Levels shot past. The wind whipped by her as she strained to keep her body upright and pencil-straight. Closer. She glimpsed the dead in numbers that galled and horrified. Then she was coming up on the midlevels. The numbers rushed towards her. Aimee wove and released the spell, and as her descent slowed, she kicked off a rail and angled herself straight into the stairwell just above her target.

She landed in a crouch. One level up and one level down, the dead rushed towards her. She set her teeth, summoned a burst of flame just past each hand, then flowed through the forms of wind and loosed a burst of air at each tongue of fire before either could dissipate.

A roaring, wind-fanned inferno erupted from just past each of her hands, blazing up the stairs and down simultaneously. The dead burned greasily, swiftly. The magic animating them ignited, discharging in multiple, red-smearing concussive blasts above and below. *Learn quickly.*

She rose from the blaze, then turning, blasted the next door open and stepped out into the midlevels. She stood in the middle of a wide street. To her right, the vast interior of *Iseult* could be seen just beyond the lip of the promenade that spanned the interior opening on this level. To her left, the street wound further past a number of gates set into the walls, and each of these had been smashed open. This, then, was the boundary of Pentus's midlevel estate. She couldn't see any of the Faceless's recently raised children, but she could hear them in the distance, along with the periodic *whump* of mystic energy projectors and the screams of people fighting back. Aimee hefted her weapon and ran towards the sounds of the chaos. She passed the third gate into the ruins of what had once been a beautiful garden, now littered with the bodies of its master's servants. Up ahead, a doorway of exquisite hardwood hung broken from its hinges.

Three of the dead came running out, eyes alight and teeth red with recently drawn blood. Aimee loosed the Radiance to burn the first to ash, but the second came upon her before she could ready it again. She jammed the shock-spear into its body and discharged its magic with a twist. As it convulsed, she wind-smashed the second in the head with the butt so hard she heard its neck crack. It spun from the impact. She turned back to the first and loosed the beam of light straight down its screaming mouth and stepped backwards through the cloud of burning dust as the second lunged through the air at her. Aimee smashed the spear-point into its chest and hit it with a dose of lightning even as she freed one hand to blast its middle into a thousand chunks of meat.

She stepped over the remnants, and charged into the late duke's stately apartments. Somewhere on the other side of this mess was the bay she needed to reach. Could she take it by herself? Maybe not, but with her backing them, the people fighting these things on the other side of the estate could push through. Flames licked at priceless works of art as she ran. Dislodged wiring and broken magic conduits sent bursts of fire across her path. She summoned shield-spells, ducked, wove, and rolled.

She was nearly through. The sounds of fighting echoed just beyond an immense window that looked down onto interior recreational grounds some fifty feet below. Across the space, downlevelers and enlisted battled against the rushing, chaotic masses of the Faceless's horde of the walking dead. No time to find a way down. Aimee took a deep breath and wind-blasted the window apart. She ran, slammed the spear into the ground, and pole-vaulted herself through the rain of glass razors, slowing her fall with magic and landing in the midst of the battle in a crouch. A downleveler jumped back, alarmed, and Aimee rose. "Hi," she said. "I'm the reinforcements."

She twisted as soon as the words were out of her mouth, and loosed the beam of white light through the center of the nearest of them, burning it to ash. Another came at her. She dropped as it swiped and slammed her palm into its chest, releasing a spell of frost before pivoting back and smashing its frozen form with the butt of the shock-spear, shattering it. Then she turned once more and said, "Who's in charge here?"

"Was one of Pentus's old armsmen," the man answered back. There was a blast from several feet away as a mystic energy projector created a hole through a garden wall. Aimee summoned a shield spell to ward off the debris.

"I last saw him charging into the press," the man said. "He didn't come back."

"Then I'm in charge," Aimee said. "The loading bay on the other side of that wall–" she gestured at the wall to his back "–we need it cleared, because backup is coming that can save the whole ship."

His eyes widened. He gave a nod and hefted the flame-lance he carried. Aimee dashed to the top of a broken bit of statuary pedestal and amplified her voice. "Enlisted of *Iseult*!" she shouted. "The skyship *Elysium* is returning with the power to save her heart from the threat of the dead! She must land in the bay on the other side of that wall!"

Eyes were on her, now. One of the dead leaped at her from the window of Pentus's estate. She struck it with her spear in the chest and blasted it away with a gust of wind, then aimed her weapon at the large cargo doors to the landing bay beyond. A shout went up from the mass of armed enlisted. It echoed through the chamber, a cry of explosive defiance. She rode the tide, letting it lift her exhausted, shaking heart.

"After me!" she shouted, and jumped from the pedestal. Her boots pounded the deck floor, and she sent beams of blazing Radiance out ahead of her, shearing through the oncoming remnants of the Faceless's minions. A wave rose behind her, men and women, armed in the defense of their home, charging at her back. The dull *whump* of the projectors sent blasts of mystic light ahead of her, blasting pathways through the enemy. Every spell she'd studied in her battle magic classes back at the academy flashed through her mind as she ran. The spells Harkon had given her since. The spear in her hand crackled with lightning. She felt the fire playing at the edge of her eyes.

Aimee de Laurent charged into the ranks of the dead at the head of an army, and let loose the fury of her magic.

CHAPTER TWENTY-SEVEN
GRANDFATHER

Elias gripped the brass rail, and held on for dear life. Winds hammered *Elysium*. The skyship bucked and spun in the storm. Through it all, Clutch held the wheel, shouting words down to Vant in the metadrive chamber. As for himself, the black knight was paralyzed by uselessness, and a mad terror of what was coming.

"ELIAS!" he heard Bjorn scream. "I need you to take the rear ether-cannons! I'm more use on the bridge!"

Jumping at the chance to act, he turned past the old man emerging out from the corridor. He gave a nod and jogged back down until he was at the top of the stairs in the cargo hold at the vessel's rear. The ladder to the gun turret was accessible at the far end of the upper level, and Elias clambered up it, nearly losing his grip. He unstrapped his sword and squeezed into a narrow, armored space. His feet found pedals, and he quickly discerned that by pushing one or the other he could swivel the small sphere back and forth.

Then he looked out the viewport of the turret, and wished he hadn't. The vast frame of *Tristan* rolled in the wind. He had a moment to take in the mesmerizing beauty of the city-sized behemoth before another limb, long enough to wrap *around* its middle, lashed from the smoky wall of the maelstrom clouds, and struck with such force that the exterior frame of the gigantic skyship dented inwards. A deep, echoing *crack* echoed above the wind, and *Tristan*'s spine snapped.

Elias's hands shook on the controls, suddenly a small boy again, held prisoner in a tiny cabin as his callous owner flew him into the outer halo of this place of havoc and chaos. But this time, it was no dream. No whispers of mindless terror or illusion assaulted his senses. Two more vast tentacles of impossible scale lashed out from the mass of vast darkness just past the dying behemoth, and started to pull the city-ship in half.

Grandfather was here. The nightmare was real.

As the ship split down the middle, a rending shriek echoed through the skies. Marble-coated buildings and scaffolds of rusted metal collapsed and spun into the wind. A series of muffled explosions detonated within the interior of the vessel in its death throes, and the rippling waves of discharging, shattering enchantments tore outward through the sky, making the black knight dizzy as he sat in the small glass and metal sphere on the back end of *Elysium*. With a final, rending *bang*, the tortured husk of a vessel split in two. A fireball larger than the central district of Port Providence flared across the sky, forcing Elias to close his eyes.

When he opened them again, it was in time to watch as the two savaged halves of *Tristan* dropped into the abyss far below, and a cloud of lighter debris hurtled towards them on the whirling winds. "Clutch!" he shouted into the communication tube. "Debris incoming from the rear!"

"Shoot down as much as you can!" her voice came echoing back. "And strap in! This is gonna make you sick!"

She didn't lie. Elias had barely gotten his seat straps into place when *Elysium*'s engines roared, and the vessel shot into a spiraling upward arc. He was upside down, he was rightside up, again and again and again.

He was going to lose his last meal all over the interior of the rear turret. Focus. He had to focus. His hands gripped the controls, first to steady himself, then to do his job. A large chunk of whirling hull-plating surged towards them. He tracked it, then set his feet and pulled the trigger. The entire mechanism of the ether-cannon jerked backwards, taking the seat with it. Bolts of blazing mystic fire blasted across the sky, striking their target and blasting it apart. Elias held on for dear life as *Elysium* spun, dived, and shot forward. He spotted another target, then let loose. Bolts of light traced across the storm-racked heavens. He pulled the trigger again, as the ship's metadrive fed raw power into her rear guns. Shredded wreckage shattered and lanced overhead and below like drops of windswept rain.

Then at once the last of it dropped away, and the skyship leveled off, pulling into an even plane before a fresh burst from her engines set her roaring straight towards her target. It took a few seconds for Elias to steady himself and calm his breathing. It was as if the walls closed around him, and again, he was the little boy: locked in a cabin, upon a slab of stone, at Roland's mercy, at Esric's, within the burning cottage where his mother had died. His heart raced. He started to hyperventilate.

He had killed the last echo of the dead Eternal Order

knight within *Iseult*'s depths. Destroyed its corpse and silenced the whispers, but he couldn't kill his own memories. "Not now," he murmured, as the surge of recollections and fear threatened to overwhelm him. "Not now, please–"

"*My sweet boy.*"

He heard the words. Whether it was the madness of the storm, or the ravaged state of his fearful mind, he couldn't begin to guess, but he heard them, and he knew the voice.

"Mother," he whispered as the wind roared and the heavens shook. Speaking the words somehow made the fear more real. "Mother, I'm so scared I can't think."

Gentle, as if from far away, came the reply.

"*Not all of your memories are wicked.*"

His eyes squeezed shut. A cottage, long ago and far away. A gentle hand. A melody sung in a voice he could barely recall. But newer, as well. The skyship on which he sailed. Harkon, standing in his cabin. A shared drink in the common room as thunder rolled in the distance. A dance with Aimee, across a gilded floor more memory than real, beneath the landless stars.

"*Noble and brave. Gentle and kind.*"

His eyes opened. His hands gripped the controls. It came for them, now, beyond the remnants of the falling debris. Not as fast as *Elysium*, no, but fast. He couldn't see the whole of it. In the immensity of the storm's edge, it was visible only as a deeper darkness, an ink-like shadow against the gray, unlit even by the intermittent, titanic flashes of lightning. He saw the outline of its limbs, more than could be counted, and beyond, a body that was long and dark, changing shape as it moved swiftly across the skies.

It followed them. And as it moved, for just a moment, Elias glimpsed something within the mass of writhing black: the flash of a single, glimmering eye.

He screamed in defiance and pulled the trigger, ineffectual bolts of weaponsfire cracking into the face of the oncoming monstrosity.

"Hang on!" Clutch screamed over the tubes. "We're coming in hot!"

Elysium turned, rotating hard and fast through the air, and suddenly Elias's vision was filled not with the titanic horror of Grandfather's visage, but with the swallowing maw of *Iseult*'s amidships loading bay door. He had a second to glimpse the chaotic battle unfolding across its massive floor, then the ship touched down hard. He felt the landing gear hit the deck with a loud shriek. The vessel tilted violently as it skidded through the middle of a packed melee. Outside, he glimpsed flashes of downlevelers battling with the dead. He angled the gun into the mass of running corpses just beyond the ship, and let loose three loud blasts, clearing the floor before them. Then he unstrapped himself, leaped out of the turret, and snatched Oath of Aurum. "Lower the bay door!" he shouted into the tube. "They're going to need me out there!"

A loud *thumping* release was followed by the drone of the bay door lowering. Elias heaved himself over the edge, dropped to the ramp, and hurled himself into the melee.

"AIMEE!" he shouted. "I'M HERE!"

He found her halfway across the bay, at the head of a surge of fighters, loosing beams of iridescent Radiance through the enemy which turned corpses to embers and ashes.

The dead were breaking, carved up now into smaller clusters being driven down by the newly armed ordinary folk of *Iseult*. He cut his way to her, and she turned in time to catch his eye as he burst through a group of them, sending their burning remnants cascading to the floor and leaving a path to *Elysium* behind him.

Aimee turned towards him, and it seemed as though a hundred feelings flashed across her blue eyes in a moment. A warm smile spread across her face, and she ran towards him, hug-tackling him with a ferocity that nearly took him off his feet. "You're late," she said in his ear.

"Got held up," he said as he pulled back. A stupid grin spread across his face. "Did you do this?"

Aimee grinned back, just as broad. "No, they did it. I just gave them impetus. Where is he?"

"Inside the bay," Elias said. "We need you in there now."

Aimee stepped past him and reopened his path through the press with a blast of wind that sent bodies flying. Then ran across the floor, up the ramp. Bjorn waited at the top, having strapped on the mystic energy projector. Its steady *whump* continued behind them as they reached the crystalline cyst of magic that encased Harkon Bright.

"Whatever you're going to do, do it quick," Bjorn said. "That monster the cult worships is bearing down on *Iseult*, and fast. It won't matter what the dead do if we don't find a way to keep their Storm-Kraken at bay."

"If I had to hazard a guess," Elias said, staring at the old mage within the crystal, "he was caught off guard, and managed to redirect the energy of the spell into some form of slumber, rather than death."

Aimee crouched beside the coffin-sized amber crystal, eyes wide. "I saw a drawing like it in one of the books in his quarters, the notes spoke of something like that, but the skill level necessary to pull something like that off in the moment is... so far beyond anything I've ever done."

"Other than opening a portal in the center of a demon's chest," Elias reminded her. "You can do this."

She flashed him a sideways look. Intent. Almost burning, then she looked at the crystalline coffin again. Bjorn's weapon blasted off twice more behind them. Aimee's lips moved as she ran through calculations out loud. Elias reflected for a moment that watching Aimee de Laurent's mind work was like watching a master paint.

"Alright, teacher," he heard her say, as she wove a simple spell that he thought he recognized as being intended for breaking enchantments, but modified, subtly, by the gestures of her swift fingers. "I don't know how you did this," she continued, "and this is the best solution I can think of, but I have to believe that you knew I could get you out of it again. Please, for the love of all the gods, don't prove me wrong."

She spoke words of magic, and pressed her hands to the surface of the crystal. A brief silence followed, as the magic dissipated, then the air was rent by the sound of a loud crack, and a flash of brilliant light as the energy of the frozen spell came undone and fell away.

And from the ashes of the broken, necromantic shell, Harkon Bright rose.

CHAPTER TWENTY-EIGHT
THE HERO AND THE HURRICANE

Harkon Bright sagged, and Aimee stepped beneath his arm, catching him. "Thank you," he said. His voice was haggard. Exhausted. "It was a gamble, but you've made it pay off in spades."

The spell had been a last ditch, creative effort. Aimee hadn't expected it to work. Elias caught Harkon's other arm, and the two held him up together. "Belit holds the wheelhouse," Aimee said. "Pentus is dead, Yaresh is no longer a problem, and the cult–"

"Worships a Storm-Kraken they call Grandfather," Harkon finished. His voice was getting stronger, as if he were shaking off a bout of bad sleep. "I know. The Faceless was prone to gloating, and he believed he'd won. I assume he's been dealt with?"

"Belit killed him," Aimee said. "With Oath of Aurum."

Her teacher's eyes widened. "Well," he said. "I suppose that explains a few things. We can discuss it all later."

"Can you stand?" Elias asked.

"I believe so," Harkon said, freeing himself from the knight. "Or at least, she will suffice. You've done magnificently, young man. Now do what you need to do."

"Vant!" Elias yelled. "Time to get this core into the chamber!"

"*Iseult* is running one subsidiary core short," Aimee explained.

Harkon sighed as he straightened. "I've missed so much. Help me reach the wheelhouse, will you? I can feel that wretched thing coming, and I fear they're going to need me soon."

The words were understated, but at their utterance, Aimee felt the flicker of a tremendous power stir within her teacher.

"Hold up," Clutch shouted behind them. "I'm coming with you. If we're going to get away from that thing, *Iseult* will need a pilot that can actually fly."

They stepped out into the bay. The dead were thinning now, but they blocked their path. Aimee put two down with the blazing spell her teacher had taught her. "Well done," he said. "Let me handle these next ones, though. We're short on time."

He turned abruptly as a cluster of charging corpses bore down upon them. His hands flickered deftly through the motions, and a *wave* of the same blazing light blasted across them, leaving stains upon the deck, and nothing more. The ripple of power jarred her, and as he draped his arm about her shoulder once again, she said, "Why didn't you teach me that one?"

"A little too advanced," he said as they moved. "Though I suspect you'll be ready for it much sooner than your teachers at the academy would have thought. Pay close attention to what happens when we reach the top, Aimee. It will all be useful in the future. Grandfather is terribly old, and terribly powerful, but there are great

spells that were designed long ago for dealing with monsters of his might."

Hope, real hope, surged within her as they reached the bay's far wall, where another doorway led to the central corridors of the ship, and from there, the way up. "You think you can drive it back?"

A grim smile crossed her teacher's face. "Dear me," Harkon said. "I'm afraid not. From what I have sensed, Grandfather is determined to devour this ship and every soul upon it. Deterring him will not be possible." He grunted, as if stretching muscles unused for a very long time. "I shall have to kill him."

By the time they reached the top level, Harkon seemed stronger. He walked on his own now, and the two sorcerers hurried up the rain-drenched central thoroughfare as the winds howled, periodic gusts ripping through the streets and threatening to dash them against the walls of fine marble-faced estates. They ran past the corpses of the storm-crazed, still uncleared from where they'd fallen. The sky overhead was split between the light clouds of the outer edge of the storm, and the flashing, chaotic darkness of its raging black wall.

"Too steep of a turn," Aimee heard Clutch say. "Too steep."

And at the edge of her senses, something immense and potent approached. They were nearly at the base of the wheelhouse when Aimee turned, and nearly froze in her tracks. She knew what a Storm-Kraken was. She had a basic understanding of the concepts underlying the myths.

Reading about a legend in a textbook of deep sky

mythology and seeing it in person were not things that could be compared. Just past the subdued glow of *Iseult*'s weakened engines, something dark and incalculably vast approached. Not quite as large as the behemoth itself, yet more than half her length, at least. From its body, a host of probing arms lashed out towards *Iseult* as she slowly turned.

"Not as much time as I hoped," Harkon said. "We need to get up to the ivory bridge. Come."

They climbed the stairs. The sounds of shouts echoed down from above. Aimee heard Belit shouting orders, Rachim barking back, and the echo of Vlana's voice as well. They burst into the wheelhouse.

"Hark!" Vlana and Rachim said at the same time, and it seemed to take everything in the former's power not to launch herself over the crystal table to hug the old sorcerer.

Clutch dashed forward, towards Belit. "Alright, Cap," she said. "I'm a guild-trained pilot. Let me take the wheel. You focus on giving those orders and getting us the hell out of here."

The look of relief on Belit's face was palpable. She stepped back, and Clutch took the wheel, immediately grunting with the strain. "I suppose," the pilot said, "I should've expected her to steer like a flying brick. Where are we going?"

"Wheelhouse?" The call came up from the engine room. "This is Vant. We've got the replacement core into the metadrive chamber, but it's going to take us a few minutes to get it plugged in. Just keep that thing from tearing the ship apart, and we'll give you the engines at maximum capacity soon!"

"Straighten our course," Belit said.

Clutch looked back over her shoulder as if Belit had just spouted incomprehensible madness. "What?"

"Level us out so we fly with the wind, along the edge of the storm," Belit said. "As long as we're trying to fight it we'll never outdistance that thing bearing down on us. At least this way we delay it! Do it!"

"Sure, talk sense to me, why don't you," Clutch said, and let the wheel go. It spun on its base, and *Iseult* lurched starboard, towards the storm.

"Navigation is still hell," Vlana said. "The damn table can't get even half of a reading with all this magic interference."

"Clutch!" Belit shouted. "Take us up! I glimpsed stars through the cloud cover before. We go high enough we might just be able to see!"

"Hang on, everyone!" Clutch shouted in reply. "This is gonna get rough!"

Her hand snapped down to a lever beside the wheel, and she pulled it down as hard as she could. There was a rumble, and the deck beneath them began to tilt as the city-sized behemoth began to climb.

"Time to go," Harkon said. "Do try to keep the ship from going completely vertical," he added to the makeshift wheelhouse crew. "This is going to be hard enough without trying not to fall. Aimee, come."

The bridge was a narrow strip of white metal between the wheelhouse and each of the watchtowers at either forward corner upon the bow. The moment they stepped out onto the rain-slick metal, Aimee had to hastily throw down a spell to keep her feet from slipping out

beneath her. The wind blew from aftward, so powerful that each step was a grueling effort, and her coat whipped horizontally out behind her. *And this is only the outer halo beyond the storm's wall,* she thought. *Within the maelstrom it would strip flesh from bones.*

She turned as they reached the middle of the expanse. Harkon seemed to have found his second surge, now. He strode purposefully through the rain, his coat whipping behind him. At the center he turned, placed one hand upon the rail, and stared to the rear of the ship with a look of terrible fury. "I will need you to defend me while I do this," he said. "Grandfather is not without his own magic, and it will not be long before he senses what I am doing."

Aimee turned. The monstrosity surged behind them, now rapidly approaching *Iseult*'s stern as the vessel climbed. Two of its shadowy arms lashed out through the wind, stretching. One struck the port corner of the stern, and the entire vessel shook.

Then Harkon Bright slammed his hands together at the culmination of a complex series of gestures. A swell of dizzying energy emanated from him, and he placed the palms of his glowing hands to the bridge beneath him. A suffusing rush of light, white and brilliant, flared outward, passing beneath Aimee and throughout the entirety of the climbing behemoth.

When Harkon spoke again, his voice was like the roar of the storm, and carried above the drone of the wind. "In the name of the First Laws, the Palimpsest of Souls, and the Empyrean Wings of Heaven, I declare *Iseult* Sanctuary against you, Devourer, Old Rain-Lurker. Turn about, and slink back to the haven of your storm-clouds. These souls are not for you."

And all at once, Aimee realized, with an arresting clarity, the focus of the primordial entity shifted. It had no face she could discern, yet its malice was directed at them, and the force of that ancient hate was mightier than any wind. She felt a pressure building in the air, then her teacher said, "A shield spell, Aimee. Like the one I taught you in Port Providence."

She stepped forward, and with flashing gestures, summoned a mandala of light into the space between the monster and her master, widening it as much as she could.

It flashed into being a moment before one of the massive limbs extended, whipped across the vast span between them, and hammered into it. The force shook the bridge upon which she stood, but the spell her master had cast somehow kept it from killing her. Aimee fell to one knee and screamed, nonetheless. She turned the shriek of pain into a howl of defiance, and shouted, "Is that all you've got, Grandpa?"

The malice of the primordial thing struck her like another gust of wind. Instead of buckling, Aimee pushed herself back up into a standing position, holding tight to her defensive spell and grinning madly into the maw of the Storm-Kraken.

"Last chance," Harkon said. The warning carried above the wind. "Turn back, or be unmade."

A terrible heat and light was growing within him, crackling beneath her mentor's skin, and when Aimee glanced back, his hands were outlines of flesh containing blazing sunlight.

The second strike of a limb loosed a spell, and Aimee was almost knocked off her feet. Her back struck the opposite rail of the ivory bridge, and the breath went out of her. Still, she held her spell. Just beyond the range of coverage of her defensive magic, the top level of the watchtower at the other end of the bridge broke in half with an ear-rending split.

"So be it," Harkon said, then he addressed Aimee. "Lower the shield spell."

Aimee blinked. "Are you *insane*?"

"Do it!"

She dropped the spell. The vastness of the Storm-Kraken spread out before her, now almost upon *Iseult*. Its limbs lashed out towards her. Aimee fought the reflex to close her eyes. She would meet death face on.

A wall of night at the end of a massive arm enveloped the entirety of the bridge in complete darkness. Aimee looked up as her world was smothered by shadow and the overpowering scent of rain.

Then she heard her teacher's voice.

"I INVOKE THE DAWN."

In the midst of the suffocating grip of the Storm-Kraken, Harkon Bright became a second sunrise.

Aimee was thrown to the deck of the bridge. The light washed over her. It tore outwards. Shadow-flesh burnt away, crisped, dissipated before the blazing white of heat, light, and the shearing corona of radiance that blasted the night away from every crevice. Clouds fled. The world was white, and through the slits of her vision, Aimee saw something vast and dark fall back into the skies, *burning*.

The flare of light died. The Storm-Kraken was gone. Aimee pushed herself up on her hands, then launched herself forward with a cry of dismay as her teacher's sagging body toppled backwards over the edge of the ivory bridge. She caught his hand, felt his limp grip nearly slip through her fingers before she tightened them around the cuff of his coat.

Then the remnants of the spell keeping her feet securely on the deck gave way, and without time for fear, shock, or any sensation but surprise, Aimee and her teacher toppled from the bow of *Iseult*, and into the open sky. She saw the abyss beneath her, dark, swallowing the rain, filled with clouds and a cacophony of lightning. The last thing doomed skyfarers saw before they fell forever.

She jerked to a stop. A hand held the collar of her coat. Not caring whose it was, she reached out with her other hand to hold onto her teacher with every ounce of strength she had. "Come on, Harkon," she swore under her breath. "It's not your time yet."

"Pull us up!" she heard Belit scream behind her, and turning her gaze over her shoulder, looked into the determined face of the swordswoman, her fist clasping the collar of Aimee's coat, and above her, Rachim, his two armsmen, and Vlana, hauling them up. The clouds high overhead broke, revealing a night sky filled with innumerable stars. Her teacher landed on the deck beside her, and she watched his chest rise and fall. He was alive.

They'd won.

Aimee let her head fall back to the deck, a reckless laugh bubbling out of her as the last drops of rain fell on her smiling face.

CHAPTER TWENTY-NINE
THE JOURNEYMAN

In the warm, fully repaired metadrive chamber of *Iseult*, Elias sat on a small stool, and watched the twin hearts of the legendary lovers glow side by side as one. A week since they returned to Flotilla Visramin, it would be wrong to say that things had returned to any semblance of normal. Belit was captain, and her ascendency had come not on a wave of support from the officer aristocracy, but from the people of *Iseult* herself. There had been politics. There had been argument, and a threat of upheaval from an angry ruling caste that rankled at having had its power bypassed. The final remaining functionaries had declared her captaincy illegitimate.

She had answered by going to the metadrive chamber, and touching the core metadrives of *Tristan and Iseult*, synchronizing them to work nearly as one. Then, two days ago, the last members of the guild's bureaucrat-priests had been exiled from *Iseult* altogether. A new council had been formed, of representatives from each of the ship's decks and districts. The downlevelers outnumbered the officer aristocrats by more than a hundred to one, on average. One of its first votes had been to strip the position of officer of its hereditary status. Elias had watched social upheaval surge through the ship, one vote after another.

And – as with her defeat of Yaresh in the square – done without a single life taken.

Every muscle in Elias's body still ached. But here and now, in this place that had once held such terrible whispers for his ravaged mind, he felt a sense of deep, abiding peace. He took a long sip from the hot tea they'd given him when he came here, and stared at the twin hearts, beating as one. He'd come here as an open wound of a person with little semblance of where he was to go, or what he was supposed to be. Since then, he'd saved lives, fought with monsters, and done enduring good.

But somehow, he felt, the vision before him, of two lovers' souls once separated, now working together to power the last of the two ships, was the thing he was most proud to have done.

"Care for company?" Harkon asked. Turning, Elias saw the smiling face of the old sorcerer. He was still walking with a cane, largely on Rachim's insistence, but looked as if he wouldn't need it much longer.

"As if I'd refuse," Elias said, moving to vacate his stool with a smile.

"No," Harkon said with a laugh. "I spent three days in a sickbed. I have no designs to sit for any longer than I've got to."

Elias didn't sit back down anyway. It felt wrong, somehow, so instead the two men stood before the vast metadrive cores with an awkward stool between them. "How are you feeling?" Elias asked at length.

"Like I turned my flesh into solar fire for a few seconds, a week ago," Harkon said with a laugh. "I'd make a joke about being too old for that, but the truth is when I was younger it would've killed me. Strange, how this sorcery business makes us stronger as we age, yet still our joints ache."

"I wouldn't know," Elias answered with a grin. "Everything hurts right now."

"Well," Harkon answered after a genuine laugh. "The difference between success and failure is preparation. I had *time*, however short, to ready myself to face Grandfather. Whereas poor Viltas—" he shook his head "—poor Viltas was able to catch me off guard. I hadn't guessed the extent to which the Faceless had taken hold of him, when I confronted him in the midst of the portal storm. Good work, that night, by the by. They tell quite the stories of what you all did, and after."

"It was mostly Aimee," Elias answered, looking up at the twin hearts of the behemoth in all their glory. He couldn't quite keep the fondness from his voice. "I supported where I was needed. I fought when there was cause. I made mistakes, but she stayed the course throughout. We'd all be dead, but for her."

When he looked back at the old sorcerer, Harkon watched him quietly, thoughtfully. Then, without any pretense, said simply, "You love her."

Silence followed. The words struck Elias, a sudden gut-punch that came without warning or time to prepare. His mouth hung open. That was absurd, he wanted to say. He was only a few weeks free from the Eternal Order's clutches. His own concept of self was still a shaky thing, informed by a lifetime of horrible memories that functioned as a guidepost for what not to be, the teachings of a newfound teacher, and six words that he sometimes heard in his dreams: *Noble and brave. Gentle and kind.*

It was insane to think that he could grasp what it was to love another person... and yet. He looked down. His eyes closed, as music, a moment in a cabin doorway, a dance beneath the stars, and words whispered hastily before interruptions that had relieved him as much as they left him confused. Aimee de Laurent had a path ahead of her. A brilliant future within the grasping reach of her own hands. He could never presume to deter her from it.

And yet.

He looked Harkon in the face, and gave a resigned shrug as the truth settled in. "Too much to ever tell her."

Harkon watched him, and a look somewhere between relief and pity stirred in his eyes. And he simply said, "I see."

The two of them sat together for a while longer in silence, as the twin hearts of *Iseult* and her *Tristan* glowed in the chamber; together, but apart.

Some hours later, Elias walked the streets of the top level of *Iseult*, alone, pulling a new longcoat lined with fur tighter against the wind. The thoroughfares had a different feel to them now. Enough officers had been killed over the past few weeks that their positions had been filled by downlevelers with sufficient skill and inclination, and a number of the empty estates were already being repurposed for the good of the vessel. As he walked down the main spinal street, the door to one of them, apparently being used as a school now, opened and disgorged a flood of bright-faced children into the streets. They ran past him, a flood of laughter and smiles.

He was nearly through them when he heard one exclaim, "It's the white knight who came from the sky!"

Were it not for Oath of Aurum strapped still to his hip, he would genuinely have believed they were talking about someone else. At once he was surrounded by a sea of laughing, awestruck faces, and a thousand questions of which he could hardly keep track. Above it all, however, was a dizzying feeling, half relief and half wonder, to have so many looking at him with something other than fear. He was just in the process of trying to extricate himself, when the familiar figure of Vallus approached up the street, flanked now by two members of Belit's Red Guard.

"Not used to children, are you?" the diplomat said, amused. He'd regained much of his color in the past week, though he was thinner, and his face had lost much of its boyishness from grief.

"Not even a little."

"Run along, kids," Vallus replied with a laugh, and soon their teacher was urging the children further down the street, leaving Elias with the man the crew were now calling the consort.

"How are you?" Elias asked, when they were alone with the shorter man's two guards in the now empty patch of street. Vallus had gone, in a very short time, from nearly giving his life to save his father, to finding out that the same man had been host to the very monster the woman he now stood beside had slain.

"Better," Vallus said at length. "And worse, both at once. It comes and goes... but I think my father would have wanted us to do better, and not dwell. And speaking of that, my lady wants to speak with you." He paused. "Specifically, she said she wanted to see her student one more time, in the training hall where he first came to her."

The training hall was quiet, lit from without by the brilliant mid-morning sunlight. One member of the Red Guard stood off to the side, wearing his armor and waiting at attention while his captain stood in the center of the hall, repeating basic cuts with her sharp, gray steel. The parting wind of the sword made repetitive sounds in the half-light, and Elias paused for just a moment to watch. Her form was still smoother than his, her posture precise. There were no wasted motions, no superfluous gestures. She might be the finest sword he'd ever met, and a small part of him rebelled at the thought of leaving his teacher.

"My lady," Vallus said, and she turned. "I found him just before he was overwhelmed by hero-worshiping children. Saved his life, really. They nearly picked him clean."

"And yet he lives," she said. The mantle of captain rested heavily on her, he could tell. There were tired circles about her eyes where none had been before, and she carried herself with the gravity of one who felt the heavy weight of a painful responsibility. "You are resilient, *junk ritter*."

Elias stood in the half-light of the training hall, and all at once, before the woman that had taught him so much in so little time, his voice was too thick to speak. He didn't know how long they had until *Elysium* departed, but somehow, it seemed to him, this was likely to be the last time that teacher and student met like this.

"Val," Belit said at length. "Can you give us a moment?"

"Aye," Vallus answered, his expression warm. Understanding. "As you wish, my lady."

The receding footsteps were followed, at length, with the closing of the door. Belit smiled. "You will leave soon."

"Yes," he said. He could hear his own pain evident in his words. A mere few months ago, it would have constituted an unforgivable weakness… time was a strange thing. "And I still have so many questions, teacher."

"You are afraid," she said.

"I am," he admitted. "A month ago I was a monster. I committed crimes without number, and now… now your people sing my praises," he said, and his voice cracked. "Children stop me in the street, not knowing how much blood is on my hands, and call me white knight. How am I to contend with both of those truths in my head?"

The grief came out of him, so sudden and sharp that he didn't notice the tears until they escaped unpermitted. "I came so close," he said, "twice, to falling under the thrall of a person I thought I'd escaped. How can I know that I will be strong enough next time?"

Belit stepped forward, and placed a hand on his shoulder. "Elias," she said, using his name. "Student. There is something you need to understand: you did not overcome the influence of the darkness through strength. It was not power that stayed your hand, not an unbreakable will that brought forth light from that blade. It was kindness, and mercy, and the determination to be gentle, even in the face of ravening hate."

He looked into her gold eyes, and she smiled. "I told you some time ago that we own what we are the moment we decide what we will be. I know you are afraid of the future, *junk ritter*. I know your broken heart is filled with uncertainty, but I am not afraid for you." The hand upon his shoulder tightened its grip. "Because you have shown me what you are, Elias Leblanc: a good man."

For a long moment, Elias couldn't summon an answer.

His teacher's words had left him silent. "There is no thanks," he finally said, "that feels sufficient for what you have done for me."

"Yes, there is," Belit said, and turning, she retrieved a leather satchel that he hadn't noticed before, opened the flap, and presented it to him. "I believe that the heroes who gave our shared art of the sword to my predecessors in the Red Guard were like you. Either fellow escapees from your former order... or perhaps students of an alternate tradition that once preceded it. I believe that they are likely still out there, somewhere, or at least their students and descendants are. I believe that they have the same gifts you possess."

"So did my former master," Elias said quietly. It was why, ultimately, Lord Roland had dispatched Azrael to destroy Port Providence and reclaim the Axiom Diamond. The dread lord's words echoed in his mind. *"The enemies we have long sought will be within our grasp."*

"You want to thank me for putting you back on the proper path?" Belit said. "Here is what I ask of you, *junk ritter*: within this satchel are all the writings I have gathered on the legends of those heroes who saved *Iseult*, the white knights that came from the deep sky, and included are my notes on the legends surrounding the grandmaster's blade that you carry. Let it serve as your starting point to understanding. I want you to train. Even if you do so alone, at first. Be the light in the training hall that keeps the demons at bay."

And here she gestured at another book in the pile, older than the others, preserved against the ravages of time by some faint magic. It was pale, written in a more archaic form of the common language. Elias sucked in a breath. It was the twin to the ancient tome over which Lord Roland had obsessed in his citadel in the House of Nails.

It was a fencing treatise of the Varengard style. The wellspring of his art. "I have memorized every word," Belit said with a smile. "And used it to teach many warriors, now including you. Take it, *junk ritter*, and continue your training."

Elias's hands delicately touched the faded, time-worn pages. For a moment, he forgot to breathe. Then he looked his teacher in the eyes, and said, "I cannot take this, it is yours."

"No," she said. "You can, and you must. It is my prerogative to give it to a student I find deserving. You will take it."

"What will you do," he asked, "should you need it again?"

Belit's smile was broad. "I already told you, *junk ritter*. I have memorized every word, every fable. Every stanza. It's time for me to do what every other student and teacher before me has done, when the time came to pass on the book. I shall take what I have learned, and I shall write my own."

He avoided everyone else for the rest of the day. His emotions were too raw, his mind too full, to want to break an outward silence that seemed sacred. There were victory celebrations still happening as the night fell. Elias stood on the landing pad of Rachim's villa, to which *Elysium* had returned, and watched as the conjured fireworks of visitors from other ships, celebrating the ascendency of a new captain, exploded across the star-laden night sky.

Other vessels in the vast flotilla sent their own riot of color bursting into the heavens. He was far away from the celebrations, but somehow, that was better. It felt good, he thought, to hang back in the peace and silence of his own, seldom calm thoughts. Enough to know that people were alive to celebrate at all.

But after a while, her last orders tickled at his mind, and he slowly made his way up the open ramp, into the darkness of the cargo bay. The others were all out, seeing to last-minute affairs, attending one of the parties, enjoying not having to fear for their lives.

The quiet and the solitude was welcome. He looked up at the darkness of the doorway to the corridor that spanned the spine of the ship, remembering some weeks back, when Aimee had appeared there, framed by light, and asked him to join the crew for a last drink.

You love her.

Too much to ever tell her.

Now he knew. And it was what it was. A reality at once euphoric and deeply painful. There was nothing to be done about the fact, so instead, he drew his sword in the empty darkness of the solitary cargo bay.

Then, finding peace in the repetition and the effort, the solitary swordsman began to train alone. And the glimmering sword cut up and down, through the air. A lone light in the dark, keeping the demons at bay.

CHAPTER THIRTY
ON EMPYREAN WINGS

Aimee spent a week and a half watching, working, learning, and obsessively studying. With Belit's position established and shored up, Harkon's role shifted to that of advisor and honored guest, and so she followed along with him, learning and working in his shadow.

After everything that had transpired since she left Havensreach, it was almost novel to return to the duties of an apprentice. Novel, but no less interesting. She was involved in an investigation deep into the bowels of the ship to suss out the extent of the damage the Children of the Empty Sky had caused, and observed as *Iseult*'s five portalmages worked together on separate daises to tear open the vast, cyclopean portal that let her jump with two other ships to continue her journey, exiting in civilized skies, far to the south. On a cool evening, she watched from the wheelhouse as the lamp-towers of the Kiscadian Republic's northern borders glimmered in the darkness.

And there were answers acquired, as well, to questions that had never been closed to her satisfaction. Viltas had been stockpiling corpses, it turned out, helped by the functionaries, to build his undead army. Harkon had begun to suspect him shortly before Pentus's Grand Ball, and had caught him outside the soiree, but he had underestimated the necromancer, and been taken off guard by his attack.

Viltas had then sent his body over to the rapidly collapsing *Tristan* on the smaller skyship that was supposed to carry a team of relief workers and officers. It had gone crewed by cult-functionaries, who had presumably all died aboard the plague ship. As for the plague that the Faceless had used to wipe out the other ship, answers remained chillingly scarce. They knew only that it had been magical in origin, and that neither Elias, Bjorn, Vant, nor Clutch bore any sign of it. But nothing else.

Between duties, ceremonies, research, book-studies, and general help, Harkon kept her so busy that she hardly saw her shipmates at all. She also slept. Gods, she had never slept so well – or so much – in her life.

The rigorous schedule didn't abate until the night before they were scheduled to depart from *Iseult*. She had said most of her goodbyes earlier in the day, and Vant and Vlana were in the common area, playing Tonk with wooden cards. Elias was nowhere to be found, Harkon was talking with Clutch and Bjorn on the bridge. She had a blessed few hours to herself. So she walked down the ramp onto the landing pad with a glass of wine in hand, and determined to set off for one last walk to take in the sights.

At length, she found herself approaching the broken remnants of the dome where Pentus's Grand Ball had been held. The ceiling was still shattered, and though the square around it had been cleaned, there were some things – like the bloodstains upon the stone beneath her feet – that yet remained. At length, she slipped through the doors she'd last passed while wearing her gown and worrying about a thousand things that now seemed small. She descended the grand staircase beneath the destroyed ceiling of the dome, and stopped at the bottom, imagining for just a moment that she could still see the whirling dancers capering across a ghostly floor.

And the last question, unanswered to her satisfaction, returned to gnaw at her mind as she stood beneath the starlight, and asked the night, "How could the Faceless know that a portal storm was coming? As powerful as he was, he could never have summoned it, and surely he couldn't have guessed precisely when it would come?"

Her voice petered out in the starlit dark. She sighed, sipped her wine, and sat down on the bottom step.

"He didn't," the night answered.

Aimee started so suddenly she nearly spilled her drink, and looking up to the source of the voice, saw the face of the Oracle. But this was no illusion, no projection at a distance. This time the woman herself stood before Aimee, or at least seemed to. She was strange to look at. Her long robe was hooded and pale white. Her face was ageless, pretty in an unsettling sort of way, and there was a strange light in her eyes.

"I owe you thanks, Aimee de Laurent," she said. "Under this captain, I no longer need fear the functionaries hunting for me. I will remain in the shadows still – I believe in discretion – but I am no longer forced to. So yes, before you ask, it is truly me, not a projection. And no, the Faceless neither caused, nor knew the portal storm was coming. He merely sensed it, I believe, and took advantage of the opportunity. The question you should be asking is whether or not that opportunity was more than serendipity to begin with."

A cold feeling cut through Aimee at this. Speaking to a deep fear, a supposition that had gnawed at her since she'd first beheld the wall of the maelstrom. "The Faceless didn't summon the portal storm," she said, "but someone else did."

The Oracle nodded. "Perhaps not someone," she added. "But something. Older than Grandfather, and much worse."

Aimee swallowed, remembering the Faceless's furious words in the moments before Belit killed it. "When we faced him," she said, "he spoke of Varengard. He spoke of the storm, and of his desire to use the deaths of two ships to give him the power to flee this world altogether." She swallowed. It was amazing, how she'd managed not to think about the necromancer's words in the days since. "He spoke of the rise of dead gods," Aimee finished. "I don't suppose any of that makes sense to you?"

"The maelstrom is old," the Oracle answered. "But, if you would believe it, *Iseult* is older. Generations beyond count have passed since my first predecessor gave up her life to give power to the heart of this cradle of her people, but we at least remember that in those days, the storm didn't exist. I do not know if I would call it alive, or even a god, but I do believe that on that night, it reached out to pluck *Iseult* and her lover from the heavens. Moreover, I can see that whatever this darkness is, you and it are not yet done with one another, Aimee de Laurent."

"That's not very comforting," Aimee answered.

"It's not meant to be," the Oracle said in turn, and gave a sad smile. "It is a warning, given in affection to one who believed in me when the hours were darkest, who proved herself a hero, and a helper of heroes, when there was need. Farewell, sky-splitter. And remember my warning. We shall not meet again."

Aimee blinked, and the strange woman in her white robes was gone, leaving her alone in the night beneath the landless stars.

"Gods, what a crowd," Vlana said the following morning. *Elysium* rose into the air through the morning sunlight. Beyond the tops of the behemoth's towers, they could see the buildings of the port city of Taresh gleaming in the light of a beautiful sunrise. Below them, Rachim's landing pad faded away as the sleek, silver skyship rose ever higher at Clutch's urging.

And beyond the villa's walls, the streets were filled with thousands of rapidly dwindling people in dress styles without number, a mishmash of cultures risen up to supersede the finery of the officers that had until just recently ruled them. It was their grand sendoff, after a week of parties and celebrations before *Iseult* put in to the port, and began to strike new trade deals of her own, independent of the guilds.

There would be pushback for that, Aimee knew. But Belit was smart, and surrounded by good people. She would do well.

"Yeah," Vant said. "I almost wish we could take something of them with us."

Something about the *way* he said it made Clutch turn her head from the wheel. "Why don't I like your tone?"

"I have *no* idea," the engineer said with a shrug. "How you respond to my tone is your problem. And I don't even have a tone! Elias? Bjorn? Do I have a tone?"

"I'm staying out of this one," the old warrior said, leaning against the rail, a mug of steaming tea in his hand.

"You have a tone," Elias said with half a smirk.

"Traitor," Vant grunted.

"Still not an answer!" Clutch said.

"Hey, hey, pilot!" Vant snapped back. "Eyes on the sky, yeah? You almost crashed us into that estate-tower!"

"Oh, I'm sorry," the pilot said, turning nearly sideways at the wheel and steering with one hand. "Do I seem too distracted to you?"

Everyone on the bridge reflexively lurched forward, and then Clutch laughed again as she righted their course just clear of another small steeple. "Suckers."

"Clutch," Harkon warned. Then, "Vant, you may as well just tell her."

"Why do that?" Vant said with a wicked grin. "When she can go look in her bed later?"

"You didn't," Clutch's eyes bulged.

"We adopted one of the squittens," Vant said. "His name is Francesco."

Clutch's eyes flashed to Harkon. "He's dead."

"Oh wow, we're getting pretty high up there, aren't we?" Vant said. "Time for me to get down to engineering! Give the little guy a hug for me when you get back to your room, will you?"

Aimee laughed, wrapping her fingers tight around her mug as she stood beside her teacher. "Where to next?" she asked.

"I'll let you know once I've gone over the atlas," he said, amused. "It's my turn to pick a destination, after all. As a matter of fact, I should probably do that." Stretching, he turned, and said with a smile, "You've done very well. Both under my tutelage and outside of it. Enjoy a bit of a break, Aimee. You've earned it. Just don't let yourself become distracted."

"What, no apocalypses to rush into?" she quipped back.

"I think we're done with those for a little while," Harkon said as he exited the bridge. "But never say never."

Clutch kept steering as Vlana fed her coordinates from her station. By the by, Aimee found herself listening to the sound of humming. Turning, she saw Elias, still at the rail, wearing his new coat and idly doodling with a charcoal pencil on a small notepad. He was humming a tune she didn't recognize, though – she had to admit – the sound was very pleasant.

"What are you drawing?" she asked, sidling up to him. Her head came about even with the lower half of his face. She made a show of peeking over his shoulder.

"Just the sunrise," he said, and turning the pad, showed her a sketch of clouds breaking over the stern of *Iseult*.

"And the song?" she asked. "Sorry, Elias Leblanc, I'm nosy today."

He shrugged his broad shoulders. "Something my mother used to sing. Came back to me recently." A warmth filled his smile. "When I needed it."

"Has anyone ever told you you're rather good at that?" she asked.

"Singing or drawing?"

"Either."

"No," he said. "And no. But thank you."

He straightened, as if to go. She didn't quite step back

quickly enough, and at once she found herself closer to the green-eyed man than she'd intended. There was the familiar scent, proximity, and confusion.

"Ah," she said. "Sorry. Going somewhere?"

"Breakfast," he said. He honestly looked like hell, she thought. Healthier than when he'd first come aboard, but the past few weeks had been rough on him. There were dark circles under his eyes. His hair was matted. He looked as though he'd rolled out of bed, thrown on a coat, and wandered up to the bridge in a fog this morning. It was hardly the height of handsomeness.

Yet a very insistent part of her refused to see it as otherwise.

She bit her lower lip, and stepped aside. *Don't get distracted.*

She wasn't distracted.

She wasn't.

"No fair trying to starve me," he said as he slipped past, and tossing her an amused wink, slipped out of the bridge. She stood in her bathrobe, holding a mug of tea, honestly considering possibilities she'd left be after what she'd written off as a flight of fancy in the aftermath of an adrenaline-filled few dances. Before the world went mad. It couldn't be anything more than that, after all. She hardly knew him, and besides, she'd been around this street before.

It occurred to her abruptly that she was still staring at an empty doorway, and she turned around. No. Not possible. Not her. Not him. She thrust her right hand determinedly into her pocket.

"You all right?" Vlana asked from her station. Outside, the sun climbed higher in the heavens, filling the bridge with a warm, golden glow. Something pricked at her fingers, and Aimee pulled her hand out of her pocket. In her palm was a single blue rosebud, dropped there after it had been put in her hair the night of the Grand Ball.

She stared at it, and her heart did a small set of calisthenics. Aimee swallowed.

Not possible, eh? Wanna bet?

"For once," Aimee said, mostly to herself, "I really don't know."

She put the rose away, and placed both hands on her drink. That was quite enough of that.

Not by a long shot.

"Vant, are we ready for a hard burn?" Clutch asked.

"You know it, crazy," the engineer's voice came back. A roar sounded behind them, and mystic power thrummed beneath Aimee's feet. And *Elysium* sailed up and up, into the dawn of the infinite sky.

EPILOGUE
THE HOUSE OF NAILS

When Kaelith reached the top of the stone steps, she felt like she'd crossed half of heaven to get there. The sole survivor of the Eternal Order's disastrous invasion of Port Providence took a moment to look behind her. The view from the top of Lord Roland's Manse was beautiful in a brutally austere sort of way. Once, all the land that spread out below her had been the royal palace of New Corinth's ruling dynasty. When the dread lord had claimed the land as his own fief within the House of Nails, they said, he had savaged the landscape. Destroyed every garden, tore down every building, and visited nightmares without number on the unfortunates left behind. Then, they'd said, he'd raised his citadel in the heart of the ruins. Most of the grounds were now overgrown with red-leafed trees. When she looked, all the foliage was red within the confines of the former grounds. Ever since Roland's burning, they said, not a single plant's leaves grew in green.

Kaelith had never flinched from orders, though – truth be told – she did not grieve for dead Malfenshir. But it was a reminder of how the most placid people often hid the deepest darkness. Lord Ogier, Malfenshir's own master, was an unabashed beast who made spectacular public executions part of his military campaigns, yet he feared Roland. And staring across the red-foliaged ruin of a palace grounds that had once covered nearly a hundred acres, Kaelith started to grasp why.

The doors opened before her, heavy oak banded with iron. Here, the cool wind of late autumn stirred curtains on the other side of the entryway, and beyond she could hear a harpist playing. Kaelith's own master had not seen fit to train her in the myriad forms of high art and court that Roland's students had received, but she knew fine art when she saw it, and the music she now heard was of a level of skill normally heard only by kings.

Glancing left, she followed the sound as she stepped through, until she saw the source, and fought down the urge to wince.

The player was a thin man with delicate fingers, plucking away at an instrument with a sort of careful grace that came from mad terror at the prospect of a single error. His face stared past her, to the far wall, the caked blood clustered at his mutilated, empty eye sockets.

Turning, Kaelith stared into the deeper darkness, and there she glimpsed the outline of a man, silhouetted against the faint glow of a brazier of burning flames. Big-framed. Wearing what looked like an evening robe.

"You are Kaelith," a smooth voice said at length.

Kaelith closed her eyes, placed the head of her great black axe upon the floor, and knelt in the presence of a superior.

"I am," she said, bowing her head. "And I bring news that I would have brought earlier, but for the request you sent to me whilst I was in the field."

"You may relax, Sir Kaelith," Roland said, dismissive. "I want truth, not platitudes. I know the Axiom is lost to us for the moment, and Coulton's flagship has been roaming the unclaimed, looking for something. Clarify, black-axe. Confirm or deny."

"As you commanded," she said, "I followed King Coulton and his fleeing court for two weeks. I sought out those they sought out, and hunted down minor nobles that have fled his increasingly unstable council of advisors. I tortured some, bribed others. His advisor, the gray sage named Silas, is losing his mind. He has embraced ever more dangerous magic, in his obsessive quest for vengeance against us. And moreover, he has Coulton searching for something, using old pathways and secrets known only to the sages. Something beyond the dunes of old pre-Imperium ruins, far out beyond the eastern edge of the Kiscadian Republic. His people are listless, a fleet of refugees floating through the unclaimed, being turned away by one petty kingdom after another."

"Good," Roland said after a moment. The sound of pouring wine reached her ears. "You may rise."

"Dread Lord," she said, still down upon one knee. "There is more."

The silence that followed was thick enough that for a moment, Kaelith could only kneel there, fighting down fear, her mind filled with visions of red-stained leaves wafting in an unending breeze.

"Go on."

"Your apprentice, Lord Azrael," she said, "lives as a traitor named Elias Leblanc. He slew Malfenshir with Prince Collum's sword, and escaped the destruction of the

Iron Hulk on a silver skyship named *Elysium*. This same crew has in their possession the Axiom Diamond."

Kaelith heard the sound of glass breaking. The silhouette didn't move for a long time. A terrible weight seemed to surround her for a moment, a roiling, powerful presence that was enough to make the knight's armored fist clench tightly about the haft of her axe.

Then it ceased, and Kaelith let out a breath she didn't know she'd held.

"So," the figure said, turning. "My wayward angel of death has lost his way, and fallen into the company of Harkon Bright."

Soft footsteps echoed as he approached. Kaelith kept her head down, trying not to think of the harpist with his bloody, empty eyes. "Yes," she said. "I believe that was his name."

He stood before her now, and Kaelith felt the touch of a gloved hand on her chin, tilting it up. The kneeling warrior raised her head, and stared into Lord Roland's face. His cold, pale eyes glittered like distant stars, and in the half-light of the apartments, she saw the ghost of a twisted smile.

"Perfect."

ACKNOWLEDGMENTS

The second step is harder than the first, but I had people without count to walk the Dragon Road with me. First, to my beloved Meaghan: without you none of this would be possible. Second, to Matt, Kirsten, David, Alice, the whole Backstage Crew, and everyone else who absorbed snippets from this beast and offered sensible advice, quick tips, or just someone to enthusiastically vent at. Loneliness kills writers, and you all kept me alive. To my parents and my sister, for everything.

To Florence + the Machine, Imagine Dragons, TSFH, Yasuharu Takanashi, and other composers without number for breathing life into the Drifting Lands a second time. To every gamer, storyteller, and poet whose shared the road with me, and swapped a story or two.

And you, for sticking with the crew of the Elysium for round two. Now go find an authoritarian and pick a fight.

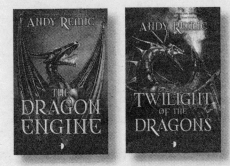

The Axiom Diamond is a myth...
and everyone wants to own it

"Non-stop fun with
unexpected moments
of real pathos."
— NEAL STEPHENSON

SKYFARER

THE DRIFTING LANDS · BOOK ONE

The Axiom Diamond is a myth... and everybody wants to own it.

JOSEPH BRASSEY